EDUCATING
CAROLINE

ALSO BY MEG CABOT

BY PATRICIA CABOT

EDUCATING CAROLINE

A NOVEL

MEG CABOT

G

GALLERY BOOKS

NEW YORK   LONDON   TORONTO   SYDNEY   NEW DELHI

G

Gallery Books
An Imprint of Simon & Schuster, LLC
1230 Avenue of the Americas
New York, NY 10020

This Gallery Books trade paperback edition September 2024
Previously published under the name Patricia Cabot

GALLERY BOOKS and colophon are registered trademarks of Simon & Schuster, LLC

Simon & Schuster: Celebrating 100 Years of Publishing in 2024

For information about special discounts for bulk purchases, please contact Simon & Schuster Special Sales at 1-866-506-1949 or business@simonandschuster.com.

The Simon & Schuster Speakers Bureau can bring authors to your live event. For more information or to book an event, contact the Simon & Schuster Speakers Bureau at 1-866-248-3049 or visit our website at www.simonspeakers.com.

Interior design by Ritika Karnik

Manufactured in the United States of America

10 9 8 7 6 5 4 3 2 1

Library of Congress Cataloging-in-Publication Data is available.

ISBN 978-1-6680-6140-4
ISBN 978-0-7434-2148-5 (ebook)

For Benjamin

Foreword

*D*ear Reader,

Oh no, a foreword! Does anyone (besides me) read forewords anymore? I hope so, because I'd really like to use this opportunity to mention how happy and grateful I am that a book I wrote more than twenty years ago is still in print and even getting a new life. And it's all because of you, dear readers.

2001—the year when this book was first published—was a very different era than the one in which we're living now, and 1870, the year in which this book takes place, was even more different.

Yet both were a time of rapid change and technological (and industrial) advances that were sometimes challenging to keep up with.

But in both times, shaming women for sex positive behavior was popular and considered perfectly acceptable. Victorian ladies, much like young women in the early aughts in the United States, were expected to be "pure" until marriage, and slut-shamed—and worse—if they were not. Women did not have the right to vote or even the right to keep money they'd earned or inherited. It all went to their husbands upon marriage.

And despite the advent of the printing press (which made

knowledge available to everyone but was viewed by many in power at the time with as much suspicion and snobbery as TikTok is today), true factual information about their bodies was nearly impossible for Victorian women to come by. Most male doctors of the age believed women were incapable of orgasm!

So what was a woman in Victorian times to do if she wanted to broaden her sexual horizons? Today she'd turn to the Internet, but back in the 1800s, it wasn't so easy, which is why virginal but ever-practical Lady Caroline Linford turns to the next best thing: a man considered an expert in the field, the notorious rake and "Lothario of London," Braden Granville, who definitely knew a thing or two about the female orgasm.

Astute readers will notice that in 2001, I used the last name of Slater in this book, as I did in The Mediator and All-American Girl series. That's because I was writing all of those books at the same time, only under different pen names! It never occurred to me that anyone would find out that my historical romances, then penned under the name Patricia Cabot, were written by the same person as my YA novels, Meg Cabot and Jenny Carroll . . . which is yet another way the year 2001 was similar to Victorian times: no one ever anticipated that what some people were trying so desperately to keep secret—like the power of the female orgasm, or even an author's secret pen names—might one day be revealed!

But I'll forever be grateful to all of you that they were . . . although perhaps not as much as Lady Caroline Linford is grateful to Braden Granville.

Thank you.

Meg Cabot

Prologue

Oxford, England
December 1869

A full moon hung in the air over the high college walls, lighting the young man's way as clearly as any gas lamp.

Not that there weren't gas lamps, of course. There were. But the glow from that round white moon rendered the amber flicker of the gaslights quite superfluous. Had all the gas lamps in England gone out, persons with business after hours—like himself—might still move about with relative ease by the light of this remarkable moon.

Or maybe it was simply that he was so drunk. Yes, it was quite likely that this moon was in no way different from any other moon, and that he was still excessively intoxicated from all the whiskey he'd drunk during the game, and that the reason he was able to find his way so easily through the midnight dark had nothing to do with the light from the moon, but everything to do with the simple fact that he had come this way so many times before.

He did not even have to look, really, where he was going. His feet took him in the correct direction. He was able, as he walked, to concentrate on other things—as fully as he was able to concentrate on anything, drunk as he was—and one of the things he was concentrating upon—besides the cold, which was considerable—was just where in hell he was going to get the money.

Not that he felt truly obligated to pay it back. The cards had been marked, of course. How else had he lost so much, in so little time? He was an excellent cardplayer. Really excellent. The cards had certainly been marked.

Which was odd, considering that Slater had been so convinced that the game was all right. Slater knew all the best games in town. Thomas had been lucky, he knew, even to have been admitted to this one, seeing as how he was, after all, only an earl—and a brand new one, at that. Why, that fellow with the mustache. He'd been a duke. A bloody duke!

Of course, he hadn't acted much like one. Particularly when, after losing yet another round, Tommy had declared the game fixed. Instead of laughing off the accusation, the way a real duke might have done, this one pulled a pistol on him. Really, a pistol! Tommy had heard of such things, of course, but he had never expected it actually to happen to him.

Thank God Slater had been there. He'd calmed the fellow down, and assured him that Tommy hadn't meant it—though, in fact, Tommy bloody well had. But you could not, Slater explained later, when they'd been alone, accuse a man of cheating without proof. And Tommy's only proof—that the design on the back of the cards looked strange, and that he'd never lost so badly before—was not particularly convincing.

He was lucky, he supposed, to have escaped with his life. That duke had looked as if putting a bullet through the brain of a fellow player was something he did every day.

Though a bullet through the brain might have been preferable to what Tommy knew he had in store for him: trying to find the thousand pounds he'd need to pay off what he now owed.

He couldn't, of course, ask his bank for it. The fortune his father had left him after his death just a little over a year before was being held in trust for him until his twenty-first birthday, and that was still two years away. He couldn't touch that money. But he could, he knew, borrow against it.

The trouble was, who to ask. Not the bank. They'd only inform his mother, and she'd want to know what he needed the money for, and he couldn't possibly tell her that.

His sister was a possibility. She was already of age, and had come into her part of their inheritance just that month. Caroline might reasonably be appealed to for a loan. She would want to know what he needed the money for, but she was quite easy to lie to. A good deal easier to lie to than their mother.

And if Tommy came up with a good enough story—something involving poverty-stricken children, for instance, or cruelly abandoned animals, since she was quite tenderhearted, his sister—he was sure of at least four or five hundred pounds.

The trouble was, he didn't like lying to Caroline. Oh, teasing her was one thing, but outright lying? That was another thing entirely. It offended his moral sensibilities, lying so outrageously to his sister, even if it meant, as in this case, saving his own hide. The fact that Caroline would surely rather pay off his debts than lose him did not ease his conscience the slightest. No, Tommy knew he would have to find someone else to loan him the thousand quid.

And as he mentally ran through a list of his friends and acquaintances, trying to remember if any of them owed him any favors, his feet, which had gone on walking, brought him to the gate to his college, and stopped there. He reached out, still without consciously thinking what he was doing, and was not at all surprised to find the gate securely locked. It had been so, of course, since nine o'clock, and it was now well past midnight.

His feet, again of their own accord, began moving once more, this time taking him past the gate, and along the high stone wall that circled the living quarters he shared with two hundred or so of his fellow academicians. He was still running over his list of friends, not even thinking about what he was doing. Because what he was doing had become quite habitual over the past few months. He was, of course, going over the wall. As soon as he came to the spot where there was a good enough toehold in the stone, that is.

None of his fellow students had any money, that he knew. They were all in the same position he was ... waiting for their twenty-first birthdays, and their inheritances. A few had fathers still living, and a few of those were occasionally the recipients of gifts of cash. But no one that he knew intimately enough to ask for a loan of a thousand pounds had been given anything like that amount lately.

It was as he was dejectedly pushing back the dead ivy that covered the wall he was about to climb, and stuffing his boot toe into a gouge in the mortar, that a voice called his name. He turned his head, swearing a bit beneath his breath. All he needed now was for the proctor to be alerted to the fact that the Earl of Bartlett was once again scaling the wall—

He turned his head, and saw that it wasn't the proctor at all, but that great ass of a duke. The fellow must have followed him from the tavern where they'd had their game. One would think that a duke had better things to do than follow penniless earls about, but apparently not.

"Look," Tommy said, leaving his foot where it was, and resting an elbow upon his knee. "You'll get your money, Your Grace. Didn't I say you would? Not right away, of course, but soon—"

"This isn't about the money," the duke said. Really, but he looked nothing like a duke. Would a duke actually curl his mustache that way? And wasn't that waistcoat, though velveteen, a bit, well ... bright?

"This is about what you called me," the duke said, and for the first time, Tommy saw that he was holding something in his hand. And in the bright white light from the moon, Tommy was also able to see precisely what it was.

"What I called you?" Quite suddenly, Tommy hoped their conversation *would* be overheard. He prayed quite fervently that that idiot proctor would overhear them and open the gate and demand an explanation. Far better—far, far better—to be sent down for being caught outside the walls after hours, than to receive a bullet through the gut—even if that bullet would likely relieve him of his debt.

"Right." The duke kept the mouth of the pistol trained on Tommy's chest. "A cheat. That's what you called me. Well, The Duke don't cheat, you know."

Tommy became aware of two things at once. The first was that it seemed unlikely a duke—a *real* duke—would possess so erratic a grasp of grammar.

The second was that he was going to die.

"Say good night, my lord," said the man-who-was-not-a-duke, and, still pointing the pistol in the direction of Tommy's chest, he pulled the trigger.

And then, quite suddenly, the bright light from the moon faded, taking Tommy's immediate troubles along with it.

1

London
May 1870

There was no light in the room other than that given off by
the flames in the ornate marble fireplace. The fire was low,
but managed to throw the couple on the divan into deep silhouette. Still, Caroline was able to make out their features.

She knew who they were. She knew who they were very well
indeed. She had, after all, recognized her fiancé's laugh through
the closed door, which was why she'd opened it in the first place.

Unfortunately, it appeared she ought to have knocked first,
since she'd obviously interrupted a moment of utmost intimacy.
And though she knew she should leave—or, at the very least, make
her presence known—she found she could not move. She was riv-
eted where she stood, staring quite against her will at the Lady Jacquelyn Seldon's breasts, which had come out of the bodice of her
gown, and were now bouncing vigorously up and down in rhythm
to the thrusting hips of the man who lay between Lady Jacquelyn's
thighs.

It occurred to Caroline, as she stood there with one gloved
hand gripping the doorknob, and the other clutching the frame,
that her own breasts had never bounced with such wild abandon.

Of course, her breasts weren't nearly so large as Lady Jacquelyn's.

Which might explain why it was the Lady Jacquelyn, and not Caroline, who was astride the Marquis of Winchilsea.

Caroline had not previously been aware of her fiancé's predilection for large-breasted women, but apparently Lord Winchilsea had found her lacking in that particular category, and had therefore sought out someone better suited to his tastes. Which was certainly his right, of course. Only Caroline couldn't help thinking he might have had the courtesy not to do it in one of Dame Ashforth's sitting rooms, in the middle of a dinner party.

I suppose I shall faint, Caroline thought, and gripped the doorknob tighter, in case the floor should suddenly rush up to meet her face, as often happened to the heroines of the novels her maids sometimes left lying about, and which Caroline sometimes picked up and read.

Only of course she didn't faint. Caroline had never fainted in her life, not even the time she fell off her horse and broke her arm in two places. She rather wished she *would* faint, because then she might at least have been spared the sight of the Lady Jacquelyn inserting her finger into Hurst's mouth.

Now why, Caroline wondered, *did she do* that? Did men enjoy having women's fingers shoved into their mouths?

Evidently they did, because the marquis began at once to suck noisily upon it.

Why hadn't anyone ever mentioned this to her? If the marquis had wanted Caroline to put her finger into his mouth, she most certainly would have done so, if it would have made him happy. Really, it was completely unnecessary for him to turn to Lady Jacquelyn—with whom he was barely acquainted, let alone *engaged*—for something as simple as *that*.

Beneath Lady Jacquelyn, the Marquis of Winchilsea let out a groan—rather muffled, with Lady Jacquelyn's finger in the way. Caroline saw his hand move from Lady Jacquelyn's hip to one of those sizable breasts. Hurst had not, Caroline saw, removed either his coat or his shirt. Well, she supposed he'd be able to rejoin the dinner party more quickly that way. But surely with the fire—not to mention the heat Lady Jacquelyn's body was surely generating—he must have been overly warm.

He didn't seem to mind, however. The hand which had gone to cup Lady Jacquelyn's breast moved to the back of her long neck, where fine tendrils of dark hair had escaped from the complicated coronet of curls atop her head. Then Hurst pulled her face down until her lips touched his. Lady Jacquelyn had to remove her finger from his mouth in order to better accommodate her tongue, which she placed there instead.

Well, Caroline thought, *That's it, then. The wedding is most definitely* off.

She wondered if she ought to declare it, then and there. Suck in her breath and interrupt the lovers in their embrace (if that was the correct term for it), make a scene.

But then she decided that she simply wouldn't be able to endure what undoubtedly would follow: the excuses, the recriminations, Hurst ranting about his love for her, Jacquelyn's tears. If Lady Jacquelyn *could* cry, which Caroline rather doubted.

Really, what else could she do but turn around and leave the room as quietly as she'd entered it? Praying that Hurst and Jacquelyn were too preoccupied to hear the latch click, she eased the door gently closed behind her, and only then released a long-held breath.

And wondered what she ought to do now.

It was dark in the corridor just outside the sitting room door. Dark and cool, unlike the rest of Dame Ashforth's town house, which was crowded with nearly a hundred guests and almost as many servants. No one was very likely to come this way, since all the champagne and food and music was a floor below.

No one except pathetically abandoned fiancées, like herself.

Her knees suddenly feeling a little weak, Caroline sank down onto the third and fourth steps of the narrow servants' staircase just opposite the door she'd closed so quietly. She was not, she knew, going to faint. But she did feel a little nauseous. She would need some time to compose herself before going back downstairs. Leaning one elbow upon her knee, Caroline rested her chin in her hand and regarded that door through the slender bars of the banister, wondering what she ought to do now.

It seemed to her that the thing any normal girl would do was cry. After all, she had just caught her fiancé in the arms—well, to be accurate, the legs—of another. She ought, she knew from her extensive novel reading, to be weeping and storming.

And she wanted to weep and storm. She really did. She tried to summon up some tears, but none came.

I suppose, Caroline thought to herself, *that I can't cry because I'm terrifically angry. Yes, that must be it. I am livid with rage, and that's why I can't cry. Why, I should go find a pistol and come back and shoot Lady Jacquelyn in the heart with it. That's what I ought to do.*

But the thought left her feeling more physically weak than ever, and she was quite glad she'd sat down. She didn't like guns, and could not imagine ever shooting anyone with one—not even Lady Jacquelyn Seldon, who quite thoroughly deserved it.

Besides, she told herself, *even if I could shoot her—which I quite positively couldn't—I wouldn't. What would be the point? I'd only be arrested.* Caroline, finding a loose crystal bead on her skirt, pulled on it distractedly. *And then I'd have to go to jail.* Caroline knew more than she'd ever wanted to know about jail, because her best friend Emmy was a member of the London Society for Women's Suffrage, and had been arrested several times for chaining herself to the carriage wheels of various members of Parliament.

Caroline did not want to go to jail, which Emmy had described for her in all its lurid detail, any more than she wanted to put a bullet through anyone.

And supposing, she thought, *they find me guilty. I'll be hanged. And for what? For shooting Lady Jacquelyn?* It would hardly be worth it.

Caroline didn't have anything particularly against Lady Jacquelyn. Lady Jacquelyn had always been perfectly civil to Caroline.

Really, Caroline decided, if she was going to shoot anybody— which she wasn't, of course—it would have to be Hurst. Why, not even one hour ago he'd been whispering into Caroline's ear that he couldn't wait for their wedding night, which was only one month away.

Well, evidently he was so impatient for it that he'd been forced to seek out someone else entirely with whom to rehearse it.

Cheating bastard! Caroline tried to think up some other wicked words she had overheard her younger brother Thomas and his friends call one another. *Oh, yes. Whoremonger!*

It would serve that whoremongering cheating bastard right if I shot him.

And then she felt a rush of guilt for even thinking such a thing. Because of course she was perfectly conscious of how very much she owed Hurst. And not just because of what he'd done for Tommy, either, but because out of all the girls in London, he'd singled *her* out to marry, *her* to be the sole recipient of those slow, seductive kisses.

Or at least, that's what she'd thought up until very recently. Now she realized that not only was she far from the sole recipient of those kisses, but that the ones she'd been receiving were quite different from the ones Lady Jacquelyn was apparently used to.

Damn! She brought up her other elbow, and now rested her chin in both hands. What was she to do?

The correct thing, of course, would be for Hurst to call it off. The marquis was invariably correct in all of his activities—well, with the exception of this one, of course—and so Caroline thought it was not unreasonable to hope that he might be the one to break off their engagement, thus sparing her the embarrassment of having to do so. *Darling,* she pictured him saying. *I am sorry, but you see, it turns out I've met a girl I like a tremendously lot better than you. . . .*

But no. The Marquis of Winchilsea was nothing if not polite. He would probably say something like, *Caroline, my sweet, don't ask me to explain why, but I can't in good faith follow through with it. You understand, don't you, old sport?*

And Caroline would say she understood. Because Caroline *was* an old sport. Lady Jacquelyn Seldon was a strikingly attractive woman, who sang and played the harp quite beautifully, as talented as she was lovely. She would make any man a wonderful wife, although she hadn't any money, of course. Everyone knew that. The Seldons—Lady Jacquelyn's father had been the fourteenth Duke of Childes—were an ancient and very well respected family, but they hadn't a penny to their name, only a few manor houses and an abbey or two scattered here and there.

That Hurst, whose family was just as noble but likewise just as poor, would have chosen to align himself with the Seldons wasn't surprising, though Caroline wasn't certain it was the most *prudent* thing he had ever done. What did he and Lady Jacquelyn imagine they were going to live on, anyway? Because unless they rented out all of those magnificent properties to some wealthy Americans, they hadn't any source of income to speak of.

But what did income matter, to two people in love? It wasn't any of Caroline's concern, anyway, how the pair of them got on. Her problem was this:

What was she going to tell her mother?

The Dowager Lady Bartlett was not going to take this well. Not by any stretch of the imagination. In fact, the news was likely to send her into one of her infamous fits. She quite thoroughly adored Hurst. Why shouldn't she? He had, after all, saved the life of her only son. The debt Caroline's family owed the marquis was enormous. By agreeing to marry him, Caroline had hoped, in some small way, to repay his kindness.

But now it was quite clear that winning Caroline's hand hadn't been any particular accomplishment for the young marquis. How humiliating!

And the invitations had already been sent out. Five hundred of them, to be exact. Five hundred people—the best of London society. Caroline supposed she was going to have to write to all of them. She began to feel a bit like crying when she thought of *that*. *Five hundred* letters. That was a bit much. Her hand usually cramped up after only two or three.

Hurst ought to be the one to write the letters, she thought, bitterly. After all, he was the one who'd broken the rules. But Hurst, who was much more of an outdoorsman than an intellectual, had never written anything longer than a check, so Caroline knew counting on any help from him in that quarter was foolish to the extreme.

Perhaps she could merely put an announcement in the paper. Yes, that was it. Something tasteful, explaining that the wedding of Lady Caroline Victoria Linford, only daughter of the first Earl of Bartlett, and only sister of the second, and Hurst Devenmore Slater, tenth Marquis of Winchilsea, was regretfully called off.

Called off? Was that the right term for it?

Lord, how embarrassing! Thrown over for Lady Jacquelyn Seldon! What would the girls back in school say? Well, Caroline consoled herself. It could have been worse. She couldn't think how, but she supposed it could.

And then, quite suddenly, it was.

Someone was coming. And not out of the sitting room, either, but down the corridor. It was someone who was looking for Lady Jacquelyn, Caroline realized, as soon as the light from the candelabra he was holding illuminated his features enough for her to recognize them.

And when she did, her heart stopped beating. She was quite sure of that. Her heart *actually stopped beating* for a moment. It hadn't done that when she'd opened the sitting room door and seen her fiancé making love to another woman. No, not at all.

But it did so now.

In spite of the candelabra, his foot hit the leg of a small table, on which rested a vase of dried flowers. When Braden Granville's foot hit the table, the vase wobbled, and then fell over, sending a number of dried petals floating down onto the carpet runner below. He cursed beneath his breath, and leaned down to right the vase. Caroline, watching him from between the banister bars, saw that he looked more annoyed than he should, for someone who'd only accidentally knocked over some dried flowers.

He knows, she thought. *Good Lord, he knows.*

This just might end in bloodshed after all.

Without conscious thought, she rose to her feet, and said, "H-hullo." Only her voice came out sounding extraordinarily breathless.

Braden Granville looked up sharply. "Who's there?" he asked.

"It's only me," Caroline said. Whatever was the matter with her voice? It sounded ridiculously high-pitched. She made an attempt to lower it. "Caroline Linford. I sat next to you last month at a dinner at Lady Chittenhouse's. You probably don't remember. . . ."

"Oh. Lady Caroline. Of course."

There was no mistaking the disappointment in his deep voice. As she'd been speaking, he'd raised the candelabra and looked at her. She knew perfectly well what he'd seen: a young woman of medium height and medium weight, whose hair was neither blonde nor brown, but a sort of sandy color, and whose eyes were neither blue nor green, but quite emphatically brown. Caroline knew she did not possess anything like the stunning dark beauty of Lady Jacquelyn Seldon, but she also knew—because her brother Thomas had told her, and brothers were nothing if not brutally honest— that she wasn't a girl to pass over without a second look, either.

But Braden Granville certainly passed her over, quite without a second look. *As if he were anything much to look at himself,* Caroline thought, with some indignation. *Conceited pig.* After all, he wasn't nearly so handsome as Hurst. Whereas the Marquis of Winchilsea was a golden Adonis, with his curly blond hair, blue eyes, fair complexion, and tall, arrow-straight frame, Braden Granville was dark as sin, broad across the shoulders to the point of being barrel-chested, and always looked as if he needed a shave, even, Caroline was quite certain, right after he'd just had one.

Braden Granville lowered the candelabra and said, "I don't suppose you've seen Lady Jacquelyn Seldon come this way, have you?"

Caroline's gaze darted toward the sitting room door. She hadn't meant it to. She hadn't meant to look anywhere near that door. But her gaze was drawn to it as surely as the moon drew the tide.

"Lady Jacquelyn?" she echoed, stalling for time.

What would happen, Caroline wondered, if she told him she *had* seen Lady Jacquelyn? That she was, in fact, just inside that door?

Why, Braden Granville would kill Hurst, that's what. Thomas had told her all about the man he referred to admiringly as "Granville." How "Granville," who'd been born in Seven Dials, the poorest, seediest district in London, had made a fortune in the firearms business. How "Granville" was as ruthless in his personal life as he was in his business affairs. How "Granville" was known for considering a bullet the swiftest way to handle problems in either area, a fact which was not hurt by his being a world-renowned crack shot with a pistol.

Why, Hurst couldn't have hit the side of Westminster Abbey with a pistol, even by *throwing* the silly thing.

"Yes," Braden Granville said, eyeing her curiously. "Lady Jacquelyn Seldon. Surely you know her."

"Oh," Caroline said. "Yes, I know her. . . ."

"Well," he said. The patience in his voice sounded quite forced.

"Have you seen her go by here? With a . . . gentleman, perhaps? I have reason to believe she was not alone."

Caroline swallowed.

How odious this was! Perhaps much more for him than for her. Because of course there was the fact that "Granville" had supposedly bedded more women than any man in London. This was not something Caroline's brother had announced at the breakfast table, but something she'd overheard him discussing with his friends. According to Thomas, "Granville" apparently had as many lovers as the infamous Don Juan. In fact, Thomas and his friends called him—with straight faces, no less—the Lothario of London.

Only lately had the Lothario finally settled down, and made an offer of marriage to the most beautiful and accomplished woman in all of England, Lady Jacquelyn Seldon. Who at that very moment was straddling Caroline's fiancé, the Marquis of Winchilsea.

Just imagine how a proud, self-made man like Braden Granville—a man who was universally admired for his skills as a lover—would feel when he found out his own fiancée had betrayed him. And with the Marquis of Winchilsea, of all people, who hadn't a penny to his name, only his very pretty face to live upon! Why, all Caroline had to do was say a word—just one word—and she wouldn't need to worry herself again with the wording of the *Times* announcement: Her wedding to the Marquis of Winchilsea would have to be called off due to his untimely death.

She shook herself. Good Lord, what was she thinking? She couldn't allow Braden Granville to shoot Hurst. Not after the way Hurst had saved Tommy.

"I did see her," Caroline admitted, finally. She pointed toward the far end of the corridor. "She went that way."

Braden Granville's face hardened. He hadn't a very handsome face to begin with, in the traditional sense of the word, and it had not been treated kindly by life—he bore the deep scar of what looked like a knife wound in his right eyebrow.

But when that face hardened with determination, it became almost frightening to look at—like looking at the face of the devil himself. What in heaven all the women he'd bedded had seen in him, Caroline couldn't imagine. She looked away, and concentrated instead on a vision in her mind's eye of the face of the Marquis of Winchilsea, which was every bit as angelic as Braden Granville's was . . . not.

"Was she with anyone?"

Caroline scissored a glance in his direction. "I beg your pardon?"

"I asked—" He took a deep breath, as if for patience. "Was Lady Jacquelyn with anyone? A man?"

Caroline replied, "Why, yes, she was." There, she told herself. That ought to get rid of him in a hurry. And thus keep him from discovering the truth, which lay just beyond that door, a few feet away.

The smile Braden Granville's lips curled into upon hearing this sent a convulsive shiver up Caroline's spine. So pleased—so diabolically pleased—did he look, that for a moment, Caroline's breath caught in her throat. Why, he really *was* a devil!

"Thank you, Lady Caroline," Braden Granville said, sounding a good deal more cordial than he had before. And then he started down the hallway, and Caroline tried to breathe again.

And found that she couldn't.

This was alarming, to say the least. But she was determined not to let Braden Granville know of her distress. No, what was important was not that she could no longer breathe, but that he go away, far, far away, so that Hurst might have a chance to escape. . . .

Only her efforts to hide her discomfort did not appear to have been very effective, since just as he passed the staircase upon which Caroline stood, Braden Granville turned and looked back at her, inquisitively.

"Are you quite all right, Lady Caroline?" he asked.

He knew, though she didn't know how. She'd made no sound. How could she? She couldn't breathe.

She nodded vigorously. "Perfectly well," she managed to wheeze. "You'd better hurry, or you might miss her."

But Braden Granville did not hurry. Oh, he looked very much as if he might have liked to. But instead he remained exactly where he was, looking at her with what, if she hadn't already caught a glimpse of that wicked smile, she might have thought was concern.

But no one with a smile as evil as that could be capable of feeling concern.

"I think you're lying," Braden Granville said, and Caroline felt as if her heart might explode.

He knows! she thought, frantically. *Oh, God, he knows! And now he's going to kill Hurst, and it will be all my fault!*

But then he said, "You aren't perfectly well. You've lost all the color from your face, and you seem to be having difficulty drawing breath."

"Nonsense," Caroline gasped. Though she was lying, of course. She was gulping in enormous amounts of air, only none of it appeared to be actually getting into her lungs.

"It isn't nonsense." Braden Granville retraced his steps. When he'd reached the stairs on which Caroline stood, he leaned over and laid a hand upon the back of her neck, just as, a few moments before, Caroline had seen the Marquis of Winchilsea lay his hand upon the back of Lady Jacquelyn's neck.

Caroline's heart, which had skipped a beat when she'd first seen Braden Granville come down the hall, now started to beat so fast, she was certain it might burst. Good Lord, she thought, irrationally. He's going to kiss me. He's going to do to me whatever it is he's done to all those women he's supposedly bedded. And I shall be perfectly incapable of stopping him, because he's the Lothario of London.

Oddly, Caroline found the thought of being kissed by Braden Granville not in the least upsetting.

Only instead of tilting her head up so that he could kiss her, the Lothario of London said, commandingly, "Sit down."

Caroline was so startled that she sat without question. She didn't suppose there were many people who would dare to disobey an order given by the great "Granville," which was undoubtedly why he was so successful a businessman, not to mention lover.

Then Braden Granville's hand on her neck tightened, and, incredibly, he pushed her head down until it was between her knees.

"There," he said, with some satisfaction. "Stay like that, and you'll be better in no time."

Caroline, staring at the beading on her skirt, said, her voice muffled against the stiff white satin, "Um. Thank you, Mr. Granville."

Her disappointment that he hadn't tried to kiss her or molest her in any way, despite her dislike of him, was profound. And disturbing.

"Think nothing of it," Braden Granville said.

Whoremonger! Caroline thought to herself, as she stared into her own lap. *I suppose I'm not good enough to seduce. After all, who am I? Oh, only the daughter of the first Earl of Bartlett. A nothing. A no one. I'm certainly no great beauty, like Lady Jacquelyn Seldon. And I don't have any manor houses in the Lake District.*

But there's one thing I jolly well do have that Lady Jacquelyn doesn't: the common decency not to sleep with another woman's fiancé.

Oh, she added, mentally. *And a bit of money, too, of course.*

She expected him to go then, but he did not. The strong hand remained on the back of her neck. It was surprisingly warm.

"Ridiculous things, corsets," Braden Granville went on, conversationally. "Ought to be abolished."

Caroline, perfectly astonished that a man as great as Braden Granville should be standing in a hallway with his hand upon her neck—and even more surprised that he should have brought up a subject as indelicate as her corset—said, into her lap, "I suppose some people think so. . . ."

Was this, she wondered, a prelude to taking her corset off her, and then—Good Lord—seducing her?

But Braden Granville only said, "I'm surprised you wear one at all. Aren't you friends with Lady Emily Stanhope?"

This was such a surprising question that Caroline heard herself say, "*You* know Emmy?"

"Everyone knows Lady Emily. She's become quite infamous for her involvement in the women's suffrage movement. I had assumed, being her friend, that you were, as well."

"Oh," Caroline said, into her skirt. "I am. I mean, I don't go to the rallies, or anything. I don't much like rallies. It's so much nicer to stay at home with a book than to go about shouting until you're hoarse and chaining yourself to things."

"I see that you are, at heart, a true freedom fighter, Lady Caroline," Braden Granville observed drily.

"Oh," Caroline said, realizing how foolish she must have sounded to him. "Oh, but I do support Emmy's cause, you know. Last month alone I paid her court penalties twice because her father won't do it anymore. And I only wear a corset because, well, I think I do look nicer in one than not."

"I see." He sounded amused. "Your suffragist leanings end where your comfort and vanity begin. At least you are honest enough to admit it."

He was making sport of her. She knew that now. So he certainly wasn't going to try to seduce her. Caroline didn't know much about men, but she strongly suspected they wouldn't bother seducing a girl they'd made sport of. She was relieved, she supposed. But it was a little insulting that he hadn't even *tried*. After all, he'd apparently seduced every other girl in London. Why not her? Caroline knew she wasn't an elegant beauty, but she'd certainly had her share of admirers, including, just that morning, a young man—a complete stranger—who'd chased her for nearly an entire city block after she'd roundly berated him for needlessly whipping his horse, only to tip his hat and say her smile was every bit as bright and pretty as a brand-new penny, and that he'd never whip another horse again.

But Braden Granville apparently hadn't noticed her smile.

And then the memory of the reason why she'd lost her breath in the first place returned in a rush. All this time they'd been in the hallway discussing her corset, Hurst had been in mortal danger of discovery! Whatever could she have been thinking?

"Hadn't you better go, Mr. Granville?" Caroline asked, trying to disguise the urgency in her voice. "If you want to find Lady Jacquelyn, I mean."

"Yes," he said. There was no kindness in his voice now. "Well, I'm sure there's no chance of that anymore."

Caroline, alarmed, asked, "No chance of what? Finding her? Oh, you're quite wrong. I'm sure she's still close." Then, realizing what she'd said, she thrust a finger toward the opposite end of the hallway. "I'm sure if you just follow her—"

"No point," Braden Granville said, flatly. Then he added, almost as if to himself, "I lost any chance I might have had at catching her out in her little game when I took a wrong turn ten minutes back, and ended up in the kitchens."

"Little game?" Caroline echoed, faintly.

Like someone recalling himself, Braden Granville said, "Never mind. Feeling any better yet?"

Caroline inhaled. Her temples tightened with the beginning of a headache, but surprisingly, she found that she could breathe normally again.

"Much better," she said. "Thank you." And then, because she was worried he might know more about the details of his fiancée's faithlessness than he was letting on—like, for instance, the identity of her secret lover—she added, "I'm sure you're wrong,

Mr. Granville. About your bride-to-be. I'm certain she isn't involved in any . . . little game. With anyone."

The laugh Braden Granville let out was every bit as wicked as
his smile had been when she'd told him—oh, why, why had she
told him?—that she'd seen his fiancée with another man.

"How very good-natured of you, Lady Caroline," he said, in
a tone that wasn't the least bit complimentary. "But please allow
me to assure you that your confidence in Lady Jacquelyn is sorely
misplaced. And when I get the name of the fellow, I'll be only too
happy to prove it, in a court of law, if necessary. You might mention
that to her, when next you see her."

Quite openmouthed at this extraordinary declaration—and
at the thought that she and Jacquelyn Seldon were anything but
the most distant acquaintances—Caroline fought to think of some
sort of reply.

She was saved, however, from making any when the door to
Dame Ashforth's private sitting room opened and the Marquis of
Winchilsea stepped into the corridor.

"Oh," Caroline said, finding her voice at last. "Dear."

2

*C*aroline was not at all certain which man looked the most surprised: the Marquis of Winchilsea, who appeared quite shocked at seeing his fiancée with her face being pressed into her lap by a man to whom she was not related, or Braden Granville, who removed his hand from her neck at once and said, "Winchilsea," in a tone of voice which suggested Hurst was not one of his favorite people.

"Granville." Hurst's voice made it clear that the feeling was mutual. Then, in a very different tone, he said, "Caroline, darling, whatever are you doing, sitting on those dirty servants' steps?"

Caroline narrowed her eyes at him through the banister-bars. How *dare* he call her darling when . . .

She shook herself. Now was not the time.

"I," she stammered. "I was l-looking for you. And it seems I grew a little faint. And Mr. Granville was very kindly helping me."

She couldn't help glancing, several times, behind Hurst, to see whether or not Lady Jacquelyn would follow him out. *Please*, she found herself praying. *Please, please stay where you are, Lady Jacquelyn.*

"And why," Hurst inquired, pleasantly, "would you go and do something as foolish as faint, Caroline?" He stretched a gloved hand toward her. Caroline took it, and allowed him to draw her from the steps. She was perfectly unable to take her gaze from his face. *Why, not so long ago, Lady Jacquelyn Seldon's tongue was in that mouth*, was all she could think.

"You're generally made of much sturdier stuff than that," Hurst was saying. "That's what I admire most about you, you know, my dear."

"Mr. Granville thought it might have been because of my corset," Caroline murmured, hardly aware of what she was saying.

"Oh, he did, did he?" Hurst laughed. Though the laugh was distinctly humorless, it took away most of the heat of his next words, which were, "I'll thank you, Granville, to keep your comments about my fiancée's undergarments to yourself. And your hands, too, while you're at it."

Braden Granville didn't say anything right away. He was looking at the marquis very curiously, Caroline thought. Almost as if . . . almost as if he *knew*!

But that was impossible. He couldn't possibly know. It wasn't as if Hurst hadn't remembered to tuck in his shirttail, or tighten his cravat. He was perfectly presentable. Maybe there was a bit more color than usual in his cheeks, but surely that wasn't indicative of anything—

"I'd be happy to," Braden commented, lightly. "If you'd be willing to return the favor."

Hurst looked startled. He said, "What? What are you talking about, Granville?"

Braden nodded toward the closed door. "That's Dame Ashforth's private sitting room, is it not?"

"Yes," Hurst said, with obvious reluctance. "What of it?"

Braden laid a hand upon the doorknob. Quite suddenly, Caroline found it difficult to breathe again. "Nothing," he said. "I am merely looking for someone."

On the word *someone*, Braden Granville threw open the door.

Caroline's knees promptly went out from under her. She sank back down onto the step and buried her face into her lap again, telling herself to breathe, just breathe, while wondering if this was the last time she would ever see her fiancé alive. . . .

And if, really, his untimely death would be such a bad thing, after all.

But of course, of *course* she did not want to see Hurst dead. Not after what he'd done for Tommy. Maimed, possibly, but never, ever dead.

But evidently, Hurst Devenmore Slater, tenth Marquis of Winchilsea, would live to see his wedding day—though the identity of his future bride was still somewhat in question—since presently, Caroline heard Braden Granville say, in a mild voice, "But I see I was mistaken."

Caroline lifted her face from her lap. Lady Jacquelyn, then, hearing their voices in the hall, must have found some other way out of the room. What a stroke of luck for them all!

"Quite," Hurst said, in a voice that was much too self-congratulatory. "You were *quite* mistaken, Granville. My dear." Hurst was drawing her up from the steps again. "Shall we go downstairs, and join your mother?"

Caroline felt as if there were sand in her mouth. Why, Hurst was speaking to her as if nothing—nothing at all—had occurred. She would have thought that a man who intended to break off his engagement wouldn't refer to his fiancée as *darling* or *my dear*. And he oughtn't, she thought, to put his hand on the small of her back. That was a bit forward, for someone who only moments before had . . .

She didn't want to think about that.

Then she happened to glance at Braden Granville, who'd come out of the sitting room, and was drawing the door of it closed behind him. Oh, of course. That was it. Hurst didn't want to cause a scene in front of anyone. Particularly, she supposed, in front of his lover's fiancé. He was going to wait, she supposed, until they were alone. Then he'd explain why it was that she was no longer the future Lady Winchilsea.

"Certainly," she said. She looked again at Braden Granville and felt, seemingly from out of nowhere, a little spurt of emotion. What, she wondered, was *that*? Not pity, surely—though it was quite true that if Braden Granville cared for Lady Jacquelyn anywhere near as much as Caroline supposed she ought to have cared for Hurst, he was going to be very hurt when he found out the truth about the lying, scheming devil-spawned whore to whom he had pledged himself.

But she didn't believe he cared for Lady Jacquelyn. Not the way he'd spoken about her and her "little game."

No, it wasn't pity Caroline had felt when she'd glanced at Braden Granville just then. But what, then? Caroline's heart was a tender one, it was true, but she did not normally feel warmly toward ruthless businessmen and heartless Lotharios.

"Good evening, Mr. Granville," she said, stifling the inexplicable emotion, and extending her hand toward him. "And thank you for your kindness."

Braden Granville looked down at her gloved hand with some surprise. Caroline had apparently startled him, and from some very dark thoughts, if the look on his face was any indication. But he roused himself and took hold of her hand, bringing it rather distractedly toward the general vicinity of his lips without actually touching it with them.

"Good evening," he said, not looking at either of them. And then he turned, and disappeared down the hall.

As soon as he was out of earshot, Hurst snorted disgustedly, and said, "Cheeky blighter!"

Caroline glanced up at her fiancé. This, too, was not the sort of behavior she might have expected from a man about to liberate himself from the bonds of matrimony.

"What did you say?" she asked, certain she had not heard him aright.

"The gall of him, mentioning your corset like that! Not that I'd have expected anything better mannered from such an upstart. You know, there's a place for men like him. Do you know what it's called? America."

"Oh," Caroline murmured. "*Really*, Hurst."

"I'm quite serious, Carrie. I tell you, I don't like it, this new habit of inviting every Tom, Dick, and Harry in London to what used to be thoroughly exclusive, private parties. I know the fellow's filthy rich, but that doesn't make him any less common than he was the day he was born."

Maybe not, Caroline only just kept herself from saying out loud. *But at least he knows how to earn—and hold on to—money. That's a skill you've certainly never managed to acquire, Hurst.*

Only of course she didn't say so. Hurst was quite sensitive about the fact that his family hadn't any money left. In fact, when he'd proposed to her, it had been almost apologetically. *I know I haven't much, Carrie,* he'd said. *But everything I've got I'd gladly give to you, if only you'd do me the honor of being mine.*

And Caroline, overjoyed at the prospect of having such a handsome, such a romantic, such a brave man—hadn't he saved her brother's life?—for a husband had uttered a resounding *Yes.*

More fool she.

"You mark my words, Carrie," Hurst went on, as they stood in the hallway, listening to Braden Granville's departing footsteps. "This isn't going to come to any good, this mingling of the classes. Interfering old women like Dame Ashforth might find it amusing, but I most decidedly do not."

And then he took Caroline's arm, and began to steer her down the corridor in the opposite direction from the one in which Braden Granville had disappeared.

As they walked, Caroline's mind turned over his words feverishly. Carrie. He'd called her Carrie, his private name for her. Why would he call her by his special name for her if he were about to break off their engagement? Why, he was calling her *Carrie* and *darling* just as if nothing had happened. Nothing at all. In fact, if she hadn't taken that wrong turn on her way from the ladies' cloakroom, heard Hurst's laughter, then seen for herself just what, precisely, he had been up to since he'd left her in the ballroom— supposedly to go and "have a smoke" with the gentlemen—she would not in a million years have guessed that he'd been with another woman.

Been *with* another woman? Good Lord, he'd been *inside* another woman. And yet now he was behaving as if he *had* only stepped into Dame Ashforth's billiard room for a few moments to smoke!

"I hope," Hurst was saying, as the sounds of the revelry below stairs grew louder, "that Granville didn't insult you, Caroline. He didn't, did he?"

Caroline, moving as if in a daze, rather like the heroines in her maid's novels always did after discovering a corpse in the hedge maze, murmured incoherently, " Insult? Me? What?"

"Well, I shouldn't be surprised if he did. He has something of a reputation with the ladies, you know. He didn't touch you, did he, Carrie? Somewhere he oughtn't?"

They were once again engulfed in the sea of humanity that flooded Dame Ashforth's ballroom. Caroline could barely hear her own reply, which was an astonished, "No!"

It was drowned out as the orchestra suddenly launched into a familiar tune.

"Good Lord," Hurst said, seizing her by the hand. "It's the Sir Roger de Coverley. I'd forgotten it was scheduled to begin at midnight sharp. Come along, Carrie, let's take our places. You know how Ashforth feels about the Sir Roger."

Caroline did, indeed, know how Dame Ashforth felt about the

Sir Roger. Nothing—not marauding Amazonian warriors brandishing spears and poisoned darts, and certainly not philandering fiancés—would ever cause her to postpone a Sir Roger. While the widow declared herself too old to take part in the lively dance, she enjoyed nothing better than watching it performed by the young people she'd invited to her home.

Her mind still awhirl, Caroline took her place in a long line of couples. Hurst stood across from her, looking coolly elegant in his fine evening clothes. His cravat was not in the least crumpled, his trousers still bore a perfect crease. How was that possible? The man had been making violent love—Caroline wasn't sure this description was accurate, but it had been mentioned once or twice in a book she'd read, and she'd rather liked the way it sounded—to a beautiful woman not a quarter of an hour ago, and yet there he stood now, looking as if butter wouldn't melt in his mouth. It was perfectly incredible.

And then—as if the evening had not gone bizarrely enough—suddenly, right before Caroline's eyes, appeared Lady Jacquelyn Seldon. Truly, there she was, her lovely head thrown back as she laughed with delight as she made her way down the line of dancers. And beside her, keeping very good time for someone not to the manor born, was Braden Granville.

Caroline stared, certain her eyes were going to pop out of her head. So he had found his Lady Jacquelyn at last, had he? And the lady, like Hurst, looked no different than she had at dinner, before their secret assignation. Incredible. Perfectly incredible. How was it possible that two people could have been engaged in doing . . . well, what the two of them had been doing . . . and then, a quarter of an hour later, be calmly dancing the Sir Roger de Coverley with someone *else*?

It was more than a girl like Caroline could assimilate in one evening. When it came time for her and the marquis to promenade, she did so with all the grace of an automaton, hardly aware of what her feet were doing beneath her. Hurst did not seem to notice, however. He was in very high spirits, and swung her about most energetically, whispering endearments into her ear whenever her head came close enough for him to do so. He called her a pretty little thing and said, again, that he couldn't wait until their wedding night to make her his own. Caroline heard what he said, and yet she did not respond. What could she say?

Because of course she knew now there would be no wedding night. Not for the two of them. For whatever reason—and Caroline suspected very strongly that the reason had a good deal to do with the size of the inheritance she'd come into recently, and the fact that Hurst had no income at all—Hurst was not going to break off the engagement.

Which meant only one thing: Caroline was going to have to do it.

It wasn't going to be easy, of course. Her mother would be furious. After all, they owed Hurst Slater ... well, *everything*. If it hadn't been for him, Tommy would have died that chilly December night, bled to death on the street outside his college.

But it couldn't be helped now, could it? How could she possibly marry a man whose kisses had, for so many months, been making her feel as if she were the luckiest girl in the world. . . .

Only to realize he'd been saving his *real* kisses for someone else?

Just once did Caroline come to life during the rowdy country dance, and that was when she happened to find herself partnered momentarily with her brother Thomas, who took the opportunity to give her arm a pinch and say, "Cheer up, puss! You look like someone just told you the punch was poisoned."

"Tommy!" Caroline cried, startled out of her misery by the sight of him. "What do you think you're doing, dancing like this? You know what Dr. Pettigrew said—"

"Oh, Dr. Pettigrew," Thomas said, scathingly. "I wish he'd sod off."

But before she'd had a chance to rebuke her brother, she was whirled away by—of all people—Braden Granville, looking very nearly as grim as she was certain she did, and she clamped her lips shut and said not another word until the reel was over.

But if she'd hoped to escape without further communication with Mr. Granville, she was sorely disappointed. At least if her brother, who stepped forward abruptly and took hold of her arm, had anything to say about it.

"Come on, puss," Tommy said. "Someone sneaked a shrimp onto Ma's plate at dinner, and now she's gotten herself a hive. She's waiting for us in the carriage. Oh, *hullo* there, sir."

Even if she had not happened to have glanced his way, Caroline would have known Braden Granville was still somewhere about from the worshipful way in which Thomas had spoken the word *sir*. The fact that he was standing so *very* near, however—right *beside* her, actually—was rather startling, since she'd thought certain he'd drift away once their dance was over.

"How do you do, Lord Bartlett?" Granville nodded at the younger man. To Caroline, he said, "Lady Caroline. I trust you are feeling better than when we last met."

Caroline, feeling color creep into her cheeks, said quickly, "Indeed," and, in an effort to keep herself from looking a bigger fool in his eyes than she was certain she already did, vowed to say nothing more. . . .

Until, absolutely unbidden, the words, "I see you found the Lady Jacquelyn," tumbled from her lips, almost before she'd realized she'd said them. *Idiot*, she berated herself. Why was it that sometimes she could not force her tongue to move, and at other times, she could not keep it still?

"Yes," Braden Granville replied, as his gaze followed Caroline's to rest upon his fiancée, who stood chatting gaily with Dame Ashforth, looking coolly beautiful and not at all like a woman who'd rather recently been ravished. "I did, indeed. It seems she'd stepped out into Dame Ashforth's garden for a bit of air."

"Granville" then added, noticing Hurst rushing toward them, "I see that you are being sought. I'll keep you no longer."

"Oh," Thomas began, "but it's only *Slater*. . . ."

His protest came too late, however, since Braden Granville had disappeared back into the throng of revelers. Hurst, his handsome face a mask of concern, burst urgently upon them.

"Carrie," he cried. "What's this I hear about your leaving, and so early? I won't hear of it!"

Thomas, put out at his tête-à-tête with his hero being interrupted, rolled his eyes. Caroline shot him a disapproving look. Sometimes it was quite hard to remember that only six months earlier, her brother had been on the brink of death.

"Our mother isn't feeling well, Hurst," she said. "We've got to go. But please, *you* must stay."

Hurst heaved a dramatic sigh. "If you insist, my sweet. Until tomorrow, then." He leaned down as if to kiss her. Caroline just barely kept herself from averting her mouth. The thought of those lips, which had so recently been on Lady Jacquelyn's, touching her own filled her with revulsion—almost as much as the thought of Braden Granville kissing her had earlier filled her with such inexplicable excitement.

But she needn't have worried. Hurst didn't attempt to place his mouth anywhere near hers. Instead, he kissed her lightly on the forehead. Caroline's relief was such that she was halfway down the steep steps that led from Dame Ashforth's town house to the carriage waiting on the street below before she even realized it.

"Good Lord," she heard her brother cry just as one of Dame Ashforth's footmen was handing Caroline into the carriage.

Caroline, thinking that her brother must have forgotten something inside, and dreading the thought of spending another minute more at this house that would forever hold such unhappy memories for her, settled herself onto the seat beside her mother before asking, "What is it, Tommy?"

"That phaeton that just pulled up behind ours." Thomas, leaning over them for a better look, jostled Caroline and her mother dreadfully. "That's Braden Granville's phaeton. Look at the team he's got pulling it, Caro. Perfectly matched bays. We wouldn't have been able to drag Pa away from them."

Caroline, despite her impatience to get away, turned in her seat to look. Their father had been a great horse lover and had passed his passion on to Caroline—somewhat to the embarrassment of her mother, because Caroline was as incapable as her father had been of remaining silent while a horse was being shabbily treated by its owner. This led to frequent and sometimes quite vocal arguments with the drivers of hackney cabs and coal carts, and Lady Bartlett often hid her face in shame at Caroline's unladylike behavior when she came across a team in bearing reins, which were so popular with the more fashion-conscious members of her set, and of which she strongly disapproved.

Braden Granville, however, had not put his team in bearing reins, which caused Caroline to say, approvingly, "Very nice," before she remembered that she didn't want to think about Braden Granville anymore. She almost said so out loud, but her mother beat her to the chase.

"Braden Granville, Braden Granville, Braden Granville!" The Dowager Lady Bartlett, pushing testily at her crinoline, which her son's antics had set askew, let out an exasperated sigh. "Can't you speak of someone else for a change, Thomas? I am sick to death of hearing about Braden Granville."

"Hear, hear," Caroline said. And, at the time, she quite meant it, too.

3

$\mathcal{A}$s it happened, Lady Caroline Linford and her mother were not the only people sick of hearing about Braden Granville. Braden Granville himself was a bit tired of hearing about Braden Granville.

When, the following morning, he opened up the *Times*, and found that he was staring at a story about himself, he shuddered slightly, and set the paper aside. There had been a time, of course, when seeing his name in the *Times*—particularly accompanied, as it was that morning, by the words *wealthy industrialist*—had given him a certain thrill. After all, he had not always been wealthy, and he had not always borne the title industrialist. Once upon a time—very long ago, but still alive in his memory—he had been quite poor, and had been called, by the boys with whom he'd daily roamed the streets of London, in search of mischief and often worse, Dead Eye. Not, of course, because he had one, but because he *was* one, having taken out a rat at the age of five with a slingshot and a pebble, at a distance of fifty paces.

He had seldom, since that illustrious day, looked back, and he didn't care to do so now. But nor did he care, necessarily, to dwell upon his current successes. After all, many of those who fawned over him today had been the selfsame people who'd vilified him a few years back. He was, he knew, neither the genius they thought him now, nor the failure they'd considered him then. The truth, Braden had decided long ago, was somewhere in the middle, and it was best simply not to dwell upon it.

Accordingly, he gathered up the correspondence his secretary had laid upon his desk and began to read it.

A knock upon the door to his private offices interrupted him before he'd finished a single line. He looked up and said, tolerantly, "Come in."

Ronnie "Weasel" Ambrose, a copy of the same newspaper Braden had been looking at a few moments before tucked beneath his arm, slipped into the room and closed the door behind him in the manner of someone who was attempting to appear as inconspicuous as possible to whomever was standing in the other room.

"Sorry for the 'trusion, Dead," he said, as soon as the latch was safely secured. "But *she's* here."

Braden didn't need to ask who *she* might be. He said only, in tones of some surprise, "It's quite early for her, surely. Only just past ten."

"She's got her feathers on," Weasel said, sauntering across the room and collapsing heavily into one of the leather seats across from his employer's massive desk. "You know, the ones she wears to shop in."

"Ah," Braden said. "That explains it."

"Right." Weasel took the paper from his arm and said, casually, "You see the paper today, then, Dead?"

Braden replied, in his deep voice, "I did."

"Did you?" Weasel turned the paper round so that the section which featured his employer faced the man himself. "See this part, here?"

"Indeed," Braden said. "I did."

"Calls it 'elegant.'" Weasel turned the paper to face himself again, and read aloud, not very fluently, but in a voice which was fairly shaking with excitement, despite his seeming nonchalance. "'From the inventor of the breech-loading revolver comes this elegant new pistol, which promises to be this year's most desired model for the discriminating gun collector.'" Weasel glanced at his employer. "Care to hear how many orders for it have rolled in this morning alone?"

Braden said, "Quite a few, I would imagine. Remind me, Weasel, to send the author of that piece a case of brandy."

"And that's not all." The secretary was doing a poor job now at hiding his excitement. He leaned forward eagerly in his chair, wrinkling the pages he held. "Who do you think we received an order from, just a little bit ago? Who do you think, Dead?"

"I couldn't begin to imagine," Braden said, a distinctly uninterested drawl in his voice.

"*The Prince of Wales*, Dead." Weasel's face was flushed, his eyes bright. "*The Prince of Wales* is going to be carrying a Granville pistol this season!"

"The Prince of Wales," Braden said, returning to his correspondence, "*needs* a Granville pistol, he's such a foul shot."

"Dead." Weasel rose to his feet and went to lean upon his friend's desk, the newspaper forgotten, crumpled in one fist. "Dead, what's the matter with you? You just received the most glowing recommendation for one of your guns you've ever had, and in the London *Times*—the *Times*, man, read by more people worldwide than any other newspaper—and you sit there and act as if it were nothing. What in God's name is wrong?"

"Don't be an ass, Weasel." Braden tugged on the lapels of his impeccably cut morning coat. "Nothing is wrong. I'm just a bit done for this morning. Long night last night, don't you know."

Weasel laughed. Few men would have had the courage to laugh at the great "Granville," but Ronald Ambrose had the advantage of twenty years' acquaintance with the man. Why, he'd rubbed Braden Granville's nose in the dirt more times than he could count. That, of course, had been well before his friend's court-appointed apprenticeship had plucked him from the Dials; before his career had consequently taken its meteoric path to its current state; and well before Braden Granville had grown to his full height of several inches over six feet tall.

Still, Weasel, even at a comparably diminutive five feet eight, suffered no compunction in teasing his best friend and employer.

"Oy," he said. "Worn out, are we, from chasin' after the Lady Jackie late into the night?"

Braden growled, "Not that it's any of your business, *Weasel*."

Weasel laughed again, this time at the reminder of how he'd come across his nickname. "Well, any luck then?"

"If you mean, did I discover the identity of the man with whom my fiancée is conducting an illicit affair, the answer is no," Braden said. "At least, nothing that would be admissible in a court of law, if she happens to sue me for breach of promise—"

"*Happens* to sue you?" Weasel hooted. "You think that if you break off your engagement to her, Jackie Seldon isn't going to sue you for everything you've got? My God, Dead! It's less than a month till the wedding."

"I am," Braden said, drily, "well aware of that, Weasel."

Weasel dropped his voice conspiratorially. "I've heard of judges awarding thousands of pounds to brides whose blokes have cried off, some of 'em a solid year before the blessed day. And you're thinking you can get away without 'er suing?"

"I know she'll sue," Braden said, with careful patience, "and I know she'll win, too, unless I have better proof of her faithlessness than badly explained disappearances—like last night—and these infernal rumors that have been floating about."

Weasel shook his head. "Rumors," he said, disgustedly. "You'd think we was back in the Dials, the way these blighters talk about one another. Still, you can't prove nothing from a rumor."

"That," Braden said, "is why I've been having her watched."

"And the boys still haven't come up with anything?"

"Oh, there's a man, all right," Braden said, grimly. "But either the boys've lost their touch, or the fellow is a ghost. Apparently, he can melt into shadows and lose himself in crowds almost as if—"

"—he were one of us," Weasel finished for his employer. He whistled, low and long. "Think he could be?"

"Of course not," Braden said. "How would a duke's daughter get herself involved with a bloke from the Dials?"

"Excepting yourself, you mean?"

Braden barely suppressed a grin at that one. "Obviously," he drawled. "No, I'm reckoning the fellow's married, and is hoping to keep the wife from finding out."

"Or you, more likely," Weasel said. "Probably doesn't want to get his pretty little head blown to bits. Still and all, Dead, wouldn't it be simpler just to let'er sue? You are richer than Croesus, you know. You can easily afford to throw a few thousand pounds her way, and have done with it. And her."

The grin was wiped from Braden's face. "No, I don't think so," he said, as politely as if refusing a cup of tea. "I'm not handing over a farthing more to Lady Jacquelyn Seldon than I have to. Not that way."

Weasel raised his eyebrows. Braden supposed he couldn't blame him. His refusal merely to "have done with" Jacquelyn Seldon puzzled even himself. Pride was clearly what was at work here. His pride, which he'd never before considered so fragile a thing that a mere woman could shake it.

Then again, he'd never before given his heart away.

It was his own fault. He'd been so stunned that such a beautiful, accomplished, and—it might as well be admitted—highly born a woman could ever be interested in him, he'd fallen for her, intoxicated by all that she represented, instead of seeing her for what she was.

He'd learned soon enough. Their engagement had hardly become official before Jackie began to get careless, not being where she'd said she was going to be, or arriving absurdly late for the assignations she did manage to keep with him, and oftentimes looking . . . well, like a woman who'd just been tumbled. And not by him. It was then that Braden began to realize that what he'd neglected to take into consideration was the fact that Jacquelyn was, for all her beauty and rank, still just a woman, as capable of fecklessness as any doxy back in the Dials.

More fool him for not realizing before the announcement was posted.

Weasel heaved a sigh. "It's a cryin' shame, I tell you. What's this world comin' to when a man like Braden Granville—the Lothario of London—can't keep his own fiancée from cheatin' on him? It's almost . . . what do they call it? Oh, right. Poetic justice."

Braden regarded his old friend with a wry smile. "Your keen insight into the ironies of my life is invaluable, Weasel. However, rather than standing there, pontificating upon them, hadn't you better send her ladyship in? There's no telling what Snake and Higginbottom might get up to out there, trying to impress her."

Weasel said, suddenly querulous, "All right. I'll send 'er in. But I'm telling you right now, Braden, I don't like it. I've never seen you this way. Not about a woman. She's not worth it, you know. She may have a title, but she's as fast a piece of baggage as I ever saw."

"Careful, Mr. Ambrose," Braden said, lightly. "That's my future wife you're talking about."

Weasel rolled his eyes. "I'll believe it when I see it."

"Go on with you, Weasel," Braden said, feeling more tired than ever. "Send her in. And find me some coffee, will you? My head feels as if it were in a vise this morning."

Weasel sniffed at this dismissal. "As his serene highness requests." Then, his head held high, but his lips betraying a distinct tendency to curl upward at the corner, the secretary exited the room.

When he was gone, Braden sat for a moment looking out the window to the left of his desk. The view, which was of busy, bustling Bond Street, was as fine as could be purchased in London, and yet Braden didn't see it, not just then. He saw instead, as he often did when he was disturbed about something, his mother's face, as it had looked before the disease which had taken her life had ravaged her pretty features. Those few years before her death had been the happiest ones in Braden's memory. And after she'd gone. . . .

Oh, his father had tried. But Mary Granville had been the light of Sylvester Granville's life as well as her son's, and once she was gone, the old man had become a shell of his formerly vigorous self, half mad, and known to disappear for days at a time in his pursuit of parts for the various and absurd contraptions he invented, leaving Braden alone with affectionate but not very attentive aunts. Was it any wonder he'd fallen in with an unsavory crowd?

Thank God one man, at least, had been there to rescue him from what he might have become. . . .

It was those days before his mother's death that Braden often thought of whenever his career took another dramatic upswing, as it had that morning. Because he had realized, from the moment he'd made his very first hundred pounds—and what a staggering amount it had seemed back then—that it didn't matter. It didn't matter how much money he made. Money didn't matter. All the money in the world wouldn't have saved his mother.

And all the money in the world wouldn't bring her back.

"Braden," declared a flutey, highly cultured voice. "Whatever are you staring at?"

Braden shook himself, and was only slightly surprised to find he was not by the hearth in the room in which he'd grown up, but rather the comfortable office he maintained on Bond Street, not far from the Mayfair town house in which he lived. And the woman addressing him was not his mother, who'd suffered a prolonged and painful death twenty years earlier, but the very much living Lady Jacquelyn Seldon, whose fine figure and even finer face was currently the toast of London.

"I'm jealous," Jacquelyn said, teasingly, stretching her gloved hand across his desk so that he could lay a kiss upon it. "Who is she?"

He stared at her. She was in a new ensemble this morning, one he had never seen before, which seemed to rely heavily upon marabou feather. He could hardly see her face, for all the feathery fronds that were embracing it. Still, what he could see was heartbreakingly beautiful.

"She?" he echoed, taking her hand quite automatically and laying a kiss upon it before returning it to her.

"Yes, silly. The one you were sitting there thinking of. Don't try to tell me it wasn't a woman." Jacquelyn seated herself confidently upon the edge of his desk, oblivious to the dangerous way her crinoline tilted upward as she did so. Then again, she might have been perfectly aware of what she was doing, and was hoping to show off a new pair of pantaloons. She was quite coquettish, in that way.

"It was a woman," Braden said, slowly, taking his seat again. He had risen as soon as he'd realized she was there, as a gentleman ought to do. Though he was not, if truth be told, completely convinced she was a lady. Oh, by birth, certainly. But not by nature. Which had been, at one time, part of her appeal: the daughter of a duke who was decidedly not above behaving quite indecorously . . . what more could a man hope for in a wife?

Quite a bit, Braden was discovering, if that wife chose to behave indecorously with more than just her husband.

Or husband-to-be, as in this case.

"I *am* jealous," Jacquelyn said, her lower lip jutting out to form a fetching pout. "Who is she? Tell me, now. You know what a horrid possessive creature I am, Granville. And you've such a reputation.

I know scads and scads of women have been in love with you. Just who have you gone and added to your stable now?"

Braden said nothing. He rarely needed to, when Jacquelyn was in the room. She did quite enough talking for the both of them.

"Let me see." She tapped a finger to the side of her chin. "Who did I see you talking with last night? Well, Dame Ashforth, of course, but she's much too old for you. I know she's quite besotted with you, but hardly the type of woman a man would sit about, mooning over. So not Dame Ashforth. Who else was there? Oh, yes. The little Linford girl. But she's much too plain for a man of your discriminating taste. Whoever could it be, Granville? I give up."

"You give up too easily," he said, easily. "But I shall tell you anyway. It was my mother."

"Oh." Jacquelyn made a moue of disappointment. "I'd never have guessed *that*. You never speak of her."

"No," Braden said. "I do not." Not to her. Not now. Not ever. "So, my lady. Supposing you tell me what I could possibly have done to earn the honor of your presence so early in the day. I have it on rather good authority, having spent enough nights with you to know, that it is only the most vital of reasons that will compel you from your bed before noon."

Jacquelyn smiled at him archly. "You think you know me so well then, Mr. Granville? It's quite possible, you know, that I still have a few secrets."

"Oh," Braden said. "I know you do. And when I finally catch you out in them, my dear, I shall make my lawyer a prodigiously happy man."

Jacquelyn's smile faded. "W-what?" she stammered. Under her rouge—only the lightest powdering, all a lady of Jacquelyn's position would allow herself—she went visibly pale. "*W*-whatever are you talking about, my pet?"

Braden, sorry he'd spoken so flippantly—and not at all sure what had prompted the outburst, save the prickle of irritation he'd felt at her catty reference to Lady Caroline Linford, a girl with whom he had only the most passing acquaintance, and in whom he certainly had not the slightest interest—and half fearful he'd tipped his hand, said quickly, "I do apologize, my lady." The last thing he needed was for her to grow suspicious, and, in her suspicion, more careful in arranging her assignations with her lover. "I spoke in jest, but I realize now it was not, perhaps, in the best of taste. Now, to what do I owe the honor of this early morning visit?"

Jacquelyn continued to eye him uneasily, but his demeanor, which he kept purposefully bland, seemed to disarm her, and the color soon returned to her face. When she'd fully recovered, she cried, blithely, "Oh, Granville, *darling*, it's the strangest thing, but Virginia Crowley's come down with one of those troublesome spring colds, and she was supposed to have her appointment today with Mr. Worth. Well, you know I couldn't get one, due to . . . well, that incident last time I saw Mr. Worth, concerning Father's credit. But suddenly Virginia said I might have hers, and you know, Braden, I do so want to look like the sort of wife an important man like yourself deserves, but my trousseau, such as it is, is hardly fit for a knacker's wife, let alone the wife of someone like—"

Braden reached into his waistcoat pocket. "How much do you need?"

"Oh." Jacquelyn looked joyous, then immediately became thoughtful. "Well, I need just about everything, hats, capes, gloves, shoes, stockings, not to mention underthings. . . . I suppose this much will do." She held the index finger and thumb of her right hand about half an inch apart.

Braden handed her a pile of bills of approximately the thickness she'd indicated. "Give my regards to Mr. Worth." Better this now, he thought, than thousands more later in court fees.

"Oh, *thank you*, darling." Jacquelyn leaned across the desk, her lips puckered to accept a kiss from him, the money having been tucked quickly into her reticule. Braden raised his face, intending to pass his mouth lightly across hers, a quick, good-bye kiss. But Jacquelyn evidently had other ideas. She reached out, seized hold of his lapels, and pulled him toward her, thrusting her tongue between his lips and pressing her not inconsiderable bosom boldly against him.

Braden, who'd quite thoroughly enjoyed the Lady Jacquelyn's forward ways in the past, did not appreciate them nearly so much now. For one thing, the marabou was a bit problematic, flying about as it was, and tickling his nostrils. For another, he knew quite well that he was not the only man upon whom she practiced them.

Which was why it was so vitally important that he discover some proof of her perfidy, and get it to Mr. Lightwood—who'd handle the breach of promise suit she'd undoubtedly bring about as soon as he ended the engagement—posthaste.

"Well," he said, after Jacquelyn had finally leaned back again, breaking the kiss. "That was . . . nice."

"Nice?" Jacquelyn hopped off his desk, looking annoyed. "There wasn't anything *nice* intended. Quite the opposite, as a matter of fact. Really, Braden, but I think you've changed."

"Changed?" Braden couldn't help grinning at that. *"I've* changed?"

"Yes, you have. Do you know it's been a month—well, very nearly—since we last . . . well, spent the night with one another?"

He said, easily, "Ah, but Jacquelyn, you know things are different now that we're engaged. We can't be as wild as we once were. People will talk."

"You didn't used to care what people thought." Jacquelyn spoke with some bitterness. "In fact, if I recall correctly, your motto used to be 'Bugger what people think.'"

"Yes," Braden said, carefully. "But that was when I had only my own reputation to think of, not that of my future bride."

She sighed, and looked heavenward. "Well, if you should happen to change your mind," she said, as she sailed toward the door, "you know where to find me."

And then she was gone. But she'd left behind ample evidence of her presence, in the form of a cloud of rose-scented perfume, and a few stray marabou feathers, which settled, like fallen autumn leaves, upon his desk.

It seemed as if no sooner had Braden Granville's fiancée left the room, however, than his father barreled into it, a very irritated Weasel Ambrose on his heels.

"Braden, my boy," Sylvester Granville cried, one arm spread wide in greeting, the other clutching a familiar leather-bound book. "Congratulations!"

"Congratulations?" Braden glanced at Weasel, who could only shake his head. Standing orders were that the senior Granville was to be admitted to his son's office whenever he wished . . . though generally some attempt was made to announce him beforehand.

Today, however, Sylvester Granville was clearly too excited to wait for such formalities.

"You can't mean you haven't heard?" Sylvester lowered himself into one of the leather seats before his son's desk. "I saw the Lady Jacquelyn leaving just now. I hope you don't mind that I shared the happy news with her."

Braden sank back into his chair, from which he'd risen politely while bidding adieu to his bride. He was tired, and his head still ached. He wondered what had happened to the coffee Weasel had promised him.

"What news?" he asked, without much interest.

"Why, the news I heard this morning. It's all over town. On account of the newspaper story, about that new gun of yours."

"What about it?" Braden asked.

"Oh." As his son's bank account had grown, so had Sylvester Granville's waistline, and now he wriggled a bit in his chair. He was by no means obese. Still, he was a man who'd spent most of his life going to bed at least a little bit hungry, and the weight he'd put on in the past few years seemed occasionally to take even him by surprise.

"Don't you know, then? Well, they say it's a sure thing you'll be offered a letter of patent by the end of the year. A baronetcy, most likely." Sylvester shook his head dreamily. "Imagine. My son, a baronet. And married to the daughter of a duke! My grandchildren will have blue blood in their veins, as well as titles before their names. A man couldn't ask more for his only progeny."

Braden stared at his father. The old man had, of course, become a bit unhinged after the death of Braden's mother, but his madness had always been more whimsical than anything else, with him fancying, for instance, that he'd invented a contraption in which a man might fly, or a potion that might make him invisible. Sylvester Granville's recent fixation with the nobility—as illustrated by the book of peerage he clutched in his hands—had seemed harmless in comparison. Now Braden wondered if he ought to have been more worried.

"A baronetcy?" Braden echoed. "I don't think so."

"Oh, yes. Yes, indeed," his father assured him. " Apparently, it was the Prince of Wales's suggestion. Well, the whole breechloading business, that was what started it, I understand. And now this new gun—the Granville—well, everyone is talking about it. Why, I heard the young Duke of Rawlings shot a fellow at Oxford with one, just last week. Now, let me see." He opened the leather-bound book in his lap, and turned to his favorite page, the one which listed the births and deaths of the Seldons, Lady Jacquelyn's family, the one upon which, in a future printing, his son's name would appear—if Braden ended up going through with the thing, that is. "I do hope you manage to receive the title before the wedding. Then the wording will be Jacquelyn, only daughter of the fourteenth Duke of Childes, married to Braden Granville, baronet, June Twenty-ninth, Eighteen Hundred and Seventy. . . ."

Braden realized, with something akin to horror, that there was no madness to this. None at all. His father was speaking the God's honest truth.

Weasel, still standing in the doorway, asked with extreme politeness, "You still want me to bring you that coffee, my lord?"

"Yes," Braden said, in a strangled voice. "And add a bit of whiskey to it, will you, Weasel?"

4

The Dowager Lady Bartlett looked up from her breakfast tray and asked, "Why is it that there isn't a servant in our household who can follow a simple instruction? I asked for a three-minute egg, and what do they bring me?" She lifted the brown egg from its silver cup and tapped it illustratively against the tray resting over her lap. "Listen to that," she said. "Completely hard-boiled. Don't you think if I'd wanted a hard-boiled egg, I'd have asked for one?"

Caroline hesitated. Conscious that her mother had not felt well the night before, Caroline had waited until morning to break her unhappy news. But it appeared clear that now was not a particularly good time, either. Was there ever a good time to break the news to one's mother that five hundred wedding invitations had to be rescinded? Probably not. Accordingly, Caroline took a deep breath and said, "Mother, something horrible has happened."

"More horrible," Lady Bartlett said, "than my ruined breakfast? That I cannot imagine."

Although she was propped up in the massive bed she'd shared with her husband up until an apoplexy had felled him, Lady Bartlett looked no less formidable than usual. She had always been a beautiful woman, and even now, in her forties, was still enormously sought after, and not necessarily for purely pecuniary reasons. The fortune her beloved husband had left her and their children was considerable, but there were many gentlemen to whom the Dowager Lady Bartlett's glowing white skin and piercing blue eyes—which, though they might now sport tiny creases at the corners, were still opined by many to be the finest eyes in England—were even more appealing than her inheritance.

Lady Bartlett, however, would have nothing to do with these gentlemen. She claimed it was because she had not yet gotten over the death of the earl, only two years gone, but Caroline suspected that her mother rather enjoyed playing the role of the rich widow.

"Well," Lady Bartlett said, narrowing those fine eyes now at her daughter, who unfortunately had inherited neither her mother's white skin—Caroline's had an unfortunate tendency to tan—nor her fine eyes, Caroline's being the dullest shade of brown, without even any interesting mahogany or russet bits. "What is it?"

Caroline stood twisting the ring on her left middle finger. It was the ring Hurst had given her, his grandmother's ring. It was beautiful, all heavy gold with a large blue sapphire in the middle, a sapphire that was every bit as blue as Hurst's eyes. Caroline knew she would have to give it back to him now, and was not as saddened by the prospect as she suspected she ought to have been. The ring was very old and valuable, and she'd been frightened she might lose it, as she had a tendency to do with her own belongings.

"It's Lord Winchilsea," Caroline said, unable to meet the penetrating directness of Lady Bartlett's famous gaze. "I'm afraid . . . I'm afraid he has not been faithful to me, Mother."

Caroline's gaze went to the vial of smelling salts at her mother's bedside. She was fully prepared to leap forward and unstop the cork the moment her mother fell into a swoon. But Lady Bartlett did not faint. Instead, she buttered a slice of toast, quite calmly, Caroline thought, under the circumstances.

"Oh, dear," Lady Bartlett said, after she'd taken a large bite. "Well, that is unfortunate. However did you find out?"

Caroline was not quite sure she'd heard her mother aright. "Unfortunate?" she repeated, her voice rising a little. "*Unfortunate*, did you say, Ma?"

"You needn't shout, Caroline. And I've asked you and your brother not to call me Ma. You know how vulgar it sounds. It was all right when we were living in Cheapside, but now. . . ." She shuddered delicately. "And yes, I do think it's unfortunate. I would have thought the marquis had more sense than to throw it up in your face." She added a dollop of jam to her toast. "But then, I'd also thought you'd have more sense, Caroline, than to upset yourself over something so trivial."

"Trivial?" Caroline burst out. "Trivial? Mother, I *walked in* on him! I *walked in* on my fiancé with—with this other woman! And not to be indelicate, but they were . . . well, sharing a moment." Caroline's mother was a scrupulously tidy woman who did not like mess, and tended to consider the human body one of the messiest things of all. For that reason, she chose to discuss its various functions as little as possible, and most especially avoided all references to functions performed in the boudoir. Caroline, respecting this, did not elaborate regarding just what, exactly, she'd seen her fiancé doing. It was enough for her to reiterate, significantly, "A *moment*, Mother."

"Oh, dear." Lady Bartlett sank back against her pillows. "My poor Caroline. My poor dear Caroline." Then, as if rallying herself, she said, "Caroline, darling. I know you must be very hurt. But you're really taking it much too hard. You can't have thought a man like the marquis wouldn't have a mistress."

"A mistress?" Caroline repeated. Tears, which had evaded her for so long, seemed to surface all at once, and in such copious amounts that it was almost as if they were making up for lost time, flooding her vision, and making her feel as if she were melting, a singularly unpleasant sensation. "A mistress? No, I never thought

Hurst had a mistress. Why should I? And why should *he*? What does he need a mistress for, when he has *me*?"

On the word *me*, Caroline broke down completely, and threw herself upon her mother's bed, causing the coffee on Lady Bartlett's breakfast tray to slosh dangerously. Lady Bartlett lifted the cup to keep it from spilling further as her daughter's sobs racked the bed.

"Now, dear," Lady Bartlett said. She reached out with her free hand and patted Caroline's tumbled hair fondly. "Don't take on so. I know it must be a shock to you, and for that I blame myself. I just assumed you knew. I had no idea you were such a little innocent, Caroline. But you see, darling, that's how men like the marquis *do* things. That's what all these titled fellows do, you know. Keep mistresses on the side."

"Papa didn't," Caroline said fiercely, into the comforter.

"Well, of course your father didn't, Caroline. He *loved* me."

Lady Bartlett uttered this last as if Caroline was dense not to have realized it already. But of course she'd known it perfectly well. Caroline's father had quite doted on his little family, but especially upon his wife, whom he'd always said had had her pick of suitors. Why she'd chosen him, Lord Bartlett had often mused, he couldn't guess, though Caroline was fairly certain that her mother's eyes were not only very fine, but very farsighted, as well. She had known perfectly well that young Hiram Linford was destined for greatness. And he had not disappointed her, except perhaps by not living long enough to see his grandchildren . . . if either she or Tommy ever produced any, which at this point, Caroline was rather beginning to doubt.

"Mistresses weren't the thing at all in Cheapside," Lady Bartlett said. "Your father was different, Caroline. He came into his title late in life. He wasn't *born* into nobility, like your marquis. And that's quite a different kettle of fish, being *born* into it, you know."

"He isn't *my* marquis," Caroline said, even more fiercely, though she still didn't lift her head from the bed. "Not anymore."

"Don't be ridiculous," Lady Bartlett said. "Lord Winchilsea is still yours, Caroline."

"He isn't," Caroline said. "*I don't want him.* And you know he only wants me for my money, Mother."

"Caroline, how can you say such a thing? After what he did for your brother—"

Caroline raised her tearstained face from the bed. "I *know* what he did for Tommy, Mother. How could I forget? I'm reminded of it every time Tommy walks into the room. If it weren't for Hurst—if it weren't for Hurst—"

"Your brother would be dead," Lady Bartlett finished for her daughter. "And now you're ungrateful enough to say you won't marry him, just because he made one little mistake—"

"Not ungrateful," Caroline declared, wiping her eyes with the cuff of her sleeve. "I'm *very* grateful for what he did for us, Mother. Only I don't see—I just don't see why—"

"Besides," Lady Bartlett said, as if Caroline hadn't been speaking, "Even if we didn't owe him Tommy's life, it's much too late to drop him now. The invitations have already gone out."

Caroline sniffled. "I thought—I thought we might put an announcement in the paper, calling the wedding off."

Lady Bartlett set her coffee cup down again, not very carefully, and some more of it sloshed over the side, onto her breakfast tray. "*Take out an announcement in the paper?*" she echoed. "Have you lost your mind, Caroline? Hasn't it occurred to you that if we did any such thing, the marquis would be perfectly within his rights to take legal action against us? And do you have the slightest idea the kind of talk it would generate? My God, people would think us the most ungrateful creatures in the world—"

"Legal action?" Caroline shook her head. "But what for? *He* was the one who had his tongue in someone else's mouth, not *me.*"

Lady Bartlett, hearing this, heaved a shudder of distaste, but went resolutely on, like a soldier picking his way across a battlefield littered with his fallen comrades. "And are you prepared to mention that in a civil court, young lady? Are you prepared to humiliate yourself by publicly admitting such a thing? Do you imagine, my dear, that any girl who did have the ill judgment to admit such a thing would ever have another marriage proposal from anyone respectable *ever again*?"

Caroline felt a fresh wave of tears sting her eyes. "B-but . . ."

"Certainly not. Besides thinking you the most ungrateful, hardened girl who ever walked—abandoning at the altar the man who saved your brother's life—you would be the laughingstock of London. We would never find anyone remotely suitable for you. You'd die an old maid."

This did not sound to Caroline like such a terrible fate, considering that the alternative was marrying a man who it turned out was not the least bit in love with her.

"I shouldn't mind that," she said. "I know quite a few old— well, spinsters. And many of them seem to lead fulfilling lives, performing good works for the poor, and striving to put an end to workhouses, and—"

Lady Bartlett looked appalled. "What, in heaven's name," she demanded, "have you been doing, mingling with women like *that*? Lord, this is Emmy's doing, isn't it?"

Caroline stuck out her chin. "It hasn't anything to do with Emmy. You know perfectly well that some mornings I attend lectures at the—"

"No daughter of mine," Lady Bartlett said, fixing Caroline with a very stern gaze, "is going to end up a spinster. Good Lord! Your father would spin in his grave at the very thought. How we scrimped and saved for you to go to that ladies' seminary, before he made his fortune! Why, those dancing slippers of yours alone cost a small ransom. If you think I intend to let all that go to waste . . ." Lady Bartlett's voice trailed off threateningly.

Caroline could not help scowling. She had certainly never

asked to be sent to the expensive and exclusive school her parents had insisted upon her attending, nor had she enjoyed her time there. The other girls—including none other than Lady Jacquelyn Seldon, who'd been a few years ahead of Caroline—had not been very welcoming of the "upstart from Cheapside," as they'd called her . . . all except Emmy, of course, in whom Caroline had found a sympathetic comrade.

Still, she had to admit her schooling had been occasionally useful. She now knew how to say, "Please stop beating your horse," in five languages.

"The fact is, Caroline," Lady Bartlett went on, not noticing her daughter's scowl, "that as usual you are troubling yourself over nothing. What you ought to be is grateful."

Caroline choked. *"Grateful?"*

"Certainly. The fact that Lord Winchilsea has a mistress means he won't be asking you to do anything . . . well, unpleasant."

Caroline narrowed her eyes, wondering what her mother meant, and knowing it was useless to ask. Lady Bartlett would only sputter and turn red, as she always did when Caroline questioned her about the sexual act. Was having a man shove his tongue into one's mouth *unpleasant*? Lady Jacquelyn certainly hadn't looked as if she'd thought so. Was straddling a man, and riding him as if he were a pony *unpleasant*? Lady Jacquelyn had looked as if she'd been enjoying it immensely.

Were these the sort of things Caroline ought to be grateful Lord Winchilsea wouldn't be doing to her?

"Now," her mother said briskly. "Pull yourself together, Caroline. I've had a letter of regret from the McMartins, which means we can pull someone up from the B list. Who do you want more, the Allingtons, or the Sneads? The Allingtons ought to give you a nicer gift, but the Sneads do own a country place where the Prince of Wales frequently stays—"

Not believing what she was hearing, Caroline stared at her mother in horror. "Ma," she said, "I can't marry a man who is only marrying me for my money. You know I can't."

Lady Bartlett blinked her fine eyes. "Caroline Victoria Linford," she said, not without some indignation. "What on earth makes you think the marquis is only marrying you for your money?"

"Oh, I don't know," Caroline said fiercely. "Perhaps it's because I saw him last night *with another woman's legs wrapped around his waist.*"

Lady Bartlett blanched, and Caroline knew at once that she had gone too far. "Caroline Linford!" her mother cried.

"Well," Caroline wailed, "it's true!"

Regaining some of her composure, Lady Bartlett said, fussing with her negligee strings, "I would think, Caroline, considering the novels I've found in your room, you of all people would hardly find such a scene very shocking."

"That isn't the *point*, Mother. Hurst only wants to marry me for my money," Caroline said, between gritted teeth. "You know it as well as I do."

"If that," Lady Bartlett said, "is true, I can only say it's your own fault, Caroline."

"*My* fault?" Caroline's voice cracked. "How on earth is it *my* fault?"

"If he doesn't love you, it's only because you haven't worked hard enough at it. Men don't simply fall in love, Caroline. They have to be pushed into it. And I haven't noticed you doing any sort of pushing at all where the marquis is concerned."

"Mother—"

"Are you in love with him?"

Caroline's mouth fell open. "What?"

"It's a simple question, Caroline. Are you in love with the marquis?"

Caroline closed her mouth and swallowed. "I thought I was," she said. "Up until last night. How could I *not*? He's—" Caroline's throat closed up, making it impossible for her to say more.

"He's extremely charming," Lady Bartlett said, knowingly. "And not only charming, but handsome, and incredibly brave. The way he chased off those footpads who assaulted your brother that night—"

"And stopped up Tommy's wound," Caroline murmured. She'd heard the story so many times, she could utter it quite by rote. "With his own handkerchief, saving him from bleeding to death before the surgeon arrived. And stayed with us, the whole time Tommy was recuperating. . . ."

"There," Lady Bartlett said, warmly. "The man saved your brother's life. Of course you're in love with him. How could you not be?" She reached out and patted Caroline's hand. "I wouldn't be able to resist him myself, if I were your age. So I'm afraid you're going to have to face facts, Caroline: You're going to have to fight for him."

"*Fight* for him? And precisely how do you suggest I do that, Mother? Challenge his mistress to a duel?"

Lady Bartlett frowned. "Remember what I said about sarcasm, young lady. Nothing is more unattractive in a lady. No, by fight for him, I mean use the weapons God gave you. That brain in your head, which, despite the tripe you've been feeding it, is a good one. And your body, which, if I do say so myself, is the spitting image of the one I had at your age, and which I used to excellent advantage in securing your father, may he rest in peace. These are very important pieces of advice I'm giving you, Caroline. You ought to be writing them down. Do you want to run and fetch some paper?"

Caroline frowned right back at her mother. "No. You mean I ought to throw myself at him?"

"Good Lord." Lady Bartlett looked heavenward. "No, Caroline. Exercise some womanly wiles. You know how."

"I—"

"You *know* how. Every woman does." Lady Bartlett glanced down at her breakfast and sighed. "I know he's handsome, Caroline, and I know he's a marquis. But you just have to keep in mind that you are every bit as pretty as he is good-looking. Well, very nearly. And your father was an earl."

"Ma," Caroline said, impatiently, "Papa was only made an earl because the queen was grateful to him for installing new *plumbing* in the palace."

"*Revolutionary* new plumbing," Lady Bartlett reminded her daughter. "That made it possible for the queen to have hot water whenever she pleased, with the turn of a faucet, no small feat in a building as old as the palace is. That is nothing to speak so scornfully about, Caroline. Your father was a plumbing *genius.*"

Caroline looked at the ceiling. "I know Papa was a genius, Ma. But they're a bit different, Papa's title and Hurst's title. You've got to admit it."

Lady Bartlett shrugged. "Apples and oranges, Caroline. Apples and oranges. Now run along. I've got to dress. Oh, and Caroline?"

Caroline, who'd reluctantly pushed herself up from the bed and gone to the door, turned to look back at her pretty mother, so small, so alone and fragile-seeming in that massive bed. "Yes?"

"Do remember that life is not a penny dreadful." Lady Bartlett smiled at her quite sunnily. "In reality, happy endings—like your father's and mine—are actually quite rare."

Caroline nodded, but inwardly, she was thinking furiously, *We'll see. We'll just see about that, won't we?*

*T*he Lady Jacquelyn Seldon was a prodigious shopper. She shopped with an intensity of purpose and sense of concentration—charting routes and tactics well beforehand—that a military strategist might have envied. When Lady Jacquelyn Seldon shopped, everything else seemed to cease to exist, with the exception of Lady Jacquelyn, the product for which she was searching, and the amount of cash that was in her purse.

Which was why it wasn't until she'd stepped into the dressing room of a stylish shop on Bond Street that she realized she had been followed. Imagine her astonishment when the shop clerk threw open the dressing room door and said, with a wink, "There you are, my lady," and Lady Jacquelyn stepped into the room to find it not quite empty.

There was a man, his face hidden in the folds of a cloak that was much too heavy for springtime, seated upon the brocade-covered bench across from the full-length mirror.

Lady Jacquelyn drew in breath to scream, but before she could utter a sound, the man threw back the cloak, leaped up, and flung a hand across her mouth.

"Devil take you, Jackie," the Marquis of Winchilsea hissed.

"There have to be half a dozen starchy old matrons out there. Do you want them to hear?"

Jacquelyn, panting hard, whispered as he lowered his hand, "What in heaven's name is the matter with you, Hurst? Are you mad?"

"I'm sorry, Jackie," Hurst said, sinking back down to the bench again. "I hadn't any choice. I think . . . I think I'm being watched."

"Watched? By whom?" Jacquelyn demanded, settling herself down upon the bench beside him, tugging on her bonnet strings. "Here, darling, see what you can do about this. It's turned into a dreadful snarl."

Hurst obliged, albeit perfunctorily, plucking at the knot in the silken bonnet strings. "If I knew who it was, I'd do something about it, now, wouldn't I, love? And I'm sorry to burst in on you like this, Jacks, but I couldn't wait. I had to see you. I simply had to."

Jacquelyn, keeping her chin raised so that Hurst could reach the knot, couldn't help but smile. Really, but it was delightful, the way he couldn't seem to get enough of her. She'd have thought their little interlude at Dame Ashforth's the night before would have satisfied him for a bit, but evidently not. A far cry, she thought, her smile fading a little, from Braden Granville, who lately did not seem to remember that she was even alive.

"Darling," he said, when he'd got the knot undone at last, and she'd whipped the bonnet from her head, and turned to the mirror to examine the extent it had ruined her coiffure.

"Yes?" she said, absently, noting how well their reflections looked together. Pity Hurst hadn't Granville's money. The two of them would have made such a striking couple.

"Does he know?" he asked, worriedly.

She blinked, the rich forest of her lashes momentarily hiding her gaze from him. "Does *who* know, Hurst?"

"Granville," he hissed. "Granville! Who do you think?"

Jacquelyn's perfectly plucked eyebrows lowered. She wasn't

going to tell him. What was the point? That remark Granville had made about his lawyer . . . he had been joking. Of course he had been joking. Not in very good taste, of course, but then what else could one expect of a man who'd been so coarsely reared?

"What are you talking about?" she asked her lover, lightly. "Of course he doesn't know."

"Are you sure?" Hurst looked uncertain. "Because last night—I could have sworn he'd found us out."

"Yes," Jacquelyn agreed, forcing a giggle. "That was close, wasn't it? We'll have to be a good deal more careful in the future. But it was worth it, wasn't it?"

"Of course it was," Hurst said, but his tone was hurried. "Did he say anything to you afterward? Anything to indicate he might . . . know."

"Don't be silly, darling," Jacquelyn said, easily. "Granville hasn't any idea. I've only just come from his offices. He's as blissfully ignorant as ever. Look, he even gave me this." She reached into her reticule, and pulled out the large pile of notes she'd wheedled from her fiancé. "Do you think if he knew anything about the two of us, he'd have parted with so much so easily? I tell you, he has no idea." As she said it, she willed herself to believe it.

"Hasn't he?" Hurst's impossibly handsome face wore an expression Jacquelyn didn't like. She didn't like it at all. "Are you certain? Because I'm certain someone's been following me."

"Following you? Oh, Hurst, really. You can't think . . ." Only then did Jacquelyn's self-assurance slip just a little. "Well. . . . He has been a bit . . . standoffish, lately."

Hurst reached out and grasped her shoulders in a painful grip. "What do you mean?"

"Well, not to put too fine a point on it, he hasn't wanted to . . . you know. In quite a while." Jacquelyn hoped it didn't show, how much this fact bothered her. She wasn't in love with Braden Granville— heaven forbid!—but it bothered her, the fact that he no longer seemed as smitten with her as he'd once been. It bothered her more than it should.

Hurst looked alarmed. "But that won't do. That won't do at all. You've got to keep him interested, Jacks. We can't have him calling it off." He gave her a little shake. "Not now."

"I know that." She blinked at him. "Do you think I don't know that? Don't worry. I have a grand seduction planned."

"When?"

"After the Dalrymples'."

"But that's not for—"

Jacquelyn laid a finger over his lips.

"Don't worry," she said, again. "Jackie has it all under control. You will wed your rich little plumber's daughter, and I will wed my wealthy gunsmith, and the two of us will meet in secret in Biarritz every other month or so, and everything will be just the way we planned—"

Hurst let go of Jacquelyn suddenly, and leaned forward until he'd sunk his face into his hands. "Oh," he said, into his fingers. *"God."*

"Darling?" Jacquelyn laid a hand upon his shoulder. "You don't like Biarritz? I suppose we *could* go to Portofino, instead."

"It's not that," he said, with a groan. "It's nothing to do with that."

"Then what is it?"

But he couldn't tell her, of course. He'd look such a fool. And he never wanted to look that way, not in front of her.

"Darling? What is it? Do tell me." Jacquelyn gazed concernedly down at him. As she did so, she happened to catch a glimpse of her own reflection in the dressing mirror, and she thought to herself how very well a look of concern became her. Perhaps she ought to look concerned around Granville. Then he might notice her a bit more. "Is it just that you think you're being followed?"

Hurst sunk his fingers into his eyelids, massaging them. "Yes," he said, into his hands. "Yes, that's it. It's just that I'm being followed. That's all."

"La, that's nothing," Jacquelyn said, tucking a stray curl of her midnight black hair back behind a shell-like ear. "So long as you haven't let them see you coming from my place."

"Of course I haven't," Hurst said, into his hands. "You know how careful I am. Even before I was sure, I always took care not to be seen."

Jacquelyn smiled. "Well, then, what does it matter? As long as Granville doesn't suspect—"

Hurst lifted his face. He wasn't certain how much longer he could take all of this.

"But what if it isn't Granville?" Hurst exploded. "What if it's . . . someone else?"

Jacquelyn burst into bright, tinkling laughter. "Well, who else could it be, darling? You can't have *two* jealous husbands-to-be after you, can you?"

"You don't understand," Hurst murmured, despairingly. "You don't understand at all."

"Understand what?" Jacquelyn tore her gaze from her reflection and looked at him. "Darling, whatever is the matter?"

He only shook his head. How could he tell her? How could he tell anyone? It was an impossible situation, and, loath as he was to admit it, it was all his own doing. But how could he have known? As a brash nineteen-year-old, he'd stumbled into it, drawn in as innocently as a lamb to the slaughter.

Well, maybe not that innocently. Lambs did not, of course, play cards.

But Lewis's invitation had been irresistible. There weren't many card games at Oxford that offered the kind of stakes that Hurst, an inveterate gambler, was looking for. The fact that the one Lewis mentioned took place in the back of a less-than-reputable tavern ought to have been his first clue. And the fact that the dealer called himself The Duke, when he was clearly anything but, should have sent him running.

But he'd stayed. He'd stayed because he was the best player in his circle—a circle made up of privileged, titled young men like himself—which made him believe he was the best player in the world.

But the best player in the world could not beat these fellows.

At first Hurst did not know why. He'd lost, and then he'd lost some more. And since he hadn't had anything much to begin with—not even the promise of a few thousand pounds when he turned twenty-one, since his family had nothing, nothing except their good name and a few abbeys—he hadn't the slightest hope of paying back what he owed.

But The Duke hadn't been angry. In later years, Hurst had seen The Duke angry, and that night was nothing in comparison. The Duke had been quite calm. Since Hurst could not pay him back in money, he'd pay him back by taking over Lewis's job of luring more innocent, privileged young Oxford men—like he himself had been—into the game.

Only, The Duke had added, with a smile, it would be better if the innocents Hurst brought him actually had the funds to cover their losses.

For a while, it had not been a bad arrangement. Hurst had proved quite good at his job. And when he had finally learned why he'd lost so badly, he'd felt as if he'd been brought in on a valuable family secret. He was not even resentful. He applied himself to his task with even more vigor. It was comforting to know he was not the only young man in England who'd been so easily duped.

And when he'd finally been obliged to leave Oxford—his family's limited funds could not be stretched far enough to allow him more than a year there—he'd continued in The Duke's employ, advising the young Oxford-bound boys he knew of the "best game in town," and often making the trip from town for the express purpose of escorting them to that game.

It had all been going far better than anyone—least of all Hurst, who knew himself to be quite without any employable skills whatsoever—had expected, until the night the young Earl of Bartlett had accused The Duke of cheating. Then it had all ended, in a shower of blood and bullets.

For a while he'd thought he was safe, that The Duke didn't know . . . how could he? The two of them hardly traveled in the same circles, and The Duke certainly did not read the society pages.

But now, he was certain. He'd seen the man—the man with the walking stick, the one who'd been trying so desperately not to be seen—as he'd left his mother's place earlier that morning. He wouldn't have thought anything of it had he not seen the man again, outside his tailor's.

That cinched it. He'd been found out. He was going to be made to pay for what he'd done. . . .

Because if it wasn't Granville's men that were following him—and, oh, how much preferable if it were!—it could only be The Duke's. And while the thought of Granville sussing out his affair with Jackie and ruining his chances with Caroline was unsettling, the thought of The Duke finding out the truth about what he'd done was terrifying.

"Hurst, darling." Jacquelyn sounded concerned. "Let me help. You know how good I am at making you feel better."

He wrenched his hands away from his face. "You can't," he cried, aware that he sounded like a wild man, and not caring. "All right, Jackie? This is one time there's nothing—nothing—you can do to help."

Jacquelyn raised her eyebrows.

And without another word, she leaned down and lifted the hem of her skirt, revealing her long legs, clad in stylish lace-trimmed pantaloons. Pantaloons which, she soon showed him, were quite easily removed.

"Nothing?" Jacquelyn asked, as she brought his head down toward her lap.

Hurst gazed at the thick black patch of down between her legs. "Well," he admitted, reflectively. "Maybe something."

6

"Unpleasant how?" Lady Emily Stanhope asked, as the birdie struck her racket with a satisfying *poing*.

"I don't know," Caroline said. She darted forward to return her friend's serve. "She didn't say. I suppose she means that his mistress will do . . . you know. The sort of things wives don't."

"And what sort of things are they?" Emily asked, lunging to return Caroline's lob. "Dammit," she said, when the birdie stuck to the net.

"I don't know," Caroline said, again. She approached the net, the racket swinging loosely from her hand. "That was quite an easy one. How could you have missed it?"

"Shut up," Emily said. "And stop trying to change the subject. What sort of things?"

"I told you, Emmy. I don't know."

Emily looked impatient. "Well, all right, then. I want to know what's so lucky about it."

"Lucky?"

"You said you were lucky. You're about to marry an adulterous cad. What's so lucky about *that*?"

"Lord, Emmy," she said. "Do you have to shout it? Someone might hear, you know. I told you in the strictest confidence—"

"It seems I must shout it," Emily declared, "since evidently, you don't understand. There's nothing lucky about it, Caroline. Nothing at all. You are saddled with an oppressor, the lowest of the low, the kind of man against whom we at the society have been fighting for years. . . ."

"I'm just saying," Caroline explained, through gritted teeth, "that it's lucky Lady Jacquelyn got out of Dame Ashforth's sitting room by the back way, or surely Hurst and Mr. Granville would be meeting with pistols at sunrise."

"A pity they aren't." Emily, who'd untangled the birdie from the net again, backed up, and struck it with a vicious backhanded serve better suited to tennis than to a friendly game of badminton. "You can't marry him now, Caroline. He's a lecherous swine. And there's no telling what diseases he's picked up from that cow."

Caroline ran for the birdie, sending it sailing effortlessly back toward Emily's side of the net. "Honestly, Emmy," she said. "You can't go about calling the daughter of the Duke of Childes a cow."

"Why can't I? She disgraced herself with someone else's fiancé, didn't she? That makes her worse than a cow. A slut, actually, is what she is, daughter of a duke or not."

"That's a bit of a double standard, don't you think?" Caroline stood still and let the birdie Emily had just hurried to send over the net fall neatly onto her racket. "Lady Jacquelyn is a slut because she was with a man to whom she's not married, and yet Braden Granville, who's been with just about every woman in London, is universally admired for his bed hopping."

"Not by me." Emily missed the shot. She was a pitiful badminton player. "Your point. And I still don't understand why you didn't simply tell Granville the truth. Then he'd have murdered Hurst, and it would be all over and done with, and everything could be back to normal again."

"Everything would *not* be back to normal," Caroline said, as she backed up for her serve. "Don't you see, Emmy? I don't want Hurst dead."

"Why not?"

"You *know* why, Emmy."

"Not *that* again." Emily rolled her eyes. "Lord, you all act as if he did something miraculous."

"He did. He saved Tommy's life."

"For God's sake, Caro, all he did was stuff a handkerchief in the wound and yell for a surgeon. Anyone who'd happened along at that particular moment would have done the same."

"At two o'clock in the morning?" Caroline demanded. "Just who do you suppose would happen along at that hour of night, except more of the same footpads who'd attacked him in the first place?"

"Have you ever stopped to wonder," Emily asked, pointedly, "what Hurst Slater was doing in Oxford that night?"

"We've discussed this before," Caroline said. "You know as well as I do that he was attending an astronomy lecture."

"At two in the morning?"

"When else are you going to have an astronomy lecture? They were looking at the stars."

Emily shook her head. "Have you ever heard Hurst express the slightest interest in astronomy, Caroline?"

Caroline said, softly, "He once said my eyes shone as brightly as the Pleiades."

Emily clutched her stomach, which, since she was not wearing a corset, as was her custom, was on prominent display beneath the front of her satin gown. "I'm going to be sick."

Caroline tapped her racket irritably against her hip. "Well," she said. "You asked. And that isn't all Hurst did, and you know it. You saw yourself how concerned he was for Tommy all during his convalescence. Why, I don't think a day passed that Hurst didn't stop by and stay for a few hours at Tommy's bedside, trying to buck up his spirits. You know how depressed he was after the attack. Hurst's little visits helped immensely."

Emily snorted. "Certainly they did. They helped *Hurst* immensely. They got him a wealthy bride."

Caroline looked aggrieved. "Please, Emmy," she said. "You yourself said it was sweet, how devoted Hurst was to Tommy."

"That was before I knew what an irreligious dog he was, underneath that saintly facade." Emily glared at her friend. "From the start," she declared, "you have mishandled this entire situation."

"Oh, you think so?" Caroline folded her arms across her chest. "What would *you* have done, then?"

"First of all," Emily said, "I wouldn't have walked out of that sitting room without saying a word."

"But I *couldn't* say anything, Emmy," Caroline said. "I'd never seen such a thing in my entire life. Her *tongue* was in his *mouth*. And that's just what I could *see*. There's no telling what was going on beneath all those petticoats of hers, which were covering them both up below the waist—"

Even in the bright sunshine, Caroline could tell that Emily had lost some of her coloring. "Oh, Lord," she said. "I really do think I'm going to be sick."

"It isn't exactly the way sheep do it, Emmy," Caroline went on, quite without compassion. "She was on top, for one thing."

"I've got to sit down," Emily said, and she collapsed onto the lawn.

"And that's not all," Caroline said, but Emily held out a hand.

"Yes," she said, "that is all. As far as I'm concerned, that's all. Caroline, you have got to break it off."

"I can't." Caroline slumped down onto the grass beside her friend. "You know I can't. Besides the fact that we owe him Tommy's life, Ma says Hurst would be within his rights to take legal action against me if I break it off."

"So what?" Emily glowered. "You'd win."

"At what expense?" Caroline rolled over onto her stomach, enjoying the feel of the sun-warmed grass beneath her. "After I've stood up in front of a whole room of people I don't know and told them that I wasn't woman enough to please my fiancé? That certainly wouldn't be humiliating, Emmy."

"It has nothing to do," Emily said, "with your lack of womanliness."

"Yes, it does, Emmy." Caroline stared down at the ground. "Hurst has never—not once—kissed me the way he was kissing Jacquelyn Seldon. Until I saw him with her last night, I thought ... well, I thought we were happy. You know I did. I thought ... I thought he loved me."

How could she have been so wrong? That was the question she kept asking herself. All those times Hurst had found her hand beneath the dining table and squeezed it ... all those times he'd caught her alone and stolen one of those quick, laughing kisses ... had it all been for show? Had all the sweet things he'd done—bringing her flowers, introducing her with so much pride to his mother— been done solely to capture himself a rich bride? Had all the things he'd said—that he loved her, that he couldn't wait to make her his own—been outright lies?

Emily reached out and patted Caroline on the shoulder. "I'm sure he does love you in his way."

"Which is nothing," Caroline said, bitterly, "like the way he loves Jacquelyn. Oh, Emmy, if only I could get him to love me like *that*. Everything would be all right then."

"How?" Emily wanted to know.

"Well, because then I could marry him, and Ma would be happy, and—"

"You worry," Emily said, matter-of-factly, "far, far too much about making other people happy. What about *you*, Caroline? What do *you* want?"

Caroline blinked at her friend. "Me? Why, to marry Hurst, of course. At least"—she frowned—"that's what I wanted up until last night."

"And now?"

"Now?" Caroline shook her head. "I just told you, Emmy. It doesn't matter what I want. I've got to go through with it. I owe it to him, for what he did for Tommy. Besides, the invitations have already gone out. Don't you see? I've just *got* to get him to love me."

Emily looked as if she would have liked very much to say something else, but all she said was, "And how do you intend to go about doing that?"

"I've been giving it some thought," Caroline said, "and I really think Ma might be right. If I use my womanly wiles, I just might be able to win Hurst back away from Jackie. The trouble is, I'm not exactly sure how to go about doing it. Exercising something I'm not even sure I have."

Emily snorted. "I'm certain it can't be particularly hard, Caro. If Jackie Seldon can do it, surely you can. She's a complete idiot. And we both know most men are nothing but great ignorant rats—"

"You called?"

Thomas, the second Earl of Bartlett, strolled toward them across the lawn, his hands in his trouser pockets, a tuft of blond hair falling down over one eye.

"Why, if it isn't the king of the rats now." Emily rose up to her elbows and grinned at the earl. "And what are you doing out here, pray, Your Majesty? Didn't your mamma forbid you from strolling about in drafty gardens? You might, after all, endanger your fragile health."

Thomas lowered himself until he was seated beside Caroline in the grass. "Sod off," he advised Emily.

"Tell me something, your lordship," Emily said, plucking up a blade of grass and inserting it between her teeth. "What is it that makes men completely incapable of maintaining a monogamous relationship with a woman? Can you tell me? Because I would really like to know why it is that one woman isn't enough to satisfy you people."

"Of course one's enough," Thomas said, affably. "If she's the right one. That's the trouble, you see. Finding the right one.

"The thing of it is, it's damned hard to tell with you girls." Thomas found his own blade of grass, and began to suck it contentedly, speaking out of the side of his mouth. "Your fathers keep you under lock and key until your wedding day, so it's almost impossible for us to tell if we've got a rum'un until our wedding night, and by then, well, it's too late, if you turn out to be a dud."

"That," Emily said, removing the grass blade from her mouth, and holding it toward him as if it were a sword, "is the vilest thing I think I have ever heard anyone say."

"But it's true, don't you think?" Thomas shrugged. "I mean, it's perfectly ludicrous. Two people pledge to live with one another until death parts them, and they've never even gone to bed together beforehand. A man wouldn't buy a pair of trousers without trying them on first, but everyone expects him to commit the rest of his lovemaking days to this one woman he's never even—"

"How are we supposed to know how not to be a dud?" Caroline demanded. "How can we know, when no one will talk about it?"

Tommy looked confused. "Talk about what?"

"You know." Caroline glanced around the garden darkly, then whispered, *"Lovemaking."*

"Oh," the Earl of Bartlett said. "That."

"Yes, *that.* You know Ma won't discuss it. So how am I supposed to know how to keep a man, let alone not be a dud in bed, when no one will tell me what it is that most people—particularly people like Lady Jacquelyn Seldon—already seem to know?"

"I say," Thomas said. "This conversation has just taken an oddly personal turn. What's Jackie Seldon ever done to you?"

EDUCATING CAROLINE · 73

"Nothing," Caroline said, quickly, even as Emily was sucking in breath to tell all. "I just meant that, you know, *figuratively*. After all, Lady Jacquelyn must be incredibly . . . well, in order to have snared Braden Granville, who, according to you and your friends, has the most discriminating taste in, um, lovers, Lady Jacquelyn must be very . . . sure of herself."

Thomas stopped looking at the sky, and instead, eyed his sister. "I suppose you could call it that."

"Oh, stop it." Emily threw away the blade of grass she'd been chewing, and sat up. "That isn't what she means at all. It comes down to this, Thomas: We need to know what goes on between a man and a woman in bed."

Thomas looked as if he thought he might like to be somewhere else all of a sudden. "Why are you asking *me*?"

"Because I need to know," Caroline insisted. "And Ma won't help."

"Well, there must be someone else you can ask. If Ma won't tell you, surely Emmy's mother—"

Emily let out a great, whooping horse laugh. "*My* mother? You must be joking, Tommy. When I asked my mother where babies came from, she told me the fishmonger finds them in the bellies of the day's catch. To this day, she still maintains it."

Thomas winced. "Well, surely one of your teachers, then, back at school—"

"Oh, which one, Tommy?" Caroline wanted to know. "Miss Crimpson, who was so afraid the coal man might rape her, she wouldn't open the door without one of us standing behind it, with the firepoker at the ready? Or Miss Avalon, who declared the waltz a dance created by Satan that would bring about the ruination of society as we know it?"

"Might one of the maids—?"

"Tried it," Caroline said. "They all curtsy prettily and say it's something I really ought to 'discuss with the Lady Bartlett, beggin' your pardon, Lady Caroline.'"

"I don't suppose you could simply ask your fiancé—"

"*Hurst?*" Caroline's voice rose incredulously. "You want me to ask *Hurst* how to make love to a man? Are you mad?"

"Well, what's so wrong with it?" Thomas wanted to know.

"Because then he'll think I'm what you said . . . a dud!"

"Why would he think that?"

"Because I don't know what I'm doing," Caroline said, thoroughly exasperated with him by now. "That's exactly what I'm trying to avoid, don't you see?"

"Really, Tommy," Emily said. "Don't be ridiculous. She can't possibly ask Hurst. She would hardly be asking *you* if she hadn't exhausted all other possibilities. And it isn't like she's asking so much."

"Right," Caroline said. "All I want is to make Hurst fall in love with me."

Thomas looked confused. "But he is in love with you, Caro. He asked you to marry him, didn't he?"

"Yes, of course he did," Caroline said, impatiently. "And I know he's fond of me. But don't you see, Tommy? That isn't *enough.*"

Thomas was beginning to look alarmed. "It isn't?"

"No, of course it isn't. Men are *fond* of their *dogs*. I want the man I marry to be completely and helplessly in love with me. So, you see, I just need to know how to avoid being—well, a dud, like you said. Which means I've got to learn how to make love. What men like. That sort of thing. So why don't you just tell me? It would save me a lot of time and trouble, Tommy, it really would. It's so *tiresome* being a virgin. You have no idea."

Thomas leaped to his feet suddenly. "You know," he said. "I believe I've forgotten an appointment—"

Caroline furrowed her brow. "Tommy, whatever is the matter with you? Is your wound bothering you?"

"Really, Tommy," Emily said. "You look positively green about the gills."

"It's just," Thomas said, reaching up to run a hand nervously through his sand-colored, overlong hair as he strode away, "that I've got this appointment—"

Emily made a sudden gulping noise. "My God, Caro!" she cried, not taking her eyes off the young earl.

"What?" Caroline looked around, alarmed. "Is there a bee?"

"No." Emily's green eyes were dancing. "I think I know why his lordship is so hesitant to discuss this particular topic."

"Emmy." Thomas froze, and turned back toward them. There was a warning tone in his voice.

"His lordship doesn't want to discuss it," Emily said, in a loud stage whisper, "because he's never *done* it."

"That isn't true," Thomas said, coming back toward them very rapidly indeed. "Now, Emmy, that just isn't—"

"Thomas!" Caroline's eyes went as wide. "Is that true? You've never done it?"

"I didn't say that," Thomas blurted. "I—"

"You're saving yourself, then," Caroline interrupted, sweetly, "for your one true love? How positively adorable!"

Thomas said an extremely bad word.

"I suppose your brother figures," Emily said, "if he's got to take the trousers without having tried them, he oughtn't try on any others first, since that might spoil him, you know, for the final fit."

Caroline was unable to reply. She was laughing too hard.

"It's not true," Thomas said, with extreme indignation. "Caro, it isn't true. I've made love with *scores* of women. I just don't choose to discuss the details of my many conquests with my sister."

"Oh," Emily said, between guffaws. "Certainly not!"

Thomas, realizing the two girls were completely beside themselves, turned around and strode back into the house, his spine very straight, his head held unnaturally high.

After a while, Caroline stopped laughing, and she said, wiping tears from her eyes, "Oh, Emmy. We oughtn't to have poked such fun at him. He was so sick, after all."

"Pshaw," Emily said. "He's been healthy as a horse for months now. You and your mother really do have to give up babying him."

"Oh, I couldn't," Caroline said. "He came so close to dying. . . ."

"Yes, yes," Emily said, disgustedly. "I've heard about it quite enough, thank you. He was never going to tell you anything, anyway. Even if he had actually had something to divulge, he wouldn't. They don't, you know, as a rule."

Caroline looked confused. "Who won't? What are you talking about?"

"Men. They won't tell us anything. Us women, that is. That's how they maintain their power. The only time they tell us anything is when they want something from us. At least, that's how it works between my mother and father."

Suddenly, Caroline didn't feel in the least like laughing anymore. In fact, she felt a little the way she had the night before, at Dame Ashforth's party, right before Braden Granville had made her put her head between her knees. She wondered if perhaps she was fainting again.

"Do you think that's true, Em?" she asked, breathlessly.

Emily had found another blade of grass, and was now attempting to form a whistle from it, by holding it between both thumbs and blowing on it energetically. "Do I think what's true?"

"What you just said. That a man won't tell a woman anything, unless he wants something from her."

"Certainly." Emily threw the blade of grass away, and leaned over to select another. "Why do you think the queen's always in such a foul mood these days? Mr. Gladstone doesn't keep her informed about what's going on in the Cabinet. And he's the *prime minister*. But I'm sure he's thinking, 'Well, why should I tell her anything, when there's nothing she can do for me in return?'"

Caroline, however, barely heard her. A different voice entirely was sounding in her head.

And when I get the name of the fellow, Braden Granville had said, *I'll be only too happy to prove it, in a court of law, if necessary.*

Braden Granville, she realized, wanted something. Wanted something badly enough, Caroline thought, to do just about anything for it.

An insidious plot was hatching inside her head. It wasn't something, she was quite certain, she ever would have thought of if she hadn't been pushed to the brink of desperation by the sight of the love of her life in the arms of another. Or rather, the legs of another. But since she was, after all, so bitterly unhappy, it only seemed natural that these ideas—the sort that never would have occurred to her under normal circumstances—came popping up into her head, the way goldfish came popping up to the surface of the lily pond at Winchilsea Abbey, now and again.

It was a despicable thing, what she planned to do. But really, had she been given any sort of choice? No. Her mother, her brother, her own fiancé had left her with no other alternative.

Besides, her mother had told her to fight for the man she loved, and to use her womanly wiles. Wasn't that precisely what she was doing now?

Well? Wasn't it?

A man's voice, quite different from Braden Granville's, startled her from her dark, devious thoughts.

"Lady Caroline," the butler said, gravely.

Caroline started, and squinted up at the tall man, who looked extremely forbidding in the bright sunlight.

"Oh, hullo, Bennington," she said. "Is anything the matter?"

"Indeed, my lady. Her ladyship, your mother the Lady Bartlett, begs me to remind you that earls' daughters do not, generally, sit upon the grass, and she has sent me to ask you if you require a chair."

Caroline looked past the butler's shoulder, and saw her mother, quite clearly, gesturing frantically to her from an upper-story window.

Oh, dear, Caroline thought. If she thinks *this* is bad. . . .

raden Granville took careful aim at the target. Located some fifty feet away, it was nothing more than a six-foot board, covered with the paper outline of a man, leaned up against the back wall of the cellar. Braden had already drilled two holes into the paper figure's head to represent eyes, and another for a nose. He was finishing off the mouth—a series of small holes in the shape of a crescent moon, the corners of which he'd made turn whimsically upward—when someone tapped him on the shoulder. He turned around and saw Weasel standing there, fanning black smoke away from his face, and saying something.

Braden removed the cotton wool from his ears.

"—won't take no for an answer," the secretary was saying. "I told her you were busy doin' valuable research on your new pistol, but she said she'd wait."

Braden nodded to the young boy who'd been assisting him all afternoon. The boy hurried down the length of the cellar to fetch the paper target.

"I'm sorry, Weasel," Braden said. "I only caught that last bit there. What were you saying? One of the neighbors, again? Offer her a gun, would you, as a token of our esteem? Wait, on second thought, better not. I don't need housewives taking shots at me in the street because I've woken their precious infants—"

"This ain't no housewife," Weasel said. "And deep as we had this cellar dug, the only folk you're wakin' is the dead. No, this is a lady."

"A lady?" Braden took the target the boy brought to him, and held it up for his secretary to see. "There, Weasel. Look at that. Are you still accusing me of being out of sorts? I drilled six of his teeth out."

"Right," Weasel said, drily. "Next time a man stands perfectly still with his mouth wide open, you'll be able to hit his back molars, all right. This lady ain't from next door. Name of Caroline Linford."

Braden lowered the target and stared at his old friend. "Caroline Linford? *Lady* Caroline Linford? What in the devil does Lady Caroline Linford want with me?"

"Didn't say." Weasel took the target from his employer's suddenly limp fingers. "Doesn't look like the sort that usually comes a'callin' on you, Dead, which is why I came down to check with you. This one's got her maid with 'er."

"Her *what*?" The cellar was thick, it was true, with smoke, but Braden could not believe that was what was making it so difficult for him to process this information.

"Her maid. Sittin' there right beside her, all prim and proper-like." Weasel shook his head. "You know I've never been one to give advice—least not in the romantic arena—but this one just don't seem right, Dead. I'd send her packing, right quick. She's bound to have a nervous papa with one of your pistols in his pocket. . . ."

Braden Granville had already begun to take the stairs two at a time. "No nervous papa," he tossed back, over his shoulder. "A fiancé, though. The Marquis of Winchilsea."

Coming up the stairs behind his employer, Weasel raised his eyebrows. "Winchilsea? You could take *him* easily enough."

"Get your mind out of the gutter, Mr. Ambrose." Braden stepped into his study and went to a mirror to adjust his cravat, then found that the creases were filled with gunpowder. *"Damn,"* he said, tearing the cloth away, and reaching into a drawer for a new one. "There's nothing going on between the Lady Caroline and myself. Not that way. But the girl did see something the other night at old Ashforth's place—"

"The night Jackie got away from you?"

"Right. I asked her if she'd seen Jacquelyn go by, and she said she had, and that Jackie hadn't been alone—"

"So you reckon she's here to . . . to *what*?" Weasel shook his head. "I don't get it."

"I don't either," Braden admitted. "She's probably here to thank me for my kind attentions to her that night. She got a little light-headed, and I—" Weasel cackled knowingly, but Braden silenced him with a look. "—I stopped to *help* her," he continued, sternly. "It's because of her I lost the pair of them—Jackie and her swain."

"And you didn't try to get any information out of her?" Weasel looked appalled.

"She was *ill*," Braden said.

"Well, she don't look ill now," Weasel said, with a wink. "I think this is your chance, Dead."

"My chance?"

Weasel groaned with frustration. "To find out what the bloke looked like! The one with Jackie!"

Braden smiled. "I might ask a casual question or two," he said. "If the subject happens to come up. But you know I would never take advantage of a lady. . . ."

Weasel groaned again, and, grinning, Braden made quick work of his second cravat, then eyed his handiwork critically. It would do. He swept his fingers through his dark, slightly overlong hair, and pulled on the ends of his waistcoat. "There. How do I look?"

Weasel frowned. "You need another shave."

Braden Granville made an impatient face. "I'm not out to rav-ish her, Weasel. I'm gathering evidence. Valuable evidence. I want to look comforting, the kind of man a young girl could confide in. So. Do I pass?"

Weasel looked dubious. "I don't think I'm the one you ought to be askin'. Maybe we should get the maid in here—"

"Just—" Braden took a deep breath, uttered a silent prayer for patience, and then exhaled.

"—send her in."

Weasel nodded, and left the room. A minute later, he returned, this time in the company of the young woman Braden recognized from Dame Ashforth's dinner party a few nights before. Only something wasn't right. Because no sooner had Weasel escorted the Lady Caroline into the room than the two of them threw themselves at the door, apparently in an attempt to keep out a third party, who was trying to come in after them.

"Violet, really," Lady Caroline was saying, as she thrust her weight against the door, "it's quite all right. Mr. Granville and I are just going to have a little chat, and then I'll be right out. I promise nothing forward at all will occur while I'm in here—"

"Your mother, the Lady Bartlett," a strident voice behind the door declared, "is going to hear of this, my lady. Don't you think for a minute that I'm going to be party to anything smacking of deceit!"

"There's no deceit here, Violet," Lady Caroline insisted. "I swear it. I am merely trying to have a word in private with Mr. Granville—"

"Ha!" said the voice from behind the door. "I know all about *him*! Don't think I don't!"

Lady Caroline, apparently despairing of ever winning this par-ticular battle, turned her head, and saw Braden beside his desk.

"Well, don't just stand there," she said, as she leaned all her weight against the door. "Come and help us."

Braden, thoroughly confused, nevertheless did as the girl bid, and joined his secretary pushing against the door.

"I say," he observed, after a moment or two. "Whoever is on the other side of this door is uncommonly strong. Who the devil is it?"

"My maid," Lady Caroline said, as she struggled to keep her footing on the slippery parquet. "And I must say, that wasn't exactly what I meant by helping."

Braden and Weasel exchanged glances. "I tried to keep 'er out," Weasel said, "like the lady asked, but she's a big'un."

"Lady Caroline," the maid shouted, from beyond the partially closed door. "No good will come of this! Mark my words!"

"Oh," Caroline groaned. For some reason, she glared accusingly at Braden, as if it were all *his* fault. "Correct me if I'm wrong, but I thought that you were supposed to be skilled in this sort of thing, Mr. Granville. Haven't you any ideas?"

Braden said, politely, "You'll have to help me here, Lady Caroline. I have no idea what particular 'sort of thing' it is we're talking about."

"Chaperons," she burst out. "Violet is my chaperon. We've got to find a way to get rid of her. I must see you *alone*."

"Oh." Abruptly, Braden stopped pushing, and straightened. "That's simple. Why didn't you say so before?"

Taking hold of Caroline's shoulders, he moved her neatly out of the way, then signaled for Weasel to step aside. The secretary did so, and suddenly, the door gave way, and Braden found himself standing before a large, determined-looking woman, wearing a flowered bonnet that was strangely frivolous when contrasted with the extremely indignant expression on her face.

"Ah," Braden said. "Miss Violet. It's you. Yes. I'm so sorry, we thought you were someone else. How are you today? And might I compliment you on that lovely hat?"

"Mr. Granville," Violet began, stridently. "You'll not put me off that easily. I know all about you, sir. You're not to have a moment alone with my lady. No, sir. Not while I've got—"

"Violet," Braden said, in a low voice, wrapping an arm around the woman's formidable shoulders. "Your mistrust wounds me. Truly, it does. I don't blame you, of course. You can't help, I suppose, but believe what you've heard. But don't mistake what a jealous few are whispering with the truth. I am not the vile monster they'd have you think. Why, Violet, I'm just like you."

Violet blinked up at him with large, suspicious brown eyes. "I beg your pardon, sir," she said, indignantly. "But I don't think so."

"No, really," Braden went on. "Do you think I always lived amongst such grandeur? Why, hardly, Violet. My childhood was spent in the Dials, Violet. Have you heard of the Dials, Violet? I'm sure you haven't. What would a lovely young woman like yourself know about the foulest section of London? Well, suffice it to say that I played amidst the dust heaps there as a boy. Until one day, fortune plucked me from them. With hard work and perseverance, I made myself the man you see before you. Is it any wonder, Violet, that there are those, envious of my success, who might speak ill of me?"

Violet's gaze began to look a little less determined—just a little. Seeing this, Braden pressed his advantage.

"It's unconscionable," he went on. "I know. But when people like us—you and I, Violet—pull ourselves up out of the dust heaps of this world, why, there's nothing—nothing at all—that can stop us. And that, Violet, is very frightening to those in power. They feel that their position in life is being threatened. So of course they say horrible things about us. I've been called all sorts of things, you know. I've even heard some people accuse me of being"—he took a deep breath—"a Lothario. But it isn't true, Violet. I'm just a man. Just flesh and bone. Like you, Violet. Just like you."

Lady Caroline, who'd been watching him with a very skeptical expression on her face, rolled her eyes at this. But her maid was not nearly so hard-hearted. She reached out and seized Braden's right hand in both her own.

"I had heard, sir," Violet said, earnestly. "I had heard things—horrible things—about you. But I see now why they lied. Jealous, all of 'em. And all I can say is . . . God bless you!"

Braden bowed his head modestly. "Thank you, Violet. Weasel—I mean, Mr. Ambrose—please show Miss Violet to the kitchens, and see that she is provided with tea and cake."

"It would be my honor, sir," Weasel said, the corners of his mouth twitching. And he led the woman—still gazing at Braden in a besotted manner over her shoulder—away.

Braden, smiling, closed the door behind them, then turned to say, "Now, Lady Caroline. What can I do for you today?"

Only his voice dried up in his throat. Because Lady Caroline was staring up at him with a furious expression on her face.

"What," she demanded, "did you do to my maid?"

He looked down at her curiously. She was not, as he'd correctly observed the night of Dame Ashforth's dinner party, a beauty. Her hair was neither dark nor fair, her figure neither voluptuous nor slim.

And yet Jacquelyn had been wrong to dismiss the Linford girl as plain. She wasn't plain at all. There were some women who had looks like Lady Caroline's, looks that, while they might strike the viewer as plain at first glance, grew oddly more appealing as time passed. These kinds of looks, Braden knew, were dangerous—more dangerous even than a beauty like Lady Jacquelyn's—since, because they were ever changing, a man could fall into the trap of wanting to be continuously about, in order to observe the subtle shifts as they took place. . . .

Not that such a thing had ever happened to him. Nor would it.

Still, Lady Caroline had something that even a jaded admirer of feminine beauty like himself had to admit was irresistible. And that was a pair of very large eyes, that, though brown, struck him as enormously expressive. Even now, they were fairly brimming with emotion. And they were staring up at him most reproachfully.

"Tell me," she said, accusingly. "Tell me what you did to her."

"Clearly," Braden said, moving toward his desk, mostly to get out of range of those enormous, liquid eyes, "I didn't do anything to her. I spoke to her as one rational human being to another, that's all."

The girl followed him, not just with her eyes, but with her whole person. She stood before his desk and glared at him some more.

"That's *not* all," she declared. "You . . . you *mesmerized* her!"

"I most certainly did nothing of the sort." Braden shook his head. "I appealed to her better judgment, and won."

"I think," the girl said, her eyes narrowed with suspicion, "that you bewitched her."

Braden sat down. It was rude, he knew, but the girl seemed fractious, and he hoped that, if she didn't have to keep craning her neck to look up at him, it might prove calming. He also hoped that the desktop might serve as a sort of shield against her agitation, which he could see was extreme.

"Lady Caroline," he said, severely. "This is the year eighteen hundred and seventy. Do I really need to remind you that there is no such thing as witchcraft? Besides, you were the one who brought her. If you didn't want her to come in, why'd you bring her in the first place?"

"Because I'm not allowed to go anywhere without her," she said, with just enough asperity to show him that she thought him very dull witted indeed.

"Not allowed to . . ." He digested this. "Good God. Are you under some sort of arrest?"

"No," she said, and though she didn't utter them out loud, he was quite certain he read the words *You stupid man* in those dark eyes. "I am not allowed to go anywhere without a chaperon. Young women in this city are often preyed upon by nefarious evildoers, and Violet is supposed to protect me from them."

"Well," Braden said, a bit taken aback by this information. "I must say, she's built for it."

Caroline looked down at him angrily. "It isn't right. What you did to her. You made her think . . . you made her think things that weren't true."

"According to whom?" he countered. "That's a matter of opinion, don't you think? I might just as well ask you if it's right to cause a scene at someone's place of business. I could easily have lost a customer, you know, due to that woman's hysterics. That's money out of my pocket, you know. Out of Wea—Mr. Ambrose's, as well. All my employees, as a matter of fact. How am I to pay their salaries if your maid drives away all my customers with her hysterical behavior?"

That got her. The reproachfulness left, and was replaced, in those brown eyes, by a flood of guilt.

"Oh," she said. "I *am* sorry. Only I had to see you, and I went to your home, and they told me you were here, and I thought. . . . Well, in a way, what I need to discuss with you *is* business-related. So I thought I'd just slip in and . . . Of course I didn't realize Violet would be so very insistent on coming in with me. I meant it to be private, you see, our interview. I *do* apologize."

He was a bit disturbed to discover that he'd missed another one of her charms that night at Dame Ashforth's: her voice. It was a pleasing voice, very low-pitched and rather more boyish than girlish, which was a relief. Girls had, Braden had noticed over the years, a rather unnerving tendency toward shrillness.

"Well," he said. "I suppose I can find it in my heart to forgive you. Now, why don't you have a seat, and tell me what it is that your Violet could not be privy to."

She looked behind her, and saw the chair he'd indicated. She lowered herself into it, and sat for a minute, pulling at the buttons on her gloves, but not unfastening them. She was, he saw with approval, very simply dressed in a white morning gown, covered with a blue pelisse. She carried a matching white parasol, and her blue bonnet was tied beneath her chin in a large white satin bow. She looked quite presentable, even becoming, though she was without any of the feathers or similar fripperies Jacquelyn seemed to think necessary for the well-dressed woman of fashion.

"I suppose," Lady Caroline began, in her pleasing voice, as she continued to pull at the button on the back of her wrist. Braden could not help noticing that between the glove and the cuff of Lady Caroline's sleeve was the exposed skin of her wrist. That skin was awfully golden in color for someone who bore the title of lady. It suggested a good deal more time spent out of doors than was commonly considered proper. Lady Jacquelyn Seldon, by contrast, spent almost no time out of doors, and had the milk-white skin—all over, as he could well attest—to prove it.

"I suppose you remember, um, speaking to me the other evening at Dame Ashforth's," the girl said.

"I do." Braden watched as she fingered the button. In a little while, it would fall off, from her worrying it so much. "I hope you haven't had a recurrence of the malady that struck you that night."

"Oh." She released the button, and focused the full of her attention on his face. It was rather like having a white-hot spotlight suddenly fastened upon one—or so he imagined, not having ever spent any time on a stage.

"Oh, no, no," she said. "No, I'm much, much better. Only that night, if you'll recall, you asked me whether or not I had seen Lady Jacquelyn, and if she had been with anyone."

Quite suddenly, he found himself leaning forward in his chair.

"Yes," he said, trying not to sound as eager as he felt. "Yes, I remember."

"Well, as you know, I did see her, and she was with someone.

And the two of them were engaged in what you might call . . . a compromising embrace."

He raised a questioning brow. *Calm*, he told himself. *Mustn't seem too eager.* "Really?"

"Yes." Her cheeks, he noted, had turned a little pink. *"Highly* compromising."

"I see," he said, trying to keep his tone neutral. "Do go on."

"You mentioned something when I last saw you," Lady Caroline said, "that led me to believe that the identity of the gentleman with whom your fiancée was . . . engaged in this embrace might be important to you."

Braden stared at her. No. It wasn't possible. After months of frustration, he was finally going to have an answer to the question that a half dozen of his best men had been unable to provide him—and from this girl! This quite unprepossessing girl!

Really, this was just too good to be true. It took all the self-control he possessed to keep from leaping about the room with joy. Instead, Braden rifled through a few of the papers on his desk, as if what she'd said was not of the least consequence.

"Yes, actually," he said, with what he fancied sounded like supreme indifference. "Good of you to go to all the trouble of seeking me out. I'd have asked you myself that night, only you seemed out of sorts, and I didn't think . . . well, I didn't think you'd have known him."

"Oh," Caroline said. "But of course I did."

"Well, then," Braden said. He stopped messing about with his papers and smiled. Then, worried that perhaps his smile might contain a little too much of the self-congratulatory glee he was feeling, he tried to control it, turning it instead into a businesslike frown. "With whom did you see her, Lady Caroline?"

Caroline looked up then. This time her expressive dark eyes were filled with something he could not put a name to. "Oh, I can't tell you that," she said, looking shocked.

It was Braden's turn to stare at her, and he did so admirably, quite certain his own eyes, which were every bit as dark as hers, did not reveal half as much emotion. "You can't—" He shook his head. "I'm sorry. I thought you said you knew him."

"Oh, I do. Only I can't tell you his name, you see." Once more, she gave him an apologetic smile. "I know you managed to mesmerize Violet with that little speech about how she mustn't believe the things people say about you, but I'm afraid it didn't work with me. You see, I *completely* believe the things people say about you. And one of those things is that you are rather quick to settle your personal difficulties with a pistol. If I told you the name of the man I saw with your fiancée, you'd doubtlessly try to kill him. Well, I won't have a man's death on my conscience, thank you very much."

Braden, struck dumb by this admission, could only stare at her.

"But if you think about it," Caroline went on, blithely, "it doesn't really matter who the gentleman is. You believe your fiancée is involved with another man, and you would like to break off your engagement with her, but you fear that she will bring a breach of promise against you. Isn't that correct?"

Braden had been staring so fixedly at her, he'd quite forgotten to blink. "Yes," he said, slowly, wondering whether or not she was a lunatic, and if she was, how he was going to get rid of her. It was a pity, really, because she was turning out to be quite a pretty little thing. But mad, clearly. Stark raving mad.

"And in order to have any hope of winning this breach of promise suit," Caroline said, "you need proof of your fiancée's faithlessness."

"Yes," he said, again. "That's right. Which is why—"

"Wouldn't the testimony of a witness who saw your fiancée in the arms of another be enough proof?"

Braden said, reluctantly, "It would depend on the credibility of the witness, of course—"

"Do you think *I* would be considered a credible witness?" she asked.

He hesitated. A lunatic would not, of course, make a good impression on any judge. But despite her behavior, Lady Caroline certainly didn't *look* like a lunatic. In fact, she looked quite respectable. Fetching, even.

Fetching. Good Lord, what was he thinking? She was *Lady Caroline Linford*.

"I believe," Braden said, slowly, "that with adequate coaching, you might pass. But—"

"I thought as much," Caroline said. "So it doesn't really matter, in the end, if I put a name to the man in question. The simple fact that I saw her with anyone"—she flung him a significant glance—"and I do mean *with* in the intimate sense—ought to be enough proof, don't you think?"

"Lady Caroline." He could no longer maintain his facade of indifference. He'd given it up some minutes ago, but only now sagged against the back of his chair, utterly drained with disappointment. "Please don't take offense, but I don't believe you've familiarized yourself adequately about the law. Lying in court—which is what you're telling me you intend to do—is called perjury, a crime that is punishable—"

She interrupted him. "I know what perjury is, Mr. Granville."

"Well," he said, testily. "If you know what it is, then I don't see how you think you can get away with—"

"Mr. Granville." Her gaze was perfectly steady. In her luminous brown eyes, he could not detect a trace of insanity. But he was perfectly convinced it was there. Because only a madwoman would suggest something so ludicrous. "If I know Lady Jacquelyn—and I do, from school—she is going to deny that she had a lover, whether or not I put a name to the man. So it hardly matters if I say I didn't recognize him—except that it will matter a good deal to the man involved, as it will keep him from getting a bullet through his hide."

"Lady Caroline," Braden said. "I'm afraid you don't understand. Lady Jacquelyn will undoubtedly secure very competent lawyers, who will question you very closely—"

"Yes," Lady Caroline said. "I'm aware of that. But I feel confident that I will be able to answer their questions truthfully, up to a point. When it comes down to the man's identity, I shall simply say I did not get a good enough look at him to say for certain who he was. But I think I shall give him a French accent." She smiled to herself. "I think that's quite a believable little detail, don't you? I could quite see Lady Jacquelyn with a Frenchman."

Braden stared at her. He knew he was being rude, but he couldn't help himself. He could not, for the life of him, figure out what she was about. What kind of woman, he wondered, would so cheerfully volunteer to perjure herself for a man she hardly knew? No woman he knew—not from Mayfair, and not from the Dials, either.

"Of course," Lady Caroline said, "before I agree to act as your witness, Mr. Granville, there is the question of my compensation."

Braden shook himself. Good Lord! There it was! There it was at last, the reason the girl had come to him. He felt a curious relief wash over him. So she wasn't mad. Not mad at all. She wanted something.

Why this should be a relief to him, he could not imagine. What did he care whether or not the girl was in full possession of her wits? She was nothing to him.

He told himself it was merely the relief any man would feel at finding out that he was not, after all, in the company of a lunatic, then wondered what Caroline Linford—who, from what Braden knew about her, which was admittedly not much, had everything any Mayfair society miss could wish for, including a generous inheritance, a pretty face, and a handsome husband-to-be—could possibly want from him.

"Your compensation?" he asked, curiously.

"Well, yes." She gave him a look which suggested she thought him rather dense for asking. "If I am going to perjure myself—not to mention engender the outrage of my entire family by agreeing to participate in anything so scandalous as a breach of promise suit—I am going to have to be compensated."

He stared at her, feeling oddly disappointed. This time, he didn't have to ask himself why he felt as he did. He knew perfectly well why he was disappointed: Because there she sat, looking so young and lovely and innocent, when the truth was, she was no different from any of the other women of his acquaintance. She was like the candied flowers he'd admired as a boy from outside the baker's window—they'd looked succulent enough, but once he'd finally scraped up the money to buy a few, he'd discovered they were not actually very good at all. Like so many of the things in Mayfair Braden had once admired, Caroline Linford, upon closer inspection, turned out not to be quite the tasty morsel she'd first appeared.

Which was a shame, though why he should feel it so deeply, he could not imagine. Again, she was nothing to him.

He wondered, cynically, what kind of trouble she'd gotten herself into. Gambled away her fortune, perhaps? He'd heard her younger brother, the earl, was fond of cards—and quite good at them, too—but he'd never have guessed that the Lady Caroline was particularly keen at loo. But he'd known a few women who'd possessed faces as equally innocent as Lady Caroline's, and who'd squandered tens of thousands of pounds at the gaming table, so he supposed it was certainly possible.

Disappointed as he was, at least he was on surer footing now than he'd been before. Business was something he had always had a head for, the same way, the first time a revolver had been put into his hand, he had instantly understood its workings, and had begun at once to devise ways to improve it.

And so he opened a drawer and pulled out a small box, in which he kept the bulk of his ready cash.

"I see," Braden said. "May I ask how much, Lady Caroline?"

He heard her sudden gasp, and when he looked up inquiringly, he was surprised to note that her cheeks had gone red.

"Not *money*," Caroline cried, clearly horrified. "I don't need *money*, sir!"

Braden closed the cash box quickly. He had offended her. He wasn't quite certain how. Jacquelyn had always been ready enough to accept money from him, but apparently, Lady Caroline Linford was of a dissimilar turn of mind.

"I see," he said, confusedly, though in truth he did not. "But you did say you would need to be compensated—"

"But not with *money*," Lady Caroline cried, looking appalled.

Braden, realizing that she was genuinely upset at the suggestion, made haste to put the cash box back in its drawer. He had fumbled, he knew, but he could not imagine how. Then again, society misses were not a segment of the population with whom he'd ever spent great amounts of time.

"I beg your pardon," he said, in what he hoped was a soothing tone. "I see now that it was not pecuniary interests which guided you here. May I ask just what it is you meant when you said compensation?"

She'd dropped her gaze. She seemed perfectly unable to look up from her lap. Which was odd, because she'd looked him straight in the eye the entire time she'd been discussing her plan to perjure herself, with a directness he'd rather admired.

He was, he had to admit, intrigued. She had gone from being a candied flower in his mind to something a good deal more tantalizing. A peach, perhaps. Peaches, when they were ripe, rarely disappointed. And Caroline Linford looked very ripe indeed.

"There must," Braden said, after watching her struggle for

nearly a minute to put whatever it was she apparently wanted into words, "be something. As you said, your testifying in court on my behalf will certainly make you an object of some . . . notoriety. It is not a position for any young woman to enter into lightly—"

"I know." She looked up suddenly, and he was again seized by a sensation of being under a bright spotlight, her gaze was that intense, her eyes that bright.

No, not a peach, he thought to himself.

"Only it isn't financial compensation I want," she said, hesitantly. "It's . . . it's something I want you to *do*."

"Do?" He returned her gaze with interest. Definitely not a peach. "Well, what is it, then?" Again she ducked her head, and seemed to be debating something quite fiercely within herself. He noticed she'd begun worrying the button to her glove again. Recalling the tan—and unable to keep from wondering, quite inexplicably, how far up those well-shaped arms that tan extended—he thought perhaps she might be interested in outdoor sport, and said, "Shooting lessons, perhaps? So you don't have to drag about that maid of yours? You could shoot at the—what did you call them? Oh, yes—nefarious evildoers, rather than depend upon your maid for protection—"

"Oh, no," Caroline interrupted quickly, looking up again. "I hate guns."

He blinked at her, not certain whether to laugh or feel insulted. "Really," he settled for saying. "I'm sure you wouldn't feel that way if someone were assaulting you, and I drove them away with a six-shooter."

"Well, of *course*," she said. "But firearms are so rarely used for protection. Mostly, they're used by people like you, to settle a stupid disagreement—"

He had to restrain himself from pointing out to her that he hardly considered his disagreement with his fiancée's lover stupid.

"—or by footpads," she went on, "threatening poor unarmed

people—like my brother—for their purses." He did not miss the throb in her voice when she mentioned her brother. "He . . . he very nearly died, you know," she went on. "And all because of a single bullet."

Braden said, kindly, "But he's all right now. I saw him the other night at Dame Ashforth's, and he was—"

"Fine," Caroline interrupted, bitterly. "Yes, I know. Thanks to Hurst."

Braden raised an eyebrow. "Hurst? The Marquis of Winchilsea, you mean?"

"Yes. He was the one who found Tommy. He chased away the footpads, and stopped him from bleeding to death on the street. Tommy would surely have died, if it weren't for Hurst's quick actions."

Braden, who was passingly acquainted with the marquis, found it hard to believe that the handsome dandy he knew, and the man of action Lady Caroline described, were one and the same. "Indeed?" he said, diplomatically.

"Oh, yes," Caroline said. "It took months of nursing, of doctors coming in and out at all hours of the night, and through it all, Hurst hardly left Tommy's side. That's how . . . how he and I came to be engaged. Because we were thrown together so much after Tommy's injury—" She broke off and glared at him, accusingly, almost as if she thought him responsible for her brother's shooting. And her next words indicated that, in a way, she thought he was.

"Really," she said, "I think a man like you, who happens to be a genius—at least, that's what my brother says you are—ought to turn his mind toward inventing something we actually *need*, rather than a new style of—of killing machine. My father, you know, invented a hot water delivery system that can be installed in just about any home. That's something *useful*."

"I see," he said, after clearing his throat. "I will take that into consideration. And now, Lady Caroline, if you don't mind, I'd like to know what it is that you believe I *can* do for you. You want me to find the men responsible for your brother's injuries, perhaps? See that they're brought to justice?"

She frowned at that. "No," she said. Then, after glancing about the room, as if to ascertain that they were well and truly alone, Caroline Linford finally leaned forward in her chair, and, dipping her voice conspiratorially, said, "Well, actually, Mr. Granville, what I need is . . . what I need is for you to teach me how to make love."

8

She wasn't certain, but it seemed for a moment or two that Braden Granville might suffer an apoplexy. Caroline was very alert to apoplexies, as a particularly severe one had carried off her father. And so she leaned forward even farther in her seat, and asked, "Mr. Granville, are you quite all right?"

Braden continued to stare at her, however, with his mouth slightly ajar, and his brown eyes—which, unlike her own, *did* have interesting flecks of mahogany and russet in them—fixed unblinkingly upon her.

"Shall I run and fetch your secretary?" Caroline asked. "Or would you like a glass of wine, or some water, perhaps?"

She'd actually risen from her chair, and was about to go tearing for the door for Mr. Weasel, when the man behind the desk finally stirred, and, shaking his head, said, in a voice that was quite reminiscent of a growl, *"Sit down."*

Caroline wondered who he could have been speaking to, since no one in her life had ever spoken to *her* that way. When it finally hit her that of course he'd been speaking to her—there was, after all, no one else in the room—Caroline sank back down into the chair she'd vacated, but more out of astonishment than any desire to do as the very commanding gentleman had ordered.

"My goodness," she said, with more temerity than she was actually feeling. "You needn't order me about as if I were a schoolgirl."

"Why not?" Braden Granville inquired, in that same growly voice. "You're acting like one."

"I most certainly am not," Caroline said, genuinely hurt. She felt she'd comported herself with a good deal of composure. "And I must say, if this is how you conduct your business affairs—by insulting your clients—then all I can say is, it's a wonder to me you've ever sold a single gun in your life."

"Yes!" Braden Granville stood up, and pointed a finger at her accusingly as his deep voice rolled across the room like thunder. "That's it! That's it precisely. I sell *guns*, young lady. I do not sell *myself*. I am not a paid escort."

"I never said you were," Caroline assured him, all temerity fleeing in the face of this sudden explosion. "Especially considering the fact that I don't even know what that means."

"A paid escort," he said, slowly and distinctly, "is a man who makes love to women for pecuniary gain. It is the male equivalent to a whore."

Caroline blinked. She was well used, of course, to foul language, having spent an inordinate amount of time eavesdropping upon her brother and his friends. But she had never before had such foul language hurled in her direction.

And then, quite suddenly, Caroline realized why Braden Granville was so angry.

"Oh," she gasped. "Oh, no. You don't think—"

He glared at her stonily from where he stood behind his desk. *Oh, yes*, she said to herself. *He does think—*

"I assure you," she said, with all the dignity she could muster, with her cheeks turning a steady crimson, "that you are mistaken.

I most decidedly did not come here to ask you to . . . to . . . do
that."

She broke off, speechless with embarrassment.

It wasn't as if, she told herself, as she sat there, feeling the fiery
blush creep over her face, it hadn't taken every ounce of courage
she possessed merely to walk through the front door to Braden
Granville's offices. And it wasn't as if she'd lain awake for hours the
night before, asking herself if she was really doing the right thing.
Because while she'd quite convinced herself that Braden Granville
was the answer to her problem with Hurst, she knew perfectly well
that she could never—never in a million years—

It didn't matter. The color that had flooded into her cheeks
explained it all. Well, not all of it, but enough so that behind the
desk, Braden Granville seemed to relax a little. Some of the stoni-
ness left that face—that face that looked as if it had been chiseled
from granite—and he took his fists off his desk. He even came out
from behind the wretched thing, and leaned his backside against
the front of it, and looked down at her with his arms folded across
his chest . . . which didn't actually make her feel all that much better, since without that vast expanse of desktop between them, she
felt quite vulnerable. He was, after all, such a very large, uncom-
promising figure of a man. Somehow she had managed to put that
little detail from her mind, in remembering that night at Dame
Ashforth's.

"To be honest," he said, his voice no longer growling or thun-
derous, but somewhere in between, "I wasn't at all certain *what* you
meant, Lady Caroline. But now that it's clear that what you meant
was not what I thought you meant, I think we had better try again."

Then he grinned. At her. Braden Granville grinned at her.

What shocked her wasn't so much that he'd done it—grinned
at her—but what she felt when she saw that grin. Which was nothing like what she'd felt when he'd grinned at her that night at Dame
Ashforth's. Quite the opposite, in fact. When he grinned down at

her now, she was not put in mind of the devil at all. All she could think was that Braden Granville was actually rather nice looking, in a dark—sinfully dark—menacing sort of way.

Good Lord! Nice looking? *Braden Granville?*

"Although I do want you to know," he went on, conversationally, apparently not in the least aware of her discomfort, "that my initial reluctance was not based on any sort of repugnance at the idea, but rather shock that a young lady such as yourself would suggest such a thing."

Caroline glared at him. She told herself that what she was feeling was not attraction. Not at all! No, it was indignation. She was terrifically angry at him, of course. Why, he'd thought she actually wanted him to make love to her! As if she were so wanting for admirers, she had to go about blackmailing them. Which wasn't the case at all. Why, Caroline could have had any man she wanted. Really, she could have.

It was what she was supposed to do with them after she got them that she wasn't exactly clear about. That was where *he* came in.

"But that," she heard herself grumble, "is the whole problem."

He regarded her quizzically from the desk. A quizzical look, she was dismayed to see, became him every bit as much as the grin. "What is?"

"Everyone thinks of me as just that. A young lady. I'm *tired* of being a young lady." What was the point? She'd already made an ass of herself. Why not let the humiliation be complete? "I want to be a *woman*. Only no one will explain to me how it's done."

He stopped looking quizzical in exchange for looking annoyed. "Forgive me, Lady Caroline, if I admit that I am not at all flattered that you came to *me* in quest of lessons in how to become more womanly."

"But don't you see?" Caroline leaned forward in her chair. "Thomas—my brother—he says that you've had more lovers than any man in London."

Braden Granville looked more annoyed than ever. But even a look of annoyance, Caroline was amazed to see, looked rather nice on him.

"Well, I'm afraid you're going to have to tell your brother that news of my romantic prowess has been greatly exaggerated," he snapped.

"But you do admit you've been with hundreds of women," Caroline persisted.

"Well, *hundreds* is perhaps a bit of a—"

"Scores, then. You've been with scores of women, at least, haven't you?"

Those obsidian eyes looked heavenward. "All right. Scores. We'll settle for scores."

"Well, you must know *something*, then, about what makes a woman attractive to a man."

"What makes a woman attractive to a man," Braden Granville said, dropping his gaze back to hers, and meeting it steadily, "you have in abundance, Lady Caroline. Believe me."

"I *don't* believe you," she said, instantly dismissing his assertion as an attempt to patronize her. "Because if that were true. . . ." If that were true, she would not have discovered her fiancé between the legs of Lady Jacquelyn Seldon. But she couldn't, of course, tell *him* that. "Well, trust me, it isn't true. Don't you see, Mr. Granville? I don't want to be a wife."

He raised a single dark eyebrow, the one, she couldn't help noticing, with the scar in it. "You don't?"

"No. Well, not *just* a wife." It was so utterly awful, admitting these things to a man who managed to fill out his coat so nicely. She obviously had not gotten a very good look at him that night at Dame Ashforth's, if she could have thought him so very ugly. Still, she had come this far. She had no choice but to continue. "I also want to be a mistress."

The first inky black eyebrow was joined by a second. "A mistress."

"Yes," she went on, resolutely. "Wife and mistress, at the same time, to the same man. That way, you see, he'd have no reason to stray. Do you think that's possible, Mr. Granville? Do you think it's possible that a man could love just one woman, if that woman was both wife *and* mistress to him?"

Braden Granville opened his mouth, and then closed it again. Then he said, "It's been known to happen. In very rare cases. But there have, I believe, been precedents."

"That's what I want," Caroline said, jerking a finger toward herself. "That is what I want you to teach me. How I can be wife and mistress both to my husband. Do you think you can help me, Mr. Granville? Because you are truly my last hope. No one else will even discuss it with me."

"Well," he said, drily. "I can see why. It's a bit of a sensitive subject. And you're a bit . . ."

She tensed. "I'm a bit what?"

"Well, it's just that you're a bit . . ." His voice trailed off.

This was far worse than she'd ever imagined. Plain. That's what he was going to say. She knew it. She was a bit plain to pass as a mistress. Well, better to get it out in the open. "A bit *what*, Mr. Granville?"

"It isn't a bad thing," he assured her, hastily. "It's just that you're quite young—"

Young? Did he think he could fool her? She knew what he'd been going to say. "I happen," she said, stiffly, "to be twenty-one years old."

"Really?" He seemed inordinately surprised by this information. "You seem a good deal younger. That's part of the problem—"

There it was. Plain. It was on the tip of his lips. Those supremely masculine, yet oddly sensitive-seeming, lips.

"What problem?" Caroline choked.

"Well, just that you seem"—he shrugged those massive shoulders—"a bit *virginal* to be a mistress."

Virginal! Virginal! Well, maybe it wasn't as bad as plain, but ... *virginal*?

Seeing her horrified expression, he added, "Virginity isn't a bad thing, Lady Caroline. Most men, as a matter of fact, require it in a bride."

"But not in a mistress," Caroline wailed, wanting to bury her burning face in her hands.

"Well," he said. "No, I suppose not. But there are some men who prefer—"

"Certainly," she said, with a good deal of bitterness. "Men who don't care to try their trousers on before they buy them. And what kind of fool does *that*?"

"Trousers?" Braden Granville looked puzzled. "Who said anything about trousers?"

"I suppose you tried *yours* on before you bought them. Jacquelyn Seldon doesn't exactly strike me as the virginal type."

Braden Granville's dark eyebrows rose again. "I believe," he said, "that you have just slandered my future bride."

"We both know, Mr. Granville, that your future bride is hardly an innocent," Caroline said, still stung at the *virginal* slur. "I happen to know for a fact that that's the *last* thing she is."

She wasn't expecting it, so when he suddenly leaned forward, his wide torso blocking everything else from view, and those large fists of his reaching out to grasp the arms of her chair, effectively trapping her, she let out a little yelp of surprise. She looked up, and found her entire field of vision filled with the furious face of Braden Granville.

And Braden Granville's face, she discovered, definitely did not qualify as nice looking when it was twisted with fury.

"Tell me," he barked at her. "Tell me who you saw her with, or by God—"

Much as he intimidated her—and by now, Caroline had decided that Braden Granville intimidated her very much indeed: she felt like kindling in the heat of his fury—Caroline could not but be impressed by the fact that everything she saw before her—the lushly furnished office on the most expensive stretch of commercial property in London; the busy front rooms, filled with employees; even the impeccably cut morning coat and intricately tied cravat he wore, had been earned by the labor of the hard hands on either side of her. It was something that could be said of few men of her acquaintance. It wasn't something that could be said of Hurst, that was for certain. In fact, just about the only man of whom it could be said, besides Braden Granville, was Caroline's own father.

But that was no reason, she decided, he ought to get away with such churlish behavior.

"For heaven's sake, Mr. Granville," she said, and was proud when her voice didn't shake. "I don't think in this particular case violence will get you what you want."

He released her chair so suddenly that a wind seemed to rush in and cool all the places that he'd singed, previously, with his nearness.

"Forgive me, Lady Caroline," he said, in that familiar growl, his back to her, his hands buried deep in his pockets, as if to keep them still. He seemed to be trying to regain his composure. Caroline welcomed the brief respite from that darkly penetrating gaze. It gave her a chance to catch her breath. Even an act as simple as breathing seemed, for some reason, to become very difficult for her whenever Braden Granville was around.

"That's quite all right, Mr. Granville," she said, hoping her relief that the storm was over didn't show in her voice. "It was my fault. I should not have said anything so . . . inflammatory about your fiancée."

He swung upon her again, only this time, he wore an expression of contrition, not fury. Even more surprising was her realization that contrition became Braden Granville. His features had softened just enough so that they might have almost passed for handsome—

not in the common, blond-haired, blue-eyed way, like the Marquis of Winchilsea—but in a rugged, more earthy sense.

"The fault is mine," he said, sounding genuinely apologetic. "Not yours."

"Still," Caroline said. In spite of herself, she was moved. Who would have thought that the great "Granville" was a man capable of such humility? Not her.

"You have a right to be angry. You love your fiancée," she said, in a gentle voice, "every bit as much as I love mine, and I'm certain it must hurt you very much indeed to hear that she has been unfaithful—"

He interrupted, quite drily, considering his earlier emotion. "You mention your fiancé. He hasn't, I suppose, any idea that you've come to me with this . . . interesting proposal?"

Caroline's jaw dropped. "Of course not!"

"No." He nodded. "I thought not. Though I take it that the reason you're in such dire need of this information is that you intend to use it upon him."

"Well," Caroline said. "Of course. Who else?"

"Who else, indeed?" Braden asked, in a thoughtful manner. "And yet I hardly think, Lady Caroline, that he will be at all pleased when he learns what you've done."

Caroline said, "Oh, but he won't. I certainly shan't tell him. And I am trusting that you, sir, will be discreet—"

"Ah," Braden Granville said. "But what will you say when he asks how it is you happen to have come by your newfound knowledge?"

"Simple," Caroline interrupted, with a shrug. "I shall tell him I learnt it all in a book."

"A book," Braden Granville repeated, looking as if he did not believe her.

"Yes, a book. There are such books, I believe. I have never read one, but Tommy told me he saw one, up at Oxford—"

"Your brother," Braden Granville muttered, taking his hands from his pockets and beginning to pace impatiently, "talks a good deal too much. But that was not precisely what I meant to ask. I meant, what do you think your fiancé is going to think when you inform him that you will be acting as a witness on my behalf at Lady Jacquelyn Seldon's breach of promise suit?"

She bit her lip. This was, of course, something she'd thought long and hard about. Because Hurst would not be happy about it. No, indeed. The idea of his wife—for she would, she was quite certain, be his wife when the trial took place, since court cases moved so slowly—taking part in anything so scandalous would surely horrify Hurst.

But the fact that she would be testifying against his lover . . . well, that was going to be interesting, to say the least.

But it seemed so far away, Braden Granville's court date—for all she knew, it might never come. Her hope was that, by the time it did, she would have Hurst well in hand, besotted with her, as he should be, and perfectly mortified at the thought that he had ever so much as looked sideways at Jackie Seldon.

That, at least, was what she told herself. To Braden Granville, she said something quite different:

"Mr. Granville, I must say, you are not living up to your reputation as either a Don Juan or a businessman. I have made you a perfectly sound offer. Let me do the worrying over what I am going to explain to my fiancé . . . such as how I feel it is my duty to share with the court what I know. Hurst understands that I frequently volunteer my time for charitable causes. This is no different."

Caroline tried to maintain an air of casual indifference. She didn't want Braden Granville to see how worried the thought of testifying made her. Her mother, she knew, would be furious with her, and Hurst wouldn't like it—not in the least. Even if she told her family what she intended to tell the court—that the face of the gentleman in question had been turned away from her—Hurst would always wonder if she really knew. How could he help but wonder?

But maybe, she thought, a little wondering would do him some good.

When Braden Granville didn't say anything else for a little while—though several times she thought him on the verge of doing so—Caroline finally said, hesitantly, "So. Will you help me, Mr. Granville? In exchange for my helping you?"

Braden Granville, looking thoughtful, strolled toward one of the tall windows on the far side of the room. He stood there for a moment, apparently admiring the view, and Caroline, standing behind him, did the same. Because, truthfully, Braden Granville did have a very impressive physique. Rarely did Caroline see such a broad and powerful back, such wide shoulders, such muscular thighs, in the circles in which she traveled. At the smithies, maybe, when she took her horses for shoeing. Or in the stable yard, when feeding time came around, and the oats were being divvied out by strong-armed stable boys. But certainly not in the ballrooms, where Caroline was required to put in such regular appearances.

But then, Braden Granville, as the marquis had reminded her so bluntly that night at Dame Ashforth's, was *not* one of them. He was an outsider, and would always remain so, even if—*especially* if—he ended up marrying the daughter of a duke.

"If your fiancè truly loves you, Lady Caroline," Braden said, not turning from the window, and speaking in a voice that was so soft and low that she found herself leaning forward a little in order to hear it, "then, I feel obligated to inform you, nothing I can teach you will be of any use at all. However unskilled you might consider yourself in the bedroom, he will only find you enchanting if he loves you. But if"—here the voice lost all of its silkiness, and became hard as flint again—"he is only marrying you for your money—"

Caroline sucked in her breath. Really, this was getting worse and worse! Certainly the man was purported to be a genius, but why had no one bothered to mention that he was also a mind reader?

"Yes?" she asked, trying not to sound too eager. "What then?"

He turned to face her. The bright sunlight, pouring in from outside, threw his face into shadow. "Then, Lady Caroline, nothing you do or say will change that. You cannot force someone to fall in love with you. Oh, you might tantalize him, for a time. You might win his respect, even his admiration. But love . . . true love. . . . That's something few find, and even fewer are able to hold onto, when they do happen to find it."

She stared at him, feeling oddly deflated. He sounded so sad, so . . . fatalistic. Could this be the man Thomas admired so much, the great Braden Granville, the man who could do no wrong? Braden Granville, waxing eloquent on the mystery of love? Braden Granville, whom nothing, no one could stop, telling her to give up?

Well, she wouldn't give up. *He* might be willing to abandon his fiancée, but Caroline didn't have that luxury. How could she leave Hurst—now, with the invitations already out, and more gifts arriving every day? Everyone would think her the most ungrateful girl in the world, forsaking the man who'd done so much for her brother, for her family. True love. What did Braden Granville know of true love? Not so bloody much.

There, she'd said it. Well, to herself, anyway. Not so *bloody* much, did he, with his own fiancée going about, making a fool of him all over London . . . just as Hurst had made a fool of her, with those endearments he'd whispered in her ear, the secret hand holding beneath the table, all those kisses. . . .

Those kisses he hadn't meant. Not a one.

Well, she'd make him mean them. See if she didn't.

She lifted her chin, preparing to tell Braden Granville exactly what she thought about his treatise on true love, when something in his expression silenced her. Quite suddenly, she knew. She knew even before she asked, "You aren't going to help me, are you, Mr. Granville?"

"No," he said, gently. She could not tell what he was feeling. He might as well, she thought, be refusing a tea cake, his face was that impassive. "I'm extremely grateful, Lady Caroline," he went on, "for your more than generous offer, but I think I would prefer not to drag you into this rather . . . tawdry situation between myself and my fiancée. You are a very respectable young lady, and it would be unconscionable of me to allow you to tarnish your reputation for my sake. So I hope you will understand when I say I'm afraid I cannot accept your terms."

She set her jaw. "I see," she said, coolly . . . though in truth, she felt very much like crying. Still, she held back the tears, and went on, bravely, "Well, that is unfortunate. Especially since, from what I understand, the only person in England with more experience with women than you, Mr. Granville, is the Prince of Wales. And I'm not at all sure he'll see me."

And then, with her head held high, she turned, and left his office.

9

*A*nd then she was gone.

As unexpectedly as she'd appeared, she was gone. And Braden was left to wonder whether or not everything that had seemed to occur while she'd been there had, in actual fact, happened. Had this seemingly guileless girl actually asked him to teach her how to make love? And had he, in fact, actually said no?

What in God's name had he been thinking?

He was still asking himself that question when Weasel came bustling in, his thin face fairly atwitch with questions. But all the secretary said was, "Got her off all right, her and her maid. Not such a bad sort, that Violet. You did lay it on a bit thick, though. Practically turned her into a bleedin' anarchist with all that power to the people tripe."

Braden stood in the same spot in which he'd been frozen since she'd sailed from the room. He'd watched the street below as the girl'd stepped into her carriage, a neat, unpretentious little contraption, with a set of healthy-looking grays to pull it. Then, after the carriage had pulled away, he'd stared at the spot where it had stood.

And yet, even though Braden had seen the girl leave, he couldn't help but continue to feel her presence in the room. Not that he could smell her, the way he could Jacquelyn, whenever she vacated a place, always leaving behind the cloying rose-scented odor of her perfume. And there were no telltale bits of plumage floating about, either. Just a faint hint of something . ... something not quite the same as it had been before she'd come in, like ripples on the surface of a pond after a pebble had been thrown into it.

It was not particularly settling, this feeling that a woman who'd left the room was still there, somehow.

"So." Weasel lowered himself onto the leather couch, and drew a cigar from his waistcoat pocket. "What'd she want, then?"

Braden shook his head. "You wouldn't believe me if I told you."

Weasel chuckled. "She don't want you to shoot nobody for 'er, does she?"

"Certainly not. She's quite opposed to violence, particularly any involving pistols."

"Oh. Too bad." Having thoroughly licked his cigar all over, Weasel inserted it into his mouth, and lit it. "Well, looks as if I owe Snake a quid." Weasel puffed on his cigar. "I bet that's what she come for. What *did* she want, then? And did you get anything out of her about what she might've seen the other night?"

"Indeed," Braden said, with thoughtful care. "She claims to have seen Jacquelyn in a highly compromising situation with a gentleman other than myself."

Weasel brightened. "She got a name for you?"

"She says she does."

"So." Weasel spoke slowly. To an outsider, it might have sounded as if he were conversing with someone slow-witted, but that was not a term that came to mind when Braden Granville was involved. Weasel was speaking slowly because he'd learned, over the years, that it was best to choose his words carefully when "Dead Eye" was in the sort of mood that seemed to have overtaken him now. "Who was it?"

"She won't tell me." Braden observed that the hour must have been approaching teatime, since the pedestrian traffic on Bond Street all seemed to be heading in the direction of the nearest eateries.

"Won't tell you?" Weasel stared incredulously. "Why the hell not?"

"Doesn't want me to shoot the fellow, for one thing," Braden said. "Claims she doesn't want his death on her conscience."

"Then what the devil did she come here for?"

"She said she'd be willing to testify," Braden said, "if I call off my wedding and Jackie brings about a suit, that she saw her with someone. Someone she didn't recognize, but who certainly wasn't me."

Weasel removed the cigar from his mouth and whistled, low and long. "Jackie must've really done something to that one, to get her so riled."

"Not at all," Braden said, mildly. "The lady has nothing—that I can tell—against Jacquelyn. She was only willing to testify in exchange for compensation."

He could almost hear Weasel's jaw drop. "How much does she want?"

"Oh, it isn't money she wants, Weasel."

The older man shook his head. "What then?"

"She wants me," Braden said, still not quite able to believe it, "to teach her how to make love."

Weasel began to cough uncontrollably. He plucked the cigar from his mouth and choked until Braden presented him with a hastily poured whiskey and water.

"Thanks," he said, taking the glass and downing its contents in a single swift gulp. That seemed to help somewhat. In a few moments, he was able to ask, "Are you serious, Dead? That little girl what was here? The one with the gloves? *She* wants you to . . ."

"Apparently." Braden thought a whiskey of his own might not

hurt. Accordingly, he downed a glass, but found it did not help very much. His mind was still in a whirl. It had been mightily difficult to think straight ever since the moment Caroline Linford had made her extraordinary demand.

What was he saying? He hadn't been able to think straight since the moment she'd stepped into the room. Still, there was no denying that that handful of words— *What I need is for you to teach me how to make love*— had thrown him into a maelstrom of confusion.

Not that he hadn't had similar requests before. Caroline Linford was simply the first who'd ever used the words *teach me how*. Of course, there was also the uncomfortable fact that she'd made it clear—not from the outset, but as soon as she'd realized what conclusion he'd jumped to—that she did not actually want to make love with him. No, apparently she only wanted him to *tell* her how it was done. That was a first—at least, in *his* experience with women.

It wasn't that *all* women were attracted to him—only men with looks like the Marquis of Winchilsea were that fortunate. But though he wasn't as traditionally handsome as some of his peers, there was something about Braden Granville that drew many women to him—which was fortunate, because he had always genuinely liked women. Until Jacquelyn, that is.

"It can't be," Weasel said, suddenly, interrupting Braden's musings. "She ain't the type."

Braden blinked at him. "I beg your pardon."

"That Lady Caroline ain't the type," Weasel said, again. "I may not know much, but I know types when I see 'em, and that one . . . she's what we used to call, back in the Dials, a one-man woman. Remember?"

Braden said, "I vaguely recall that there used to be women who fell into that category, when we were growing up. But I'd come to the conclusion that fidelity had rather lost its allure of late."

"Not with girls like her," Weasel asserted. "She's a corker."

A corker. Braden smiled. Lady Caroline Linford was a corker, at that. He recalled her last remark to him, the one about going to the Prince of Wales. She'd intended the comment to be biting, evidently unaware that no one could possibly take offense at anything uttered by such a sweetly upturned mouth. She would, he thought to himself, always have difficulty disciplining servants, since no one would ever be the least bit intimidated by her.

Quite unlike his fiancée, who could—and occasionally did—frighten her maid with a single glance.

"And Jackie?" Braden asked his secretary, just to hear someone else say it. "What's she, Weasel?"

"You know good and well what Jackie is," Weasel said, with a grunt.

Well, that was the truth. He'd known perfectly well what he was getting himself into where Jacquelyn was concerned—or thought he had. When he'd turned thirty, not too many months ago, it had seemed only logical that he begin to think about marrying and siring an heir. The problem, of course, began as soon as he looked about for a suitable bride. Since Braden Granville was first and foremost a businessman, it was imperative that he find a bride who would not only make the perfect wife and mother, but also the ideal hostess, someone who could share gentle gossip and sympathize with the wives of the wealthy men he frequently entertained. That someone would necessarily have to be in the same social class as these women, or they would look down upon her and speak cattily behind her back, as women, Braden Granville knew, were wont to do.

So that categorically ruled out any candidates from his old neighborhood. Nor could he, he soon found, abide the marriageable misses he met at the various functions he attended: their prattle caused his head to ache, and the simpering attentions of their mammas, clearly aimed at getting their hands on his purse and not his person, were loathsome to him.

But in Lady Jacquelyn Seldon—beautiful, confident, silver-tongued Jacquelyn—he thought at last he'd found a soul mate. She came from a family with an age-old title and significant social connections, but no money, whereas he had all the money in the world, but no title, and hardly any connections. They were, he thought, the perfect match, made all the more appealing by the fact that Jacquelyn was untroubled by the stifling morality that made other girls her age so unappealing to him. She had always, from the first moment he'd met her, been perfectly willing to toss up her skirts and throw a leg around him, a habit quite appealing in a person with whom one planned to spend the rest of one's life.

Too late, of course, he'd come to realize that this habit was one that Jacquelyn did not necessarily reserve solely for his appreciation.

Too late as well he'd realized the reason why Jacquelyn felt she could get away with this sort of behavior. He'd learned it one night, when he'd arrived unexpectedly at Jackie's home, and entered her bedroom unannounced, only to overhear her saying conversationally to her mother, "If Granville is such a great genius, why did I see him use his fish fork to butter a roll at dinner the other night?'

And a man who'd commit a crime as heinous as the one she described was not at all likely to suspect a refined lady like herself of anything as base as philandering.

How wrong she'd been. And how much he longed to prove it to her.

Still, his engagement to the daughter of a duke had already brought him unquestionable benefits, not the least of which was an endorsement from the Prince of Wales. Not that Braden didn't think he'd have won that on his own merits, but his connection with Jacquelyn, whose father had been a longtime adviser to the prince, hadn't hurt.

And of course, there was the fact that his own father was over the moon with joy at the prospect of blue-blooded grandchildren. Doubtlessly any grandchildren would have delighted Sylvester, but given his current obsession with lineage, the fact that his son might produce an heir with a descendant of a duke thrilled Sylvester more than any flying machine or invisibility potion ever could.

But the benefits, Braden was beginning to find, did not outstrip the drawbacks of being married to a woman like Lady Jacquelyn.

"So," Weasel said, folding his hands beneath his head. "When's the first lesson?"

Braden eyed the soles of the shoes his secretary had swung up to rest on the low table in front of the couch where he lounged. "There aren't going to be any lessons," he said, tersely. "And put your feet down. That wood's over—"

But Weasel had already straightened up in his seat, dropping his feet to the floor.

"Not going to be any . . . Dead, you turned her down?"

"Of course I turned her down." He turned back toward the window. "What do you take me for?"

"A bloody fool," was Weasel's prompt reply.

"No," Braden said, still staring at the traffic going by in front of his offices. "Not a fool." A fool would have accepted her offer. Accepted her offer and found himself sinking deeper and deeper into those warm eyes. Eyes like that weren't easy to climb out of once a fellow had sunk into them.

"Yes, a fool!" Weasel sprang up and began to pace in front of the leather sofa. "What are you thinking? Lady Caroline Linford, with her little white gloves and parasol, would make the perfect eyewitness in your case against Jackie!"

"I'm aware of that," Braden said, woodenly.

"So what'd you turn her away for?" Weasel was practically shouting.

"I should think that would be obvious," Braden said, slipping his hands into his trouser pockets and standing with his shoulders hunched. "You saw her."

"Damned right I saw her," Weasel said. "I told you. She's a corker!"

"She's also," Braden pointed out, "the sort of girl who goes about with a chaperon. She's marrying that idiot Hurst Slater because he apparently saved her brother's life, or some such. She's impossibly young. And I don't mean in years, either."

Comprehension dawned. Weasel gaped. "She's a *virgin*?"

"Well, of course she's a virgin." Braden threw him an annoyed glance. "What did you think?"

"I'll tell you what I think," came Weasel's prompt reply. "I think you're scared."

Braden raised that single scarred eyebrow. Usually this gesture had the effect of silencing whomever he happened to be conversing with. Unfortunately, it had never worked on Weasel.

"Don't pull that eyebrow trick with me," Weasel said, disparagingly. "Admit it. You're scared. Because you never had one before. A virgin, I mean."

Braden rolled his eyes. "For God's sake, Weasel," he said. "She didn't want me actually to physically *show* her how to . . . you know. She claimed she only wanted me to *tell* her—" He was interrupted by Weasel's explosive bark of laughter. Braden frowned. "It isn't," he said, "funny."

"Oh," Weasel cried, clutching his stomach. "But it is, mate! It is! You may be able to hit a rat at fifty paces, but you ain't got the slightest idea what makes a female tick, have you?"

Chagrined, but not completely insensible to the humor in the situation, Braden waited until his secretary had calmed down before asking, "Well, if that's true, why am I known as the Lothario of London, while you're just called Weasel?"

Weasel wiped tears of laughter from the corners of his eyes. "Your success with the fairer sex has always been overrated, in my opinion."

"You think so?" Braden drawled. "Well, I haven't noticed any virgins throwing themselves at you, begging you to educate them in the ways of love."

Weasel snorted. "I haven't time to run around after every pretty woman that passes my way. I'm too busy looking after *your* correspondence, and running your bloody business."

"Is that what you do all day?" Braden inquired, mildly. "I always fancied you were generally at the gaming tables, gambling away *my* hard-earned money."

"Don't try to change the subject," Weasel growled, clearly trying to steer his employer away from that particular topic. "You had a perfect shot at Jackie, Dead, and you flinched."

"For now," Braden said, calmly. "But that doesn't mean I've put away my guns."

"But *Lady Caroline Linford,* Dead," Weasel persisted. "You couldn't ask for a more credible witness."

"Perhaps not," Braden said. "But I won't drag her into this. It's a dirty business, and no place for a girl like Caroline Linford." Trying to block the memory of those reproachful eyes, he squared his shoulders and said confidently, "We'll catch Jackie out eventually, mark my words."

Weasel looked annoyed. "I sincerely hope so. It's my night to follow her. I have to tell you, Dead, I'm getting tired of lurkin' around, hoping to catch a glimpse of that bloke of hers. Why can't you just tell her the wedding's off, chuck a pile of money at her, and be done with it? If you paid her enough, I doubt she'd go squealing to her lawyers."

Braden was growing tired of explaining the reasoning behind his action—or inaction, as the case happened to be. "The principle of the thing, Weasel! The principle of the thing! Why should I pay her for making a cuckold out of me?"

"Christ, Dead, you've given her a bloody fortune already for her trousseau. What's a few thousand more?"

Braden shook his head. "You don't understand. The trousseau, the ring—all of that is contractual. She doesn't get to keep it if the marriage doesn't take place. And it isn't going to." His expression went steely. "You accused me of not knowing what makes a female tick. That may be true, but I can tell you a lot about what makes Jacquelyn Seldon tick. She thinks that because I grew up in the Dials—because I only recently came into my fortune—because I earned it, instead of the method preferred by her set, inheriting it—that I am a fool. She thinks that because I grew up poor, she can play me like that harp she sometimes drags out at parties and plucks. Well, I'm out to prove her wrong. And I will prove it, as soon as I have some better proof than a faceless stranger my men may or may not have seen leaving her house in the dead of night."

"They *did* see him!" Weasel stabbed a finger at his employer. "I tell you, they saw him! Is it their bloody fault the bloke's slippery as a cat? I swear, it's as if he were a phantom, or something." Then the secretary grinned. "Too bad we didn't have him workin' for us, huh, Dead? Back when we were in a different kind of business, if you get my meaning? We'd never have gotten caught, if we'd had Jackie's boy on our side. Wonder if he's workin' for one of our competitors these days?"

Braden did not return the smile. "Our competitors," he said, severely, "are the Americans. Remember? A company called Colt? We're walking on the right side of the law these days, my friend." He turned back toward the window. "And as for Jackie's lover being a phantom," he said, his voice nothing but a rumbling growl, "we know now that's not true. Because Caroline Linford's seen him."

10

"But," the Dowager Lady Bartlett said, "Peters says he waited for you for almost an hour."

"Oh, Mother." Caroline leaned against the balcony railing, scanning the crowd through her opera glasses. "It was nothing, all right? Only an errand. I say, Lady Rawlings is looking particularly rotund this evening. Can she be having *another* baby? How many is that now? My God, she seems to be trying to give the queen a run for the money."

"I'll thank you, miss," Lady Bartlett said, acidly, "to save your comments about the queen and her baby-making habits until you're fortunate enough to have produced a baby of your own. And stop spying on people through those things. They're to see the performers, not the public."

"That tears it." Caroline lowered the mother-of-pearl and gold glasses, and turned to Emily Stanhope, who sat in the chair beside hers. "Lord Swenson dyes his hair. There isn't a doubt in my mind anymore. No one has hair that black. No one."

"Except maybe an Egyptian," Emily agreed. "And Lord Swenson is most definitely *not* an Egyptian. His people all come from Surrey."

"An errand?" Lady Bartlett, from the seat behind her daughter's, would not let the matter rest. "What kind of errand takes an hour to complete? And at the offices of Braden Granville, no less? I simply don't understand it."

"Oh, really, Ma," Caroline said, lifting the glasses again, and training them on the people taking their seats below. "Peters is exaggerating. It was more like twenty minutes."

"But what were you doing at Braden Granville's offices in the first place?"

Caroline lowered the opera glasses and rolled her eyes at Emily, who had turned away with a smirk. "I *told* you, Ma," Caroline said, for what seemed the hundredth time. "I went to buy Tommy one of those new guns. You know, the one that's been in all the papers. I wanted it to be a surprise for Tommy's birthday."

"A gun?" Lady Bartlett was appalled. "For Tommy? Caroline! You? I don't believe it."

Emily, beside Caroline, started to snicker. Caroline gave her a swift kick on the side of the ankle, and the snickering turned to a yelp of pain.

"You know he's going back to school in the fall, Mother," Caroline explained, "and I think he ought to have something that he can protect himself with. Oxford obviously isn't as safe as it once was, and a Granville—"

"I don't like it." Lady Bartlett fanned herself energetically. She was dressed in one of her newest gowns, an elegantly cut creation in shiny red satin, with real roses pinned to the sleeves. Her son, upon seeing her in it, had had the impertinence to inquire whether she was certain she was only going to the opera, and not actually performing in it, a remark that had put the Lady Bartlett into the foul mood from which she still suffered.

"And I must say, I'm surprised at you, Caroline." Lady Bartlett shook her head until her curls swayed. "You have always been most outspoken in your condemnation of violence. And now suddenly you're saying it's all right—"

"To defend oneself," Caroline pointed out. "That's all."

Her mother, however, wasn't listening. "And Braden Granville, of all people," she went on. "You had to go to see Braden Granville about it. Well, he isn't like us, you know, Caroline, however much Tommy might like to think otherwise." Lady Bartlett always acquired a box every season, so that she could sit in it and say whatever she wanted to about anyone, without fear of it being overheard. "He was born poor, and you know what they say. . . ."

"You can take the man out of the slums, but you can't take the slums out of the man." Caroline and Emily mouthed the words along with Lady Bartlett, since they'd both heard her utter them so often. Then they looked at one another and burst out laughing.

"It really isn't at all like you, Caroline," Lady Bartlett went on, ignoring the girls, "to buy your brother a *gun*. A *gun*! Why, what if it goes off accidentally, and he ends up shooting himself?"

"That's why I'm buying him a Granville," Caroline said, when she'd managed to catch her breath again. "They're supposed to be safer—"

"And I'm not convinced," Lady Bartlett continued, relentlessly, "that Tommy ought to go back to school in the fall. I don't think he should be attending an institution where the students aren't safe to walk the streets at night. You know what Dr. Pettigrew said. Tommy isn't to excite himself unduly. Any strain on his heart could potentially be hazardous to his—"

Emily Stanhope's elbow connected solidly with Caroline's arm. "*Look*," she whispered, urgently, when Caroline, rubbing her arm, turned to see what was the matter. Caroline followed her friend's gaze, and saw, in the box across the theater from theirs, a familiar face. She instantly lifted the opera glasses to her eyes, and peered through them.

It was Braden Granville, all right, looking absurdly imposing for someone who was only dressed in evening clothes, same as every other man in the place. Why was it that on him, however, the ubiquitous black coat appeared to make his shoulders look so very massive? He must, Caroline decided, have an excellent tailor.

Well, and why not? He had everything money could buy. Including, apparently, the ability to track down the identity of his fiancée's secret lover without Caroline's help, thank you very much.

"Look at him." Emily, to whom Caroline had related the truth of what had really occurred while Peters had been waiting outside Granville Enterprises, leaned forward, obstructing her view through the binoculars. "Just who does he think he is?"

"I believe," Caroline said, rising in her seat so she could see above Emily's head, "that he thinks he's Braden Granville."

"Braden Granville," Emily muttered. "King of everything."

"Emily," Caroline warned.

"Well, seriously, Caro. Imagine the gall of him, turning down an invitation to teach you to make love! You! Lady Caroline Linford! Why, you're the prettiest girl I know. What could he have been thinking?"

Caroline tore the opera glasses from his face, and threw a hasty glance at her mother. *Emily! Not here. We are not going to discuss this here.*

"Oh!" Emily cried, reaching for the glasses. "Look who's joining him!"

Caroline looked. A woman whose creamy shoulders and magnificent bosom were well displayed by her dangerously low decolletage had joined Braden Granville in his box. In fact, when she bent to smooth her skirt beneath her before sitting down, Caroline was awarded a view of her breasts that was every bit as unimpeded as the one she'd had a few nights earlier, at Dame Ashforth's.

Lowering the glasses with a scowl, she asked, beneath her breath, "Why is it that my mother treats it as a mortal crime if my decolletage slips so much as an inch, but Jackie Seldon can get away with going about bare breasted as an Amazon?"

"That's easy enough," Emily said. "Look at *her* mother."

Sure enough, the dowager duchess, taking a seat behind Lady Jacquelyn, had on a gown almost as indecent as her daughter's. As the older gentleman who was sitting beside her illustrated, by eagerly holding the dowager's program while she adjusted her skirts, Lady Jacquelyn's mother was as irresistible to the opposite sex as her daughter.

Caroline sighed gustily. "It isn't fair. Why do girls like Jacquelyn Seldon get all the men? Don't they know she's incapable of fidelity? And from what I remember from school, she always treated her horses very shabbily indeed."

"Men don't care about things like that," Emily replied, with a shrug. "All they care about is whether or not their knob is being polished on a regular basis."

Caroline made a face at her friend's crudeness. "Not *all* of them," she pointed out. "Tommy doesn't care about that."

As had been happening regularly since the earl's startling revelation a few days earlier, Emily grinned widely at the mention of his name. "That's because he hasn't tried it yet," she said. "Wait until he does. He'll be addicted to it, just like all the others."

Caroline, whose relationship with her brother was not always an easy one, nevertheless said, with sisterly loyalty, "Not Tommy."

As she spoke, she'd continued to gaze through the opera glasses into Braden Granville's box. Only now, she realized with a start, someone was staring right back at her through a pair of opera glasses of his own.

Not just any someone, either, but Braden Granville himself.

Caroline lowered her glasses with a start, feeling her cheeks heat up. What, she wondered, had *he* been looking at? Not *her*, surely. Though it had certainly *looked* as if it had been her Braden Granville had trained his glasses upon. But that was impossible. He hated her! Her scandalous offer had repulsed and offended him. She was quite sure it had. Why else had he turned it down?

Maybe he'd been looking at Emmy. Yes, that had to have been

it. Everyone looked at Emmy, who had always steadfastly refused to wear a corset. Her loose-fitting gowns were actually very pretty—much prettier than the horrid poofy trousers she'd worn briefly, inspired by the design of the American Mrs. Bloomer, until her father had finally put his foot down, and threatened to cut off her allowance if she appeared in them in public again. But no matter how pretty Emmy might look in her waistless gowns, she did not look conventional, and that was always reason for someone to stare.

Yes, Caroline comforted herself. That had been what had so caught Mr. Granville's interest on this side of the theater. Emmy and her corsetless frock. Certainly not Caroline. Never Caroline.

And yet when, a few seconds later, she slid her gaze toward his box, she found that he was still—yes, *still*—staring at her! Her, not Emmy at all! Her!

"And that's another thing." Lady Bartlett leaned forward and seized the back of her daughter's chair. "Braden Granville has an execrable reputation where women are concerned. Why, Lady Chittenhouse told me she saw him at Ascot two seasons ago in the company of a *married* viscountess. And they were *not* behaving as one might think a married viscountess and an eligible bachelor ought. I want you to promise me, Caroline, that you will not go to Braden Granville's again."

Caroline, her cheeks still burning, said nothing, though it occurred to her that if she were never again in Braden Granville's presence, that would be quite all right with her.

A new, unmistakably masculine voice filled the box. "Not Braden Granville once again," the Marquis of Winchilsea said, as he and Caroline's brother, smelling of cigar smoke, took their seats. "Has Caroline been talking corsets with him tonight?"

"Talking corsets?" Lady Bartlett fanned herself rapidly. "Caroline, what is the marquis referring to? Tell me at once. I must know."

"Oh, Mother." Caroline gave her fiancé a sour look—careful

not to turn her head in the direction of Braden Granville's box. "It's nothing. Just a passing remark Mr. Granville made last week at Dame Ashforth's."

"I didn't know you were acquainted with Granville, Caro." Thomas took his seat behind Emily, and immediately began to tear off bits of his program and roll them into small balls, in preparation for the opera's more dramatic moments, during which he would hurl them into Emily's lap, as was his custom. "I mean, not more than to say how-do to."

"I'm not acquainted with Mr. Granville more than to say how-do to," Caroline insisted, wishing it were true. "Really, Hurst, I wish you wouldn't give my mother ideas. You know how excitable she is."

"Excitable?" Lady Bartlett was fanning herself more energetically than ever now. "Don't be ridiculous. I swear I don't know where you get your ideas sometimes, Caroline. I am not excitable. I can't help wondering, however, why it is so very wrong of me to be *concerned*—and that's all I am, concerned—when I hear that my only daughter is engaging in conversation about underthings with strange men. It is, after all, my maternal duty to protect her. Don't you think so, my lord?"

"Indeed, madam," Hurst said, lifting Lady Bartlett's hand, and kissing the back of it lightly. "And might I compliment you on the exemplary job of it you've done thus far?"

Lady Bartlett giggled coquettishly. "Why, thank you, Lord Winchilsea."

Disgusted, Caroline slumped down in her chair—as much as her corset would allow her to, anyway—and concentrated on hating Braden Granville.

That's right, she hated him. Now more than ever, seeing as how he seemed intent on publicly humiliating her with that pointed stare—yes, he was still looking her way, though thankfully he'd lowered the opera glasses.

Oh, yes, she quite positively hated him now. Not that she'd any liking for him before. Why, the man was nothing but a hypocrite! Imagine, him seeming so shocked by her proposal, when everyone knew what a wicked reputation he had.

And yet he hadn't seemed at all wicked to Caroline. He had seemed like a fairly normal, rather thoughtful man—a little on the forceful side, maybe, but she supposed that was only natural, since he was, after all, in charge of such a large and prosperous business. In fact, if she hadn't heard as many rumors as she had about his conquests, she would never have guessed he was a ruthless predator of her sex—which was what men like him were called in the novels she liked.

Well, that wasn't, she supposed, strictly true. There'd been a moment when he'd hung over her chair, and she'd felt the heat from his body, and had seen up close the strength in those great hands, that she'd caught a glimpse of the Lothario. And that glimpse was what had made her feel, as she had that night at Dame Ashforth's, as if she'd never again be able to breathe quite normally.

Only what kind of Lothario turned a young woman, eager to be indoctrinated in the ways of love, away?

The answer was easy enough, but regrettably unflattering: a man who wasn't the least bit interested in her. So uninterested in her, in fact, that even the promise of a reward—in Braden Granville's case, her promise to testify on his behalf if Jacquelyn Seldon brought a breach of promise suit against him—had not been enough incentive.

Except, if he really did find her so repulsive, why did he keep *staring* like that?

"*Ouch!*" Emily swung her attention away from Tommy and glared at Caroline. "What did you pinch me for?"

"Look at Mr. Granville's box," Caroline whispered. "And tell me if he's still looking this way."

Emily looked. "Good God. He *is*. He's positively *staring*."

"I knew it," Caroline murmured, sinking more deeply into her seat with a groan. "He hates me."

"I wouldn't say that *hate* is the first thing that comes to my mind when I discover a man is staring at me," Emily said. "Besides, how could he possibly hate you? He doesn't even *know* you. Why are you wasting time even thinking about him? I thought you'd given up on this ludicrous plan of yours to learn how to be a whore."

"Mistress," Caroline hissed. "The word is mistress, or, if you insist, courtesan. And I have *not* given it up. I've merely given up on Braden Granville."

"Oh," Emily whispered. "So if you're not going to get your education—" She said the word with quite unnecessary malice, Caroline thought. "—from Braden Granville, then who are you going to get it from, eh?"

Caroline opened her mouth to reply, but was interrupted by Hurst, who leaned forward to seize the glasses Caroline was holding.

"Oh, I say, Carrie," her fiancé said. "Thanks. There's something I want to take a look at."

Caroline had no choice but to release the glasses. A second later, she saw Hurst training them in the direction of Braden Granville's box. Well, how could he have helped himself? He, like every other man in the theater, could not have failed to notice Lady Jacquelyn's cavernous decolletage.

But would he notice that Lady Jacquelyn's fiancé seemed preoccupied with someone else entirely?

Fortunately at that point the lights started to be put out, and the orchestra conductor strode out from the wings. The audience applauded politely, including Hurst, who had to pass the glasses back to Caroline in order to do so.

She took them and brought them at once back to her eyes. Braden Granville was no longer looking at her, but at the stage, a fact over which she knew she ought to be rejoicing—why would she want that odious man's attention on her?—but which made her feel oddly let down instead.

She slumped in her seat. Why? she asked herself miserably. Oh, why had she gone to him in the first place? It had been a mad scheme, simply ridiculous. Braden Granville was quite right: She couldn't hope to force Hurst to love her, any more than she could salvage the shattered pieces of the love she'd felt for him—until that night at Dame Ashforth's—and glue them back together. She was simply going to have to marry him and put up with his loving someone else.

Maybe it was better that way. Maybe things like gratitude and friendship were better for a lasting marriage than mad, passionate love, anyway.

"Well?" Caroline whispered to Emily an hour later, when the curtain descended for the first interval. "Is he still looking this way?"

Emily looked at the box across the way. "That's strange," she said. "He's gone."

"Gone?" Caroline flung a glance toward Braden Granville's now empty seat. "Where on earth could he have gone so quickly? The lights only just came back up."

"He must have slipped out before the act ended. Oh, Tommy!" Emily noticed all the balls of paper Thomas had tossed into her lap during the performance, and began furiously to sweep them off.

Tommy had a hearty laugh at Emily's expense, then hurried off with Hurst to enjoy a cigar in the smoking room. Lady Bartlett declared a desire for a bit of air, which Caroline knew meant she wanted to show off her new gown, and Emily mischievously volunteered to join her, which dampened Lady Bartlett's enthusiasm somewhat. Her new gown would not draw nearly as much attention with Lady Emily Stanhope, in all her un-corsetted glory, standing beside her.

Still, there was nothing Lady Bartlett could do about it, except command Caroline to walk with them, in the obvious hopes that Emily's odd ensemble might be lost between the enormous crinolines both Lady Bartlett and her daughter wore.

"I'll be right there, Mother," Caroline said. She was trying to gather up as many as she could of the tiny wads of paper her brother had so thoughtlessly scattered across the floor of the box, so she could dispose of them where they rightly belonged . . . in her brother's coat pocket.

Which was why she was quite alone—although she had been so for barely a moment—when suddenly a pair of men's shoes appeared just beside the fan she was using to sweep the pieces of paper into her hand. Caroline did not recognize these expensive evening slippers, gleaming with polish, as Hurst's bore silver buckles, and Tommy's tassels. These bore neither.

Her glance sliding slowly up the trouser legs attached to the shoes, Caroline began to feel uncomfortable. And when her gaze flicked over a beautifully stitched but subdued satin waistcoat, then paused to take in the wide breadth of shoulder encased in a perfectly tailored evening coat, she didn't need to look up any farther.

She knew who it was. She knew exactly who it was.

11

"*L*ady Caroline." Braden Granville's deep voice was filled with concern. "Are you quite all right?"

Why? she wailed to herself. Why was it that every time Braden Granville came into her presence, he managed to catch her performing some act of utter inanity? *Why?*

"I'm perfectly fine," Caroline replied, keeping her head resolutely ducked, so she would not have to look into those dark eyes. "I'm only . . . my brother played a little joke, and I'm just picking up after him. He thinks he's very amusing, but I highly doubt his sense of humor is very much appreciated by the people who are paid to clean the theater at night."

From behind the velvet curtains that separated their box from the corridor beyond it, Caroline heard her mother call her name. She answered, "Coming, Mother," and started to climb to her feet, aware that her cheeks were burning as hotly as fire pokers left too long in the flames.

Her blush deepened as she felt his hand cup her elbow, helping to steady her as she rose.

"Lady Caroline." Braden Granville's voice was cool, but there was something urgent in his tone. Caroline supposed that, whatever it was he'd come to say, he wanted to get it said as soon as possible, so he could return to the side of the Lady Jacquelyn, who might otherwise get up to mischief in his absence.

Either that, or he wished to avoid being seen by Caroline's mother, a sentiment for which she could not help feeling thankful to him, when she considered what her mother would have to say if she happened to step back into the box and see him. . . .

"I was hoping I would see you tonight. I wished to talk to you about what we were discussing in my offices the other day—"

Caroline could not help but look up at that, bringing her startled gaze to his face.

"I've reconsidered." His gaze met hers steadily. She could read nothing in his face but seriousness. "I'd like it very much if you would be able to stop by Granville Enterprises again tomorrow. Would four o'clock suit you?"

Caroline stared at him, not at all certain that she'd heard him correctly. It seemed to her that he'd said—no, she did not think she could be mistaken about this—that he had changed his mind, and that he would entertain the idea of coaching her in the art of lovemaking.

But that was impossible. Because hadn't he made it more than clear that Caroline was entirely too virginal—read, repulsive—for him to do any such thing?

"Lady Caroline?" He stared down at her, puzzled by her silence. She wondered what he'd thought she'd do upon hearing his announcement that he'd changed his mind. Whoop for joy? "Did you hear me?"

"I heard you," Caroline said, conscious that her heart was beating frantically beneath her corset stays. He'd said yes. He'd said yes. Good Lord. He'd actually said yes.

Braden Granville's serious expression did not change. He said, "If tomorrow is inconvenient, another time would be quite all right. It really doesn't matter to me, Lady Caroline. I am at your disposal. The next day, perhaps, would be more convenient for you?"

It was on the tip of her tongue to say yes. To say yes to this man who possessed such a miraculous ability to steal her breath—not literally, of course, but it did seem as if no sooner did he come near her than she was fighting to breathe, fighting to keep calm, fighting not to notice little things about him, like the way the dark hair at his neck curled against his high starched collar, or the fact that his eyelashes were coal black and almost as long as her own. . . .

But what did *he* think of *her*? What did the great Braden Granville think of Lady Caroline Linford? When she came near, what went through *his* mind?

She knew. And what she knew kept her from saying yes. He'd humiliated her— *humiliated* her—that day in his office, and now he thought he could simply walk up to her and say he'd changed his mind, and everything would be all right?

Both of Caroline's hands were balled into fists, at the center of one was all the wads of paper she'd collected from the floor. She was so furious, that for a moment she considered flinging them in Braden Granville's face, but as this would have been much too childish a gesture, she settled for saying, in what she hoped were tones of ice, "No, the next day is not convenient for me, Mr. Granville. There is no time, Mr. Granville, that will ever be convenient for me to see you. In fact, if I never saw you again in my life, I would die a very happy woman. Good evening, sir."

Whereupon she attempted to glide from the box with all the dignity of one of the queen's naval ships at full sail.

Unfortunately, she'd forgotten Braden Granville still had hold of her elbow. He tightened his grip, and managed to keep her firmly anchored at his side.

"I beg your pardon, Lady Caroline," he said, sounding somewhat taken aback. "Have I done something to offend you?"

Good God! Was he serious? Evidently he was, since Caroline

could trace not the slightest hint of irony in his face at that particular moment.

"Mr. Granville." She fought to keep her voice from becoming shrill. The last thing she needed was to attract the attention of the opera patrons below them, or worse, her mother. "The . . . *discussion* . . . we had the other day is one that I would sincerely like to forget, if it's all the same to you. And I certainly don't care to continue it, or even refer to it, ever again. And I am frankly appalled that you would care to do so, especially in so public a place. After all, it certainly won't do your reputation any good, being seen with someone as *virginal* as I am."

The bewilderment left his face, to be replaced by amusement. Amusement! He actually thought her indignation with him humorous!

"So that's what's bothering you," he said with a grin. His hand still hadn't left her elbow. While his strong fingers weren't hurting her, she could not help but be aware of the gentle pressure they were exerting. She could feel the heat from his skin straight through the silk of her evening glove, all the way up her arm, and throughout her entire body. "You know, there are a good many women in this world who would take a remark like that as a compliment."

"Well, I am not one of them. I don't suppose it has ever occurred to you, Mr. Granville, that being a virgin is extremely tiresome, and that having it constantly thrown up in one's face is actually quite irritating." Caroline jerked her arm from his grasp as if he'd stung her. "My offer to you the other day, Mr. Granville, was ill considered. I realize that now, and withdraw it. Now, if you will kindly step out of my way, my mother is waiting for me."

But Braden Granville did not step out of her way. Instead, he regarded her thoughtfully with those inscrutable brown eyes. The grin, she saw, was gone.

"It is ill advised, Lady Caroline," he said, in a tone that was, Caroline noticed, carefully neutral, "to put so much emotional stake in business dealings. You seem to have taken my declination of your generous offer very personally. But there was nothing personal about it, Lady Caroline. At the time, it struck me as an unsound venture. I have since had time to re-evaluate it, and I feel somewhat differently than I did—"

She shot him a shrewd glance. "You mean something happened," she interrupted, tartly, "that's made you anxious to rid yourself of Lady Jacquelyn once and for all. What was it?"

He merely shook his head. "That's not it at all. But I don't want to trouble you with the details—"

"Well," Caroline said, wondering furiously what could have occurred to make the great Braden Granville change his prodigious mind, if not some recent outrage of his fiancée's. "I'm sorry, but I no longer have a need for your . . . services, so—"

"Have you found someone else?" he demanded, sharply enough to cause Caroline to stammer, "Of course not!"

Then she regained her composure, and added rudely, "Not that it's any of *your* business. The fact is, I have merely decided to take your advice."

"*My* advice?" He looked, if such a thing were possible, even more surprised than he had before.

"Indeed. Weren't you the one who warned me that is impossible to force someone to fall in love?"

"Well," he said, looking chagrined, "that is true, but—"

"But now it doesn't suit you to have me throw it up in your face?" She told herself that she felt fiercely gratified to have disappointed him every bit as much as he, that day in his office, had disappointed— no, *humiliated*—her, though if truth be told, she did feel a tiny bit of regret. She didn't like causing anyone pain, even heartless businessmen like Braden Granville. "Well, I'm very sorry, Mr. Granville, but I think it quite sound. My fiancé and I have a good deal of esteem for one another, and I believe that is all that is necessary for a successful marriage. And now, if you don't mind, I must join my mother."

Caroline's mother, she knew perfectly well, had forgotten all about her, and was probably deeply engrossed in conversation with some friend or other, but she knew if she didn't get out of his presence, and soon, the disappointment on his face was going to drive her to do something rash, like agree to meet with him. She gathered her skirts to get by him. . . .

Just as the bell sounded to indicate the end of the interval.

"Oh," Caroline said with some dismay, stopping in her tracks.

"I see that I had better return to my seat," Braden Granville said, gravely, "before you are rejoined by your family. But I'd ask that—your esteem for your fiancé aside—you'd consider what I've said, Lady Caroline. I believe we are each in a position—completely unique to this situation—where we might be of great help to one another. I apologize again if I said anything to offend you, and hope that you will not let your pride stand in the way of making what could be a very profitable venture—for us both."

He left then. But before he left, he did something so shocking, Caroline still hadn't recovered by the time the others returned to the box. Because what Braden Granville did—*all* he did—was reach out as he was leaving, and run the tip of his index finger along the side of Caroline's long, bare neck, from her collarbone to just beneath her ear, as casually as if he were a child running a stick along a fence.

But there was nothing childlike about the jolt Caroline felt through her entire body as a result of his light, almost nonchalant touch. And she had thought Hurst's kisses thrilling! Why, all Braden Granville had done was touch her—just *touch* her—and she'd experienced a physical sensation quite unlike any she'd ever felt before.

"Where were you?" Emily demanded, as she sank back into her seat. "Did you get lost in the crush?"

Hardly aware of what she was saying, Caroline murmured, "Yes."

"Hurst, too, it looks like. He'd better hurry, the curtain's going to go up in a minute. How are our friends across the way?" Emily aimed the opera glasses at Braden Granville's box. "Ah. He's back, I see."

It was true, Caroline thought to herself. It was true, all those things Tommy and his friends had said. Braden Granville knew things. Tricks, like that one with his finger. What if Caroline could learn a few of those tricks? Just a few?

"But what's this I see?" Emily focused the binoculars. "No Lady Jacquelyn? No, and the lights are going down. Hmmm. Hurst is missing. Lady Jacquelyn is missing. Careless of them."

"Caro." Tommy leaned forward in his chair. "Where are all my bits of paper? Did you pick them up? What am I to throw at Emmy now?"

Supposing, Caroline mused, she used that finger trick on Hurst. He likely wouldn't waste another second with Lady Jacquelyn. Not if she could make him thrill to her touch the way Braden Granville had thrilled her. . . .

"Quiet, both of you," Lady Bartlett hissed. "The curtain! Oh, where's your fiancé, Caroline? He's going to miss the first number."

"Aria, Mother," Tommy said, tiredly.

"Number, aria." Lady Bartlett began to fan herself. "Is anyone else overwarm? Tommy, are you feeling warm? Would you like to borrow my fan?"

Fortunately, the music swelled, drowning out Lady Bartlett's voice. But it could not drown out Caroline's thoughts, which were centered around the extraordinary interview she'd had with a man she'd quite firmly put out of her mind just a day or so before. Braden Granville's touch hadn't just awakened Caroline physically; it had also awakened something she had almost given up—hope.

And hope was something she very badly needed, particularly when, midway through the second act, Emily elbowed her, and indicated Braden Granville's box. Jacquelyn Seldon was making her

way toward her seat. A few minutes later, Caroline felt a distur-
bance in her own box, and glanced over her shoulder to see Hurst
sinking into his own seat.

"Beastly long line," he informed them, under his breath, "at
the refreshment table."

Caroline darted a quick glance in Braden Granville's direction.
Had he noticed? Had he seen that his fiancé and hers had both
been gone from their seats for the same amount of time? Evidently
not. He was examining his program in the light from the stage, and
no matter how many times she looked at him throughout the rest
of the evening, she never once caught him looking her way again.

Well, and why should he? She had put him in his place, hadn't
she? Given him a well-deserved dressing down.

So why did she feel so terrible about it?

And yet, when the opera had finished up, and they'd been
descending the grand staircase to the lobby, Braden Granville—
whose party had happened to be taking the stairs at the same time
as hers—nodded to her politely, and said, "Good evening. I hope
you enjoyed the performance."

Caroline, who had been expecting him to ignore her as stonily
as she'd planned on ignoring him, stammered, "Oh, um, well, it
was all right, I suppose."

"All right?" An older gentleman behind Braden Granville
stared at Caroline as if she'd said something sacrilegious. "It was
the most moving performance of *Faust* I've ever seen!"

Braden looked at the older man and said, calmly, "That's the
only performance of *Faust* you've ever seen, Pa."

"Um," Caroline said. "Maybe if it had been in English . . ."

"Caroline." Lady Bartlett's voice was unnaturally high. "Come
along, dear. Peters has brought the carriage round."

"Braden, my boy." The elder Granville was grinning in a way
that Caroline thought slightly . . . well, off. "Aren't you going to
introduce me to your friends?"

And then Braden Granville was saying, in the most patient tone imaginable, "Father, may I present to you Lady Caroline Linford and her fiancé, the Marquis of Winchilsea. Thomas Linford, Earl of Bartlett, and his mother, Lady Bartlett. Oh, and this is Lady Emily Stanhope, daughter of Lord Woodson. . . . My father, Sylvester Granville."

"Lady Bartlett," the elder Granville murmured, reaching for the lady's hand, and bowing low over it. "Sylvester Granville, at your service."

"Mr. Granville." Caroline's mother, for once in her life, did not seem to know where to direct her gaze. She, too, Caroline realized, recognized that all was not well with Braden Granville's father. "How . . . charming to meet you."

Sylvester Granville straightened and released Lady Bartlett's hand, a slightly silly expression suffusing his face. Why, Caroline thought, her heart swelling with pity, the great Granville's father is mad! Perhaps not violently so, but clearly to some extent. The poor, poor man.

And poor Braden Granville, to whom she had just been so unforgivably rude!

Lady Jacquelyn's mother, the dowager duchess, did not seem particularly troubled by the mental state of her daughter's future father-in-law. Instead, all of her attention was focused on Lady Bartlett, a woman of about her own age, but whose fine skin and eyes put hers to shame—and the duchess knew it.

"How sweet," she drawled, not taking her gaze off the milk-white skin Lady Bartlett's red satin gown showed off to such an advantage. "A family outing to the opera, just like ours."

Lady Bartlett's fine eyes came into sharp focus then, the lids around them narrowing dangerously. "Ah," she said. "How nice to see you again, Your Grace."

The dowager duchess's eyelids did some fluttering of their own. "Pardon me, but have we met?"

"Oh, Mother," Lady Jacquelyn said, in a bored voice. "You remember Lady Bartlett, surely? Her daughter Lady Caroline and I were in school together—"

Caroline, who was becoming alarmed by the bizarreness of the situation, seized Lady Bartlett by the arm and said, "Come along, Mother. The carriage is waiting."

"Oh." Lady Bartlett seemed startled by Caroline's sudden eagerness to be away. "Well, good-bye, then, Your Grace, Lady Jacquelyn, Mr. Granville, and, er, Mr. Granville."

But unfortunately, that was not the last Caroline was to see of Braden Granville's party. Because as they approached their own vehicle, a carriage bearing the crest of the Duke of Childes pulled up behind, and caused Caroline to freeze where she was.

The marquis saw the duke's brougham at the same moment Caroline did, and he reached out and placed a restraining hand upon her arm. But it was far too late. Shaking herself free of her fiancé's grip, Caroline forgot all about the evening's awkwardness and turned toward the dowager duchess with a stricken expression, crying, "Bearing reins? Your Grace, what can you be thinking?"

The duchess raised her carefully groomed eyebrows. "Bearing what?"

"Bearing reins." Caroline pointed accusingly at the team of fine grays that were harnessed to the duchess's carriage. Standing with their heads erect, their necks curled, the horses looked as alert as if they were marching on parade.

But the effect was deceiving. The animals were not holding their heads high due to any sort of equine pride. Their heads were being pulled back by a second pair of reins, attached to a double bit that forbade the horses from relaxing their necks, tossing their heads, and even, Caroline knew, from breathing or swallowing properly.

"*Look*," Caroline said. She gestured toward the mouth of the nearest horse, which was foam flecked. "Do you see that? Do you see how it's pink, the foam? That's blood, Your Grace."

The duchess, who'd leaned forward to see what Caroline was indicating, recoiled. "Is the animal ill?" she asked, her repugnance evident in not only her lovely face, but her voice as well.

"No, they aren't ill." Lady Bartlett spoke quickly. "You must forgive Caroline, Your Grace. She has a soft spot for horses, and she can't bear to see them in even the slightest discomfort—"

"There's nothing *slight* about the discomfort of a bearing rein, Mother," Caroline snapped. "I should like to know how you would feel if *you* had one in your mouth, your head pulled back so far you can hardly breathe—"

Lady Bartlett, embarrassed by the scene her daughter was causing, tittered nervously, and before her son could stop her—and Thomas, always supportive of his sister, tried—was saying apologetically to the duchess, "She takes after her father, I'm afraid. Quite mad for horses, he was. Why, he must have fired half a dozen drivers because he thought they were too rough on his little darlings, as he called them. He'd stop men on the street and lecture them if he thought they were being cruel to their mounts. Caroline's no better. You know, she's actually acquired quite a little collection of nags she's saved from the knacker's yard. . . ."

Lady Bartlett's voice trailed off as the dowager duchess and her daughter exchanged glances.

"How interesting," Lady Jacquelyn said, coldly. "But I'm of the opinion that it isn't anyone's business how my mother keeps her horses."

Caroline declared loudly, "It's the business of any human being with an ounce of compassion, Lady Jacquelyn. It's unconscionable, really unconscionable, for your mother to allow these animals to suffer in this manner."

"But," the duchess said, confusedly, "Lady Bartlett said they aren't ill—"

A deep voice interrupted her.

"The bearing reins are cutting their mouths." Braden Granville had stepped forward and laid a hand upon the unnaturally arched neck of the nearest horse. He spoke not to the duchess, but to the brougham's driver, perched behind the horses, whip in hand. "Have they stood like this all night?"

The driver nodded, looking apologetic. "Her Grace don't like a horse with a droopin' head, my lord."

"Yes," the duchess said, emphatically. "Yes, I like a smart-looking horse—"

"Well, they won't be smart-looking for long." Braden Granville spoke with grim authority. "They'll be of no use to you in a year or two. You're damaging their windpipes. It's a shame, too, because these are fine animals."

"I should certainly hope they're fine animals," the dowager duchess said, imperiously. "I paid enough for them." Then, with an impatient gesture at her driver, she said, "Well, don't just sit there, man. Remove the things. Remove the things at once!"

The driver climbed down from his seat with alacrity, and, with the help of one of the duchess's footmen, began to remove the second set of reins from the horses' heads.

"I say, Caro," Thomas leaned down to whisper in his sister's ear. "Well done!"

But Caroline knew it wasn't because of anything she'd said that the dowager duchess had capitulated so suddenly. It had been Braden Granville's influence, far more than hers, that had liberated the horses. Accordingly, she flashed him a grateful smile—

But he had already turned away, and was busy handing his fiancée, now wearing a pretty scowl upon her heart-shaped face, into the carriage.

Which was, Caroline told herself, just as well. She didn't want, after all, to give him false expectations. Because, ill father or not, nothing had changed. She was most certainly not going to his offices tomorrow at four o'clock. Most decidedly *not*.

12

Braden Granville pulled his pocket watch from his waist-coat for a third time. He shook the twenty-four carat gold and diamond instrument, then held it to his ear. Then he examined it again, glancing at the ormolu clock on the mantel across from his desk.

It was five minutes past four o'clock in the afternoon. There was no question in the matter. His watch kept perfect time, and Weasel made sure the mantel clock was wound every evening before they left the office.

There was no doubt about it: She wasn't coming.

Not that he'd expected her to. Not really. It had been, he knew, reprehensible of him even to mention it to her last night. He had not intended to speak to her. Had told himself, firmly, not even to entertain the idea of speaking to her, once he'd noticed her in the box opposite his.

He hadn't even come close to taking his own good advice.

In his own defense, however, his interest in Caroline Linford was only partly due to the fact that ever since she'd stormed from his office a few days earlier, he'd found it perfectly impossible to put her out of his mind. She was certainly one of the most original women he'd met in some time.

But that, he knew, wasn't quite it. It was something else.

What he couldn't decide was exactly what that something was.

But then there was what had happened the evening after her extraordinary visit to his offices . . . the evening Weasel had come home with a badly bleeding leg wound, having been stabbed by a man who, like himself, had been following Jacquelyn Seldon's mystery lover.

Braden found it astounding that the man could have had *two* people following him, but Weasel was adamant.

"He asked me," Weasel had said, through tightly gritted teeth, as the surgeon had probed at the ragged hole in his thigh, "who sent me. Who I was with."

Braden, wracked with guilt despite the doctor's assertion that it was only a flesh wound, and that his secretary would be on his feet again soon, had urged his friend to save his strength, but Weasel had insisted on telling him everything.

"I told him it wasn't none of his bloody business who sent me," Weasel went on, between swigs from the flask of whiskey Braden had given him. "And then I asked who'd sent *him*. And that's when he up and stabbed me. He'd have killed me, too, if I'd given 'im half a chance. But I didn't. I ran—probably left a trail of blood all along the road after me, but I ran faster than I've ever run in my life. I lost him eventually. I don't think he knew the area at all."

"I don't understand." Braden sat slumped in a chair beside Weasel's bed. He would not soon forgive himself for sending others to do his dirty work. Granted, his face was recognizable enough—thanks to the frequency with which sketches of him appeared in the *Times*—that he attracted far more attention on the street than he liked. That, coupled with his height and large build, made him a pathetic tail—he would have been found out at once.

But that his friend should have suffered for him . . . that he would not allow, not ever again.

"Who was he watching, this other fellow?" Braden asked, swallowing down his self-loathing for the moment. "Was he spying on Jacquelyn? Or her lover?"

"The lover." Weasel looked at the surgeon, who was threading a needle with businesslike precision. "'Scuse me, but is that going to leave a scar?"

"Almost certainly," the surgeon replied.

"Good," Weasel said. Like many men who'd grown up in the Dials, Weasel equated scarring to manliness, and did not mind in the least acquiring new ones. To Braden, he said, as if there'd been no interruption, "He came on foot, from out of nowhere, I swear it, Dead. The bloke who came callin' on Jackie, I mean. Slunk down to the servants' entrance this time, almost before I even noticed he was there. She opened the door for 'im—I saw her face in the light that fell from inside the house. He had on another one of those blasted hoods, so I couldn't see anything but his nose—"

"Of course," Braden commented, drily.

"Of course. A second or two later, this other git shows up, panting like he'd been followin' the first bloke—Jackie's bloke—for a while. But moving real quiet-like. He was a professional, Dead, I'm sure of it."

"And you're sure you'd never seen him before?" Braden had asked his old friend.

"He wasn't from the Dials," Weasel had assured him. "I didn't recognize him from the docks, or the track, or any of the tables I've been to lately. He didn't talk like . . . well, any Eastender I ever met. I don't think he was even from London, Dead. But he was good. He was damned good."

He'd have had to be, to have caught Weasel so off guard. Ronald Ambrose had not earned his moniker merely for his persistence. He was also ferocious in a fight—when he was not taken by complete surprise, that is.

It was the unwarranted viciousness of the attack that worried

Braden most. Most men who struck out with violence did so because they were afraid. But Weasel hadn't done anything at all to threaten this man he'd encountered. And yet he'd assaulted him with a brutality that shocked even Braden Granville, used as he was to violence.

Which was why he was calling his men off. He was not willing to risk any of his friends' lives, simply so that he could have the name of his fiancée's lover. There was another way to achieve something like the same end.

Not one he particularly liked. He wasn't looking forward to employing it. But now he had no other choice. He could not let Jacquelyn win. He could not let her come away from their relationship with any of the money he'd worked so hard to earn . . . especially when it was so clear that she held the fact that he'd had to work for it in so much contempt.

Which was where Caroline Linford came in. Lady Caroline Linford, with her shocking proposal, was the only chance Braden had now of winning his case against Jackie. Though it galled him, the idea of going along with such an ill-conceived, completely ludicrous scheme as hers, what other choice did he have?

It might not have been so bad, if it had been some other woman. But no, it had had to be Lady Caroline Linford, who, with her white gloves and her chaperon, was exactly the sort of society miss Braden had made such an effort to avoid when he'd been shopping for a bride. Having encountered so few of them in his life, virgins quite thoroughly terrified him—when they weren't boring him senseless.

Well, Caroline Linford had never once bored him since she'd burst so boldly into his life, but her naiveté *was* a bit terrifying. She was demanding to be taught how to make love, when it seemed extremely likely to him that she had never even been properly kissed. How in God's name was he going to explain to such an inexperienced girl the fine art of seduction?

But there was nothing else for it. The game had got too danger-ous. He had to end it any way he could, and the sooner, the better.

But was Lady Caroline still willing to help him? She certainly hadn't appeared so the night before. Her ire had been raised by his initial rejection, and he could only pray that the finger he'd run along her neck had done what he'd intended—piqued her interest again. A man who could generate such sensation with the merest touch of his finger, he hoped she was thinking, must be in posses-sion of a wealth of other such sexual secrets.

Little did the poor girl know that he'd been counting on her being as ticklish as she looked.

But what did that matter? What was important was that she came.

Only it didn't look as if she were going to.

He glanced at the clock. Twelve after. She most definitely wasn't coming.

Which was a shame. He'd been looking forward, in an odd way, to seeing her again—and not just in order to test his theory that Caroline Linford was one of those women whose looks seemed to improve upon acquaintance. He'd already come to that conclu-sion, especially since observing her at the opera the night before. Though once again simply dressed in a white gown, with very little on in the way of jewelry, she had caught his eye and held it so long, he'd had to force himself to keep from staring. Even when pros-elytizing on the perils of bearing reins, a habit that might prove obnoxious in a less attractive woman, Caroline Linford was well worth a second look.

She was, if nothing else, an original. There weren't many women of his acquaintance who'd rebuke a duchess for cruelty to animals. There were even fewer who'd have the temerity to admit to having been bored by *Faust*.

And none, that he knew of, would approach a virtual stranger, requesting lessons in lovemaking.

That, he'd decided, was her appeal, and why, truth be told, he'd been relieved that Weasel's stabbing had given him the excuse to contact her again. That she was like no woman he'd ever met before. That, he told himself, was why, ever since that afternoon in his office, he'd been unable to put the memory of her completely from his mind, why often, completely unbidden, her image appeared in his mind's eye. It had nothing to do, he assured himself, with that sweet mouth or haunting eyes of hers. Nothing to do with them at all.

And then, just as he'd abandoned all hope, and was preparing to go home and spend the evening entertaining the infirm Weasel, most likely by losing to him at cards, there was a tap on his office door, and Snake, who'd volunteered to take over Weasel's duties, poked his head round it and said, "There's a Lady Caroline Linford to see you, sir."

And there she was, eyeing him warily as she approached his desk, a closed parasol swinging from one wrist, and a beaded reticule from the other.

"Mr. Granville," she said, without a smile, after Snake had closed the door behind her. She stood before his desk radiating indignation, much like a recalcitrant schoolgirl brought before the headmistress for disobedience.

He hadn't even had a chance to stand. He had been rendered completely immobile, dumbstruck first by her sudden appearance, then by the fact that—yet again—she looked nothing like she had that first time he'd noticed her, when she'd been sitting on the stairs at Dame Ashforth's. Then she'd been a plain-faced, mousy-haired thing, with an unremarkable figure and a doleful expression.

Now there wasn't anything at all plain about her face. She was, and clearly always had been, doe eyed and dewy lipped. Her hair glowed with flashes of gold and amber, and her figure was all that was light and pleasing.

The Marquis of Winchilsea, he thought, not for the first time, was a fool, if her claim that he was not in love with her was actually true.

He said—stupidly, he later thought—the first thing that came into his head: "Where is Violet?"

"Oh, Violet." She reached up and began undoing her bonnet strings. "She's outside. The spell you put her under still hasn't worn off. She trusts you implicitly now."

"But you"—he watched as she placed first the parasol and then her bonnet on a small table beside one of the leather chairs in front of his desk—"don't share her feelings about me, I take it?"

"Trust you, you mean? Why should I?" Caroline dropped into the chair, and began stripping off her gloves. "You obviously don't know your own mind."

"What about you?" he couldn't help asking. "You told me last night not to expect you today."

She busied herself with digging through her reticule, her honey-colored curls hiding her face, her hair being slightly mussed. None of Jacquelyn's elaborate coiffures, he thought, had ever been so fetching.

"Yes," she said. "Well, I don't think either of us was perfectly honest last night." From her reticule, Caroline produced a small leather-bound book, a pencil, and something wrapped in a handkerchief. "I said I wasn't coming, and you said nothing had happened to make you particularly anxious to rid yourself of Lady Jacquelyn." Caroline didn't look at him. She was busy unfolding the handkerchief. "We both know that neither of those statements was true."

The object successfully unwrapped, Caroline removed it, and settled it over her nose. It was, to Braden's astonishment, a pair of spectacles.

"Now," Caroline said, opening the book—a diary, he realized, from its blank pages—and holding her pencil poised over the first page. "Shall we begin?"

He could not take his eyes off the spectacles. They were rimmed in gold wire, quite small and feminine, but most definitely . . . well, *spectacles*. Behind them, her already sizable brown eyes looked enormous. He said—stupidly, he realized, but he couldn't help himself—"What are you doing?"

She looked down at the diary, and then up again. "Well," she said, blinking those luminous eyes. "Taking notes, of course."

"Taking *notes*?" he burst out.

"Well, yes, of course." She reached up to lower the spectacles a little, and examined him over the rims. "I shouldn't want to forget anything. And this way, you won't have to repeat yourself."

He stared at her. The spectacles, while giving her the appearance of a very young—though not very strict—governess, did not actually alter her looks to the extent that he'd have thought such a hideous accessory might. In fact, they leant her a surprising air of attractiveness.

"I haven't at all long," Caroline said, apologetically. "Only an hour or so before anyone notices I'm gone. So if you don't mind, Mr. Granville, I should like to begin by asking you what made you change your mind."

"Yes," he said. "Well, that's fair, I suppose. And it's something you should know, anyway, seeing as how you say you are acquainted with the gentleman in question. Perhaps you could deliver a warning from me to him."

She raised her eyebrows inquiringly. "I beg your pardon?"

"The man with whom you said you saw my fiancée engaged in that highly compromising embrace." Braden regarded her seriously from across his great expanse of desktop. "I am afraid he might be in a good deal of danger."

Her small mouth dropped open, and her eyes, above the rims of her spectacles, widened perceptibly. "From whom?" she demanded, with a good deal of suspicion, when her astonishment had ebbed enough to allow her to speak. "I thought I made it clear to you that I would not tolerate—"

"Not from myself," Braden hastened to assure her. "I don't even know who he is."

"Then how do you know he's in danger?"

"Because I've been having Lady Jacquelyn's household watched," Braden explained, a bit sheepishly—though why he should feel sheepish in front of her, he could not fathom. She was all too well acquainted with his romantic troubles. "And last night, the man I had stationed there was viciously attacked by another man, a man whom it seems was following . . . your friend."

"My friend," Caroline repeated. "A man whom you sent to spy on your fiancée was attacked by another man, whom you say was following my friend . . . the man with whom your fiancée is having an illicit affair."

"Yes," Braden said. "That's precisely it. So you might want to tell your . . . friend to have a care. Especially if he is at all dear to you."

The eyes, appearing larger than ever behind the magnifying lenses of the spectacles, regarded him archly. "Dear to me?" she echoed.

"Yes," he said. "If, for instance, he is your. . . ." Was it his imagination, or did those eyes grow larger yet? ". . . brother?"

She erupted in peals of laughter. "You think my *brother* is having an affair with your fiancée?"

"Well," he said, with some asperity. "You did mention he'd been shot before—"

"By footpads," she said. "Oh, Mr. Granville. You could not be more wrong. My brother quite worships the ground on which you walk. Besides, Jacquelyn would *never*—"

He held up a hand to keep her from finishing. What she said was entirely true. It had been only a fleeting suspicion, but still, one he'd felt compelled to mention.

"Well, in any case," he went on, "this fellow seems to mean business. I am calling off my own men, for the sake of their safety.

Not," Braden added, on a lighter note, "that I imagine your friend should have any difficulties dealing with him. Your friend does seem to possess an uncanny ability to evade detection. My men are convinced he doesn't exist at all, but is some sort of phantom, the way he darts in and out of shadows, disappearing at will."

Caroline's stare, he thought, had gotten rather incredulous, so he wasn't surprised when she said, "My friend. You mean the man I saw with Lady Jacquelyn?"

"Yes. That's precisely who I mean."

"The man I saw with her at Dame Ashforth's? *That* man?"

A little impatiently, he nodded. "Yes. That man."

To his utter astonishment, Lady Caroline burst out laughing again.

"I find it hard to believe," Braden said, after listening to her helpless giggles for a minute or so—this was, he knew, his punishment for agreeing to do business with a virgin—"that this man is such a great friend of yours, if you find the idea that his life might be in mortal danger by a hired assassin so amusing."

"Assassin!" This sent Lady Caroline into another fit of the giggles, until she was obliged to lift off her spectacles in order to dash tears of laughter away from her eyes. "Oh, God," she said again, panting from her humorous outburst. "I'm sorry. But the thought . . . the thought of anyone calling him a *phantom*—"

Fearing that she was going to burst into a fresh batch of giggles, Braden said, hastily, "Well, I felt it only fair to let you know. Whether or not you choose to relay the information to your friend is your business, of course—"

"I don't think I shall," Caroline said, still smiling. "It seems highly unlikely that your phantom and my friend are one and the same man. Has it ever occurred to you that Jacquelyn might have more than one lover?"

"Thank you for the suggestion," Braden said, unable to keep a hint of dryness from creeping into his tone.

All of the laughter was immediately wiped clean from Caroline Linford's face. She said, looking guilt stricken, "Oh, I did not mean . . . I did not mean to suggest that Lady Jacquelyn is . . . oh, dear. I *am* sorry."

He waved away her apology impatiently. "Never mind," he said. "We both know what my fiancée is. It's why we're here. I am afraid I have no other option now, Lady Caroline, than to accept your proposal. While I do not like the idea of you involving yourself in my affairs, I am afraid I can no longer risk the lives of my men trying to ascertain for myself the identity of my fiancée's lover."

He glanced at her, suddenly fearful that the excuse sounded as false to her ears as it did to his own. But if she thought he might have any other motive in accepting her offer—such as, say, a chance to spend more time in her intoxicating presence—she gave no sign.

And why should she suspect him of any such thing? He had, as he knew only too well, made it quite clear he was not interested in girls of her ilk.

More fool he.

"Well, then," he said, clearing his throat. "I take it I am to proceed with, um, a lecture of some sort?"

Caroline, her glasses settled back over her nose, nodded vigorously. "Yes, please."

He cleared his throat. "And just precisely how many . . . lessons do you think you are going to require, Lady Caroline, in return for your testimony?"

Caroline looked a little dismayed. "Oh," she said. "Well, I suppose that depends. How many do you think it will take before I am fully . . . versed?"

"That depends, I suppose," he said, slowly. Inwardly, however, his thoughts were moving without a hint of the sluggishness. What, he was thinking, if I were to rip those spectacles from her nose, toss them to the floor, pull her from that chair, and kiss her? What then? Would she storm from the room? Slap me? Or kiss me back?

"Well," Caroline said, interrupting his frantic internal monologue. "Why don't you simply begin, and we'll go from there."

"All right," he agreed, reluctantly. And he cleared his throat again.

He had, of course, prepared a lecture for the occasion. An elegant lecture, quite well thought out. He'd come up with it during the opera the night before. Well, he'd needed something to keep him from spending the whole of the evening staring at Caroline.

Unfortunately, he had not truly believed she would show up this afternoon, and so he had left his program from the opera, on which were penciled his notes, on his bedside table.

"All right," he said, again. He felt unaccountably nervous, though why this should be so, he could not think. Unless it was the fact that he had never imagined himself in this position, explaining something so . . . well, intimate, to a young lady who'd been so gently and carefully reared.

And to whom he was finding himself more and more attracted.

Fortunately, the subject he'd picked for his first lesson was fairly impersonal.

"Well, you see, Lady Caroline," he began, "the intimacies which occur between a man and a woman in the privacy of the bedroom cannot adequately be described in a setting such as this one. We are, as you're undoubtedly aware, in an office, an atmosphere hardly conducive to romance."

That sounded good. He decided to expound upon that theme.

"I cannot stress enough the importance of atmosphere to the romantic liaison. There are those who say that love should not be made during the daylight hours, as sunlight is not conducive to appropriately romantic feelings. And while I've found that this proves true with some women, who are perhaps timid about their shape, I've also found that there is nothing more liberating than the shedding of clothing, as well as inhibitions, in the bright light of day—"

"Pardon me," Caroline interrupted, her pencil stilling on the page.

He paused, and eyed her. Curse him if she didn't look as fetching as a naiad on a riverbank, with her golden hair and fresh-skinned beauty. Well, a naiad in spectacles.

"Yes?" he said.

She smiled politely. "As I said before, I only have an hour. Could we perhaps save this discussion on atmosphere—which is fascinating, believe me—for another time, and go straight into kissing?"

He raised his eyebrows. "Kissing?"

"Yes," Caroline said. "Kissing. And then I should like to discuss that thing you did last night, with your finger."

He coughed. So much for impersonal.

Well, he'd brought it upon himself. Think of Jacquelyn's face, he thought. Think of how she's going to look when Lady Caroline Linford appears as a witness upon his behalf. . . .

He could, he felt, keep control over his baser instincts for the pleasure of seeing that.

"All right, then," he said. "Kissing. Very well. One hears, of course, about kissing all the time, but what one may not know is that kissing is a very important part of the—"

Lady Caroline interrupted him. "There is a particular *kind* of kiss I'd like to discuss, one that I've had occasion to observe. It is the kind in which the persons engaged in it stick their tongues into one another's mouth."

He could not help staring at her own mouth as she said this. It was a very pretty mouth, rosebud pink and imminently kissable. He dragged his gaze from it with an effort. "You've observed this."

She nodded emphatically. "Oh, yes. There is certainly such a thing. I've seen it done."

He wondered if he had ever, even in his childhood, been as absurdly innocent, and then decided that it was unlikely.

He cleared his throat. "Yes. Well, that particular kind of kissing you've described is rather . . ."

"Disgusting," she finished for him, with a knowing look.

Braden blinked at her. He couldn't help it. Really, what was wrong with that fiancé of hers? Braden had always rather thought he might be a fop. It was certainly the only reason he could think of why the fellow had yet to bed Lady Caroline. He was either a fop or a fool, or possibly some combination of both.

"It isn't disgusting," he said, keeping his tone impersonal with an effort. "It isn't disgusting at all."

"Well," she said. "I don't see what could be pleasurable about it. Having someone ram his tongue into my mouth, I mean."

"No one should be *ramming* his tongue anywhere," Braden said, impatiently. "If that's how Slater goes about kissing you, I shouldn't wonder you find it disgusting."

Caroline looked prim—a look that wasn't hard for her to accomplish in those spectacles. "If by Slater," she said, "you mean my fiancé, the Marquis of Winchilsea, then the answer is no, Mr. Granville. He has never kissed me like that."

Well, that was certainly unsurprising. What did surprise him, a little, was the wistfulness in her voice as she made the confession.

"Well," he said, quickly. "One day he doubtlessly will, and it would be good for you to be prepared. That type of kiss, Lady Caroline, is known by the French as the soul kiss, because it is thought that by engaging in it, a couple passes their souls back and forth to one another."

Caroline's mouth dropped open. "How perfectly morbid," she said.

He shrugged. "The French," he said, with an apologetic shrug. "Now, I ought to warn you, this kind of kissing has quite caught on in this country, and I'm afraid if you are sincere about your desire to be both wife and mistress to your husband, you will have to learn it."

Caroline sighed resignedly, turned the page of her notebook, and readied her pencil. "Very well. How is it done?"

From any other woman, it would have been an invitation. It certainly affected him as such. He was seized by such a sudden and powerful desire to kiss Lady Caroline that his arms seemed to shake with the effort to keep them at his sides. He did not make a habit of going about, snatching up girls who had made their disinterest in him very clear indeed, and kissing them.

And yet there it was. He wanted to kiss her, in spite of the fact that kissing her was undoubtedly one of the most ill-considered ideas he had ever had.

Still, he fought it.

"Perhaps," he said, in a voice that he hoped she wouldn't notice did not sound at all like his own, "we ought to return to the subject of creating a romantic atmosphere."

"Kissing, please," Caroline said, tapping her pencil impatiently against her book.

Good Lord. This wouldn't do at all. Even the way she said the words—*Kissing, please*—in that bored tone was arousing him.

Well, and so what if it was? What harm would one little kiss do? Really, what harm?

"It isn't the sort of thing one can describe," he said, his gaze on her mouth once more. It was a mouth completely bare of any sort of cosmetic rouge, quite unlike any of the mouths he remembered kissing in the past few years. "Perhaps it would be better if I showed you."

She laid the pencil down. When he lifted his gaze from her mouth to her eyes, he saw that she was looking at him very seriously through the lenses of her spectacles.

"Mr. Granville," she said, severely. "Perhaps you've misunderstood. I did not come here out of a desire to be added to your harem. I am not at all interested in having a love affair with you. I am, as you know, engaged to be married."

He felt a strange spurt of delight shoot through him. It was quite inexplicable. He had never felt anything like it before in his life.

"As am I, Lady Caroline," he said, spreading his hands wide. "But you don't see me quibbling over the propriety of my teaching you these things. Why should you quibble over the propriety of learning them? After all, *you*, Lady Caroline, came to *me*."

"But," she said, in a voice that was a good deal fainter than the one she'd used before, "I don't see why you can't just *tell* me—"

"I told you." He pushed back his chair and stood up. "Because it isn't the sort of thing you can tell." He came around his desk quickly, before he could talk himself out of it, and while he still had her flummoxed. "I have to show you. It's the only way," he said, bending down to take the notebook and pencil from her limp hands, "you'll learn."

"But," Caroline said, weakly.

"You want to impress the marquis, don't you?" He'd taken her hand, and now he pulled her firmly up from her chair.

"Yes," she said, in the same unsteady voice. "But—"

The spectacles, he realized, would have to come off. He reached up, and gently disengaged them, speaking to her in the same low, reassuring voice, the sort of voice a groom might use on a nervous horse.

"Everything will be all right," he said. "You'll see. You might even enjoy it."

"I don't think so," Caroline said, anxiety written plainly in her enormous, expressive brown eyes.

"Well," Braden said, "I do." He reached up and swept a wayward amber curl from her forehead. While she was distracted by that, he stooped down, and with a feeling of urgency, pressed his mouth against hers.

13

*C*aroline could hardly believe what was happening. One minute, it seemed, she'd had the situation perfectly under control, and the next, Braden Granville was kissing her.

How had it happened? How had she allowed things to get so out of hand, when she had been on such vigilant guard against this sort of nonsense? After all, Braden Granville was the most notorious rake in all of England. It was only to be expected that he would try something like this.

Only he had made it so clear, that first day she'd come to him, that he wanted nothing to do with her. She had thought he quite disliked her, that she'd horrified him with her forwardness, that he thought her a stupid, foolish virgin not worth a second glance.

And now, here she was, with her face cupped in Braden Granville's enormous, calloused hands—she could feel the callouses, rough upon the skin of her cheeks—and instead of feeling gratified that he obviously didn't find her as repulsive as she'd first thought, she felt only panic.

Because he was kissing her in a manner quite unlike any she'd ever experienced before. Not that he'd thrust his tongue into her mouth—not at all. He was merely moving his lips over hers in the lightest, gentlest kisses imaginable. His lips, unlike his hands, weren't at all hard, which was a surprise. He certainly *looked* as if he'd be very hard, all over, but his lips were shockingly soft.

There was strength behind that softness, though, and it was that strength which Caroline found herself responding to. There was something seductive about it, about the restraint he was exercising. She could sense that restraint in the careful way he held her head, not allowing his hands to go roaming anywhere else—sense that it was only with an effort he did not snatch her closer to him, bend her body back, and crush her against his rock-hard frame.

And it was that realization which caused her to relax. Her arms, hanging limply at her sides, seemed suddenly impossible to lift. Her knees seemed to have gone the consistency of butter. She felt as if Braden Granville's hands alone were keeping her upright.

Even her mouth, which she'd been holding tightly closed, seemed to loosen under the petal-soft caresses of his lips. She felt her lips part, and then go slack, as if he had uttered some magic word, and opened them.

But no mere word could have made her feel so deliciously languorous, and yet so thoroughly alive. There was magic involved, no doubt about that . . . but that magic lay in Braden Granville's gently persuasive lips, not in anything he had said.

And then, before she was even aware of what was happening, he had neatly, expertly—the work, clearly, of a master—slipped the tip of his tongue through her moistly parted lips. Just the most fleeting of contact, and then it was gone, and Caroline, hardly knowing what she was doing, opened her mouth even farther . . .

. . . and there it was again, his tongue, flicking against her own.

How extraordinary! Because it didn't feel disgusting at all. In fact, quite the opposite. She reached out with her own tongue, shyly at first, and then with growing confidence as she realized, wonderingly, that it really *was* like he was drawing her soul into him. She could feel it spilling from her, tumbling from her mouth into his mouth, until he tossed it back again. It was a lovely feeling, really. Miraculous, almost.

Even more miraculous was what Braden Granville's kiss was doing to her below the neck. Because she was feeling things down there she'd never felt before—a strange tingling sensation over most of her skin, as if she were a cat someone had stroked the wrong way. It caused the tips of her breasts to harden into sharp little peaks, and her thighs to tighten defensively against a sudden rush of warmth where they joined together. *What*, she wondered, fuzzily, *is happening to me?*

But she'd barely had a chance to marvel at her own reaction to what Braden Granville was doing to her before he abruptly stopped doing it. Just like that, he broke the kiss, releasing her face and tearing his mouth from hers. Caroline, whose eyelids had drifted closed, opened them bewilderedly at the sudden rush of cool air where his lips and hands had been, and almost fell down, since her knees hadn't yet recovered. Braden thrust out an arm to steady her, and Caroline, clinging to it as the only steady object in a universe that had, just a second before, been spinning out of control, lifted her dazzled gaze to meet his.

"There," he said. Was it her imagination, or did his voice not sound quite as steady as it had before? "That wasn't so disgusting, now, was it?"

It was her imagination. It had to be. Braden Granville was a jaded man of experience. He would not be feeling as Caroline did because of their kiss, as if she couldn't speak. Her lips felt numb, her tongue heavy as lead. *All* of her felt heavy as lead. In fact, as she plunked back down into the chair from which he'd pulled her, it occurred to her that she needed to rest a minute.

"Now," Braden Granville said, reaching for her notebook and pencil and thrusting them back at her, "write that down. Are you sure you got the feel for it? If you want, I could do it again."

Caroline shook her head stupidly. She felt as if there were

cobwebs in her skull. "No," she said, faintly. "No, I think I've quite got it."

"Good." Braden Granville, instead of going back to his seat behind his desk, sat down in the chair beside hers. But not, she was quite certain, because his legs felt as if they contained no bones, as his kiss had made her feel. "You're quite a quick learner."

Caroline heard herself murmur, "I always got very good marks in school."

"Excellent. Well, what shall we go over next? You asked about my, er, touching you last night just here—" He raised a finger toward the base of her ear. She must have flinched, however, since he quickly dropped his hand, and said, "Unless you'd rather go back to the topic of designing a romantic atmosphere for your seduction. . . ."

"I think," Caroline said quickly, closing her notebook, "that that's enough for one day. Perhaps we should meet again tomorrow—"

He rose politely as she climbed, not very steadily, to her feet. "That would be fine. But are you certain you're feeling all right, Lady Caroline? You look—"

She bent to retrieve her gloves, which had slipped off her lap when he'd pulled her from the chair. He said, "Allow me," and scooped them up before she had a chance to touch them, then presented them to her with a gallant flourish.

"Thank you," Caroline murmured.

"Don't be offended," he said, reaching down to help her gather up her bonnet, parasol, and reticule, which also lay scattered about the floor beneath her chair, "but your color's quite . . . high. Perhaps you ought to stay and have some tea. I could ring for it—"

"No, no," she said, quickly. "I can't stay. And I was, um, playing badminton the other day, and it was quite sunny, so I suppose I'm only a little burnt—"

"That must be it." He handed over her reticule, and she slipped the pencil and notebook into it. "So. Same time tomorrow, Lady Caroline?"

"Um," she said, as she pulled on her gloves. "Yes. I think so. If it's all right with you."

"Perfectly fine," he said, passing her bonnet to her. "Thank you."

Her bonnet secured, she reached for the parasol he held. "Thank you," she said, politely.

"And will you," he asked, "be attending the theater again to-night? Perhaps we'll be seeing one another again."

"No," she said. "We've a private dinner party to go to, I think. Good day, Mr. Granville."

She started to go, thinking that, except for the fact that she'd obviously been blushing quite a bit, she really hadn't handled the situation too badly. But his deep voice arrested her midstep.

"Lady Caroline?"

She turned and blinked at him. He certainly was a terrifically large man, quite imposing. It wasn't hard to imagine him as a boy, eking out a rough existence in the squalid Seven Dials district, where Thomas had told her he'd grown up. He'd have had to be quick with those massive fists, simply in order to survive.

And yet, for all his size, he'd been surprisingly gentle with her.

"Yes, Mr. Granville?" she said.

He held something out toward her. "You forgot your spectacles," he said.

"Oh," she said, stepping forward to take them from him. "Thank you. I, um, only need them, you know, to read. And write. And so on."

"And so on," he said, with a grave nod. "Of course."

"Well," Caroline said. "Good-bye again."

She hurried out this time, before he had a chance to call her back, or even to say another word.

It was with a good deal of relief that Caroline found herself standing with Violet on bustling, familiar Bond Street. But no sooner had the door to the offices of Granville Enterprises closed behind them than the magnitude of what she had just done hit her.

Good God. She had kissed Braden Granville. She had *kissed Braden Granville.*

Not just Braden Granville, either, though that was quite bad enough. No, she had kissed another man, a man to whom she was not even engaged.

Never mind that barely a week earlier, she herself had stood and watched her fiancé do a good deal more than simply kiss another woman. This wasn't, she told herself, about Hurst. Well, except in a roundabout way. This was about her. This was about her and a man with whom she had made a bargain.

A bargain which had very expressly included a no touching clause.

She hadn't the slightest idea what compelled her to do what she did next. She only knew that one minute, she was standing on Bond Street, and the next, she'd asked Violet to wait a moment, and was stalking back toward the great black door.

She did not bother ringing the bell. She laid a hand upon the latch and shoved, and the great portal swung neatly open. She did not pay the slightest bit of attention to the questioning looks she received from Braden Granville's many employees. She paid no heed to the little man who asked if she had forgotten something. She merely stalked toward the door through which a few seconds ago she'd exited, and threw her weight against it.

Braden Granville turned from the window where he'd been standing alone, his hands stuffed into his trouser pockets.

"Lady Caroline," Braden Granville said, in tones of great surprise. "Have you forgotten something?"

"Indeed I have," Caroline said.

She strode up to him, brought her right arm back, and struck him across the face a good deal harder than she had ever swung a badminton racket.

The resulting sound of her skin smacking against his was quite loud, and extremely satisfying. And when she brought her arm down again, Caroline had the further satisfaction of seeing an imprint of her hand, starkly white, against his cheek. An instant later, the white mark filled with hot color.

She said, "Consider that *your* first lesson in lovemaking, Mr. Granville."

Then she turned and stalked from the room again.

14

So it hadn't gone according to plan. So what? If there was one thing Braden Granville had learned during the course of his rise to wealth and fame, it was that things often didn't.

Go according to plan, that is.

And when a woman was involved, well, things were nearly guaranteed to go awry. Particularly when they involved a woman like Caroline Linford, who was clearly. . . .

Well, not normal.

Braden assured himself of the young woman's abnormality all the way through dinner that night with his fiancée and her family. Really, there wasn't any doubt about it. No normal woman would have reacted the way Caroline Linford had. There was something seriously wrong with the girl. She had asked him—*begged* him, practically—to teach her the art of lovemaking, and then, when he'd made a sincere and purely scientific attempt to do so, she'd turned on him, viciously as a little alley cat.

Granted, she had made it clear from the start she wanted no actual physical contact. But he'd asked her permission before kissing her, hadn't he? And she'd given it . . . reluctantly, perhaps, but she'd given it. So what right had she to slap him? What right?

Every right. He had been thoroughly manipulative, and unforgivably rude. His only chance at redeeming himself for his callous behavior was to vow never again to touch, or even go near, her.

A vow that was more easily kept, he immediately found out, when she was not within sight. Because as soon as he spied her in the crowded ballroom to which he was dragged that evening by his fiancée, his resolve crumbled. Within seconds, he was tapping her dance partner—who, thankfully, happened to be her brother, a youth to whom the name Braden Granville was synonymous with Hero—on the shoulder and saying, "Pardon me. But may I?"

The young Earl of Bartlett nearly fell over himself in his haste to surrender his sister, who looked none too happy about the exchange. In fact, she had the nerve to vocalize her chagrin, and quite loudly, too.

"Tommy," she said, in a dangerous voice.

"Really," the earl was saying, to Braden. "You take her. I was going to sit this one out, anyway, but Ma made me ask her, since no one else had—"

"*Tommy,*" she said, and Braden couldn't see how her brother failed to hear the warning in her voice.

But Thomas Linford only said, "Have a nice time, you two," and ran away, leaving his sister—who looked like such a sweet, defenseless young thing—alone in the arms of the infamous Braden Granville.

Defenseless. *Ha!*

"You had better stop scowling and start moving," he said, as he wrapped one hand around her waist, and took up her right fingers in the other, "or your mamma is going to come scooting over here, wondering what's wrong. And I might just be compelled to tell her."

The brown eyes, so deceivingly guileless, stared daggers at him. "I'll *bet* you would," she said, bitterly. "What are you doing here? Do you have men following *me* now, as well as your Lady Jacquelyn?"

"Don't be ridiculous." He moved her expertly across the crowded floor of the ballroom. "Of course I'm not having you followed. I'm here with Jacquelyn."

"Well, then why on earth aren't you dancing with *her*?" Caroline demanded. "She's the one who agreed to marry you. What are you bothering *me* for?"

"Because I'd like to apologize," Braden said, calmly.

She eyed him suspiciously. "For what?"

"You know very well," he said.

"For insulting and degrading me, you mean?"

He nearly stopped dancing, he was so appalled.

"Let's not go too far," he said, when he'd recovered himself. "It was only a kiss, after all, Lady Caroline."

"Was it? Or were you trying to seduce me?" Her look was pointed.

He did stop dancing, at that. "I most certainly was *not*. My God, whatever gave you that idea?"

"Either dance or escort me off the floor," she whispered. "Don't just stand there. People are looking."

He began to move his feet again. "You and I, Lady Caroline," he said, trying to keep his voice steady, though, truth be told, he felt like shouting, "have a business arrangement—or at least, I thought we did. Where in God's name did you get the notion that I'm out to seduce you? Simply because of that kiss?"

"You forget," she said, "I have a brother who worships you. I know all about you, *Mr.* Granville. And your horrid ways."

She put a rather insulting stress on the word *mister*, as if to suggest he was not worthy of the title.

"Now see here," he said. "You came to me *because* of my horrid ways. Against my better judgment, I agreed to help you, in exchange for your help with my . . . situation. Now it suddenly seems as if you're going back on your part of the bargain."

"Why shouldn't I?" Caroline demanded. "When it's clear that

your intention is to add my name to the list of fools who've fallen for you over the years?" She pulled away from him suddenly. "Well, I thank you, Mr. Granville, but that is one honor I think I can do without. You had better consider this dance *over*, Mr. Granville."

She didn't just mean the waltz, either, and he knew it.

Suddenly frightened she might actually escape, Braden snatched her to him, pulling her so close against him that Caroline could feel the fob of his watch chain through the whalebone stays of her corset . . . his watch fob, and his heart, which was slamming as hard as hers was against his ribs.

To her mortification, she felt her cheeks heat up again. Not at the inappropriateness of the way he held her, in a very public embrace, but at the myriad of sensations she experienced at the close contact: the scent of him—which she remembered all too well from that afternoon—an extremely masculine combination of soap and, faintly, gunpowder; the warmth that emanated from beneath his coat, almost singeing her through the material of her gloves; the faint bluish tinge of the skin along his jaw, already prickled with razor stubble; that devilish scar in his eyebrow . . . all of these things seemed to prey upon her resistance.

But she *would* resist him. She had to.

"I haven't the slightest intention of seducing you," Braden growled. His hot breath caused shivers to ripple up and down her spine, the same shivers she'd felt when he ran his finger along the side of her neck. Worse than the shivers, however, was the fact that she felt her nipples hardening in the lace cups of her corset. *Oh, no*, she thought. *Not again.*

"Unless of course," he went on, "you happen to decide you want me to."

Caroline said, quickly, "I can assure you that *that* will never happen."

"Prove it, then," he said, "by staying and finishing this dance with me. I promise I will behave like a perfect gentleman."

She continued to hesitate, until he added, "Of course, if you choose to storm off in a huff, it will only draw the attention of people who might inquire as to why you are so angry with me. And I might be compelled to explain our arrangement. . . ."

"You wouldn't!"

She could see by his expression, however, that he would, and reluctantly she put one hand back upon his broad shoulder, and slipped the other back into his fingers.

"So this is why you're so successful with women," she commented. "You *blackmail* them."

Braden couldn't help frowning at that. This was not going at all the way he'd intended it to. But what had, since he'd met her? Caroline Linford seemed to bring out the worst in him. It was a battle just to remember he was supposed to be a gentleman now, and not some ham-handed ruffian from the Dials, besotted for the first time.

Besotted? Hardly. What was he thinking?

Interested. That's what he was. She interested him. She interested him very much indeed. And he'd hoped to make a better impression on her than he evidently had that afternoon.

"Believe me, Lady Caroline," he said, moving her expertly across the dance floor. "If I wanted to, I could make you so eager to dance with me, *you*'d blackmail *me* if I didn't ask you."

But all she said in reply to that was a bitter, "Hurst was right about you."

But not, Caroline had to admit, about everything. His dancing, for one thing. Braden Granville did not dance like a man better used to reels than to waltzes. Why, for a man his size, he was almost graceful! Usually when she found herself being partnered by one of London's society bucks, Caroline had to fear for her slippers, but in the shelter of Braden Granville's strong arms, she felt her toes might, for once, be safe. Her only possible objection might be that, unlike herself, he wasn't wearing gloves, and occasionally she felt his bare hand press not against her waist, but the smooth bare skin of her back, between her shoulder blades. That contact was just a little too intimate for a ballroom in which Caroline's fiancé was standing just a dozen yards away. Not, of course, that she'd expect Hurst to notice. But her mother certainly might.

"Was he, now?" He didn't sound in the least pleased to hear it. "And what did the marquis say about me?"

"He told me what an uncouth upstart you are," she informed him. What she neglected to add was that, when Hurst had said it, she'd objected to the harshness of his condemnation. Now, however, she conveniently left out that part of their conversation. "And he warned me to stay away from you."

"Oh, he did, did he? So, why," he inquired, "aren't you following his advice?"

"Because you've got hold of my hand," Caroline snapped, "and you won't let go of it, *obviously*."

He threw back his head and laughed, and Caroline, startled, blinked up at him. It was unnerving how handsome Braden Granville looked when he was smiling. And he certainly wore evening clothes well. Why, his cravat was as frilled as any of Hurst's!

Reminded of her fiancé, Caroline glanced around. Hurst, normally the most laconic of men—which was why she'd found Braden Granville's description of this " phantom" lover of Jacquelyn's so hilarious—wouldn't have cared if she'd been dancing with a bandit chieftain . . . particularly tonight. He'd been moody and distracted all evening, to the point that she'd asked him if he felt well.

Yet suddenly, she noticed, he was alert enough not only to recognize that she was dancing with Braden Granville, but also to take exception to the fact. He was already striding toward her mother, his mouth open in a complaining bleat and his finger pointing in her direction.

Good Lord, Caroline thought to herself. Could it be. . . . Was it possible that her fiancé was actually *jealous*?

It couldn't be. Hurst didn't care about her—not in that way. He only, she knew, hated Braden Granville with a passion, for his low birth and immense wealth and, unquestioningly, choice of bride. Which reminded her . . .

"If you think," Caroline snapped, "that we're going to continue these so-called lessons of yours, may I just point out that you, sir, are sadly mistaken."

"Oh, but you're wrong, Caroline," he said, quietly, looking down at her with such heat in his gaze, Caroline could not look away. "We *are* going to continue them. I've already started planning tomorrow's lesson."

Caroline swallowed. She didn't dare ask what might be on the syllabus.

"If you so much as lay a finger on me again," she said, "I'll tell Hurst."

"For someone who claims to be in so much debt to the marquis, you are certainly hasty to put his life in the way of danger. I haven't been called Dead Eye for most of my life for nothing, you know."

He was smiling broadly now. The scar in his eyebrow, coupled with the smile, leant him a distinctly devilish air that once again caused Caroline to feel a little breathless. She wondered if she was going to have to put her head between her knees once more.

"It would be a shame," he said, in a voice that was as much of a caress as the hand he moved slowly once more across the bare skin of her back, "for your fiancé to have go down the aisle with an arm in a sling—or worse yet, in a coffin."

She sucked in her breath. She couldn't help it, any more than she could help the tears that sprang suddenly into her eyes. "Stop it," she said, jerking herself once more from his arms. "You—how *dare* you?"

He knew even before he heard the sob and saw the tears that he'd gone too far. Belatedly, he remembered her brother, and cursed himself. The scare the boy had given her and the rest of his family was still too fresh even to joke about death. He was instantly contrite, moving to lay a comforting arm across her shoulders, an arm she immediately shrugged off.

"Caroline," he chided her, gently. "I'm sorry. I would never shoot your marquis, even if he did call me out. I know how much he means to you."

For some reason, however, these words of comfort seemed to have the exact opposite effect he'd intended. For suddenly, Caroline turned and stalked from the room.

Fortunately, the waltz was already ending, and so no one—with the possible exception of her mother—noticed how abruptly Caroline Linford left her partner. Her shoulders stiff with rage—not shame. It certainly wasn't shame, or so she told herself as she turned around, and began marching blindly away, heading straight for a set of French doors that, she assumed, led out into the garden. She felt a sudden and overpowering need to escape the heat of the room—and Braden Granville's gaze.

Braden Granville, however, was not about to let her escape that easily, and he hurried after her.

"Oh, Lord," Caroline said, not very encouragingly, when she saw that he'd followed her. "Why are you doing this?"

"Doing what, Caroline? I'm not doing anything. I was only joking when I said that about shooting your fiancé. I certainly didn't mean—"

"No, not that," she said, with an impatient stamp of a slippered foot. "Why are you here, talking to me? I know you think I'm nothing but a simpering schoolgirl. So why do you bother seeking me out?"

Braden hesitated, taken aback by the question. He ought to have expected it, of course. Caroline Linford was nothing if not direct. Braden knew he could not reply with anything like her candor, however. He couldn't possibly tell her the truth—that he had been unable, since he'd first noticed those enormous brown eyes of hers, to get them completely out of his mind. That, unlikely as it might seem, he felt an odd sort of kinship with her—felt it since that night he'd held her head to her lap, and listened to her describe her utter lack of commitment to her friend Emily's cause. And most of all, that he had found, during that highly erotic kiss they'd shared in his office—the first and only kiss, he was convinced, that she had ever had in her twenty-one years—that he wanted her in the worst way.

And so he replied, quietly, "The truth is, Caroline, that you . . . interest me. And when someone interests me, I make an effort to get to know her better."

Caroline stared up at him in disbelief. "Interest you?" she echoed, her voice breaking. "I *interest* you?"

"Yes." He nodded seriously. "You do." But since he could tell by her expression that she did not believe him, he decided to prove it to her. And so he seated himself upon a nearby stone bench, and said, "Tell me about it."

The clouds abruptly parted, and in the few brief seconds the moon was unobscured, he saw her expression in its light.

She looked confused.

"Tell you about what?" she asked.

"Your brother's accident."

Whatever it was she'd been expecting him to say, it wasn't that. He could tell by the way her mouth fell open. Then the moon disappeared again, and he could see only the outline of her, silhouetted against the balustrade that separated the promenade from the garden.

"His. . . ." Her voice was faint. "His accident?"

"Yes. You told me he was shot. At Oxford, wasn't it?" He patted the empty seat beside him on the bench. "Sit here and tell me about it."

She took a step toward him, and an arc of light, falling from one of the tall windows looking into the ballroom, fell across her. He could see that her look of confusion had deepened to one of suspicion.

"Why do you want to talk about what happened to my brother?" she asked, warily.

"Because," he replied, "you *interest* me, remember? And though he seems to have a made a full recovery, I can tell that the earl's accident—or any mention of it, or of guns in general—still seems to upset you. And I'd like to know why."

"Because he nearly died," she said, in a tone that suggested that this should have been obvious.

"Did he? Was it a single wound, or multiple shots?"

"Just the one," she said. "Only the bullet went through here." And she pointed to an area just below her heart.

Braden, though he wasn't certain whether or not she could see him, sitting in the shadows, as he was, nodded. "Yes. I imagine that must have been very frightening."

And then she was on the bench beside him, seated, if he wasn't mistaken, with one foot tucked beneath her. She was so close that he could smell the lavender scent she wore. It mingled with the fragrance of rain and roses that hung so heavily in the air.

"They couldn't move him," she said. "And we had to stay in Oxford for several weeks—all through Christmas until past Candlemas—until he was finally strong enough to come home. Even then, we weren't certain—we couldn't be certain he'd live through the trip. But Ma only trusts London surgeons, and so she thought it worth the risk."

The earl, Braden learned, survived the trip, in large part thanks to the efforts of the Marquis of Winchilsea, without whom, Caroline asserted, her small family would have been lost. Her mother sunk half the time in hysterics, the marquis had been a godsend, making all the necessary arrangements at inns along the way, seeing to the changing of the horses, everything, almost as if Thomas had been his own brother.

Never had there been such a devoted friend. The kindness of the marquis could never be repaid by Caroline and her family.

"And so," Braden said, when she fell silent, her narrative complete, "you had no choice but to say yes when he asked you to marry him."

He felt, rather than saw, the foot she'd tucked beneath her shift, until both her slippers were again on the ground.

"That isn't how it was at all," Caroline informed him, in a prim little voice. "I had been . . . fond of Lord Winchilsea for some time before he proposed. I was delighted to accept his offer of marriage."

And he imagined she had been. It had undoubtedly been her first. He couldn't help noticing that Slater's proposal coincided rather neatly with Caroline's first season out after inheriting her share of her father's fortune.

"It's no small wonder, then," Braden observed, in a carefully neutral tone, "that you are so anxious to please your future husband."

He could not tell for certain, but he thought from her silence that he had made her blush. It had been years, he realized, since he'd last been with a woman who blushed as easily as Caroline Linford seemed to.

"Now that I am fully aware of how very much you owe the marquis," he went on, hardly knowing what he was saying, he was so conscious of her closeness, the warmth radiating from her, the sweet smell of her hair, "I think I'll have a better idea what topics we ought to cover during your lessons."

"About my lessons, Mr. Granville," she said, without the slightest bit of rancor in her husky voice. "I truly do believe that what happened this afternoon was a mistake. A horrible, terrible mistake. I think we'd do better—far better—not to continue the, um, lessons."

"*I* don't think it was a mistake," he said.

And before she knew what he was about, he'd snaked an arm around her waist, and pulled her—not roughly, but emphatically—against him.

"I don't think it was a mistake at all," he said, and she could feel his deep voice reverberating through his chest.

Her face just inches below his, she stared up at him, into a pair of eyes every bit as dark as hers, only with little licks of flame in them that her own eyes, she knew, sadly lacked. Those firelit eyes were examining her as closely as she was studying him, only whereas there was nothing but resentment in her gaze—or so she told herself—Braden Granville's seemed to be filled with something else entirely.

"Mr. Granville." For some reason, she found herself whispering. Why, when she ought to have been shouting with fury? But all that came from her throat was the weakest of pleas. "I would really prefer it very much if you released me, sir."

"No," he said, and for once, his deep voice was a little unsteady, "I really don't think you would."

Caroline had been staring, with a sort of hypnotic wonder, at his lips as he spoke. They weren't exactly nice lips. Far from it. Not that they were ugly. Not at all. What they were, she thought, were lips that had done *a lot* of kissing.

"Really, Mr. Granville," she said, unable to drag her gaze from his mouth. "You simply cannot go around *grabbing* people like this—"

Then those lips, which a second before she'd been admiring, were on hers, and she couldn't think of anything at all.

15

*I*t was happening all over again. Just like before, only worse somehow now, because Caroline really ought to have known better this time. She knew, she knew how her body would react the second it came into contact with his! But instead of pushing him away, instead of screaming for all she was worth, anything, anything to keep it from happening again, she just sat there, knowing it was going to happen all over again, and letting it. Letting it!

And she'd thought Jacquelyn Seldon was bad. Why, she was no better.

But that knowledge didn't stop her from feeling as if a flame had been lit inside her the moment his mouth touched hers. Nor did it keep her body from melting into his until it seemed as if she was only kept upright by his embrace alone. It didn't do any good at all at keeping her arms from sliding up around his neck. Nor was she able to keep from sighing just a little . . . which left her lips open just enough for that questing tongue of his to launch another exploration of the inside of her mouth.

And this time, she met that thrust with a knowing flick of her own tongue, just to see what would happen. . . .

What happened was a lot more than Caroline had bargained

for. Braden Granville let out a groan, muffled against her mouth, a sound she might have confused with a grunt of pain, except that he didn't push her away. Far from it. Instead, he tightened his grip on her, drawing her so close to him with one hand, she was almost pulled into his lap, while his other hand rose, skimming the bodice of her gown, running up along the smooth skin of her arm, until his fingers came to rest on the place where her heart was drumming hard against her chest.

Caroline started as she felt the searing heat from his hand over the curve of her breast. She had never been touched there before, not by anyone. With his tongue still playing hide-and-seek with hers, she couldn't say anything, though she tried to draw away from him reflexively, knowing that things were going too far, too fast.

He wouldn't release her, however. He wouldn't give an inch. Those taunting fingers startled her even further by dipping beneath the lace of her extremely modest decolletage, until he was cupping the soft firm flesh of her breast in his hand, her nipple already hard against the center of his palm.

At this, Caroline tore her mouth from his.

"What—?" she started to demand, then gasped as his fingers began to knead that sensitive part of her, exerting a gentle but inexorable pressure that almost had her crying out with wordless appreciation, as, she now realized, he had when she'd started kissing him back.

"Caroline."

Just her name. That was all he said, just her name, and that barely recognizable, he'd uttered it so gutturally. His thumb moved over the hardened peak of her nipple, causing another wave of desire to slam through her. She was conscious that she'd gone damp everywhere, but mostly between her legs, where she felt the same tenderness she'd experienced that afternoon in his office.

She blinked up at him, her breath coming in quick, hiccuppy gasps. *Oh, Lord,* she thought. *I can't breathe again.* She could feel something very hard indeed pressing through the front of his breeches and against her hip.

So this is what it's like, she thought, hazily. *What it was like for Hurst and Jackie. Well, that explains it, I suppose.*

And then his fingers were tightening on her breast again, and his mouth lowered over hers once more. . . .

It wasn't until she heard her name being called from inside the house that sanity returned. Bracing both of her hands against his hard chest, Caroline shoved with all of her might. Braden, who'd been so caught up in the embrace that he was taken completely unaware, would have fallen off the bench entirely, and into a potted hydrangea if he hadn't righted himself at the last minute.

"What—" he started to demand, but broke off as the Marquis of Winchilsea stepped through the French doors, irritably calling Caroline's name.

"Oh, *there* you are," her fiancé cried in relief. "Your mother and I've been looking *everywhere* for you, darling."

Caroline backpedaled until she came into contact with the rough stone balustrade that guarded the steps leading down to the gardens. Her guilty gaze was fastened on Hurst's face, but it was apparently too dark for him to notice either the hectic color playing on her cheeks or the fact that her chest was rising and falling as rapidly as if she'd been running.

Nor did he seem to register the fact that there was a man standing a few feet away from her, flicking hydrangea petals from his coat and adjusting his trousers to accommodate that thing Caroline had felt but hadn't quite been able to identify.

"Whatever are you doing out *here*?" Hurst demanded, going to Caroline's side. "I had the devil of a time finding you. Where did that—" He finally noticed Braden, who'd straightened to his full height and was watching them with his arms folded across his chest, and an inscrutable expression upon his dark face.

"Oh," Hurst said. The disappointment in his voice was so evident that Caroline would have burst out laughing if she hadn't felt such mortification over what Hurst, if he'd been a few seconds sooner, might have seen. "It's *you.*"

"It is," Braden agreed, tersely. What in God's name did Caroline see in this annoying parasite? he was asking himself. He was going to have to do something to get rid of him, and fast. Braden wondered if pouring gunpowder into one or two of the man's cigars would count, in Caroline's mind, as extreme violence.

Caroline cleared her throat. "Hurst," she said. "Mr. Granville and I were just . . . just . . ."

"Discussing," Braden said, calmly, "the situation in France."

Hurst's handsome face crumpled with perplexity—which was all right, because perplexity became the marquis.

"*France?*" he echoed.

"Indeed," Braden said, gravely. "They have such a unique way of—"

"Fighting the Prussians," Caroline finished for him. "Really, quite revolutionary, those new guns they've been using."

"New guns?" Hurst shook his head, clearly bewildered. "The two of you were out here, talking about *guns?*"

"Well, what else? Mr. Granville is, after all, an expert on the subject." Caroline slipped her hand through the crook of her fiancé's arm and said, "I suppose Mother must be ready to go. Is that why you were looking for me, Hurst? Because Mother is ready to go?"

He said, "Er, yes. Yes, she is."

"All right." Caroline hugged his arm to her. "Well, Mr. Granville, this is good night, then."

He only looked at her.

In a way, she supposed, that look was worse than anything he could have said. It was an enigmatic look, completely devoid of expression. And yet, seeing it, she suddenly felt that same odd little spurt of emotion that she'd experienced the night she'd looked at him at Dame Ashforth's.

What was it she was feeling? Pity? For the great Braden Granville?

But that was ridiculous. He didn't need her pity.

Or did he? It wasn't as if he fit in anywhere. He was too wealthy now to remain in Seven Dials. But because he was only newly wealthy, he would never be accepted into the social circle in which Caroline traveled so easily. Even *she'd* had trouble getting invitations to certain events before her engagement. After all, her father had only been the *first* Earl of Bartlett, a title so new that most people sneered at it. Thomas, as the second earl of Bartlett, had an easier time of it. What people had made of Braden Granville, when he'd first started coming round, Caroline could not imagine, but she supposed that his engagement to Jacquelyn Seldon had helped gain him a good deal of social acceptance.

Truth be told, they were not so very different, Caroline Linford and Braden Granville. Was that why she felt this strange sort of kinship with him? She ought, she knew, to be angry with him for kissing her again—especially after she'd made it so clear to him that she did not welcome his advances. She had managed to work herself into a fine rage after he'd kissed her the first time in his offices. Why couldn't she do it now?

"That," her mother hissed into her ear, a few minutes later, after Hurst had led her back into the ballroom, "is the last time you are to speak to that man. Ever. Do you understand? It is unconscionable, a man like that, and a girl like you—an engaged woman—alone. In a garden. At night! Why, I've never in my life heard of such a thing. What must the marquis think of you? And the Dalrymples! They're mortified! In the garden of people whom the Prince of Wales holds in such high esteem. How could you?"

Caroline pointed at her brother. "*He's* the one who let him cut in," she said.

Thomas held out both hands in a *Who, me?* gesture. "He asked," he said. "What was I supposed to do? Say no?"

"Really, Ma," Caroline said. "That would only have caused an even bigger scene."

"I . . . don't . . . care." When she was angry, the Dowager Lady Bartlett's lips had a tendency to all but disappear, she pursed them so hard. They were nowhere to be seen at that moment. "You are never to dance with him again, Caroline. Not dance with him, nor speak to him, nor even be seen within a ten-foot radius of him. If it happens again, I'll . . . I'll send you to the country until your wedding. And as it is, you can plan on spending all day tomorrow locked in your room!"

Caroline and her brother exchanged glances, trying not to laugh out loud. Their mother's wrath had always been a source of great amusement for them.

The Dowager Lady Bartlett, however, happened to catch this particular exchange, and, made even more furious by it, declared, "And not only that, young lady, but I shall sell off all your horses!"

Caroline felt no urge to laugh after that.

"You *wouldn't*!" she cried.

"I would." Lady Bartlett held her chin high. "All of them. The ones you keep here in London, as well the ones you think I don't know about, those horrid cart horses you've been going about, buying up, and sending to Emily's place in Shropshire."

"Ma!" Caroline stamped her foot. "You can't!"

"I can, and I will," Lady Bartlett said, primly. Satisfied that she'd done her maternal duty, Lady Bartlett let out a little yawn. "Lord, it's late. Where *is* Peters?"

Caroline, completely appalled by very nearly everything that had taken place in her life in the past twenty-four hours, was far too absorbed in her own self-pitying thoughts to object when her fiancé suddenly appeared, and begged for Lady Bartlett's permission to take her son and daughter home. Lady Bartlett was only too happy to give it, undoubtedly because it meant she wouldn't have to look at Caroline's mutinous expression all the way home.

Caroline, for her part, couldn't have cared less who took her home, so long as someone did. She wanted to get out of her tight corset and into a hot bath at once, where she could sit in absolute privacy and try to figure out how she felt about having had Braden Granville's calloused hands on her most private parts. Well, maybe not her *most* private parts, but nevertheless, a place no one had ever touched before, but which he'd handled without the slightest compunction.

And she had let him! That was the most shocking thing of all. She had sat there and let him.

And *liked* it!

Oh, what was the matter with her? Braden Granville was a skirt chaser. Braden Granville was a man ruled by his temper. Braden Granville was responsible for the manufacture and distribution of thousands of firearms that could very well end up being used in violent crimes like the one committed against her brother. She shouldn't *like* being touched by such a man.

And yet . . .

And yet he'd been very kind in the garden, listening to her talk about Tommy. He had seemed genuinely to care. He had seemed genuinely interested—interested in her!

"Caroline."

She looked up, and saw the Marquis of Winchilsea looking at her very seriously from where he sat beside her on the carriage seat.

"Are you all right, Caroline?" The marquis's pretty blue eyes—so very unlike the dark, unsettling eyes of Braden Granville—were filled with concern. It might, for all Caroline knew, have even been heartfelt.

"Me?" Caroline blinked. Tommy had abandoned them as soon as they were safely out of Lady Bartlett's line of vision, eschewing Hurst's offer of a ride home for a more interesting one with the pretty daughters of a neighbor. Her chaperonless state did not worry Caroline, as the phaeton's top was up, due to the threat of rain, and it wasn't likely anyone would spot, much less comment upon, the Marquis of Winchilsea and his bride-to-be alone in a carriage together.

"Yes, you," Hurst said. "You haven't said a word since we started."

"Oh," she said. "Yes, I'm all right. Are you taking me home?"

"Of course I'm taking you home," the marquis said. "Where else would I be taking you?"

Where indeed. Certainly not back to his rooms to ravish her, the way marquises were always doing to heroines in books.

But Caroline knew perfectly well she wasn't anything like those heroines. In the first place, they didn't have faithless fiancés, like hers. And in the second place, even if they did, they wouldn't go around asking perfect strangers to teach them how to make love, so that they could win their fiancés back again. Instead, it all ended up being some dreadful misunderstanding, and everyone lived happily ever after in the end.

Caroline highly doubted she had misunderstood what she'd seen in Dame Ashforth's sitting room.

Impulsively, she turned in her seat to wrap both hands around the marquis's firm, but not really very pronounced, bicep. "Hurst," she said, tugging on the arm.

He was concentrating on steering his team—a smart pair of grays that Caroline had purchased for him, to go with the phaeton—around an overturned orange cart. "What, Caroline?"

"Hurst." She waited until he had successfully navigated the orange cart, then gave his arm another tug. "Hurst, kiss me."

Obligingly, he turned his head, and placed a swift kiss on her temple, before turning his attention back to the road.

"No," Caroline said, with a feeling of something akin to despair. "I mean, pull over and kiss me properly."

Hurst, looking very surprised, nevertheless did as she asked. He pulled the phaeton to a stop, turned in his seat, and stooped to press his lips to hers.

Caroline, who had not lied when she'd confessed to receiving good marks in school, remembered with perfect clarity exactly how Braden Granville had kissed her. And so, accordingly, she let go of Hurst's arm and reached up, taking his face in her hands. Then she pressed quick, eager kisses all across the marquis's mouth.

Only instead of letting his lips fall open under the sensual onslaught of her mouth—as Caroline had, when Braden had kissed her like that—Hurst pulled his head back, and eyed her as if she had just escaped from an asylum.

"What," he said, "do you think you're doing, Caroline?"

She sank back into her seat dejectedly. "Nothing," she replied.

Well, and what had she been thinking? That she could somehow recapture the excitement she'd used to feel when Hurst kissed her, back before she'd found out about him and Jackie Seldon? Back before Braden Granville had shown her what a proper kiss was?

No. It was over. There was no hope for it now. Esteem and friendship, she told herself. There was nothing wrong with esteem and friendship.

Hurst stared down at her. Then, to her perfect astonishment, he said, "Caroline, I understand from your mother that you've been spending some time lately in the company of Braden Granville."

She said, quickly, "Well, yes, but just because I'm purchasing one of his guns, you know, for Tommy, for when he goes back to school. To defend himself, you know. It isn't anything more than that. Really. I swear it."

"Oh, I believe you," Hurst said. "That's not why I'm concerned."

She felt a completely uncharacteristic spurt of violent anger. The devil take the man!

"It's just that I was wondering," Hurst went on, thoughtfully, not looking at her now, but at the twitching flame of the gaslight they were parked near. "In all of your conversations with him, has Braden Granville . . . well, has he mentioned anything to you about . . . well, me?"

Caroline's eyes flew wide open. Why, Hurst was fishing for information! He was actually trying to find out how much Braden knew about his affair with Jacquelyn Seldon. If only, she thought, he knew. If only he knew what Braden Granville and his man thought him—a phantom! The phantom lover!

The story Braden Granville had told her—about his man being attacked by someone who'd been following Jacquelyn Seldon's lover—plucked at her conscience. But it could not, she knew, have any relation to Hurst. No one could possibly wish the marquis harm. The streets of London, Caroline knew, were disgracefully unsafe—and the criminal element was spreading, as she knew only too well, all the way up the hallowed halls of the country's leading academic communities. Braden Granville's man had no doubt been attacked by a footpad like the one who'd nearly killed her brother.

"Mr. Granville?" She kept her voice light. "Ask about you, Hurst? Whatever for?"

"Oh," Hurst said, with elaborate casualness. "I was just wondering."

I'll bet you were, Caroline thought about saying. Instead, she said, "Why, no."

"Oh." Hurst picked up the reins, and whistled to the horses. "He's a strange one, Granville. Your mother's quite right, you know. You're better off staying away from him. Did you really order a gun from him for Tommy?"

She'd told so many lies lately, she was having trouble keeping track of them all. She supposed she had said something along those lines to someone, and said, "Why, yes."

"I'll pick it up then, when it's ready. All right? I don't want you going near that fellow again."

Caroline sat quite still for the rest of the ride home, and said very little. What was there, after all, to say? She had already learned everything she needed to know.

Which was that when Braden Granville kissed her, every single one of her senses came alive, until it felt as if someone were lighting firecrackers—yes, firecrackers!—inside of her.

But when her fiancé kissed her now, she felt nothing. Absolutely nothing at all.

My God, she couldn't help thinking. The trousers.

The trousers *don't fit*.

16

It was after midnight when Braden Granville rang the bell to the front door of the stylish Mayfair town house. Despite the late hour, however, only a second or two passed before the door was swung open, and when it was, a giant of a man stood behind it, broad across the shoulders as a fireplace mantel, and with a face that looked as if it might once have been used as a horseshoe anvil.

That face crumpled with relief when it recognized Braden.

"'S' bout time you showed up, Dead," the butler cried, in tones of rebuke. "This place's been busier than a Covent Garden whore on a Saturday night—"

"Please, Crutch." Braden threw his balled-up gloves into his top hat and handed the hat to the butler as he stepped through the door. "Not now. I'm not in the mood."

"You're goin' to be in even less of one," Daryl "Crutch" Pomeroy said, as his employer moved toward an inside door, "when you see who's waiting fer you in your—"

But Braden only waved the giant's warning aside. "Unless it's the tax collector, I couldn't care less. Bring me a whiskey, will you, Crutch?"

"You're goin' to need a lot more'n a whiskey before this night is through," Crutch muttered menacingly. But since Braden had been listening to Crutch Pomeroy's dire warnings for more than twenty years, he ignored him, threw open the door to his library . . .

And was more than a little startled to see his father sitting in the exact chair upon which Braden had been looking forward to enjoying his nightcap.

"Braden!" Sylvester Granville cried, his favorite book resting in his lap, his stockinged ankles crossed on the ottoman before the fire. "Thank goodness. I've been waiting all night. Come here, my boy. Come here and see what I've done!"

Behind Braden, Crutch muttered, "Told you so. Insisted on waitin' up for you, he did. Said 'e's got somethin' to show you." Then the butler left the room, closing the door firmly behind him.

"Come, boy!" Sylvester patted the arm of the leather chair beside his eagerly. "Sit here!"

Sighing—he really was rather tired—Braden moved from the door to the seat his father had been saving for him.

"Good evening, Pa," he said, as he sank into the deeply cushioned chair. "What is it you wanted to show me?"

Sylvester held up his somewhat battered leather-bound book of the peerage. "I've written it in myself," he said, excitedly. "They may not put out another edition for a year or more, you know. Have a look."

Obligingly, Braden leaned forward, and looked where his father pointed. There, on the page listing the descendants of the Duke of Childes, he saw his own name beside Jacquelyn Seldon's. But before his name, his father had written the word *Sir*, and afterward, the letters *bt*.

"For baronetcy," the old man explained, enthusiastically. "For likely you'll be made a baronet. Which isn't nobility, you know, but it is definitely gentry. Quite definitely gentry. Now, if Her Majesty's feeling particularly generous, and makes you a baron . . . well, that will be quite a different kettle of fish."

But Braden hardly heard his father. He was staring down at the book, at the name his father had linked to his. Jacquelyn. Jacquelyn Seldon. His bride.

"Pa," he said, slowly. "What if it weren't to come off? Would you be very disappointed?"

Sylvester looked up from the book, the firelight casting an orangey glow to his whiskers. "The letter of patent? Oh, but my boy, I have it on certain authority that it will."

"Not the letter of patent," Braden said, with a quick shake of his head. "But the wedding. To Lady Jacquelyn. Supposing I were to marry . . . well, someone else, instead."

The senior Mr. Granville looked concerned. "Not marry Lady Jacquelyn? Oh, but my boy, whyever not? She is the loveliest creature."

Lovely. Yes, Lady Jacquelyn Seldon was lovely, all right.

"Supposing I married someone else instead," Braden went on—quite brashly, he knew, but he'd been feeling somewhat brash ever since leaving the Dalrymples' ballroom. "Supposing I were to marry, instead, Lady Caroline Linford."

Sylvester's gray eyebrows rose to their limits. "The daughter of Lady Bartlett? Lovely Lady Bartlett, whom we met at the opera?"

Braden nodded. "Yes. That Lady Bartlett. Her daughter."

Sylvester immediately began to flip through the pages of his book. When he came to the Bs, however, he was sadly disappointed.

"Why, there's no Bartlett here," he said, looking stricken. "None at all! Could the publisher have made a mistake?"

Braden sighed. "No, Pa, no mistake. The Earl of Bartlett is rather newish. I believe he was only granted the title a few years ago, thanks to some unique plumbing he invented."

"Plumbing?" Again, Sylvester looked stricken, but his affection for his son won out, for once, over his obsession. He reached out and patted Braden fondly on the hand. "My boy," he said, kindly. "If you want to marry the plumber's daughter, you go right ahead.

Only you had better think of a pretty gift for Lady Jacquelyn, for she will be sorely disappointed!"

Braden didn't doubt that. And since the chances of his actually marrying the plumber's daughter were, after all, moot, he told his father not to worry, and helped him up the stairs, and saw Mr. Granville Senior tucked finally into bed. It wasn't until Braden threw open the door to his own bedroom that he discovered what Crutch had meant when he'd asserted that the house had been busier than a Covent Garden whore on a Saturday night.

For there, curled in the center of Braden's canopied bed, a sheet just barely covering her to her milky white shoulders, was the Lady Jacquelyn Seldon.

She smiled at him coyly and said, "Well, it's about time you came home."

While it was a fine thing to be able to provide steady, legal employment for one's friends, Braden thought, occasionally, as in this case, doing so proved problematic. A professional butler would have mentioned, upon Braden's return, that his fiancée had demanded entrance, and was currently holed up in his bedroom, naked as the day she was born. Crutch, however, having spent most of his life as a hired thug, and not a gentleman's servant, had couched the information in such colorful terms that Braden had completely missed the implication.

He would have been hard-pressed, however, to miss the implication in Jacquelyn's next action, which was to fling back the sheet to reveal that she was, indeed, as naked as he'd suspected.

"Aren't you coming to bed?" she asked, with a mischievous smile.

The Lady Jacquelyn Seldon, it had to be admitted, was every bit the jewel the *ton* had proclaimed her. Braden, who'd had occasion to observe her in most every condition and environment over the course of their year-long courtship, could testify to the veracity of this. Slender limbed and yet generously proportioned where being generously proportioned mattered, Jacquelyn Seldon's dark beauty was universally admired. Her unerring taste in fashion, which always showed off her considerable assets to an advantage, was heralded wherever she went. High-spirited and vivacious, Lady Jacquelyn's name was rarely left off any guest list, and happy was the hostess whose home the only daughter of the late Duke of Childes chose to grace with her presence. She was, in short, perfect in all the ways that mattered—at least in the opinion of the beau monde—and Braden Granville should have been gratified and flattered to find her sprawled across his bed in a state of extreme undress.

What he was, however, was annoyed.

"For God's sake, Jackie," he said. "What are you doing here?"

Jacquelyn traced a small circle on the linen sheet beneath her with one tapered fingernail. "What," she said, her eyelashes sooty against the high curves of her cheekbones, "does it *look* like I'm doing here?"

He felt another keen burst of annoyance. What was the use, he wondered, of having a lock on his front door, if anyone who wanted to could come barging in, and make themselves at home?

"Well," he said. "You can't possibly stay here." He knew he sounded churlish, but he didn't care. He felt he'd been sorely tested these past two hours, first by Caroline Linford and her infernal fiancé, and now by his own. He was not certain, actually, how much more pushing he could take before he pushed back.

And Braden Granville was not a careful pusher.

"What do you mean?" Jacquelyn lifted her dark-eyed gaze to meet his. "Why can't I? I've spent the night before, Braden. Plenty of times."

"Certainly," he said. He had to speak with a patience so forced, he was surprised she didn't notice it. "But that was before."

"Before *what*?" The dark eyes narrowed, just slightly.

"Before we got engaged, of course," he amended, hastily.

"Things are different now. I told you that the other day. Now get your clothes back on, and I'll have someone run you home."

Jacquelyn, instead of doing as he asked, let out a humorless little bark of laughter. "You can't be serious, Braden," she said.

"Jackie," he said, "I thought I made it clear to you that this sort of thing"—his gesture incorporated her clothing, scattered carelessly about his floor, as well as her magnificently nude body— "has got to stop."

Jacquelyn laughed again, a sound that was more shrill than he was sure she'd aimed for. "Goodness, Braden, but you have gotten terribly proper lately. Whatever is the matter with you? I can remember a time when you would have been delighted to find a naked lady in your bed. This isn't a bit what I thought our married life was going to be like, you ordering me *out* of bed, rather than into it."

She was trying to be amusing, but Braden was in no mood for levity.

"Come on," he said, reaching down and scooping up her pantaloons. "I'm tired, Jacks. It's been a long day. Let's go."

This had been a miscalculation on his part. Normally, Braden had as keen an insight into the human psyche as he did the mechanical workings of just about any machine. But in this particular case, he had been too impatient, too out-of-temper to go carefully. He might, on any other night, have been able to cajole Jacquelyn out of her sulk and out of his bed, with no hurt feelings whatsoever. But this time, he trod too quickly.

"I'll go," she snapped, snatching the pantaloons out of his hand, and regarding him through eyes that were no longer flat, but quite heated. "A long day, eh?" Wriggling into the pantaloons, which happened to be a pair he had purchased for her, silk ones, trimmed with Venetian lace, Jacquelyn did not take her gaze off him. "Yes, and I suppose you're all tired out from dancing at the Dalrymples'. Not, of course, that you bothered to turn a single reel with *me*. But *Lady Caroline Linford*, on the other hand—"

Braden frowned at the mention of the name. He couldn't help it. That name had been very much on his mind of late, the more so since he had happened to get a good deal closer to its owner than he'd ever expected to. Lady Caroline Linford, at close proximity, had a rather devastating effect on his equilibrium.

Worse, the sight of Lady Caroline with someone else—in this case, the Marquis of Winchilsea—had proven to have a curiously unsettling effect on him. He knew he was being ridiculous, but when Slater had come and led Caroline away, all Braden had been able to do was glare at him, at his patrician profile, his nose that looked as if it had never once been broken, his thick blond curls, his cloying, precious blue eyes.

He wasn't jealous of the man. Far from it! Slater was so utterly beneath contempt, so vapid, so self-involved, that Braden couldn't feel jealousy toward him. No, what he had felt instead was fury toward Caroline, who had gone and gotten herself engaged to a man in every way her inferior.

Not that Braden fancied himself as a much better catch. He had, after his mother's death, and his father's descent into gentle madness, run pretty much wild in his youth, and had suffered numerous run-ins with the law, most of them deservedly. If it hadn't been for the patience and kindness of one man—Josiah Wilder, the gunsmith to whom the courts had assigned him as an apprentice, the man who'd dragged him, quite literally, out of a life of crime, treated him as a second son and shown him, in the years before Josiah's eventual death from old age, that there was another way to live—he might be in Seven Dials still, hiding from the law or, more likely, drinking himself to death, a common and fairly well-respected practice there.

Still, even he had to be a better choice for a husband than Hurst Slater, who couldn't open his mouth without letting out some inanity. So what if he was good-looking, with his blue eyes and un-broken nose? There was more to a man than looks. So he was a mar-quis? What was a title, anyway? Anyone could have one. Even, if his father was correct about that letter of patent, Dead Eye Granville.

Of course, the man had managed somehow to save her broth-er's life. That was one fact that could not, unfortunately, be over-looked. Hurst Slater might well be vapid. He might well be vain. But there was no question that toward Caroline's brother, he had acted with generosity and self-sacrifice—undoubtedly in an effort to win the affections of the boy's suddenly wealthy sister—but he had done it, just the same.

Such nobility would appeal to a girl like Caroline Linford. It would, in fact, be almost impossible to resist. Coupled with a few well-placed compliments and the occasional peck on the cheek, and Slater soon found himself with a very wealthy bride. Of course she had said yes when he'd asked her to marry him. What else was she going to say? The marquis wasn't just handsome. He wasn't just attentive. *He had saved her brother's life.*

No woman in the world would have said no to such a man—with the possible exception of a woman like Jackie, who had never, Braden was now certain, felt gratitude or sympathy in her life.

"What were you talking about, anyway?" Jacquelyn demanded, interrupting his private musings. "You and Caroline Linford, back there in the Dalrymples' garden? And don't deny you were there with her, Braden. I *saw* you two together."

"Guns," he said, automatically. "We were talking about guns."

She paused as she worked an ivory button. "Guns. You and Caroline Linford were in the garden—in the dark—talking about guns."

"That's right."

Jacquelyn stopped dressing and looked at him. There was no heat at all in her gaze now. Her dark eyes were back to being flat and dead.

"Caroline Linford," she said, quietly, "hates guns. She's quite morbidly obsessed with getting rid of all of them, because of what happened to her brother."

"Yes," Braden said. "I know."

But he was not really attending to what Jacquelyn had said. He was still thinking about Caroline.

It had finally gotten so bad, there at the Dalrymples', watching her with Slater, that he'd been forced to leave. It was true what he'd told her, that he was interested in her. But it would have been more truthful to say that ever since she'd come to his office that first time, and shocked him so thoroughly with her highly unladylike proposal, he'd wanted her. In his arms. In his bed. In his life. More than any other woman he had ever known.

And why not? There was no doubting she was the most genuine woman he'd met since he'd left the Dials. She didn't seem to care a whit for convention, said exactly what she was thinking (most of the time, anyway) and once she got an idea in her head, clearly couldn't let it alone, and to hell with the consequences. Caroline Linford had all the qualities he had most admired in the girls back in Seven Dials—loyalty and an almost brutal honesty amongst them—and none of the affectations of the girls of the so-called polite society he so despised, coupled with a disarming sense of humor and a red-hot temper. All that, and the fact that she was, it had to be admitted, the most easily aroused woman he'd ever had the good luck to lay his hands on, convinced him that this was a fight worth fighting, no matter how high the body count rose.

Except, of course, for the fact that he was supposed to be marrying somebody else by the end of the month.

The somebody else who was, in fact, glaring at him very unhappily indeed that very moment, as she struggled back into her crinoline.

Jacquelyn said, "I think you should know, Braden"—she pulled the steel cage up around her hips—"that I have every intention of suing. If you call the wedding off."

The scarred eyebrow rose, just a fraction of an inch. "And what," he asked, kindly, "makes you think I would ever want to do something so rash as to call off our wedding?"

"Maybe," Jacquelyn said, with a toss of her night-dark hair, "because you haven't touched me in over a month."

"Merely observing the social niceties," he said, "considered so important by you and your friends."

The lifeless eyes narrowed. "I mean it, Braden. It won't be pretty. I'm talking about all of it. The men I've turned down since I've been with you. The emotional anguish—"

"Don't worry, my dear," Braden said, almost gently. "If it should come to that—my calling off the wedding—you can be sure I shall have very good reason for doing so. The sort of reason that holds up very well indeed in court. Get dressed, Jacquelyn." There was no gentleness at all in his tone now. "I'll have someone drive you. I'm sure Crutch will be delighted to do it."

Or would be, once Braden pressed a few pound notes upon him. It was too bad, really, that Lady Jacquelyn wasn't so easily appeased.

17

The ninth Marquis of Winchilsea had not left much, it was true, to his children. He had not, poor man, had much to leave, except of course for his title, and a run-down abbey in the Lake District.

But one thing he had managed to leave for Hurst was a membership in his club, a rather exclusive men's club, for which the marquis had, it was true, not paid dues in some time, but which was so exclusive that no one dared mention this to the new marquis, who, it was hoped, could be appealed to for the back dues when his impending marriage to the wealthy Earl of Bartlett's daughter became fact.

But it was not his tardiness in paying his dues that had earned the new marquis the contempt of the club's employees. Rather, it was his inherent stinginess, not tipping, even so much as a ha'penny, the grooms who kept his horses brushed while he was enjoying luncheon, or the sommelier who brought him his claret.

Worse, for all his stinginess, the new marquis was exacting to the extreme, complaining if a bay leaf was found in his stew, or if he had to wait so much as five minutes for anything.

So it wasn't perhaps to be wondered at that the club employees would not hesitate to declare the marquis "in"—when every other member was always, without question "out" to anyone who came calling (with the exception, perhaps, of the Prince of Wales)—to a man who called himself Samuel Jenkins, but who was, in reality, The Duke.

And to show a man like The Duke to the marquis's chair, in which he'd been slumping, staring dully into the fire—well, that was a sign that Hurst was very unpopular with the club staff indeed.

"Hello, there, my boy," The Duke said, as he lowered his impressive bulk into the leather chair opposite the marquis's. "Been a while, hasn't it, then?"

For almost a full minute, Hurst could only stare at the man sitting across from him, rendered completely speechless at the sight of him. So it was true. It was true after all, the thing which he'd most feared. He'd told himself over and over again that he was being ridiculous. The Duke couldn't know. The Duke couldn't possibly know what he'd done. Who'd have told him? It wasn't as if the two of them traveled in the same social circles now, was it?

But someone had told. Someone had to have told. Because The Duke had come to London. Come to London, and apparently come to London in search of Hurst. It had been The Duke who'd put the tail on him. The Duke, and not Granville.

Oh, Lord. If only it had been Granville.

Hurst shot the hireling who'd led the corpulent man over to his chair a look of rage, which the servant pointedly ignored, choosing instead to bow politely to The Duke—from whom he'd already received a pretty tip, just for showing him in—and inquire, "Brandy, Mr. Jenkins?"

"Yes, I think I will take a brandy," The Duke said. "You, my lord?"

Hurst shook his head, much too stunned to speak. The Duke—whose real name Hurst did not know; it certainly wasn't Jenkins—was risking a great deal, showing his face in London, where, if the marquis wasn't mistaken, he was wanted for a vast number of crimes, not the least of which was capital murder. And what in God's name was he doing in Hurst's club, where anyone—even a criminal court judge—might happen by, and spy him?

Well, at least, Hurst thought, running a finger under his cravat, which suddenly seemed a bit too tight, he could not possibly intend to kill him. Not here, in front of all these witnesses. . . .

"Now," The Duke said. "I think we've some things to discuss, you and I."

Hurst found that his palms were sweating. As it was quite cool in the room where they sat, he could not blame this on a sudden change in temperature.

"If it's about the money," Hurst burst out, "I still haven't got it. But I'll get it. In about a month, I'll have it."

"Now, my lord," The Duke said, with a good deal of fatherly patience, for a man known to have such a violent temper. "You know perfectly well it isn't about money. Well, except in a roundabout way."

"I don't"—Hurst looked about the room. Was there no one at this club who could recognize a member of the underworld when he happened to be seated right in front of him? Would no one come to his rescue?—"know what you mean."

"Don't you?" The Duke lifted the delicate ballon of brandy the waiter had brought to him. The graceful piece of crystal looked ludicrous in the sausagelike fingers, and he held it the wrong way, by its tiny stem. Burying his thick nose into the mouth of the glass, he tasted the amber liquid with his plump lips, found it acceptable, and nodded to the waiter, who left with a smile and a little extra change rattling in his pocket. "I'm not surprised to hear it. It's been some time, ain't it? Since before Christmas, most like. That's the last I seen of you, anyway."

Hurst's grip tightened on the arms of his chair. "I—I had a friend. He fell ill. I had—had to see that he was looked after."

"Ah," The Duke said. "I'd heard that, actually. Do you know what else I heard?"

"N-no. . . ."

"I heard your sick friend was someone I thought I'd taken care of. That bloke you brought round. What was his name? Oh, yes." The Duke eyed him over his brandy snifter, which he held with his pinky finger in the air. "Linford."

Brains had never been something much appreciated by Hurst's clan, who preferred a fellow who could hunt over a fellow who could philosophize. But he flattered himself that he was at least as intelligent as The Duke. Which was why he attempted to prevaricate.

"Oh, yes. Lord Bartlett," he cried. "Yes, yes, of course. Yes, Lord Bartlett was the, er, gentleman with whom you had that disagreement—"

"He called me," The Duke said, his voice dropping to a low growl, "a cheat."

"I remember, I remember." Hurst leaned forward in his chair and spoke to The Duke in a low voice. "But that's not why I left Oxford, you know. Lord Bartlett's not my friend, you see. It was another fellow, back here in London. Dueling injury. Quite serious, really. I meant to send you a note, but it must have slipped my—"

"Don't play games with me, Slater. I've had you watched, you sodding bastard. I know it was Linford. You're marrying the bloke's sister come June. It was in all the papers. You may think me illiterate scum, but I *can* read. Next time you try to run from me, boy, I recommend you stay out of the social pages."

Hurst realized his attempt to prevaricate had not succeeded. He shifted tactics.

"All right," he said, coolly, leaning back in his chair. "Yes, all right, then. I'm the one who fished Linford out of the gutter. I'm the one who saw that he was patched up and shipped home. I did it for you, you know. You ought to be thanking me, instead of sitting there, reviling me."

"Thank you?" The Duke glowered at him. "Thank you for what?"

"For saving the poor bloody boy. What were you thinking, shooting him like that? He owed us a thousand quid!"

"He called me a *cheat*."

"So you tried to kill him," Hurst said. "Very bright. Very intelligent. How did you plan on collecting the thousand quid?"

"I planned," The Duke said, "on wringing it from your scrawny neck. You're the one who brought him into the game in the first place."

"If you had just let him win a few rounds now and then—"

"What?" The Duke's porcine eyes, half hidden between folds of sunburned fat, glittered. "If I had just let him win a few rounds now and then, *what*?"

"He wouldn't have gotten so suspicious," Hurst said, in a calmer voice. "He's an excellent player. That's what you wanted, right? Good players, confident in their ability, who'd bet high. Well, he bet high. And he lost big. Too big, too many times. He knew something wasn't right."

"Of course he did." The Duke sipped delicately at his brandy again. "That's why I shot him."

"I warned you. I warned you before. If you didn't let them win a few rounds, they'd get suspicious."

The Duke grinned at him. "*You* didn't," he pointed out.

"Yes," Hurst said. "But I was quite drunk. . . ."

"Not as drunk as Linford was."

Hurst frowned. This was true, of course. He hadn't been as drunk as the earl, yet he'd never suspected a thing. He'd lost, and lost, and lost, and kept right on playing, until he owed more . . . well, more than he could ever hope to pay back in a lifetime.

But that hadn't mattered, in the end. Because he had something other than money, something The Duke and his friends needed badly: connections. Connections with other young men like himself, only wealthier. Much wealthier. Hurst knew he wasn't a clever man—not nearly, he knew, as clever as the Earl of Bartlett—but he was blue-blooded, by God. And breeding always won out over brains, any day of the week. Or so Hurst had always been assured by his grandmama.

"All right," he said, testily. "All right. So you found me out. It wasn't as if I were avoiding you, or anything. I planned to come see you." A lie. A blatant lie. "Well, after my wedding, anyway. I should have the money I owe you then. I won't be able to continue working for you, of course, once I'm married. I shan't have time to make all those trips up to Oxford. But I'll still steer all the willing lads I can in your direction—"

"Aren't you just rolling in the clover?" The Duke stretched out his legs and folded his sausage fingers together across his vast expanse of belly. "Isn't everything just so bloody nice for you now?"

Hurst eyed him uneasily. "Well . . . not really," he said, but he didn't feel he could burden The Duke with his problems with Jacquelyn and Braden Granville.

"Bollocks," The Duke said, explosively.

Hurst, turning crimson, looked quickly around. A number of club patrons, and even some of the staff members, glanced up curiously at the sudden outburst the marquis's guest had made.

"Your Grace," Hurst said. The Duke liked to be addressed as befit his self-awarded title. "Your Grace, if you please, keep your voice down. This is a private club, and I—"

"Bollocks," The Duke said again, but he said it a little more quietly this time. "You've got some nerve, Slater, sittin' here in your bollocky club in them bollocky velvet pants, while you've got yourself a bollocky bride and a bollocky bitch on the side, as well. See? I know. We've kept an eye on you, Slater. And we aren't happy with what we've seen."

The Duke had a tendency to employ the royal we when he was unhappy. He appeared to be very unhappy right now.

"You know I shot Linford. You know I shot him and left him to die. He would have died, too, if it hadn't been for your bollocky interference. Well, as far as I'm concerned, you've made this mess, so you've got to clean it up."

Hurst licked his lips. A part of him was wondering how many members of his club were going to complain to the management about the number of times the word "bollocks" had been employed by his guest. Another part—a much bigger part—was concerned about just what, exactly, The Duke meant.

"Mess?" he echoed. "What mess might that be, Your Grace?"

"The Linford mess." The Duke lifted his ballon and finished his brandy in one swift gulp. "I shot him, you bloody idiot, to keep him from bleatin' to all his friends about The Duke being a cheat. Not much point in running a card game, is there, if no one'll show up to it because they've heard it's fixed."

"Oh, please," Hurst said, his heart beginning to beat with uncomfortable force beneath his shirt. "Bartlett won't tell anyone, Your Grace. He's learned his lesson. You put the fear of God into him. He'll be silent as a mouse when he gets back in the fall—"

"Yes," The Duke said. "He will be. Dead men don't talk."

Hurst's heart seemed to be hurling itself against his ribs. "Oh, no," he said. "You don't mean . . . you can't mean. . . ."

But The Duke very clearly did.

"But Your Grace—" It was all Hurst could do to keep from sliding off his chair and falling to his knees before the man. "I'm to marry his sister! You don't understand. She's got money. Lots and lots of it. I'll pay you. I'll be happy to pay you anything you like—"

"Of course." The Duke looked down at him quizzically. "You'll do that, too. And you'll have even more money than you ever supposed, because with the earl dead, his inheritance will go to his

206 · MEG CABOT

sister. You'll have quite the wealthy bride, Slater. Wealthier than you ever imagined. But first, of course, you'll clean up your mess."

"But—"

"You'll clean it up." The Duke rose to his feet. "Or we'll clean up *you*, as well."

Seeing that "Mr. Jenkins" was preparing to depart, the young man in charge of such things hurried forward with his hat and cane, which The Duke accepted with a smile and a shiny new guinea.

"Don't be too long about it, either, Slater," were the gentle-man's last words before departing. And each one seemed to strike at Hurst's chest like a blow from a hammer.

How long he sat after The Duke had left, he did not know. He had suspected, of course, that something like this was going to happen. He had not thought he'd be able to break free of The Duke and his friends with anything like ease.

But he had never thought the cost would be this high.

Later, over luncheon, a good many of Hurst's fellow club members speculated over the reason the new Marquis of Winchilsea had left his chair so suddenly after his meeting with the extraordinary Mr. Jenkins. It was generally agreed that the new marquis had over-extended himself, and that Mr. Jenkins was, perhaps, a representa-tive of one of the individuals to whom the marquis owed money.

What they did not know, of course, was that the reason the marquis quit the club so suddenly that afternoon was not so that he could go to the bank and withdraw money to pay his debts, but so that he could go to the nearest gun club, and brush up on his target practice.

18

"*H*e what?" Emily's voice cracked.

"Shhh." Caroline put a hand over her best friend's lips. "Not so loud! Ma's in her room down the hall, resting, with another one of her headaches. She's bound to hear you."

"But Caro," Emily burst out, from behind the strategically placed fingers. "His *tongue*?"

Caroline took her hand from her friend's lips and said, "It isn't as nasty as it sounds, Emmy. In fact, it was rather . . . nice."

Emily made a face. "*Nice?* Caroline, there is nothing *nice* about—how can you even . . . but that isn't the point. The point is that letting a man kiss you that way—well, it's tantamount to inviting him into your bed." Emily thumped emphatically on the mattress they sat upon, that mattress being the one belonging to Caroline's large, canopied bed. "And if you think Braden Granville is going to let you alone now that you've put that idea in his head—"

"It isn't like that," Caroline said. "He isn't how you think he is—how everyone says he is. Emmy, he's really very nice—"

"Nice?" Emily rolled her eyes. "Caroline, Braden Granville isn't *nice*. You're a fool to think it. He isn't like Hurst or Tommy. He's different. He comes from a different world."

Caroline found herself glaring at her friend. "From a little east of here. Not *China*, for God's sake."

"You misunderstand me," Emily said, a little stiffly. "Purposefully, too, I think. You know I am not one to judge a man according to whether he was born in the East End or West End of London. I believe as much in the equality of the classes as I do in the equality of the sexes. But Caro, Braden Granville has such a reputation. You know he has. You can't allow a man like that to do something as . . . intimate as stick his tongue in your mouth, and expect him to just forget about it. It wasn't an interesting social experiment to him, like it was to you. He's not going to just forget about it. Because when a man like Braden Granville sticks his tongue in your mouth, it's actually a rehearsal for sticking something *else* in you—"

Caroline snatched up one of her bed pillows and flung it at her friend. "It's *not*," she said, blushing furiously.

"Caro, it *is*." Emily caught the pillow. "And Braden Granville's not the type of man to be satisfied with a mere *rehearsal*. He's not going to let you alone until the curtain's come down and the standing ovation's begun. . . ."

Caroline tried to shrug off her friend's concern, though it wasn't easy, with her face burning so hotly. She wished she'd never told Emily about any of it. She wished it was all a secret she could hug to herself at night, like a pillow.

"Well," Caroline said, with elaborate nonchalance. "What's so wrong with that?"

Emily stared at her. "What's so wrong with that? Did you just ask me *what's so wrong about that?* Caroline, what's so wrong about that is that you are engaged to marry Hurst Slater, the tenth Marquis of Winchilsea, in less than a month."

She stuck out her chin. "So? If Hurst can have a lover, why can't I have one, too?"

Emily's jaw dropped. Seeing her stunned expression, Caroline groaned, and then, rolling over onto her stomach, let her head hang over the side of the bed. "Fine," she said, from her new, up-side down position. "You're right. I'm not exactly the type of girl who takes a lover, am I? But the plain fact of the matter is, Emmy, I've tried the pants on, and they don't fit."

Her friend dropped down beside her. *"What?"*

"I kissed Hurst last night—really kissed him—and I felt nothing."

"You used to love it when he kissed you," Emily said.

"Exactly. But now? Nothing."

"Oh, God." Emily lifted her head, her green eyes snapping fire. "This is all your own fault, you know. If you'd just told me what you were going to do when you went to see Braden Granville the first time—"

"You'd have tried to talk me out of it."

"Of course I would have. It was a perfectly ridiculous idea. *Lessons*, Caro? In how to *make love*? Only a madwoman would have come up with such a thing."

Caroline sat up. "What else was I supposed to do, Emmy? I honestly believed I could make Hurst love me."

"And now?"

"Now? Now I'm telling myself that there are worse things than marrying a man you don't love, who doesn't love you." Caroline sighed. "Snakes, for instance."

"I was wrong." Emily climbed down from the bed, and began to pace Caroline's pretty, lace-filled bedroom. "This isn't your fault. It's Tommy's. If he hadn't been stupid enough to get shot, Hurst wouldn't have had to save him, and you could marry anyone you wanted."

"But I wanted to marry Hurst," Caroline pointed out. "I was delighted at the idea of marrying Hurst. Until I found out about Jackie Seldon, and then the pants not fitting."

Emily glowered. "It's Braden Granville's fault, then. You'd never have known the pants didn't fit if he hadn't stuck his tongue in your mouth."

"Or," Caroline added, thoughtfully, "put his hand down my shimmy."

Emily cried, "He *what*?"

Caroline, startled, said, "Oh, yes. I forgot to tell you about that part."

"Caroline!" Emily looked as if she might pass out, but Caroline knew she wouldn't. Emily, like herself, had never fainted in her life. "You didn't . . . He didn't . . . Tell me you didn't!"

Caroline said, "Well, I was a little hard-pressed to stop him. I mean, he's so much bigger than I am. Besides, it felt—"

"The brute!" Emily burst out. "I can't believe the audacity of him! I'm going to tell your mother—no, I'll tell Hurst. No, I'll tell Tommy!"

In a flash, Caroline had her friend by the wrist. "Don't you dare," Caroline said, her voice almost as hard as her grip. "Tommy will try to fight him, and you know he's not up to it yet. Besides, Braden would never accept the challenge, and you know how that would—"

"*Braden?*" Emily stared at her best friend with eyes wide as saucers. "You call him *Braden* now?"

"Well," Caroline said, a little taken aback. "I should think I'm allowed. He's been a lot more intimate with me than Hurst has ever been, and I call him by *his* first name."

Emily shook her head. "Oh, Caroline," she said. "This is awful."

A knock sounded on the door.

"Lady Caroline?" Bennington's voice sounded strained. "A message for you, my lady."

Caroline rolled her eyes. Another letter of regret, she supposed, to her wedding. Well, her mother would be happy. It would mean she could bring up another couple from the B list.

"Promise me," she said, ignoring the butler, and taking her friend's hand in both her own. "Promise me, Emily, that you won't say anything to Tommy."

Emily, looking sullen, said, "All right, I promise. But you've got to promise to end it, Caroline. Now, before it goes any further."

The butler knocked again. "Lady Caroline?"

Caroline dropped her friend's hand. "Oh, dash it all," she said, impatiently. "Come in, then."

The key scratched in the lock, and then the butler, looking as if delivering messages to young ladies who'd been locked into the bedroom by their irate mothers was something he did every day of the week, came in, holding a silver salver.

Caroline picked up the neatly folded foolscap that rested on the salver, and saw that she didn't recognize the handwriting on it. Curious, she lifted her eyeglasses from where they rested on a bedside table, settled them onto her nose, then tore the missive open, glanced at the signature, and immediately turned a violent shade of red.

> *Caroline*, the note read in strong, powerful script. *It is now five o'clock. You are exactly one hour late for our appointment. Tardiness is the one thing I cannot abide. Get your spectacles and meet me outside in five minutes, or I shall force my way in and drag you out. B. Granville*

Caroline looked at the butler, her mouth suddenly very dry. "Bennington," she said. "Is there a carriage sitting outside the house?"

"Indeed, my lady," he said. "There is. An enclosed black curricle. The footman informed me that his master is within it. His attendant is waiting for your reply."

Her heart beating a bit too rapidly for comfort in her chest, Caroline slipped off the bed and went to her writing desk, moving like someone in a daze.

"Caro," Emily said, in a concerned voice. "Are you all right? You look . . . strange."

"I'm fine," Caroline said, automatically, as she drew out a piece of stationery and a pen.

Mr. Granville, she wrote, rapidly. *Even if I wanted to meet you, which I am certain would not be at all wise, I could not, since my mother has locked me into my room as punishment for having gone into the garden with you last night at the Dalrymples'.*
C. Linford

She waved the note until the ink dried, and then she folded it, and placed it on Bennington's salver. "That will be all, Bennington," she said. "Thank you."

The butler bowed, and left the room. He was careful, after he'd closed the door, to lock it again behind him.

"That letter," Emily burst out, "is from Braden Granville, isn't it?"

Caroline shushed her. "Must you shout so?" she asked. "I tell you, Ma has ears like a cat. She'll find out Bennington let you in here, and there won't be a minute's peace after that."

"It *is* from him." Emily rushed to Caroline's side. "Let me see it."

Knowing Emily would never let her alone until she did so, Caroline surrendered the note. Emily read it with an expression that grew more indignant with every line.

"Of all the conceited—" She practically threw the note back at Caroline. "I can't believe the gall of that man! First he sticks his tongue in your mouth, then he puts his hand down your shimmy, and then *this*!"

"Yes," Caroline said. She knew it was wicked, but she could not help feeling extremely pleased. She had never in her life had a man threaten—in writing, no less—to force his way into a building and drag her anywhere. There was something extremely thrilling about it. Especially considering the fact that the man in question was Braden Granville.

"It's barbaric," Emily said. "He's ordering you about as if you were some sort of servant! This is a classic example of a domineering male thinking he can assert his power over a female by threatening her with physical violence."

"Shocking," Caroline agreed, happily.

"And what does he mean, about your spectacles?"

"Oh," Caroline said. She listened for sounds, below stairs, of Braden forcing his way in. Where *was* he? "Nothing."

"What did you reply?" Emily wanted to know. "I hope you told him to go and soak his fat head somewhere."

"Of course I didn't," Caroline said. "That would only have been childish."

"Caroline." Emily's voice was cautious. "Are you in love with him?"

Caroline felt her cheeks flare up again. "What? Me? In love? With Braden Granville?"

"You heard me," Emily said, flatly. "Are you?"

Yes. That was the sorry answer, and she knew it. She didn't know how it had happened, or even when. All she knew was that sometime in between that night at Dame Ashforth's, and last night, when he'd slipped his hand down her shimmy, Caroline had fallen for Braden Granville. And fallen hard.

Not, of course, that she'd ever admit as much to Emmy. Or anyone, for that matter. "I hardly," she said with a sniff, "know the man."

"You just told me you know him a lot more intimately than you know Hurst," Emily cried, "and you're *engaged* to *him*. I don't think it out of the realm of the possible—considering that I've known you my whole entire life, and never seen you act this way before—that you might be in love with Braden Granville."

Fortunately, Caroline was spared from having to reply by another knock on the door.

"Lady Caroline," Bennington said, calmly. "The gentleman's reply."

214 · MEG CABOT

Caroline winced and called, "Come in." When the butler had unlocked the door and let himself in, she whispered, loudly, "Really, Bennington, did you have to say the word *gentleman* so loudly? Do you want my mother to hear, and put me on bread and water rations next?"

"*Really*, Bennington," Emily said, severely.

"I beg your pardon, my lady," the butler said. He kept his chin very high in the air. "You're quite right. Here is the reply."

Caroline snatched the paper off the silver salver and opened it. Scrawled on the bottom of her own letter were the words,

Do you honestly expect me to believe this ridiculous story of your being locked in your room like some sort of princess in a tower? If it is true, then all I can say is that I sadly underestimated your intelligence if a mere lock is all it takes to keep you a prisoner in your own home.

Of course, if it isn't true, then all I can say is may God forgive your lying soul, since I certainly won't. B. G.

Caroline looked at the butler.

"Will there be a reply, my lady?" he asked, in a bored voice.

"Yes," Caroline said, removing her spectacles and standing up. "But I shall be making it in person."

Emily gasped and stood up, as well. "Caroline!"

Caroline, ignoring the shocked expressions on both their faces, reached for her reticule, into which she slipped her eyeglasses.

"Pardon me, Lady Caroline," Bennington said. "But did I hear you correctly? Did you say—"

"Yes," Caroline said. She pulled a bonnet down from one of the hooks on the inside of her closet door, and secured the ribbons beneath her chin in an enormous, saucy bow. "You heard me correctly. I am going out."

"But," the butler said, "begging your pardon, Lady Caroline, I believe your mother expressly forbade you from—"

"Bennington," Caroline said, tugging on her gloves. "You've never struck a woman, have you?"

"Indeed, no, my lady," the butler said, looking a bit panicked.

"And you would never do anything," Caroline said, reaching for her parasol, "to hurt me, would you?"

"Um." Bennington swallowed hard. "No, indeed, my lady."

"Then"—she swung the parasol up until it rested on her shoulder—"I'm sorry to have to inform you that the only way you are going to stop me from walking out that door, Bennington, is if you strike me, something you just said you would never do."

Bennington lowered the salver . . . and his chin. "Very well, my lady," he said, glumly. "Only do be so good as to explain to the Lady Bartlett that I only relented under duress."

"Of course," Caroline said. "That goes without saying."

"Caroline!" Emily hurried after her as Caroline left her bedroom and started down the stairs. "Have you lost all the sense God gave you? You can't go anywhere with that man. Who knows what he'll try to do next?"

That, Caroline thought, with a flash of guilt, *is precisely why I'm going*.

"Caroline, don't you see? Don't you see what he's doing to you? He's doing to you exactly what he's done to dozens of other women—hundreds, maybe. He's seducing you."

"No," Caroline replied. "He isn't."

"Caroline, open your eyes. Of course he is. What else could he want?"

Caroline paused on the stairs. "He said I . . . interest him."

"Forgive me, Caroline." Emily looked pained. "But what could you possibly have to say that would interest a man like Braden Granville?"

Caroline considered her friend's question carefully. "Well," she said. "Let me see. We've discussed the nature of love, Tommy's accident, my mother, kissing, his fiancée's pending breach of promise suit, Hurst, and . . . oh, and the importance of creating a romantic atmosphere." She turned and gave Emily a knowing smile. "If, however, his plan really is to seduce me, I shall put up a spirited defense. Never fear."

"And I'm sure running off like this to see him is the best way to do that." Emily stood on the landing, her hands stretched out in open appeal to her friend. "Caroline, listen to yourself. He's a manipulative wretch. It's men like him—charming snakes like Braden Granville—who keep women like us from ever achieving our full potential, because he divides us, pits us one against the other—"

"Oh, Emmy," Caroline said, as she hurried down the stairs. "For heaven's sake, he does no such thing. I'm sure he's never even been *near* Parliament."

"Well," Emily amended, quickly. "You've got to admit that at the very least, if you go to him, now, in this manner, your reputation will be in shreds by sundown."

"Emmy," Caroline said. "Don't fuss so. I'll be home before Ma even *thinks* about dressing for supper. She'll never miss me, same as she never even knew you were here. When I come back, Bennington can lock me in again, and everything will be fine."

"Caroline"—Emily had to pause to catch her breath, even though it was Caroline who was wearing the restrictive corset, not her—"I don't understand. Why are you doing this? You know it can't lead to anything, except perhaps your ruin. So why are you doing it?"

Caroline did not hesitate. She threw open the front door, and stood in a shaft of late afternoon sunlight. "Because he asked me to," she called over her shoulder, then stepped outside, and tugged the door closed firmly behind her.

19

"If you weren't going to come," Braden Granville said, without even a good evening or how-do-you-do, "the least you could have done was let me know."

Caroline eyed him uneasily. Whatever else she might have been expecting when she'd allowed his driver to help her into the back of this tasteful curricle, it wasn't *this*. He looked so angry, like a summer storm cloud, threatening to unloose a torrent. In the dim light of the carriage—he had thoughtfully lowered the window screens, so that no one might recognize Caroline as they drove along—he looked more saturnine than ever.

Saturnine, maybe, but also undeniably appealing, in a way that Hurst, who was far better looking in the traditional sense, never had.

"I couldn't," Caroline said, carefully. "I'm being punished. I'm not even allowed to send a message with a servant. Ma instructed them all to—"

"For going into a garden with me?" His expression went from scornful to incredulous. "Am I an ogre, then?"

Caroline laughed at that. She couldn't help it. "No, much worse. You've got a reputation." When his only response to this was a grimace, she said, "Don't pretend you don't know that they call you the Lothario of London," and was quite pleased that the little throb of emotion she felt saying it—*Lothario of London*—didn't show in her voice. Just precisely what that emotion was, of course, she refused to admit to herself.

But Braden Granville made no effort at all to hide what he felt upon hearing his popular moniker. Both of his hands, lying ungloved on his thighs, clenched into fists, just for a moment. And then his fingers relaxed again.

Caroline, observing this from where she sat beside him on the softly padded seat, could only raise her eyebrows, feeling a quick wave of helplessness wash over her. The sight of those fists—so large, so uncompromisingly masculine—caused her to recall what Emily had said in her bedroom. He was from a different world, a world where fists and bullets and knives and garrotes were commonplace.

Not that Caroline thought he'd ever use those fists on *her*. But seeing them reminded her of the other name she'd heard people call him: Dead Eye.

What was she doing? What was she *doing* here? Emily was right. She was a fool. She oughtn't to be here. She ought to be with Hurst, who hadn't any other name than that, just Hurst, and occasionally, Lord Winchilsea, and whom she'd never even seen make a fist.

"So your mother," Braden Granville said, breaking in on her frantic thoughts, "locked you in your room as punishment for stepping into the Dalrymples' garden with the Lothario of London."

His voice was devoid of any sort of inflection. Still, Caroline rushed to assure him, "Well, it's only because she doesn't know you, except by reputation. Tommy talks of you, you know, almost incessantly."

"It's odd," he said, almost whimsically, "that your brother doesn't share your feelings about the immorality of my designing guns for a living, considering what one did to him."

Caroline nodded. "He's still quite keen on them. Stranger still, he's anxious to get back to school in the fall. You would think that after what he went through, Oxford would be the last place he'd ever want to see again, but he seems quite eager. He even suggested we take a weekend trip there not too long ago, though the doctor says he's not up to it. He's not supposed to be dancing, either, but that doesn't stop him."

"Do you think he wants to find the man who—" But he broke off, and only looked at his hands.

She looked up at him questioningly. "Man who what?"

"Never mind. I've instructed my driver to take us round the park. I felt we had things we needed to discuss, you and I. And this way, there won't likely be any more interruptions."

Remembering precisely what they'd been doing the last time they'd been interrupted—when Hurst had walked in on them in the garden—Caroline swallowed, and was careful not to look at his face as she said, "Yes. I wanted to speak with you, as well. I—I was going to write to you, as soon as my mother would let me send a note. You see—"

"You needn't say it," he said. There was a wealth of weariness in his tone. Caroline risked a glance at his face, and saw it turned toward hers, his dark eyes fastened onto hers with an intensity that sent the same shivers up and down her spine as that single finger he'd laid upon her. "The suit. I know you won't be able to testify—"

She was shaking her head before the words were fully out of his mouth. "Oh, no," she said. "That's not it at all. Of course I'll still . . . help you." And then she remembered her mother's warning from the night before, about how she'd sell off her horses, and bit her lip. "I might," she said, "need a place to put my horses for a while, however, if I do. How many does your stable hold? You wouldn't happen to have room for about twenty more, would you?"

The intense look he'd been giving her turned to one of confusion. "Twenty more horses?"

"They—" She shook her head again with a feeling of hopelessness. "Oh, never mind. I'm sure she didn't mean it. No, I promised to help you with Lady Jacquelyn's suit, and I still shall. Only I'm afraid I won't be able to continue with the, um, lessons anymore."

Slowly, that scarred eyebrow rose, and with it, one side of his mouth—just a corner. "Is that so," he said, in a tone that suggested he was only mildly interested in what she was saying.

"Yes," she said, firmly. "You see, it's just not going to work."

Again the disinterested tone. "You think not?"

"No. There isn't any point to it now."

Both the eyebrow and that single corner of his mouth dropped, until he was frowning at her. There was nothing disinterested in his tone when he asked, quickly, "What do you mean?"

Caroline shook her head sadly. "The pants just don't fit."

He looked confused. "What pants?"

Caroline sighed. "Hurst. You know what they say. Don't buy the pants without trying them on first. Well, I tried them on, and it turns out they don't fit after all. So there isn't very much point in continuing the lessons, is there?"

Though she was sitting a good six inches from him on that padded seat, with not even the edge of her skirt touching him, she felt him stiffen. She started to turn toward him questioningly, but a split second later, he'd swung round on the seat and grasped both her shoulders.

"*You had relations with Slater?*" he asked, in a choked voice.

Caroline stared up into his anger-darkened face, utterly bewildered by his accusation—and the fact that he seemed so upset. "Relations?" she echoed, shocked. "Of course not! I only kissed him, for heaven's sake!"

The grip on her shoulders loosened at once. All of the dark color that had come into his face drained out of it, and then he said, "My God," and released her, turning a broad shoulder upon her.

Caroline stammered, "I—I tried to kiss him the French way—

you know, the way you taught me—and he didn't seem to like it at all. He was quite put out with me about it, actually. So you see, besides the fact that the pants don't fit, they aren't working, your lessons. So what is the point?"

Beside her, Braden lifted a hand—one of those traitorous hands that had reached out so rashly and seized her a moment ago, despite the promises he'd made to himself that he would not touch her again—and ran it through his thick dark hair. What, he asked himself, *was* the point? He had been asking himself that exact same question as his mantel clock had struck the half hour, and he'd finally admitted that Caroline wasn't coming. What madness had induced him to order his carriage round and set off after her, he could not imagine.

He told himself it was because he wasn't a man used to being kept waiting. People simply did not break appointments they'd made with Braden Granville. The fact that Lady Caroline Linford had done so—without so much as a beg-your-pardon—had infuriated him. She had promised to come at four o'clock, and when she had not arrived, he had felt himself perfectly justified in going to her house to demand an explanation. . . .

But more than that, he supposed, he had come . . . to see. To see *what*, he wasn't quite certain. To see whether or not that fop of a fiancé of hers had figured out exactly what they'd been doing when he'd interrupted them the night before. To see if Caroline Linford, whom he hadn't taken for a coward, was hiding behind her mamma's skirts, afraid now, by the sensations he knew he'd roused in her.

Or maybe just to see if there were still sparks flying in those lucid eyes of hers.

If that was the case, he'd got his answer. There were sparks there, all right. Sparks and even, he fancied, a few bottle rockets, as well. Lady Bartlett could lock her daughter up for a thousand days, but she would never manage to put out the fire that shone in

222 · MEG CABOT

those deep brown eyes, eyes which reflected Caroline's every passing emotion, eyes in which, Braden felt, he could lose himself. . . .

Rallying, he said, as lightly as he could, "I feel the need to investigate this further."

Caroline, relieved that whatever passion had seized him appeared to have vanished, asked, "Investigate what?"

"This failure you cited." He was careful not to look at her lips. But nor could he look into those perceptive eyes. He settled for looking at her gloved hands, folded primly in her lap. "With your fiancé."

"Failure?" Comprehension dawned. "Oh, you mean the kiss? Well, it hardly matters. I told you, it's quite clear the pants don't fit. I can see now that . . . *that* aspect of our marriage"—she was much too embarrassed to say the word *sexual*—"will probably never be particularly good—"

If that were true, Braden said to himself, it was only because Slater was uninterested in the female sex. Or a eunuch.

"—so I intend to concentrate on other, more important things."

Braden had to look at her eyes then. He could not believe she was serious. But her steady gaze told him that indeed, she was so.

"More important than what goes on in the matrimonial bed?" he asked, incredulously. "And what things would those be?"

Caroline sighed. Really, it was vexatious, having to explain herself to this man all the time. Even more vexatious was that she didn't have to. It wasn't as if there was a lock upon the carriage door. She could open it and get out any time she cared to.

But she didn't care to. Which was the most vexatious thing of all.

"Furnishing our new household," she said, slowly. "Entertaining our friends. Hurst has quite a lot of them, you know. He's quite fond of cards—he and Tommy both—and we attend frequent card parties. I will have to reciprocate, once I'm Lady Winchilsea—"

"And that is more important to you," Braden said, woodenly. "Being Lady Winchilsea, and reciprocating card parties, than marrying a man who—"

He broke off. What was he doing? What was he *doing*?

She was glaring at him from her corner of the carriage. "Of course that isn't important to me," she said, angrily. The bottle rockets, he saw, were there in force. "How can you say such a thing? I told you why I'm marrying him."

"Because of what he did for your brother? Tell me something, Lady Caroline. If the man who'd saved your brother had been a dust picker rather than a marquis, or a one-eyed hunchback, rather than a golden-haired dandy, would you feel the same obligation to marry him?"

The bottle rockets turned suddenly into twin volcanoes. "Of course not," Caroline snapped. "I didn't agree to marry Hurst solely because of what he did for my brother. I loved him, too."

Then, as if realizing she'd said something indiscreet, she pressed her lips together, and turned her face resolutely away from him, until it was hidden behind her bonnet brim.

Feeling a sudden surge of what could only be called delight, Braden slid across the seat until their hips were touching— something which seemed to annoy Caroline, since she slid away, until she was pressed up nearly to the door.

"You *loved* him?" Braden reached out and lifted an amber curl that had escaped from her bonnet, and lay across her puffed white sleeve. "But you don't anymore?"

"I didn't say that." All he could see of her face was one smooth cheek, but it was most decidedly pink. "Of course I love him."

"But not, perhaps," Braden said, bringing the curl closer to his face, as if he wished to examine it, "the way a wife should love her husband. More, perhaps, the way a sister loves the man who saved her brother's life."

"If you say so," was Caroline's stiff response.

"But you loved him once in a different way," Braden said. He lifted the curl to his nose. Her hair smelled, as he'd known it would, of lavender. "Otherwise, you wouldn't have come to me with your interesting . . . proposal. I wonder what happened, Lady Caroline, to make you fall out of love with your fiancé."

She knew what he was thinking. She knew it as surely as she knew her name. He thought she'd fallen in love with him.

And was he really so far wrong? It was not, of course, what had *really* woken her from the stupor into which Hurst's kisses had placed her. If only she could tell him what had *really* happened to break that spell! That would surely wipe the knowing smile from his face.

Yes. And put a bullet through Hurst's.

She could not tell him. She would never tell him. Better to let him think she loved him than that he knew the truth.

Oh, how could she have done something so stupid as fall in love with Braden Granville? Because in spite of what she'd told Emily— that Braden Granville was not the grand seducer everyone thought him, but actually a very kind, thoughtful man, who had tried, at least, to say no to her when she'd first come to him with her ridiculous plan—there was no getting around the fact that he was a Lothario— *the* Lothario, actually. The Lothario of London.

She reached up and snatched the curl of hair from his fingers. "Nothing happened," she said, carefully avoiding his gaze. "I am not *not* in love with Hurst."

"But you just told me," he was swift to point out, "that the pants don't fit."

She cursed herself. Why had she opened her mouth to him about that? She tried a different tack.

"Well," she said. "Maybe it wasn't that the pants didn't fit. Maybe I just did it wrong."

When, a second later, he slipped one of his strong hands around the back of her neck, she knew she hadn't said the right thing.

"I think," he said, his deep brown eyes very steady and warm on hers, "you'd better show me what you did, so we can ascertain the source of the problem, and attempt to repair it."

Caroline was torn between an almost overwhelming desire to feel his mouth on hers once more, and a very strong suspicion that she was just some sort of cog in an elaborate wheel of manipulation he was spinning for his own entertainment. But really, when she thought about it, it was ridiculous to think he'd have any desire to seduce *her*. What could *she*— Lady Caroline Linford—ever do for someone like Braden Granville?

"It's only a kiss, Caroline," he said, chidingly.

"I know it." *Now* she'd summoned up some indignation.

"Then what are you afraid of?"

"You, turning wild again."

"Me?" He sounded wryly amused. "Wild? When did I turn wild?"

"Last night, in the Dalrymples' garden, of course."

"I wasn't a bit wild. I was a perfect gentleman."

She snorted. "A perfect gentleman who put his hand down my shimmy."

Now he was grinning, evidently heartily amused by her. "I rather got the impression you *liked* it when I did that."

"I did not," Caroline lied, primly. "And if I'm to kiss you now, you've got to promise not to do it again."

He sighed. "So very strict for someone so very young . . . and so very inexperienced. So be it, then. I promise not to put my hand down your—What was it?"

"Shimmy," Caroline said, beginning to suspect she was being made fun of, and not certain what to do about it.

"Ah, of course. I promise very faithfully not to put my hand down your shimmy this time. Now, why don't you scoot over a little closer to me?" He put an infinitesimal amount of pressure on the back of her neck.

Caroline obliged him—although scooting, with her stiff crinoline, was not entirely as easy as he'd made it sound. She managed to get near enough to him, however, on the curricle's narrow seat, so that her shoulder fit into the space beneath his arm, and her hip was again touching his—through, of course, layer upon layer of clothing, not to mention the steel bars of her crinoline.

"All right," she said, deciding swiftly that if he really was manipulating her, well, she didn't care. No man could manipulate her out of as many clothes as she happened to be wearing at that moment. "Now what?"

"Now," he said, "show me what you did to Slater."

She sighed to show she thought the whole thing very tiresome indeed, then, slipping one foot beneath her to give her more height upon the seat, tilted up her head and placed a series of featherlight kisses on Braden Granville's mouth.

Only this time, instead of keeping his mouth firmly set, the way Hurst had, Braden let his lips fall apart, just a little. Just enough for Caroline to slip in her tongue. She did so tentatively, perfectly conscious of what had occurred the last time she'd kissed him.

But when seconds passed, and nothing happened—nothing at all—Caroline pulled back her head and eyed him, uneasily.

"I'm doing it wrong, aren't I?" she asked. No wonder. No wonder Hurst had looked the way he had!

Braden's eyes had been closed. Now the lids drifted slowly upward, and she was surprised to see his normally sharp-eyed gaze looking a bit distant.

"I'm not sure," he said, in a voice that wasn't quite steady. "You had better try again."

Caroline nodded, and, slipping her other foot beneath her for balance, so that she was now on her knees beside him on the narrow bench, went back to work. This time, she reached up and laid a hand upon the back of his neck, for better support as she strained to reach his lips.

And when she began her second assault upon his mouth, she had better luck. The fingers he'd placed at her nape tightened a little. Caroline thought this a good sign, and proceeded to kiss him with more energy, attempting an even bolder approach with her tongue, thrusting it quite confidently into his mouth.

She was in no way prepared for the violence of his reaction.

The tip of her tongue had barely flicked his before she found herself thrown completely off her balance by the sudden introduction of his other arm wrapping around her waist. Crinoline rings collapsed and her skirt was crushed as he lifted her from the bench and deposited her upon his lap, her legs straddling his. Alarmed, Caroline tried to pull away, but he'd kept one hand on her neck, neatly preventing escape. Caroline only had time to be thankful that the afternoon dress she wore was a particularly high-necked one before she became conscious of the pressure of his mouth on hers, and felt that all too familiar melting sensation once again, and was lost.

20

*R*eally, but it had to be sinful, the way he made her feel. As if there were just the two of them in the whole world. As if there was nowhere more important she had to go, nothing more important she had to do, than sit inside this curricle and lazily explore this man's mouth, and let him do the same to her.

And yet he wasn't doing the same to her. Caroline realized too late that while she had been busy enjoying the sensual plundering he was performing of her mouth, a plundering of quite a different kind was occurring beneath those very steel bands she'd counted on to protect her. Braden Granville's hand—the one that wasn't behind her neck—had slipped beneath her crinoline and somehow found the ribbons that held her pantaloons closed.

Caroline tried to protest as she felt the bow, in which those ribbons had been neatly tied, tighten suddenly, then spring apart. She tried to say stop. Really, she did. But it was just so . . . difficult. And not only because of his tongue being in her mouth. It was because . . . well, she didn't want him to stop.

Still, it wasn't right, this business with her pantaloons. Putting his hand down her shimmy had been one thing, but *this* . . . .

"Stop squirming, Caroline," he drew his head back from hers

to say, abruptly. "The hoops from your crinoline keep sticking me in the ribs."

"What are you *doing* down there?" Caroline demanded. "You can't *do* that."

"Of course I can. I'm trying to show you something. You *asked* me—"

"I asked you to tell me whether or not I had kissed Hurst right."

Even as she spoke, her lips felt pleasantly tingly from the bruising manner he'd returned that kiss. She had kissed him right. She knew she had kissed him right. The person there was something wrong with, she'd decided, was Hurst, who had never kissed her like that, nor expressed the slightest interest in the bow that held her pantaloons closed.

"I didn't ask you," she pointed out, "to *undress* me."

"I'm not undressing you," he said. "Kiss me again."

"No, not unless you move your—"

He silenced her by doing some kissing of his own, bringing her face up hard against his with the hand he'd kept anchored at the back of her neck, and fairly devouring her mouth, it seemed, with his. Caroline, wanting not so much to pull away as to *want* to pull away, was horrified to find herself kissing him right back, hungering after his lips and tongue with as much enthusiasm as he appeared to hunger after hers.

Well, and how could she be expected to help herself? Here she was in his arms—in his *lap*, actually—surrounded by him, *enveloped* by him. He was all she could see, all she could touch, all she could taste. His breathing—somewhat ragged—was all she could hear, if you didn't count the not-very-steady pounding of his heart, which she could not only hear but feel, even through the material of his coat, and the high-necked bodice of her gown. All she could smell was the rich, masculine scent of him, mingling odors of soap and clean linen and, more faintly, gunpowder, a smell she was sure, years and years from now, would always bring back memories of

Braden Granville. It was ridiculous—totally ridiculous—to imagine that something like that—the smell of gunpowder—would make her cling to him even harder, kiss him with even more wild abandon, but that's exactly what happened. She couldn't explain it. She didn't care to explain it. There it was, and that was all.

And then she figured out exactly what his hand was doing in her pantaloons . . . figured it out when that hand brushed—and not at all accidentally, she was quite certain—a certain part of her that had lately been behaving very strangely indeed, tending to go damp quite a bit in his presence, most especially when he kissed her. It was damp now, damp and extremely sensitive, so sensitive that when his fingers brushed it, Caroline's back arched reflexively, and she tightened her fingers around his neck, and let out a murmur against his mouth. . . .

But not of protest. Not of protest at all.

As if this were a sign for which he'd been waiting, Braden let his hand slide there again. Only this time, instead of brushing casually against her, his fingers pressed there with the most definite of intentions.

And that caused an even greater sensation. Caroline, who had hardly ever touched *herself* there, much less allowed anyone else to do so, was unprepared for her immediate and very physical reaction. Instantly, she found herself flooded with longing, and that longing seemed to be rooted in a desire to press herself even more firmly against those hard, calloused fingers. So firmly, in fact, that it seemed as if one or two of those fingers might actually have slipped inside her. . . .

And *she didn't even care*. Quite suddenly, Lady Caroline Linford had been transformed—by the merest touch of a man's fingers—into a wanton thing, who could think of nothing but . . .

Well, *this*.

But who could blame her? It felt so heavenly, having his hand there, and his lips on hers, and his other hand, oh, his other hand had slipped away from her neck now, and had settled over one of her breasts, and it was too bad she was wearing so many clothes, because it felt divine, the way he was cupping her breast, but there was all that *material* in the way. In the future when she went out with him she'd have to remember to wear nothing but short sleeves and her lowest necklines and . . .

What was he doing *now?* Petting her, it seemed like. And it felt so good, the way he was petting her, so sweetly and so tenderly, only there was still that *longing*, that feeling that if he'd only put a little more pressure *there* . . .

And quite suddenly, he did.

And Caroline's world, which had been spinning quite steadily out of control, seemed to explode into a thousand shimmering bits. It was a little like the sensation she experienced every time she slid into an extremely hot bath—for a few seconds, her entire body, from the top of her scalp to the soles of her feet, felt as if it was on fire. It was almost unbearable, the sensation, but perfectly delightful, too. And, lost in the throes of it, she jerked her lips from his and clutched at his shirtfront convulsively, unable to keep from crying out. . . .

And then, just as suddenly, the fire was out, and she felt as if she were shivering all over, like something newly born.

Shivering and completely limp, dazed by it all, she slumped forward until she fell against him, panting.

"What," she wanted to know, when she could bring herself to speak, "was *that*?"

His voice wasn't so steady either. "Your lesson for the day," he replied.

"Lesson?" she demanded. "Is that what you call it?"

But she couldn't summon up any real indignation, since she felt so deliciously lethargic. If only, she was thinking, she could sit like this forever, with her cheek upon his shoulder and her arms curled around his neck, listening to his heartbeat, and the sounds of the horses' hooves as they went round and round the park. . . .

232 · MEG CABOT

A sound that, even as it was registering on her consciousness, abruptly stopped.

Braden moved his hand from between her thighs.

"Get up," he said. "You're home."

She raised her head to blink at him. "Home?" she said, stupidly.

"Yes." Even as she sat there, staring at him, he was putting her clothing back in order, neatly tying the ribbon to her pantaloons back into place, and jerking her crinoline hoops down again. "We've been gone over an hour. We wouldn't want to raise your mamma's suspicions now, would we? She might lock you in your room again, and that would adversely affect tomorrow's lesson plan."

Caroline shook her head confusedly. What was he talking about? Didn't he realize what he had done? Taken her to the heights of heaven, that was what. And now he expected her just to go *home*? To walk in her front door as if nothing had happened? As if he hadn't, as far as she was concerned, touched her soul?

"But—" she began.

"Here." He plucked at a curl that had slipped out from beneath her bonnet, doubtlessly when she'd thrown her head back in ecstasy. "You need to fix your . . ." He made a gesture around her face. "Yourself. Your hair has gotten all . . ."

Mechanically, Caroline reached up, and began tucking her hair back where it belonged. "But I don't understand," she said, as she tucked. "I only asked you to tell me whether or not I was kissing correctly."

"Oh, yes," he said. "I believe you've quite mastered kissing. That's why I moved on to the next step."

"The next step? Is *that* what that was?"

"Well, we might have skipped a few in between," he said, and there was, she thought, something distinctly odd in his expression. "But that wasn't your fault. We'll go back to them, one of these days."

"But—" Caroline shook her head, trying to clear it, and nearly undid all the hair tucking. "But you were supposed to be teaching me how to . . . to . . ." She broke off, not sure how to put into words what she meant.

He looked down at her, questioningly, one eyebrow raised. But since it wasn't his scarred eyebrow, she figured she hadn't angered him. Suddenly, she knew exactly what she meant.

"You were supposed to be teaching me how to give a man pleasure," she said, all in a rush. "You weren't supposed to be pleasuring *me*."

Up went the scarred eyebrow.

"Is that so?" he said . . . mildly enough, she supposed, for someone who looked so . . . well, intimidating.

"Yes." Sadly, the lovely glowing feeling she'd been experiencing was growing faint. "How am I supposed to learn anything about making love to a man when all you ever do is make love to *me*?"

For some reason, he seemed to find that amusing. Both corners of his mouth were twitching as he took her by the waist and lifted her from his lap, placing her onto the seat beside him once again.

"That," he said, his voice rich with an emotion she could not identify, "is the first time I have ever heard that particular complaint from anyone I've—how did you put it? Oh, yes. Pleasured." He could barely say the word, he was trying so hard not to laugh. "Go home, Caroline," he said, leaning down to give her a distinctly unromantic peck on the forehead. "We'll see to my pleasure next time. Go, before the esteemed Lady Bartlett discovers you've gone—"

Caroline didn't hesitate. She slipped from the curricle, and, after pausing just a fraction of a second to adjust her skirts, which had gotten woefully tangled, ran fleetly up the steps to her front door. . . .

And only then realized what he'd said.

Next time. They would see to his pleasure *next time*.

But there could be no next time! Hadn't she explained to him that the lessons could not continue?

She was about to return to the carriage to make sure he understood that there could be no next time when, to her consternation, the front door was wrenched open by a tight-faced Thomas.

"Caroline," he said, urgently, slipping a hand beneath her arm.

Caroline threw a hasty glance over her shoulder. The curricle hadn't moved. There was still time—

"Just a moment, Tommy," she said. "There's something I've got to—"

Tommy's hand tightened on her arm. "You've got to talk to Ma," Thomas said. "Please. I'm begging you."

"Ma?" No! The curricle was going away! Slowly, but surely, heading down the street.

"She's having one of her fits," was Thomas's surprising reply. And Caroline forgot all about Braden Granville, and swung the full strength of her astonished gaze upon her brother.

"One of her fits?" she echoed.

And then they were inside the house, Caroline undoing her bonnet strings as Thomas closed the door behind them.

"She noticed," Caroline said, trepidatiously. "She noticed I was gone, didn't she?"

"No," Thomas said. "It's nothing to do with you, for a change. It's only that I told her . . . well, I told her this afternoon that I'm going back to school. I'm going back the day after tomorrow, just for the weekend. And she went mad."

Caroline's eyebrows flew up. "Well, I can see why. You know what the doctor said, Tommy. You might feel better, but your wound's not completely healed yet, and you're supposed to be resting as much as possible—not that you ever do it. What did you expect Ma to say—Go with my blessings, son?"

"Will you talk to her, Caro? I know she'll listen to you."

Standing in the marble-floored foyer, Caroline stared up at her brother. For a long time, she'd been the taller of the two, until one memorable summer he'd sprung up four inches in three months. Suddenly, he'd been able to best her at all the games she was used to winning.

When word had come that he'd been shot, Caroline had thought that the bottom had dropped out of her world. If he had died, and left her alone, alone with their mother . . .

She would not have been able to stand it. She loved her mother dearly, but without Tommy . . .

Without Tommy, she'd have no one.

"Why is it so important to you to go back, Tommy?" she asked him. In the late afternoon light slanting through the long, narrow windows that bordered the front door, she saw that there was color in his face, freckles across his nose, because despite the doctor's orders, he would not stay inside. "School isn't even in session right now. None of your friends will be there."

She saw his tanned fingers ball into fists, and she was put in mind of another pair of fists she'd happened to observe as closely, just a half hour before.

"There's just something," Tommy said, "that I have to do there. I've been waiting and waiting—and now I think I'm well enough. Please, Caro. Go and talk to her. I need the carriage, and some pocket money. Just enough for a day or two."

"What?" Something in her brother's voice awoke the elder sister in her, ever watchful for mischief—or worse, recklessness. "What do you have to do there?"

"It isn't something I feel particularly comfortable discussing with my sister," he said, with a smirk.

Caroline eyed him. A girl? One of his masters' daughters, perhaps? She could only hope. She prayed it wasn't some blowzy barmaid—though how could it be, if what he'd said that day was true, about never having tried on any trousers before?

"It's just something that I've got to do, all right?" Thomas ran a hand through his overlong hair, making the ale-colored strands stand on end. "Something I've got to take care of. That's all."

No. She narrowed her gaze. It wasn't a girl at all. She couldn't say how she knew, but she did, quite suddenly.

"Tommy," she said. "Does Hurst know you're going?"

Something tightened in her brother's face. He seemed to go pale beneath his tan.

"No," he said. "And you're not to tell him, Caro. This isn't something I want to drag Hurst into. It wasn't his fault."

Her eyebrows went up at that. "What wasn't his fault? Whatever are you talking about, Tommy?"

He glared at her. "You mustn't say anything about my going to Hurst. Promise me, Caro."

Caroline shook her head. There was only one reason her brother would wish to go to Oxford and not tell his good friend Hurst. Because Hurst would try to talk him out of it.

"You can't ask me to keep a secret from the man I'm to marry," Caroline said, firmly. "If you aren't taking Hurst with you, I don't want you going, either. Not alone. Not after—"

"Caro, you don't understand—"

"No, I don't. I won't tell Hurst. But I'm not talking Ma into letting you go." Caroline turned her back on him, and started up the stairs to her room. "And don't bother asking me for the money, either. I won't loan you so much as a ha'penny. You're up to no good, I can tell. You had better just stay here."

Tommy stood at the bottom of the stairs. She could feel his gaze boring into the back of her neck as she took each step, but she didn't care. She kept her shoulders squared, and her head held high. She didn't like fighting with her brother—not now that they were fully grown. But what was she to do? He would go. She knew him, and just as soon as he could scrape together enough money for a train ticket, if he couldn't get their mother to loan him the carriage, he'd be gone.

Her first instinct was to tell Hurst, only how could she, when he had asked her not to?

But *why*? Was Tommy finally realizing what Caroline had? That Hurst was not the saintly creature he'd seemed when they'd first come to know him? Oh, he loved Tommy. There was no doubt about that. But now that the two of them were about to become brothers in truth, did Tommy suspect that his friend did not love his sister as well as he ought? Did he, she wondered, know about Jacquelyn? Surely not, or he'd have said something to his friend, to Caroline—she couldn't believe that her own brother would knowingly allow her to marry a philanderer.

Or was it simply that Tommy thought Hurst, too, would try to stop him from going if he were made aware of his plans?

It was madness, this decision to travel when he was still so weak—and Caroline knew that, despite his assertions otherwise, Tommy was not yet whole. He still slept every morning until well past ten, her brother who'd always been up and out of the house before the clock struck eight. And she saw him wince, occasionally, whenever his side was jostled in a crowded ballroom. He could not well command a horse, nor yet dance more than one set in a single evening. Even badminton seemed a strain sometimes.

No, he was not yet strong enough to embark on whatever mission this was that he'd assigned himself. But if he would not listen to the doctor's words of warning, or his mother's protestations, or Caroline's misgivings, however was she to induce him not to go?

It wasn't until she was back in her own room—Bennington obligingly locked her in again, after telling her that Lady Emily had finally given up waiting on her, and gone home—and she spied the piece of foolscap on her dressing table that she remembered Braden Granville.

And just like that, she knew what she had to do.

21

*H*er missive arrived at his office the next morning with the very first post, the feminine cursive with which it had been addressed setting it apart from the business letters and legal correspondence that arrived at the same time. Braden noticed it the minute he sat down at his desk, and quickly plucked it from the pile, examining the small, cream-colored envelope into which it had been folded. He recognized the handwriting at once as Caroline's. Her script was scrupulously small, each letter formed with care, as if she were still striving for good marks in penmanship.

He sat studying the envelope, strangely reluctant to open it, and angry at himself for being so. He knew what it was, of course. What else could it be? Especially after what had happened between them in his carriage the day before. What had he been thinking? What in God's name had he been thinking?

He hadn't been thinking at all. That was the problem. Something came over him when Caroline Linford was anywhere within his proximity. It was unlike anything that had ever happened to him before. Always before with women, he'd been able to keep cool control over his actions, his emotions. The wooing of an attractive female was a game, a game which he'd mastered at a young age. Or thought he had, at least. Lady Caroline Linford had showed him otherwise.

Why was it that the one woman whom he most longed to impress was the same woman who drove him to such acts of supreme idiocy? What had happened in the carriage was a prime example. What had he been thinking, mauling her about like that, as if she were some doxy he'd picked up off the docks? Caroline Linford was a lady—one of the only women he'd ever met whom he felt truly met the definition of the word. And yet it seemed that every time he got within two feet of her, his only thought was of removing as many articles of her clothing as was possible in the limited time they had together. What sort of way was that to treat a lady?

It was no small wonder she wanted to sever all ties to him. He thoroughly deserved her reproof. She was a complete innocent, guileless in her understanding of the male half of the species, and he had taken advantage of that. It was unforgivable, the way he'd treated her.

And yet he hadn't been able to help himself, any more than he was capable of stopping himself from breathing. Perhaps it was just as well she was putting an end to it. If he could not control his baser instincts in her presence, he did not deserve to have her. Maybe it was true, what Jacquelyn had said: One could take the man from the slums, but never the slums from the man.

Deciding that, no matter how eloquently she pleaded, he was not going to allow it to end this way—with a letter—he ran a finger beneath the wax seal that held Caroline's letter closed, and unfolded it. *Dear Mr. Granville,* he read. Well, of course. She'd yet to call him Braden.

But what came after the salutation was not at all what Braden had expected. He read Caroline's careful script all the way to the highly impersonal closing— *Most sincerely yours, C. Linford*—then dragged his gaze back to the top of the page, and read it again, certain he'd missed something.

But he hadn't. There was nothing reproachful here, nothing in the least indicating that she wished never to see him again. Not a word of condemnation. Nothing bitter, nothing biting. Instead of recriminations came a request. A most unusual request, but one that Braden could easily accommodate.

He took out a sheet of paper and began at once to pen a reply that would arrive, if he hurried, by return post.

It pleased him far more than it should, the thought that he might be able to do something for her—something no one else but he could do. It was sickening, this weakness he had for her. He was almost glad Weasel was holed up with his bad leg: he would have been disgusted at his employer's ingratiating behavior—the more so because it was so uncharacteristic. Braden Granville did not fall over himself in an effort to win any woman.

Until now.

But he couldn't help himself. One glimpse into those chestnut-colored eyes, and all the steely composure for which he was known was lost.

It was a little after twelve in the afternoon when he arrived, sitting tall in the saddle of an even-tempered roan, his gaze sweeping the sandy track upon which only a few gentlemen were left taking their morning exercise. Rotten Row was most crowded with equestrian traffic early in the day, but Caroline had made it clear in her letter that since his accident, her brother was rarely out of the house by midday. The late hour, however, would not keep the Earl of Bartlett from putting in his appearance at the park. He was determined not to let his injury keep him from all of the rites and traditions of the beau monde that he had come to know since coming in to his title.

And, Braden saw, after a few minutes of searching, there he was, taking it very easy on a fine looking gray. He was accompanied by a middle-aged groom, but whether this escort was not particularly to the earl's liking, or the groom was of a taciturn disposition, there appeared to be no conversation taking place between the two men, and the earl, in fact, rode a little ahead, his face turned toward the midday sun.

Braden gave his mount a gentle taste of his heels, and the mare broke into an obliging trot. He was soon neck and neck with the earl, and eased back on the reins.

"Good afternoon, my lord," he said, gravely.

The boy threw him a startled glance. When he realized who it was who'd greeted him, the earl turned a deep red—Braden saw his crimson cheeks from the corner of his eye. He was startlingly like his sister in the easy way he blushed.

"Gran—I mean, *Mr.* Granville," Thomas Linford cried. "Oh, I say. I've never seen you here before."

"No," Braden said, resignedly. "I haven't much time for riding."

"Of course." Thomas nodded. "You're needed at your business, I imagine, all the time."

"Quite." Braden turned then and looked at the groom, who was riding just behind them, with his head ducked, as if by doing so, he could stop his ears from overhearing his master's conversation. "Do you think you and I might have a word in private, my lord?"

The boy nodded again, and turned in his saddle to instruct the groom to wait for him. He would ride on a little with Mr. Granville, then return when their business had been conducted.

The groom assented, and Braden and the earl rode on in uneasy silence—uneasy on the part of the earl, since it was plain to see the boy was bursting to ask what Braden wanted, and Braden because he could not quite see how he could introduce the topic he wished to discuss without betraying Caroline, who'd asked him in her letter not to let on how he'd discovered what he knew.

Finally, upon passing a fellow who had obviously imbibed too much the night before, and had fallen asleep upon his mount, to circle round and round the park until his horse either tired or decided to take it upon itself to find its way home,

Braden remembered something, and said, "I used to come here quite often as a boy."

"To the Row, sir?" Thomas's voice conveyed his astonishment without, Braden was certain, the boy's meaning it to. "I mean—"

"I know what you mean. I didn't come to ride, of course. I hadn't a horse until I was well into my twenties. But my friends and I used to come here and look for fellows like that one back there."

"The drunken one, sir?"

"Yes, that one. They were quite easy targets. We'd wait until they passed close to a tree, and when no one was looking, we'd knock them from their mounts and take their wallets." Braden spoke as tonelessly as if he were describing a chemical experiment. "A dangerous way to make a living, but back then, we didn't know any other."

Thomas rode beside him in silence. Braden studied the boy's profile. Except for his coloring, Braden could not trace much likeness to his sister. His features were sharply drawn, most likely as a result of the weight he'd lost after his injury. Caroline's face was much softer, her nose not aquiline at all, but turned up at the end, her cheekbones high enough to give her fine eyes an upward tilt at the corners, like a cat's, without making her appear haughty in the least.

"But," Thomas said, at length, "you never shot them, did you? These men you robbed, I mean."

"Of course not." Braden turned his attention toward guiding his horse around a particularly wide stretch of track that had gone to mud. "None of us owned guns. They cost too dear. That is why—" He grunted as his mare misstepped, her hoof sinking into the deep mud, and momentarily lost her balance. A second later, she had righted herself, and seemed embarrassed by the mishap, giving an indignant whinny before moving on again. "—I find myself wondering about your story concerning the footpad."

He saw the boy's chin slide forward, and instantly recognized the stubborn gesture, as it mirrored exactly the one that appeared on his sister's face when she was at her most intractable.

"Are you calling me a liar, sir?" Thomas asked, hotly.

"Of course not. I am merely suggesting that the story you told your mother and sister about the footpad might have been a fabrication to hide the truth about how you came to be shot." Braden was careful to keep his tone neutral. Not judging. Merely stating a fact. "I don't fault you in the least for the lie. Had I a mother and sister, I would have told them the exact same thing. For they would not know—as you and I both do—that footpads rarely have access to pistols. If they do manage to find one, they generally sell it—for even as scrap, a pistol will usually fetch more than most thieves can make in a year."

Thomas was silent, but not sullenly so. He was listening to Braden intently, and seemed to be debating something within himself.

"The person who shot you," Braden went on, "was not a footpad. For not only did he have ready access to a pistol, but he was skilled with the weapon. He'd had practice, and a good deal of it. Not only that, but he respected his weapon, keeping it in good repair. If he had not, you would not be alive today, for the shot was clean, if a little low. I assume he was aiming for the heart."

Thomas murmured, "My foot slipped. I was going over the wall, and my foot slipped—"

"Good thing, too," Braden said. "For if you had held steady, we would not be having this discussion."

"It was—" The earl appeared to have drifted far away from Rotten Row—not physically, but in his mind. He murmured, "It burned. When it hit me. It flung me back, and then it burned. And then when I woke up, it hurt. More than anything I've ever known."

"Yes," Braden said, flatly. "It does, doesn't it?"

That brought him back. He flung a surprised look in Braden's direction. "You—*you*'ve been shot before?"

"Many a time," Braden said, evenly. "One does not become known as the Lothario of London without incurring the wrath of the occasional husband. But I was never stupid enough," he added, "to be run down by a footpad."

And with that, Thomas gave it up.

"It wasn't a footpad," he said, scornfully. "It was a duke."

"A *duke*?" Braden could not have been more surprised if Thomas had said he'd shot himself. "Were you dueling?"

"No. Cards." Thomas's voice was filled with scorn. "A fixed game, I'm sure of it. I called him a cheat. And so he followed me home and shot me, I suppose so I wouldn't tell anyone about the fact that the game was fixed."

"Only he failed," Braden said. "Because the marquis found you."

"Found me?" Thomas let out a bitter laugh. "Not hardly. He'd been following me. He suspected the duke might be out for my blood, and he—"

Braden's tone sharpened. "Lord Winchilsea was playing as well?"

"Of course. He's the one who let me in on the game. Highest stakes in Oxford, he said. He didn't say they'd be *this* high, though." He touched the place the bullet had gone through with a wry expression. "He hadn't any idea the cards were marked, of course."

Braden Granville felt a sudden chill, even though the day was fine. Someone had walked over his grave. At least, that's how he remembered his mother explaining the sensation.

"The cards were marked?" he asked, in a wooden voice. "You're sure of it?"

"Yes. It was difficult to see—they kept the lights low. But if you squinted and stared long enough, you could see, plain as day, the mark in the design on the back—"

"The Duke," Braden said.

"Well, that's what he said he was, only I've met dukes before, and this one—"

"Not *a* duke," Braden said, quickly. "*The* Duke."

"Right. That's what he called himself. You know him?"

Braden shook his head. When Caroline had written to him, asking if he'd be willing to try to talk her brother out of going back to Oxford for the weekend, he had never imagined this. . . .

"I know him," Braden said, grimly. "Thomas, you must tell me the truth now. Does he know that you're alive? The Duke? You haven't communicated with him, have you, since he shot you? Or anyone else who might know him?"

"No," the earl said, looking bewildered. "Just Hurst. Only he said I wasn't to tell anyone about . . . well, about what had happened. He's the one who came up with the idea about footpads. I suppose he'll be put out with me when he finds I've told you, but you're—"

"He's quite right," Braden said. "You mustn't say a word—not a word, Thomas—to anyone." He shook his head wonderingly. "It's a miracle they haven't discovered it yet," he murmured.

"What?" Thomas leaned forward in his saddle, though it was clearly not easy for him to do so, with his wound still not completely healed. "What did you say?"

Braden wheeled his mare around and urged her forward until she stood nose to nose with Thomas's mount. Then he said, in a low and urgent voice, "Thomas, I know this man, The Duke. His real name is Seymour Hawkins. He used to operate an illegal gambling hall in the Dials. He bribed the local constabulary there to turn a blind eye to it . . . until a new man, an honest man, was appointed chief constable, and wouldn't accept Hawkins's blood money. Hawkins doesn't take kindly to honest men, Thomas. He cut out the constable's tongue for calling him a liar and a cheat, and gouged out his eyes for looking at him while he did it."

Thomas stared up at Braden with a mixture of fascination and horror on his face. "Truly?" he asked, looking suddenly far younger than his nineteen years.

"Truly," Braden said. "The crime was so brutal, it garnered a good deal of attention from the press, and The Duke became a wanted man. He was forced to leave London. If he discovers that you are still alive, Thomas—if you go to Oxford—he'll see that you are permanently dispatched this time. I know it as surely as I am looking at you now. You do not cross The Duke."

Thomas said, in a voice he obviously meant to be haughty, but which came out sounding only petulant, "I cannot let a man shoot at me and get away with it. I am an earl. I cannot show such cowardice. I have my pride, sir. Now that I am well enough, I must go to him and demand satisfaction—"

"Damn your pride," Braden said. "Think of your sister, boy. She would sooner have you alive and humbled than dead and vindicated."

A scowl broke out across the young earl's face. "You seem to know quite a bit about my sister's feelings." His tone was hotly accusing.

"I will not deny," Braden said, in a wooden tone, after a moment of silence, "that I admire your sister."

"She is engaged to be married," Thomas said, quickly.

"Indeed." Braden spoke again without inflection of any kind. "And to a man who is responsible for getting you shot."

"That isn't so!" Color flooded the boy's cheeks. "Hurst is the one who saved me. I would have died if it hadn't been for his efforts."

"If it hadn't been for his *efforts*," Braden said, not quite so tonelessly now, "you wouldn't have been shot in the first place. How is it that you are so blind you cannot see that? That bullet caught you in the chest, not the eyes."

Thomas said, shakily, "Hurst didn't know. He told me a thousand times he didn't know the game was rigged. And I believe him!"

"Evidently," Braden said, the fury burning within him so hot that his mare felt it, and began to dance nervously. But it still didn't show in his voice. "Evidently you believe him well enough to entrust to him your only sister. I admit I don't think I could be so easy, knowing my sister was to wed a man who associates freely with the likes of Seymour Hawkins."

"I would sooner see her wed to him"—Thomas, for all his bluster, sounded very much as if he might start crying—"than to the Lothario of London!"

"Then you can rest easy." Braden realized he'd made the boy fractious. He hadn't set out to do so. But hearing the truth about Hurst had set his teeth on edge. "For she has no intention of breaking off her engagement to the marquis. But if you were any kind of man, my lord, you would tell her the truth. She has a right to know exactly what sort of fellow she's getting for a husband."

"I can't tell her," Thomas said, looking horrified. "If Caro found out I was gambling, she'd . . . well, I don't know what she'd do. Tell Ma, I wouldn't doubt. And she'd cut me off."

"I don't have a sister," Braden said, stiffly, "but if I did, I can assure you that my fortune would not be worth more to me than her happiness."

"Caroline loves Hurst," Thomas assured him, with a confidence Braden was not convinced he actually felt about the matter. "Just as he loves her. He's a good man. He'll take care of her. I'd stake my life upon it."

"You may have to," Braden said.

"What does that mean?" The earl's voice rose an octave. "I say, just what do you mean by that, Granville?"

Braden said only, "Swear you won't go back to Oxford."

Thomas said, "I'll do no such thing."

"Swear you won't go back, or I'll tell your sister the true story of how you were shot."

The chin slid out again. "You *wouldn't*."

"I would. I *will*, unless you swear to me you won't go anywhere near Oxford, and The Duke."

Thomas stared sullenly down at his hands. "I swear it, then," he said.

Braden's lips curled, but not in satisfaction.

Please tell my brother he mustn't go, Caroline had written in her letter to him that morning. *I don't know why it's so important to him to return to Oxford—he says there's something he must do there. But he is not as well as he thinks he is. Please tell him not to go. He'll listen to you. He thinks of you as the Great Granville. He will do whatever you say, I'm sure of it.*

But that wasn't so. The Earl of Bartlett would not do as he said. Oh, he wouldn't go back to Oxford—Braden was fairly sure of that now. But he would never tell Caroline the truth about the man she was marrying.

And he had just sworn he would not tell her either.

22

"Don't slouch so, Caroline. Pull your shoulders back."

Caroline, standing on a footstool in the center of the mirrored room, pulled her shoulders back.

"I don't know," her mother said. "It doesn't look right, but I can't say why."

Caroline looked down at the frothy white confection that threatened to engulf her. She knew precisely why the wedding gown didn't look right on her.

Caroline lifted her gaze to the reflection she saw peering back at her from nearly every direction. The girl on the pedestal in the mirror was not Caroline Linford. She had already decided that. The girl on the pedestal was someone who looked like Caroline Linford, but couldn't, of course, actually be Caroline Linford, because Caroline Linford was no longer chaste, and had no business putting on white wedding dresses.

At least, she didn't *think* she was chaste anymore. Did it count when a man put his finger in you? She thought it probably did, but she wasn't certain, and there wasn't actually anyone she could ask.

"Stand up *straight*, Caroline," her mother said again, sounding exasperated.

Caroline, already standing as straight as she could, stuck out her chest, and promptly caused the seamstress to prick herself with a basting needle.

"I'm so sorry," Caroline gasped, stooping down to lay a hand upon the girl's back. "Are you all right?"

"Caroline," her mother snapped, "stay away from her. Can't you see she's bleeding? Do you want to get blood on your wedding dress? Is that what you want? Your original Worth design wedding dress, ruined by a bleeding seamstress?"

Caroline straightened again, and looked down pityingly at the seamstress, who was sucking on her finger. "I *am* sorry," she said again.

"Never mind her, Caroline," Lady Bartlett said. "Violet? This box is empty. See if Mr. Worth has any more." Lady Bartlett handed her maid a box that had once contained bonbons, and the maid glided quickly from the room in search of more.

"I didn't like to say anything in front of Violet," Lady Bartlett said, not seeming to mind saying it in front of the anonymous seamstress instead. "But I did want to ask you—has Tommy said anything more to you about this absurd desire of his to go to Oxford this weekend?"

Caroline felt herself turning red. Incredible. Even a round-about reminder of Braden Granville, like her mother's mention of Tommy, made her blush.

Well, and what kind of girl would she be if she didn't blush? After what she had let him do in that carriage—and then the bold-faced way she'd sent him that letter this morning! Why, only a hussy of the lowest order would let a man do to her the things she'd let him do, then turn around and ask him to do her such a personal favor, as well. What must Braden Granville think of her?

She could not tell by his response to her note. Its tone had been perfectly impersonal. He had stated merely that he would be only too happy to provide the Lady Caroline with whatever aid he could.

Then he'd gone on to say that he looked forward to the day's "lesson"—and Caroline had realized, with a sinking feeling, that she'd forgotten all about his parting words as he'd let her out of his carriage the day before. He meant them to go on with the arrangement, even though she'd told him there was no longer any point to it.

And though she ought to have written back at once, reminding him that she no longer held him under any obligation to fulfill his part of the bargain, she did not. Instead, she'd opened her jewelry box and removed the false bottom, and added his letter to the notes she'd received from him the day before, putting them where no snooping eyes were ever likely to discover them.

Four o'clock. She would see him again at four o'clock. Oh, she was a wicked, wicked thing! She had no right, no right at all, to be standing here dressed in white.

"He's said nothing to me," Caroline said. "But then I haven't seen him since he went on his morning ride."

"His morning ride," Lady Bartlett said, indignantly. "He isn't supposed to be riding, and he knows it."

"He goes gently, Mother," Caroline said.

"He oughtn't go at all," Lady Bartlett said. "The doctor said so." She sighed. "He hasn't said anything more to me about this Oxford business, either. When I asked Tommy just before he went out, he told me to—"

Something in her mother's voice caused Caroline to glance in her direction. "To what?"

"To mind my own business!" Lady Bartlett's color was high. "Imagine it! His own mother! And he tells me to mind my own business! Not only that, but he called me . . ." She dropped her voice to a whisper. *"Fatty!"*

Caroline, who'd stooped to hear her properly, knit her brow. "I beg your pardon?"

"Fatty! 'Mind your own business, fatty,' he said. His exact words. I nearly fainted on the spot, Caroline."

Caroline had to try very hard not to laugh out loud. "I'm so sorry, Ma," she said. "But I'm sure he didn't mean it—"

Violet returned, looking regretful. "I apologize, my lady," she said. "But I couldn't find Mr. Worth. They say he's with another client in the next room."

"Another client?" Lady Bartlett's lovely face turned a shade pinker. "Mr. Worth takes more than one appointment at a time?"

The seamstress took her finger from her mouth and said, in a heavy French accent, "Monsieur Worth is a very busy man, Madame. If he did not take more than one client at a time, no one would ever get an appointment at all—"

Lady Bartlett cut her off. "I specifically made an appointment for my daughter's final wedding gown fitting for today. We have no intention of waiting—"

"Oh, there will be no waiting, Madame," the French girl assured her. "If Madame and Mademoiselle will step this way, I will show you some lace that has only just arrived, all the way from Vienna. Perhaps Mademoiselle still requires lace, for her veil?"

Seeing her mother's dark expression, Caroline said, "I'll go. You stay here, Mother. I'll be right back."

Lady Bartlett said threateningly, "If her dress is damaged while she's rummaging about out there, I shall expect Mr. Worth to repair it without cost."

"Of course, Madame," the French seamstress said, and she led Caroline through a narrow door, into a pleasant room filled with long tables, across which were lain yard after yard of differently patterned lace.

It was the lace that did it.

The gown hadn't done it. Standing there in all of that white froth, she had merely mused at the irony of it. But the lace . . . the lace for her veil. That somehow brought home the reality of it all.

The lace. There was so much of it. Flowered lace, lace with heart patterns in it, lace as delicate as cobwebs. How many girls, Caroline wondered, had stood at this table and fingered this lace? Hopeful girls. Happy girls. Probably not many had stood before it feeling as she did, as if she might burst into tears at any moment.

It was when she saw the lace that she knew. She pictured herself lifting the gossamer stuff from her face, turning to the man with whom she'd just pledged to spend the rest of her life, raising her lips to meet his in joyful union. . . .

That was when the vision dissolved. Because the lips she'd pictured kissing were not Hurst's. Not at all.

Oh, God. *What was she going to do?*

"Lady Caroline."

A voice, oddly familiar, sounded beside her. Caroline lifted her gaze . . .

And found herself staring directly into Lady Jacquelyn Seldon's dark eyes.

"Oh," she heard herself say, faintly.

"What a surprise bumping into you here." Jacquelyn smiled prettily. "I didn't know your wedding gown was a Worth."

Automatically, Caroline's gaze dipped below Jacquelyn's neck. She, too, was dressed in a Worth wedding gown. Only Jacquelyn's, Caroline saw in a glance, was a good deal less modest than Caroline's, cut very low over the bosom. Jacquelyn's gown was much fancier, too, with sparkly beading and even some feathers sticking up out of the poofed sleeves. Caroline's own sleeves were quite plain.

"Do you like this lace?" Jacquelyn asked, lifting a piece featuring a pattern of entwined hearts, and fingering it experimentally.

Caroline looked down at the snowy fabric. All she could think was, *Yesterday, this woman's fiancé had his hand down my pantaloons.*

And then her cheeks turned crimson. *Why*, she thought to herself, *here I've been, hating Jacquelyn Seldon for doing what she did with Hurst, and what have I been doing?* What have I been doing? *Why, I've been every bit as bad. Well, maybe not* completely *as bad, but almost as bad. I haven't any cause at all to feel superior to her. None at all! I'm every bit as wicked.*

And both of us—both of us—wearing white!

Caroline said, through extremely dry lips, "It's lovely."

Jacquelyn looked at the lace, made a face, and tossed it away. "I hate it," she said. "It's much too busy. Granville's bought me a tiara, you know, and I wouldn't want anything to detract from that. Not that anything could, of course. It's got over sixty-five diamonds in it, not a one of which is under a quarter of a carat."

Caroline made what she hoped was a suitably impressed expression, but all she could think was, *Did he go home last night and do that trick with his fingers on* her?

And then, to Caroline's horror, Jacquelyn, almost as if she'd read her thoughts, said, "You know, Lady Caroline, I couldn't help but notice you and Granville dancing together the other night at the Dalrymples'."

Caroline swallowed hard. "Yes," she tried to say, but it didn't come out right. She had to clear her throat and try again. "I mean, yes. I'm buying a gun from him. For my brother. For when he goes back to school in the fall."

"Oh, your brother," Jacquelyn said. She moved along the table, the train of her white satin gown making a swishing sound behind her. "Of course. How is he? He looks better every time I see him."

"He's doing very well," Caroline said. And if this woman's fiancé was as successful in his mission as he'd sworn to Caroline he would be, Tommy would continue to do well for some time to come—or at least until the next inane scheme that came into his head. "Thomas is very keen, you know, on Bra—Mr. Granville."

"Well," Jacquelyn said. "He's not the only one."

Caroline lowered her face, hoping Jacquelyn wouldn't notice the red hot heat suffusing it. She knew. She had to know. What else could that remark indicate? Jacquelyn knew precisely how she felt about Braden Granville.

But how could she help it? He wasn't like any other man Caroline had ever met. He wasn't like Hurst and his friends, sweetly empty-headed, thinking only of their next card game or glass of port. Braden Granville actually listened to her, and seemed to consider her opinions with some amount of seriousness—at least when he wasn't thrusting his hands down various parts of her clothing. How could any woman help being keen on Braden Granville? He was . . . well, he was extraordinary.

Lady Jacquelyn was speaking again, suddenly, cutting through Caroline's frantic musings:

"You know, Caroline, it's strange, but even though you and I went to school together, I don't feel that . . . well, that I know you very well. So I hope you won't take it amiss if I give you a little piece of womanly advice."

Caroline, her eyes very wide, echoed, "Advice?"

"Yes," Jacquelyn said. She turned around and awarded Caroline another of those frightening smiles. "Woman to woman. You see, Caroline, I know."

Caroline felt her face go scarlet again. It was not a pleasant feeling. "Know?" she managed to stammer. "Know what?"

Jacquelyn tossed her head. Her ink-black hair had been done up in a complicated arrangement of curls, many of which hung loosely down the back of her neck, swaying like the fronds from a willow tree. That's what Jacquelyn was, Caroline thought, suddenly. A weeping willow, tall and slender, bending in the wind, but never breaking. Nothing could break Jacquelyn.

"About you," the older girl said, lightly. "And Granville. You've never been very good, you know, at hiding your feelings."

Caroline's blush drained away. She must, she thought, have

gone as pale as her gown. She said the only thing she could think of, which was, "I—I don't know what you mean."

Jacquelyn's smile, which had been so sinister, suddenly turned very sweet indeed. "Don't you? It isn't anything to be ashamed of, dearest. You couldn't help it. What woman could help falling in love with him? He isn't called the Lothario of London for nothing. But that, you see, is why I wanted to give you a little advice. You are such a little innocent, I'm afraid you might get your little heart trampled on."

Caroline blinked. "You mean . . . you mean . . . ?"

"Yes." Jacquelyn smiled down at her kindly. "I know you're in love with my fiancé. Goodness, any fool could see it, just by looking at your face any time his name is mentioned. You go positively red, Caroline. And I want you to know, I'm not in the least angry about it. But I do feel obligated to warn you, Caroline, that Granville isn't . . . well, he isn't the sort of person little girls like you ought to fall in love with."

Caroline felt dizzy suddenly. She had, in fact, to reach behind her, and grip the edge of the table on which rested all those yards of lace. If she hadn't had the table for support, she was quite sure she'd have sunk to the floor, for her knees seemed to have turned to jelly.

Oh, Caroline thought. *Oh God!*

Because it was true. It was true, what Jacquelyn was saying. She did love Braden Granville. Loved him as she had never loved before. The silly schoolgirl crush she'd had on Hurst had only been just that—a pale, pathetic slip of a feeling, as easily torn in two as the lace she was gripping as she clung to the table. What she felt for this woman's fiancé was as strong and as sturdy as the thick taffeta of her skirt. It would never tear, never break. Only shears could rend it.

Oh, God, what had she done?

Shame followed quickly on the heels of the dizziness. For she knew now what she ought to have realized all along: she wasn't any better than Jacquelyn Seldon. Hadn't she been behaving just as reprehensibly yesterday in Braden Granville's carriage as Jacquelyn and Hurst had behaved that night at Dame Ashforth's?

There was no difference. No difference at all.

"I can see that I'm upsetting you," Jacquelyn said. "But you must know, darling, for your own good, that Granville . . . well, he's only playing with you. He doesn't mean it. He only finds you . . . well, interesting, I suppose. He hasn't had much experience with virgins, you know."

Caroline had to once again tighten her grip on the table, because all of a sudden it seemed to her that the floor might rush up to meet her face. She wished very hard for a chair. *Oh, God*, she prayed. *Whatever else happens, don't let me faint in front of Lady Jacquelyn Seldon. Don't let me faint.*

Jacquelyn, noticing Caroline's white-knuckled grip, cried, "Oh, the dog! He *has* been playing with you, hasn't he? Poor, poor Caroline. Well, you've been warned. And I know how sensible you are. You'll go back to your adorable marquis now, won't you? Of course you will. Think how much you owe him. Why, he saved your brother's life, I understand. Imagine the scandal if you were to break it off with him, after all he's done for you and your family. You'd have to leave town, I imagine."

Caroline, fully aware that she had not uttered a sound to dispute any of Jacquelyn's charges, tried to make her lips move. *I'm sorry*, she wanted to say. *But you must be mistaken. I'm not in love with Braden Granville.*

But no sound came from her throat. It was as if the words stuck there, the way her badminton birdie sometimes stuck in the net.

Jacquelyn raised her eyebrows. She seemed to realize Caroline was trying to say something. "Yes, my dear?"

A lie. That was why Caroline could not say the words. Because they were a lie.

But she had lied before. Many times, in fact. So why couldn't she do it now, when it really mattered?

Jacquelyn reached out and laid a comforting hand upon her shoulder. This time, Jacquelyn's smile reached almost all the way to her eyes. "Caroline." The smile widened. "I know what you're trying to say. I know you are a very good sort of person, who prides herself on things like loyalty and honesty and kindness to four-legged creatures and the like. But there's no point in denying it. You are in love with Braden Granville. It is perfectly obvious to anyone who looks into your eyes. You love him so much, it's tearing you up inside. But fortunately, there's still time to put a stop to it, before any real harm is done. Forget him, Caroline. Before you do anything stupid, anything that might damage your chance at happiness. Before he breaks your heart, like he's broken the hearts of so many girls all across London. All right?"

Damage your chance at happiness. What chance at happiness did Caroline have? Married to a man who didn't love her, for whom she could feel nothing—nothing except gratitude. What kind of chance at happiness was that?

Once it had been enough. But not now. Not now that she had come to know Braden Granville.

What was she going to do? It was despair that made her clutch the table now, hanging her head and staring down at the finger on her left hand, the one wearing Hurst's grandmother's ring. A ring she didn't doubt would look far better on Jacquelyn's hand.

Suddenly she heard her name called. Looking up, Caroline saw Violet approaching her, holding a sealed envelope.

"Oh, my lady," she said, hurriedly. "This just arrived for you, by private messenger. It is marked urgent."

Caroline looked at the folded piece of foolscap in her maid's hand. It was exactly the same size and shape as the one she'd received earlier in the day from Braden Granville. How, she wondered, had he managed to track her down at Mr. Worth's? And then, more worryingly, another thought occurred to her. Had he failed? Had he failed to convince Tommy to stay in town?

But then Violet handed it to her, and Caroline saw it wasn't from Braden Granville at all.

"Not bad news, I hope?" Lady Jacquelyn said, watching Caroline's face carefully as she tore open the seal.

Caroline scanned the familiar handwriting quickly.

Caro, it read. *Rally at Trafalgar Square at three this afternoon. Chaining myself to the statue of the lion. Bound to get arrested. Pay my penalties again? See you then. E.*

Caroline glanced at Violet. "Do you have the time?"

The maid looked at the clock face pinned to her apron. "It's half three, my lady."

Caroline crumpled the note in her hand.

"I do hope it isn't bad news," Jacquelyn said, sweetly.

"No," Caroline replied. "My maid of honor's been arrested again. That's all."

Then she turned and ran back to her fitting room without remembering to say good-bye to Lady Jacquelyn.

But Lady Jacquelyn, truth be told, did not care in the slightest whether or not Caroline had said good-bye to her. She had far more important things to worry about.

23

I don't want to hear another word about it," Jacquelyn snapped. "You've got to do it, Hurst, and you've got to do it at once."

Hurst, slumped in an uncomfortable chair that had been in the Seldon family for nearly a century, said only, "Must you shout so? I've a wretched headache."

"It appears I must shout," Jacquelyn said, as she paced before his chair. "For you are clearly insensible to reasoning. I'm telling you, Hurst, it's the only way."

"Yes, but, darling—" He raised his face from the hands into which he'd sunk it, and eyed her miserably. "It's so *drastic*."

"Drastic times call for drastic measures." Jacquelyn crossed to the marble-topped mantel and corrected the position of a Dresden milkmaid before turning around and facing her lover again. "I tell you, Hurst, you've got to do it."

Hurst pushed himself up from the chair and threw himself, instead, facedown across the more comfortable brocade of a chaise longue. "But you know I can't stand Spain."

"Well, then take her to France." Jacquelyn, beautiful as ever in pale pink muslin, stood above the marquis's head, her hands on her hips. "Take her to Belgium. I don't care where you do it. Just *marry* the stupid cow, now, before she calls it off. I'm telling you, Hurst, she's going to. She's in love with Granville. Any fool could see it—with the possible exception of Granville himself, who's so besotted with her he can't see anything at all."

Hurst rolled over on the chaise longue and gazed up irritably at his lady love. "I don't see what makes you think Caroline's in love with the brute. She seemed quite fond of me, still, when last I saw her. Even wanted me to kiss her."

Jacquelyn's look of disgust, which she'd aimed in the marquis's direction, deepened. "Of course she did," she said. "The silly girl doesn't know what she's feeling. That's why time is of the essence, Hurst. You've got to elope before she realizes what's what. You've still got a chance with her, if you act fast."

Hurst stared at the cheerful cherubs painted on the drawing room ceiling overhead. He hated the way they leered down at him, mocking him. For he knew there could be no elopement. The wedding itself would doubtless be postponed—if there were any wedding at all, after the funeral.

"You've got to do it tonight," Jacquelyn went on, relentlessly. "I'll make the arrangements. You go home now, and pack up a bag."

Hurst said, carefully, "It can't be tonight. I've something planned for tonight."

Jacquelyn stamped a slippered foot. She was not the sort of woman it was wise to anger. Had Hurst been looking at her when he'd made his reply, and not at the ceiling, he might have put it a bit differently. As it was, however, he'd still been staring at the ceiling mural, and so he hadn't seen the thunderclouds gathering on the horizon.

Jacquelyn strode swiftly toward him, reached down, and pinched his nose very hard between two perfectly manicured fingernails.

"You'll . . . elope . . . with . . . the . . . girl . . . tonight," she hissed, fiercely, "or suffer the consequences, my friend."

Alarmed, Hurst swung out an arm, and broke Jacquelyn's grip on his nose. He leaped to his feet, and, fingering his now tender proboscis, wailed, "Ow! What did you have to do that for, Jacks?"

Jacquelyn's eyes were narrowed to twin slits. "I told you. You're going to marry her, and soon, or else."

Mournfully holding his nose, Hurst asked, "What's the bloody hurry, Jacks?"

"She's in love with Granville, don't you see? And I fear he returns the feeling. And she isn't to have him! Only I. *I* am the only one to have him."

Hurst looked at her curiously. He was not prone to brilliant thinking, but at that moment, as he stood gazing at Jacquelyn Seldon, something happened in his handsome head, and he blurted, like someone coming out of a trance, "Why, Jackie! You're in love with him!"

Jacquelyn went red. "I'm not. What drivel."

But Hurst, unused to ever having inspirations of any kind, was too impressed with himself and his newly discovered insight to leave well enough alone. "No, no. You are. I can tell you are. You're blushing. And you never blush. My God, Jackie! How *could* you? *Granville?*"

Jacquelyn crossed the room so swiftly, he didn't even have time to duck when he saw the outstretched hand sailing in the direction of his face.

Smack. Jacquelyn glared up at him with eyes that were darker and yet brighter than he'd ever seen them.

"There'll be more of the same," Jacquelyn snapped, "if you ever say anything like that again. I am *not* in love with Braden Granville. I'm *not!*"

Hurst, cradling his stinging jaw in his hand, looked down at Jacquelyn with disbelief in his robin's-egg blue eyes.

"You are!" he cried, in a voice that was close to hysterical. "You've fallen for him! The Lothario of London! My God, Jackie. *My God.*"

But Jacquelyn only screeched, "Stop saying that!" And when Hurst didn't, she dashed to the fireplace, lifted the Dresden milkmaid from the mantel, and hurled it at him with all her strength.

This time Hurst had the foresight to duck. The figurine smashed harmlessly against the wall behind him.

"That's it," Hurst said, when he'd straightened again. "That's it, Jackie. I've had as much as I can take. Braden Granville. Braden bloody Granville. He hasn't any right to set foot in the homes of decent folk. You know that. The man is Seven Dials gutter trash, and hasn't the slightest idea how to behave around his betters. Why no one has taken that upstart out and given him the thrashing he so richly deserves—"

Jacquelyn, her face still mottled with rage, cried, "If you lay one finger on him, Hurst—just one finger—I'll tell the Linford girl! I swear I will. She'll never marry you then. Never."

Hurst turned around and went to the door.

"Where are you going?" Jacquelyn looked bewildered. "How dare you turn your back on me while I'm speaking. Hurst! *Hurst!*"

He slammed the door so forcefully on his way out that the Dresden milkmaid's Dresden cow trembled on the mantel, then finally plunged headlong toward the hearthstone, where it met the same fate as its mistress. Jacquelyn, observing this, let out an anguished shriek that summoned the maid, who was promptly slapped in the face for obsequiousness.

24

There was something of a circus atmosphere outside the Old Bailey that afternoon. Braden wasn't surprised. Where the criminal element gathered could usually be found the men who were paid to prosecute, defend, and hang them, and the mixing of these two crowds tended to inspire an air of sustained hysteria. Pushing his way past a bewigged judge and a lame pickpocket, who carried, for some reason, a shrieking monkey on his shoulder, Braden asked himself, for what had to be the hundredth time, what he was doing at the Central Criminal Court, a place he had not been since, as a youth, he himself had been held there.

Not that he had been done so badly by the Central Criminal Court, all those years ago. He had been lucky—far luckier than most of the boys with whom he'd grown up.

Only Josiah Wilder—the gunsmith to whom Braden had been appointed apprentice by the courts, and whose widow Braden supported and still visited regularly, fifteen years later—had taught Braden much more than the inner workings of firearms all those years ago, back in his busy little shop. For Braden, it was the lessons Josiah taught him outside of the shop that had mattered most. Josiah Wilder taught Braden Granville everything he knew that was of any sort of importance, from how to dance the Sir Roger de Coverley, to the correct way to hold a newborn baby. It was Josiah Wilder to whom Braden felt he owed everything he had, and it was that great man's memory to which he silently raised a glass at supper every night.

But that did not mean Braden particularly relished the spot where he had first met the man who changed his life.

But there was nothing for it. He'd had to come. He'd received Caroline's note, penned in obvious haste, reiterating the fact that she would not be requiring any more "lessons," and that she would not be able to meet him as he'd asked her both the day before and in his reply to her letter concerning her brother, because her presence was required at the courts.

He'd sent immediately for his carriage.

Well, what other choice had he had? Her note had maddened him. No more lessons. She had said as much the day before, but he had tried not to listen. Would not listen. Without the lessons, what hold did he have upon her? None. She would marry that blackguard Slater—whom Braden was convinced was not as perfectly innocent as her brother claimed—and be lost to him forever.

Because he had promised. He had promised not to tell her what he knew. Which meant he certainly couldn't tell her what he merely suspected, which was that to him, her fiancé's heroism smacked of a guilty conscience. Slater might be better acquainted with The Duke than he let on. Braden knew that one way Hawkins had been able to lure high rollers to his establishment in the Dials had been by employing impoverished but highly regarded members of the gentry to vouch for the authenticity of the place. Was Slater one of those pawns?

Not that it would make much difference if his suspicion was proved true. He had promised. In the Dials, a man lived and died by his word. Braden would not go back on his promise.

But nor would he give her up. Not that easily.

Which was why he was here, at one of his least favorite places in London. Old Bailey, as he knew only too well, was unpleasant enough for anyone, but it was absolutely the last place on earth a young lady like Caroline Linford ought to have been showing her face. What, he wondered for the thousandth time, could that idiot mother of hers be thinking, allowing her daughter to go there? If ever there were two things that were completely incongruous, those two things were Caroline Linford and the Old Bailey.

And yet he saw, as he strode across the squalid yard, the Bartlett carriage, pulled off to one side and with maid and driver waiting patiently atop it for their mistress. It didn't seem possible, but here was the proof: Caroline Linford was somewhere in this seamy crowd. He shouldered his way through a throng of prostitutes—creating quite a stir by politely excusing himself afterward—and approached the brougham. The maid, he saw, was, by some stroke of good fortune, Violet. He called up to her, and she looked down, clearly frightened by all that was taking place around the calm island of leather and steel upon which she sat.

"I say, isn't that you, Violet?" Braden used his deepest, most reassuring voice.

The maid spun around on the high seat, looking startled. When her gaze lighted on Braden, she brightened considerably.

"Oh," she said, looking pleased. "It's you, sir."

"Lady Caroline is still inside, I take it?" he asked, nodding his head toward the steps to the Old Bailey, which teemed with the sort of riffraff that was necessarily attracted to such places, criminals and their families and supporters, gawkers and missionaries, fruit sellers, dogs, hordes of street urchins, hoping to profit by a picked pocket or two, and, most regrettably of all, lawyers.

Violet nodded her head so forcefully that the artificial flowers on her bonnet swayed. "Yes, sir," she said. "An hour she's been already."

"She asked me to meet her here," Braden lied, reaching into

his waistcoat pocket. "There's no need for you to stay. I've brought my carriage. I'll take her home. Why don't you two go and have yourselves a nice cup of tea somewhere?"

Violet and the driver exchanged quick glances. Braden did not miss the appraising look the driver flicked at the wallet he'd drawn from his waistcoat pocket.

"Oh, sir," Violet said. "That's right kind of you, sir. Only we daren't leave. If the Lady Bartlett were to find out—"

She broke off with a yelp. The driver had obviously kicked her.

"We'd be right happy to go for a cuppa," the driver said, smiling politely down at Braden. "That's very kind of you, sir." And, when he noted the denomination on the bill Braden handed up, his eyes widened, and he added, "Very kind indeed!"

The carriage swung away a few seconds later, and Braden took up a position where it had stood, folding his arms and trying to ignore the ceaseless activity around him, much of which consisted of acts that, anywhere else in London, would have resulted in immediate arrest, but since they were in front of the courthouse, resulted only in guffaws, since all the constables were busy inside the building, restraining those who were receiving their punishments.

An ice cart pulled up, a rickety wagon drawn by a flea-bitten nag, and its driver informed Braden that he was standing in his spot. Braden only looked at him, and after a little while, the iceman decided it wasn't his spot after all, and stayed where he was, loudly hawking his product.

It couldn't have been above a quarter of an hour later before Braden's eye was caught by two spots of very bright color, and he saw Caroline and her friend, the Lady Emily Stanhope, emerging from the Old Bailey, their wide skirts cutting a swath through the crowd like sails on the open sea. He found, to his surprise, that he was waiting in some suspense to see what her reaction would be when she noticed him. Caroline Linford's reactions to things were so varied—and so imminently satisfying—that he had begun to look forward to them rather the way a child looked forward to emptying a Christmas stocking.

He was not disappointed when Caroline, coming to the place where her carriage had been, stopped dead in her tracks and asked, "But where could Peters and Violet have disappeared to?"

Then her gaze fell upon Braden, and he saw those enormous brown eyes flare wider than ever. Then, like the windows of Westminster when the sun hit them, Caroline's cheeks flared slowly redder and redder.

He grinned at her, inordinately pleased by her blush. It had been worth the wait.

"What," she cried, her voice as hoarse as if it had been her, and not her friend, who'd been rallying at Trafalgar Square a few hours earlier, "are *you* doing here? And where are my driver and my maid?"

He shook his head at her. "Tsk, tsk, tsk," he said. "So suspicious, for someone so very young. What makes you think I've done anything to your precious maid?"

"What else am I to think?" Caroline demanded. "She was here when I left her, and I come out to find her gone, and you in her place. Considering what you did to her last time—"

Lady Emily, who'd been watching the exchange with eyes only a little less wide than Caroline's, interrupted.

"What?" she asked, eagerly. "What did he do to her last time?"

"*I* didn't do anything to her," Braden replied, at the exact same moment that Caroline said, "He mesmerized her."

Emily, glancing from Braden and then to her friend and back, finally said, "I think you two must want to be alone. Caroline, thank you, but I think I'd better find my own way ho—"

To Braden's chagrin, Caroline reached out and seized her friend's arm tightly. "I don't," she declared. "I don't want to be alone with him at all."

Emily looked as if she really would have preferred to have hailed a hack and been on her way. Braden didn't blame her. He was certain he looked as desperate as he was starting to feel. Desperation was not something he was at all accustomed to experiencing when it came to women, but Caroline Linford seemed to have the ability to bring it out in him in droves.

Still, he tried to remember he was at least halfway a gentleman, and said, with a courtly bow, "I would be delighted to see the both of you home. I have my carriage, just over there, across the square. I'll be happy to drop you—"

"What have you done with Peters and Violet?" Caroline demanded.

But before he could reply, they were interrupted yet again, this time by a hack that pulled up so abruptly beside the ice cart that the street urchins—who had gathered round the back of the wagon to steal fistfuls of the cool stuff—scattered like pigeons to all sides of the square.

A second later, the driver, looking delighted at having beat out his companions for this easy fare, was helping Emily, who'd flagged him down, then broken free of Caroline's grasp, into the back of his cab.

Caroline abruptly abandoned Braden, and hurried toward her friend.

"Emmy," she said, her face filled with confusion. "Mr. Granville said he would drive us both—"

Emily flung a glance at Braden over Caroline's shoulder. "And it's really very kind of him," she said, quickly. "Thank you for your help, Caro, but I think the two of you ought to be alone to, er, work things out—"

Braden saw Caroline draw breath to argue, but Emily had already urged the driver to move on. When Caroline came back to him, her face was filled with indignation.

"Look what you did," she said. "You frightened her."

"Frightened her?" Braden was stunned. "How on earth could *I* have frightened Lady Emily? *She* frightens *me!*"

Caroline glared at him. "Nonsense. You must have lifted your wretched eyebrow at her or something to scare her off, when you know—you know perfectly well—that I can't be alone with you. Not ever again. In fact, I shouldn't even be standing here talking to you. Someone might see us together—"

"Oh?" This was an interesting—a lesser man might have said alarming—turn of events. But Braden Granville said only, taking her by the hand, "Then we had better go. My carriage is—"

"No." She pulled on the fingers he held. "No. Don't you see? That's all over. I was quite wrong ever to have come to you in the first place. I thank you for everything you've done—" She broke off, glancing up at him from under the shadow of her bonnet brim, then asked, almost shyly, "Did you have a chance to speak with my brother?"

"Indeed," Braden said, gravely. "I did. You needn't worry yourself any longer. He will not go to Oxford."

"He will—" She turned to stare up at him wonderingly. "Really? Oh, thank you! Thank you so much. Only what did you say to him to make him agree to stay in London?"

"Oh," Braden said, casually. "Nothing much. I don't think he particularly wanted to go in any case, so it was just a matter of someone pointing out the advantages in staying put."

Caroline knit her brow. "Well, I should think those would be obvious. But perhaps he needed to hear it from a man. Poor Tommy, with so many women clucking over him. He must feel quite henpecked."

"He didn't mention that," Braden said.

"Oh." Caroline seemed to realize with a start that he still had hold of her hand. She began to tug upon it again. "Well, I thank you. You've been very kind—especially about Tommy. But now I do have to go. You'll have to forgive me. I—"

She was trying to wrench her hand from his, but he was too quick for her. In a second, he had her hand tucked into the crook of his arm, where he kept it tightly imprisoned.

"What," he said, trying to sound calmer than he felt, "do we have here, then? Mutiny?"

She pulled ineffectually at her trapped fingers. "This isn't amusing, Braden," she said. "We haven't any right to be doing what . . . well, what we've been doing. It's better that we stop now and carry on as we were, and hope no one ever finds out how foolish we were being. . . ."

Her voice trailed off as she noticed the expression on his face, which must have been odd indeed, judging by the way she was staring at him. "What?" she asked, clearly alarmed. "What is it?"

He still hadn't recovered from his shock, and could not, for the life of him, stop staring at her. Nor could he let her go. Not then. Maybe not ever. "What did you call me?"

Down went her eyelids as, abashed, she looked at the ground, her feet, anything but him. "Mr. Granville," she said, breathlessly. "I meant Mr. Granville. Now let *go*— "

"That's not what you called me."

"It's what I *meant* to call you," she said, still not meeting his eyes. "*Why* won't you let go of me? I told you I can't stay here with you—"

"Say it again."

"*Mr. Granville*— "

"Say it again."

"Oh, very well!" She stopped struggling and turned to face him, her cheeks pink now not from embarrassment, but the exertion of trying to break free of him. "Braden. Are you happy? I said it. Braden. Now, will you please let go of me?"

He let go of her. Looking extremely surprised at finding herself so suddenly at liberty, she reached up and, apparently from force of habit, adjusted her bonnet.

"Now," he said, slowly. "What's this nonsense about us not seeing each other anymore?"

Dropping her gaze to her feet again, she took a deep breath, and said, "It's just that this afternoon, I happened to run into Lady—"

The sound of a whip cracking interrupted her—caused her, in fact, to jump, and Braden to throw an arm around her shoulders defensively.

25

Barely a foot or two away from Caroline, the ice cart driver lifted his arm to deliver another blow to the ragged horse hitched to his wagon.

"Come on," the iceman snarled at the mare. "Git a move on, then."

But this time when he lowered his whip, instead of hearing the satisfying snap of leather to hairy flank, he heard bones crunching. His own bones, primarily those in his wrist, which had been seized by Braden Granville's fist.

"Oy," shouted the old man. "What do you think you're doing? You're breaking my arm!"

"No more than you deserve," Braden growled, "cracking that whip so close to the lady."

"Not to mention"—to Braden's bemusement, Caroline stepped forward, and, putting her hands on her hips, confronted the iceman in a manner not unlike the mothers of his friends back in Seven Dials used to confront them after a long night's carouse—"the fact that you are abusing this poor animal. Look at her! No meat on her bones, her ribs sticking out everywhere—when is the last time you fed her a decent meal? Or let her stop for water?"

The iceman looked from the gentleman to the lady and seemed

to decide that, despite the painful grip he had on his arm, the gentleman was the more rational of the pair.

"Look," he said, in a wheedling voice. "I'm right sorry about affrighting the lady. How would you like a little free ice, sir? You and the lady? A nice little bit of ice to lick on a hot evening—"

"I think you ought," Caroline said, "to give some of that ice of yours to your poor horse."

The iceman looked to Braden for help, but he only said, "You heard the lady."

Sighing, the old man climbed down out of his seat and, after Braden released his punishing hold on his arm, shuffled to the back of his wagon. Caroline, meanwhile, had bent over, and was examining the animal attached to the wagon's front.

"Oh," she cried, clearly dismayed as she scrutinized the many oozing welts on the nag's flesh, to which flies were proving to be powerfully attracted. "Oh, Braden, look. Look at the poor thing."

Braden didn't so much as glance at the horse. His gaze was instead fully locked on the woman exclaiming over it. He was recalling, with rather startling clarity, the way in which Caroline had thrown her head back the day before, when she'd climaxed in his arms. Her throat, fully extended, had looked so long and slender, the skin ever so slightly tanned, all the way to the point where it disappeared beneath her lace collar. How far, he wondered, did that tan extend?

Caroline straightened. "This horse will be dead by next week if he is allowed to continue abusing her in this manner."

Braden recalled how, at the peak of her orgasm, Caroline's fingers had clutched convulsively at his shirt, then slowly uncurled as the shudders of pleasure lessened. Watching Caroline Linford climax in his arms had been the most erotic moment in Braden Granville's life.

"How much?" Caroline was saying. "How much do you want for her?"

Braden shook his head, trying to focus on the situation at hand. The iceman, he saw, was staring very hard at Caroline.

"Pardon?" The iceman looked confused.

"You heard me." Caroline reached into her reticule. The last rays of the afternoon sun touched her curls, setting them aflame. "How much for your horse, sir? I'd like to buy her from you, if I may."

Finally realizing what Caroline was about, Braden reached into his waistcoat pocket, not quite believing what was happening. Apparently, they were buying this flea-bitten nag.

"Allow me, my lady," he said.

Caroline looked up from the depths of her reticule. Seeing that he held his wallet in his hand, she blanched.

"Oh, no," she said. "Mr. Granville, you mustn't—"

"How much?" Braden asked the iceman.

The iceman, clearly no fool, took one look at Braden's face, and another at his wallet, and said, firmly, "Twenty-five pounds."

Caroline said, "Mr. Granville, I must insist that you allow me to—"

"Fine," Braden said, and thrust the money into the old man's hands. "Unhitch her and tie her up to the back of that curricle over there, just across the square." Then, taking hold of Caroline's arm, he began to steer her, too, in the direction of his vehicle.

But Caroline was still sputtering, even as she walked. "Twenty-five pounds!" she cried. "Twenty-five pounds! Why, I doubt he paid above three for her in the first place. And I said *I* would buy her, Mr. Granville. You simply can't go around—"

"Caroline," he said through gritted teeth, as he hustled her along, ignoring the street peddlers who, having seen him purchase the iceman's horse, seemed convinced he'd be stupid enough to buy their ill-gotten and ugly wares, as well.

"You don't understand." Caroline did not notice in the slightest how much attention they were attracting. "That horse is going to require weeks of nursing. She's been half starved and most foully abused. You must let me take her."

"Caroline," he said again, as he nodded to Mutt, his driver, who was watching with an appalled expression as the fly-ridden cart horse was tied to the back of his handsome black curricle.

"I insist," Caroline went on, passionately, "that you let me buy her from you, Mr. Granville. It's the very least I can do—"

Braden handed her into the curricle. She didn't even appear to notice that, in spite of the fact she had said she couldn't see him anymore, she was actually about to be driven away by him. Not, he supposed, that there'd have been much for her to do about it if she had noticed. Every hansom cab in the area had already been spoken for, every omnibus packed to capacity.

"I'll take her to Emmy's," Caroline was saying, as he swung into the seat beside her. "She has a country place in Shropshire, where I send all the horses I rescue. Her parents don't mind—I pay them for room and board, of course. And they've so much pasture, they hardly know the difference if there are ten or twenty horses grazing on it. They have the most excellent groom. He's done wonders with animals worse off than this one, you'll see. He'll have her rolling in the grass in under a month, I swear to you."

Braden leaned forward and said, "Home, Mutt, nice and easy," to his driver, and the carriage suddenly lurched into motion.

Caroline flung out a hand to steady her bonnet, which had snapped forward with the movement of the curricle.

"Where," she wanted to know, as if realizing for the first time just what, exactly, was happening, "are we going?"

"Home, of course," Braden said.

"Home?" she echoed. "*Your* home?"

Not liking the rising note of alarm he detected in her voice, he said, calmly, "We have to see to the horse, don't we?"

"But—" Caroline twisted in her seat, peering back the way they'd come.

"I sent your carriage home, Lady Caroline."

Caroline whipped her head around to glare at him. "Who gave you permission," she demanded, "to do that?"

"No one," he replied, with a shrug of his heavy shoulders. "But I needed to speak with you, and this was the only way I could think of to do it."

"Speak with me?" Her expression softened. "Oh. You mean about my brother?"

"That, and . . . other things."

"But he listened to you, didn't he?" Her brown eyes were warm in the half light that filtered around the sides of the blinds he'd pulled down over the carriage windows. At Braden's nod, she said, with a gusty sigh, "I knew he would. I was sure if there was anyone who could talk him out of such foolishness, it was you. Thank you."

She held out her right hand. Braden looked down at it as if it were a foreign thing. And indeed perhaps he thought it was, because it seemed exceedingly odd to him to be shaking hands with a woman whom only the day before, he'd touched in a much more intimate capacity, right in this very carriage. . . .

"Don't thank me," he said. His voice sounded strange, not his own. But he had to say it. He had done nothing to deserve her thanks. What had he done but use her, and for his own selfish pleasure? He had fought her at first, that he would admit. But as soon as things became inconvenient for him—in this case, when Weasel had been injured—he had capitulated, and ever since, had been leading her down a path that would, if he didn't put a stop to it soon, bring about her ruin.

But how could he stop it? How could he keep away from her, when every inch of him burned for her touch? It was wrong. He knew that. She was a lady, gently born and reared, while he was . . . what he was. It wasn't right.

And yet he couldn't stay away.

She reached across the seat, plucked up his hand in hers, and squeezed it, a brief, warm contact.

"Thank you," she said, then put his hand down again, and turned to peer worriedly at the nag they were pulling along.

"Does your groom," Caroline asked, "know anything about tending horses as sick as this one?"

Braden, still feeling raw, as if it were he, and not that wretched horse, who was being dragged behind a carriage, said, "I haven't the slightest idea."

"Perhaps," Caroline said, "we should take her to my house. My father often brought sick and injured horses home, and our grooms are quite—"

He could not say what made him so churlish, except that he knew if they went to her house, that would be the end. He would have to say good-bye to her, and that he would not be able to abide.

"No," he said, curtly. "She's my horse. I paid for her. She stays with me."

"Well," Caroline said, chewing her lower lip. And then, just as he'd secretly hoped she would, she said, "I had better go along with you, then, hadn't I? Just in case? I've had rather a lot of experience with injured animals like this one."

Braden had to bite down on the corners of his mouth to keep them from curling up. "If you think that's best," he said, mildly.

"I still don't understand, though," Caroline said, tearing her concern-filled gaze away from the mare, and turning it upon him, instead, "what you were doing down at the courts."

"I've been meaning to put the very same question to you," Braden said.

"But I explained what I was doing there," Caroline said. "In the note I sent you, explaining why I could not meet you today."

"You explained that you were going to post bail for Lady Emily," he said.

"That's right. And I did."

"You did not, however, explain why such a task should fall upon you." He regarded her as calmly as he could, which, considering his feelings when he'd opened her note and seen where it was she intended to go, was not very calmly at all. "There are several places in London, Caroline, where young ladies such as yourself haven't the slightest business going, and the Central Criminal Courts is most definitely one of them."

He could not keep a note of anger from creeping into his voice. She heard it, and those eyes, which had grown so soft as she'd gazed upon the injured horse, hardened.

"*That's* why you came?" she demanded. "To scold me for going?"

"To insure your safe return," he corrected her, politely.

She let out a little bark of disbelieving laughter. "Mr. Granville, I am not in need of a protector."

Braden lifted a questioning hand. "Why? Because you have one already? If that's so, I hope you won't mind my asking . . . where is he?"

Her chin slid out challengingly as she set her jaw. "Hurst didn't even know I was going down to the courts."

"He ought to make it his business to know."

To his horror, those wide, dark eyes filled suddenly with tears. The chin which had been thrust out so stubbornly trembled, and she said, looking significantly more wounded than the emaciated beast they were towing, "I *told* you. Hurst didn't know."

Braden, torn between a desire to stop the tears that were already glistening, jewel-like, in her long dark lashes, and an equally strong desire to tell her exactly what he thought of the fool she was engaged to, settled for saying, gruffly, "I'm sorry."

She didn't say anything right away, and he could no longer see her face, because she'd turned it so that it was hidden by the brim of her straw bonnet. He sat berating himself for several seconds, wondering why it was that with every other woman in London, he'd always known exactly the right thing to say, but with this one he seemed instinctively to say the very worst thing he possibly could every time.

"I apologize," he tried again, awkwardly, "if I seemed . . . censorious."

To his surprise, she let out a burbling little laugh, and the next thing he knew, she was flashing him a smile—tentative, at best, but still a smile.

"Wherever did you learn a word like *that*?"

Not certain that the tears were well and truly gone, he shrugged uncomfortably. "I don't know," he said. "I suppose I just picked it up."

"You didn't just pick it up. You don't just pick up words like that. You learned them somewhere. I know you didn't go to school. Tommy told me so. So how did you learn them? From books?"

He shrugged again, losing interest in the conversation. "A book, anyway. The dictionary."

Her eyes, which had always seemed a little large for her face, appeared to widen to the size of saucers. "The dictionary?"

"Yes," he said, impatiently. They had so little time. This was not what he wanted to be doing during it, discussing his education— or lack thereof. He'd heard about that enough times from Jackie. "The man to whom I was apprenticed owned a dictionary. I used to read it at night, before I went to bed."

"A dictionary," Caroline said, as if for clarity.

"Yes." He looked at her, and noted that her eyes were still abnormally wide. "You think that's strange." Jackie had certainly thought it strange—strange enough that he'd overheard her mention it once, in a mocking tone, at a dinner party.

"To read a whole dictionary?" she said. "And remember what was in it? Not so much strange as extraordinary."

Feeling uncomfortable, he glanced out the back of the curricle, ostensibly to see whether or not the cart horse had stumbled yet, but really to escape the penetrating quality of her bright-eyed gaze. She looked admiring. He had done nothing worthy of her regard.

"That's something that's never been a problem for me," he said, dismissively. "I've always remembered everything I've ever read."

"Everything?"

"Everything."

"What did I say," Caroline demanded, "in my note to you?"

"Which one?"

"The first one."

"'Mr. Granville,'" he said, quoting easily from memory. "'Even if I wanted to meet you, which I am certain would not be at all wise, I could not, since my mother has locked me into my room as punishment for having gone into the garden with you last night at the Dalrymples'. C—'"

Caroline, stunned, held out a hand, laughing. "Stop!" she cried.

"'—Linford.'"

"How can you do that?" she asked, bewilderedly. "How can you remember every single word?"

He shrugged. "How can anyone not? That's what I've always wondered. How is it that anyone could miss hitting a target at which they'd aimed? It makes no sense to me. Unless, of course, the weapon's faulty—"

"You," Caroline said, "are a strange man, Mr. Granville. But a good one, I think."

And then, before he had a chance to try to dissuade her of this notion—he could not be good, not where she was concerned—the curricle was pulling to a halt, and Mutt, on the driver's seat, had announced, "We're home, sir."

26

"You see," Caroline said, looking extremely pleased. "I told you. A little warm bran and some poultices over those wounds. That was all she needed."

Braden didn't say anything. He particularly didn't say what his groom had said, upon first spying the spindly-legged mare, which was, "What that horse needs is a bullet through the brain."

Fortunately, Braden's warning look had kept him from bringing up that particular idea—tempting though it was—again, and Hammer had done a fair enough job of following the Lady Caroline's orders concerning the mare's care, which seemed to consist primarily of providing the animal with food soft enough for its tender mouth to chew, and paste to keep the flies away from its oozing wounds. When they left it, Braden had to admit the mare did look a trifle better, though Hammer had still been eyeing it with something akin to horror, obviously wondering what this nag was doing in amongst the fine thoroughbreds and jumpers his master kept.

But the rescued horse's ears had pricked forward, proving they were not bent back in permanent ill temper, as Braden had feared, when she'd accepted—with surprisingly ladylike delicacy—the sugar cube Caroline extracted from the depths of her reticule and offered to her in an outstretched hand.

It was this astonishing politeness that caused Caroline, as they were leaving the stables, to say, excitedly, "I was sure, when I saw her, that she had not always been a cart horse. I fancy she was probably once a lady's mount, who got sold when her owner fell on hard times. Such a shame, how ill used she's been since! I think you shall have to call her Lady, because that's clearly what she once was."

Braden, who hadn't any intention of calling the horse anything, opened the garden gate, and gestured for Caroline to precede him through it. She did, clearly too caught up in her joy over the horse's recovery to consider what she was doing . . .

. . . which was, Braden thought grimly to himself, walking straight into the spider's lair.

He ought, he knew, to stop her. He ought to send her home at once, for her own good. If her fiancé and brother would not look out for her, he would have to do it.

But he knew that the one thing from which she needed protection the most was himself, and he could not send her away.

"So this is the home," Caroline said, as she took in the back of his town house, rising four stories high against the twilit summer sky, "of the great Braden Granville."

She didn't say it at all mockingly. The startled glance he threw her revealed that, if her expression was any indication, she had meant it reverently, as if the place he lived was a sort of monument to something.

And, if he considered it impersonally, he supposed it was a bit astonishing, the fact that all of this—the nine-bedroom house, the beautiful, high-walled garden with its fountain and gazebo, the fine stables containing the best horseflesh and fastest vehicles available—belonged to a man who had been born in such abject poverty, to parents such as his. The house was, he supposed, a monument to tenacity, more than anything else. Because to Braden, the most astonishing thing of all was that he had hung on to it as long as he had.

"Do you," Caroline asked, as she stood with her neck craned, gazing up at his house, "have a badminton set?"

He could not have been more surprised if she had asked him whether he kept monkeys in his cellar.

"Badminton?" he echoed. "Er . . ."

"Oh, you've heard of it, surely." She spun around and made a serving motion, using her reticule as an impromptu racket. Though the sky was getting dark enough for the evening star to shine, Braden could see with perfect clarity the fact that when Caroline pulled her arm back, her crinoline swayed up enough to give him quite a good view of her slender ankles beneath the hem of her dress.

"The Duke of Beaufort invented it a few summers ago," Caroline informed him, matter-of-factly. "Tommy and Emmy and I are mad for it. It's like tennis, only with a little feathered—"

"I don't have a badminton set," Braden said. Then, noting her disappointed expression—he'd not been at all wrong, when he'd taken her for an outdoors sort of girl—added, "But I have a swing."

"A swing?" Her interest, as he'd hoped, was piqued. "What sort of swing?"

"This sort," he said, stepping toward it.

It was a garden swing, hanging from a thick bough of ancient oak by two stout ropes, with an ornately scrolled wooden back, and a wide and cushioned seat, long enough to hold several people. Caroline, seeing it, drew in her breath with delight.

"Why, that's the biggest swing I've ever seen!" she cried.

"Indeed," he said, giving the seat a push, and causing it to sway gently back and forth. "When I run into a snag on whatever design I'm working on, I find it quite beneficial to come out here with a cigar and a brandy and—"

Caroline plunked down onto the swing and ran her bare

fingers—her gloves having been abandoned while preparing the poultices for the horse—over the cushioned seat appreciatively. "Oh, yes," she said, as though she had actually allowed Braden to finish his statement, "I could certainly see that. If I had this swing, I would never leave it. I'd spend all summer out here."

He shouldn't. He knew he shouldn't. And yet, unbidden, the words came to his lips.

"It's long enough to stretch out upon," he said. "I enjoy gazing up at the pattern the leaves make against the sky. It's like being in the countryside."

And Caroline, as a part of him must have known she would, raised her feet and actually stretched out on the swing, apparently too caught up in her enthusiasm over it to be conscious of the fact that her crinoline had tilted up, giving him a highly rewarding view of her pantaloons, which at that moment were displaying her shapely calves and highly appealing thighs to an advantage, all the way up to the temptingly plump V where they joined.

"Oh, yes," she said, gazing up at the leaves overhead, dark against the twilit sky. "I quite see what you mean. You wouldn't think you were in the city at all. You can't see any buildings, just trees and sky."

What happened next was entirely his own fault. He had known it was going to happen almost from the moment he'd pointed the swing out to her. It had been in the back of his mind, he was certain, since he'd seen her brother that morning. Somehow, some way, he had to make Caroline Linford forget. Forget her family, forget her fiancé, forget her upcoming wedding and what would happen to her if she called it off.

And since he could not do that the way he'd have preferred to, by telling her what he suspected her marquis had done, Braden could only hope to prey upon her weakness, that weakness only he, in all the world, had managed to suss out.

And that was that Caroline Linford was as carnal a creature as he was, underneath all of that virtuous exterior, those white gloves, and lace-trimmed petticoats. He had known it, he thought now, from the first moment he'd kissed her, when he'd realized that here, at last, was what he had been searching for all his life: a good woman, a kind and honest woman, whose wide-eyed wonder at the world was coupled by a sensuality more rapacious than any he'd ever encountered, with the exception perhaps of his own.

But how to get her to admit it, to keep off those white gloves and accept the fact that the two of them belonged together? There was no way, except to show her.

And so he tried.

He did not, he would be the first to admit, do it with much finesse. He hadn't time for that. Instead, he settled for getting straight to the point, and accordingly moved with all the speed his youth in Seven Dials had taught him. In the blink of an eye, he was on top of her, flattening the crinoline and imprisoning her hands—which she'd thrown up when she'd seen him coming—in his own.

"What," she gasped, as his weight pinned her where she lay, "do you think you're doing? You can't—"

There really wasn't any point in letting her finish. He'd found from experience that Caroline, while she usually put up a token resistance to his advances at first, soon lost all interest in denying either of them what, he was quite certain, they both wanted. And so he lowered his head and, finding her lips, silenced her on the matter.

Beneath him, Caroline struggled. Not because she didn't like what he was doing to her—his lips mesmerized her, the way his words had mesmerized her maid—but because she liked it too much. She knew, now more than ever, that his kisses, divine as they were, were also dangerous. They drove home the truth of what Jacquelyn had accused her of that afternoon—that she loved him.

Which was why she couldn't—shouldn't—let him do the things he was doing to her. . . .

All she had to do, she knew, was ask him to stop. He would. She knew he would.

But it was so hard. It was so hard to say stop, especially when, for the first time in her life, Caroline was realizing what an absolutely incredible sensation it was, having the full force of a man's weight on one. She didn't feel in the least bit like he was squashing her, or that she couldn't breathe. Instead, she felt a delicious warmth all over her body, but especially at certain points, points he wasn't even touching—at least, not directly. Not yet.

But then he *was* touching them, very directly. She wasn't certain how it came about—he was kissing her so deeply, so intrusively, that her thoughts became a jumble of brief, but incredibly intense sensations: how he tasted—of mint, how fiercely the bristles of his razor stubble scraped her face, and how likely there'd be burn marks all around her mouth, like that night after the Dalrymples'; how neatly he'd managed to pry her legs apart with his knees, and fit himself between them; how he murmured her name occasionally, in the deepest voice imaginable, whenever he lifted his head to draw a breath, before kissing her all over again.

And then, suddenly, through the fog his lips and tongue had cast over her senses, Caroline became aware that his fingers had found their way inside the bodice of her gown, and had even managed to dip beneath the lace cup of her corset. His calloused hand closed over first one burgeoning nipple, and then the next, and Caroline, beneath him, felt completely powerless to stop him—not because of his superior strength and weight, but because she didn't *want* to stop him . . . not even when, with his other hand, Braden began removing her pantaloons.

That's right, removing them. And Caroline didn't care. Everything, everything else ceased to matter—Jacquelyn, Hurst, her mother, all of it. She didn't care a whit, just kept kissing him, clinging to his enormous shoulders, and wondering how it was that she'd gone through twenty-one years of life and never felt this way

288 · MEG CABOT

288 · MEG CABOT

before, never felt as truly alive as she did at that moment, beneath the stars on Braden Granville's garden swing, which was swaying gently with the movement of their bodies.

And when he touched her, *there*, where he'd touched her the day before, well, she didn't object to that, either. How could she, when it felt so good, so *right*? She *wanted* him to touch her there, wanted him to touch her there more than she'd ever wanted anything in her life. She still gasped when he did it—it still felt so *strange*, having someone's fingers there. Strange, but nevertheless, immensely satisfying. Though not quite as satisfying, she thought, in her desire-drenched haze, as if he pressed *down*, filling her with his fingers, the way he had in the carriage. And so she moved against his hand, to show him what she wanted . . .

But then something so perfectly astonishing happened that Caroline snapped out of her amorous state. Because when she moved against him, she felt something, hard and long, press up against her thigh, through the butter-soft fabric of his trousers. And suddenly, the immensity of what was happening came home to her. Why, all he had to do, she realized, was undo a few of his trouser buttons, and there would be nothing, nothing at all to keep them from doing precisely what she'd seen Jacquelyn and Hurst doing in that sitting room, not so many nights ago—

And they would be no different than Jacquelyn and Hurst, because there could be no future for them, only momentary pleasure. . . .

Followed by—in Caroline's case, at least—a lifetime of guilt and regret.

With a ragged sob, she pushed away from him. "Oh, let me up," she cried.

Braden, thinking he'd injured her, though he couldn't imagine how, obeyed her at once. But when she'd sprung to her feet, it was clear that there was nothing wrong with the Lady Caroline—at least physically.

"Oh, God," she murmured, hastening to refasten the garments from which he'd so recently liberated her. "Oh, God, oh, God, oh, God. . . ."

Braden sat up, feeling light-headed. His heart was pounding in his chest, and he was breathing as hard and as fast as if he had been in a race. His erection throbbed, a painful reminder of his folly.

He would never get her. Not that way. He realized it now, too late.

Panting, he observed her as closely as he could in the half light. The sun had slipped entirely away, but a new moon had risen across the horizon, and turned the night sky a deep, velvet blue.

It was ignoble of him, but the words came out, nonetheless. "He doesn't love you," he said. "And you know you don't love him. So why—"

"I *told* you why." She strode forward and accompanied the word *told* with a fist to his shoulder. The blow didn't hurt, but it certainly took his mind off his aching testicles.

"Yes." The word was a hiss in the darkness. "Tommy."

"Yes. Tommy. And then there's—" She shook her head, her hair, mussed from his rough contact with it, coming down from its pins. She couldn't tell him, of course. She couldn't tell him what she'd come to realize. It was too humiliating. But she could tell him part of it. "I saw Lady Jacquelyn this afternoon, and—"

He was up and off the swing in a second.

"And what?" he demanded, urgently. "What did she say to you?"

"She thinks . . ." Caroline said to her feet, perfectly unable to meet his gaze. "She thinks . . ."

He told himself not to panic. There was no telling what lies Jackie might have told her. She was capable of anything. But it couldn't have been that bad, or Caroline would never have allowed what had just happened on that swing. "Tell me what she said."

"She said . . . oh, Braden. Don't you see? If we do this, why, I'll be no better than she is."

He relaxed. Guilt. That was all. Jacquelyn hadn't told her anything. Caroline was suffering from nothing more than a guilty conscience.

"Well," he said. "I wouldn't worry about it, sweetheart. Whatever she said, she only said because she's jealous. She's seen how I look at you. She must know—"

Caroline wrenched away from him. "But don't you see?" she cried. "What does that make *me*? Something horrible! You and I aren't any better than Jacquelyn and . . . her lover are. We might be even worse, because for all we know, Jacquelyn and . . . the man I saw her with might be in love. They might not have been able to help themselves. They might feel an uncontrollable passion for one another, a burning passion they have to deny, while we're—"

He quirked up an eyebrow. "We're . . . ?"

"We're just playing a game." Caroline spoke to the garden floor.

He regarded her profile thoughtfully. "Is that what you think this is, then? A game?"

Not to me. That's what she wanted to say. But Lady Jacquelyn's words were still too fresh in her mind. A game. It was all just a great game to him. And she was too naive, too inexperienced to have known better. No, she'd had to go and fall in love with him, and ruin it.

Finally, she felt able to look at him without weeping. "Well," she said. "What else would you call it? It's not as if you and I are . . . madly in love with each other."

"Aren't we?"

The question was so softly put that at first she wasn't certain she'd heard him right. It was as if the leaves, moving in the light breeze over their heads, had sighed the question, not him.

But it had been him. Unquestionably it had been him. She could see it in the way he looked at her, expectantly waiting an answer. She could see it in the tense way he held himself, ready to spring forward, it seemed, and snatch her up again, and make her feel and feel—oh, the things he made her feel!

And all of a sudden, she was afraid, more afraid than she'd ever remembered feeling. Two little words—*Aren't we?*—and her world, which he'd already managed to turn upside down, went plunging yet again, around and around until she did not know left from right, night from day, up from down.

And then, quite suddenly, everything righted itself again, when Sylvester Granville popped up on the terrace just off the library.

"Braden, my boy," he called. "*There* you are. I've been looking everywhere for you. Heard another rumor today about that letter of patent. I say, who's that you've got there with you, eh? Lady Jacquelyn?"

Braden anticipated her flight a split second too late. He stepped forward, knowing she would run, reaching out to seize her shoulders to prevent it. . . .

And found himself clutching only air. Caroline, her skirts hiked up nearly to her knees, was dashing away from him, toward the silhouette his father made against the library windows.

"Oh," she cried, as she ran. "Oh, Mr. Granville, it's me, Caroline Linford. Would you mind terribly—could I trouble you to call a hack to take me home, please?"

"Caroline," Braden said. He could not quite believe this. He could not quite believe this was happening, and in this way.

She ignored him, and raced up the stone steps to the terrace.

If Sylvester Granville was surprised to see Lady Caroline Linford barreling toward him through the warm evening air, he didn't show it. Instead, he lay down the Baronetage, which he'd been carrying, and patted the hands Caroline had wrapped tightly around his arm.

"Of course, my lady," he said. "Whatever you wish. But we needn't call you a hack. I'm sure my son's driver would be only too happy to take you home. Would you like for me to escort you?"

"Oh, yes," Caroline said, throwing a nervous glance over her shoulder. Braden was now climbing the same steps she'd just raced up, wearing an expression which she found forbidding, to say the least. She turned quickly back toward Sylvester. "If we could go at once . . ." she said, the urgency in both her tone and the grip with which she held his arm mounting.

"Caroline," Braden said, his deep voice cutting through the night air.

Sylvester, however, was enjoying his newfound role of champion, and said, "I'm taking Lady Caroline home now, Braden. I'll see you when I return."

Braden ignored the older man, addressing Caroline, instead.

"This isn't over, you know," he assured her, in his lowest, steadiest voice.

If Caroline heard him, however, she gave no indication. She continued to cling to the elder Granville, allowing him to lead her through the house and toward the front door, where the carriage he'd called soon pulled around.

"Did you hear me, Caroline?" Braden demanded, with feelings of increasing desperation, as he followed the pair. "Did you hear what I said?"

At the carriage door, Sylvester turned, having handed the Lady Caroline safely into the vehicle. "My boy," he said, with a chuckle. "Of course she heard you. But she's obviously a bit put out with you right now. I'd leave it, if I were you. You know how women are. Call upon her in the morning. I'm sure she'll be pleased to hear from you by then."

And then Sylvester banged on the brougham's ceiling, and the vehicle rolled away, taking Caroline with it.

It is doubtful that in all its years of existence, Park Lane ever heard language the likes of which Braden Granville let loose at that particular moment.

27

Jacquelyn was sitting at her dressing table, practicing facial expressions in a great, gilt-framed mirror: this was the expression she'd wear when Braden Granville turned at their marriage ceremony and presented her with the emerald and diamond-encrusted wedding ring she'd requested; this was the one she'd wear when she pulled off her glove and flashed that ring in Lady Caroline Linford's face, first opportunity she got.

She was deeply absorbed in the expression she'd wear while receiving the necklace that matched the wedding ring as a first anniversary gift, when quite suddenly, the door to her bedroom—which Jacquelyn always carefully locked whilst she was preparing her toilette, for fear someone might actually catch her without her rouge on—burst open.

Not just burst open, but exploded open, flying right off its hinges and splintering apart. Jacquelyn let out a shriek and clutched the marabou trim of her wrapper tightly to her naked chest.

But Braden Granville, who was apparently the person who'd knocked the door down, since he was the one who came stepping across its wreckage, appeared not in the least interested in Jacquelyn's state of undress.

"Well, Jackie," he said, as soon as he'd safely crossed the recently created sea of wood shards and brass hinges. "What did you say to her, then?"

Jacquelyn looked from the ruins of her bedroom door to the dangerous expression on Braden Granville's face, and then back again. She apparently considered it safer to address the damage he'd just done than his question, since she said, with a good deal of indignation, "Braden! Really! It's a jolly good thing my father's dead, or he'd quite call you out for such boorish behavior. As it is, I suppose the staff are suffering apoplexies out in the hallway. Did you do the same to the front door, as well?"

"I did not," Braden said. "Your mother let me in herself."

Jacquelyn rolled her eyes. "She would. But I highly doubt she knew you were going to break down my bedroom door."

Braden Granville, however, said only, "What did you say to Caroline Linford when you saw her today at Worth's?"

"Caroline Linford?" Jacquelyn knit her brows, looking at Braden as if he'd just stepped from Bedlam, and not from his fashionable residence, which in a scant few weeks, would also be hers . . . if she played her cards close enough to her chest. "*Caroline Linford*? You broke down my door to ask me a question about *Caroline Linford*?"

"That's right," Braden said, coolly. "You heard me. What the devil did you say to her?"

Jacquelyn stared at him. She had heard, of course, that Braden Granville's temper was a dangerous thing—as dangerous as one of his pistols, in the wrong hands. But she had never actually witnessed firsthand one of her future husband's rages. It was, she saw now, not a pretty sight. Braden Granville was all that was manly, it was true, but he wasn't handsome. And when his face, as it was just then, was twisted with wrath—the muscles in his square jaw leaping, that devilish-looking eyebrow, the one with the scar, lifted practically to his hairline—it was downright frightening.

"I only told her the truth," she said, defensively. She had not risen from her dressing table, but could merely sit on the tasseled stool before it, quite immobile with trepidation.

"The truth?" Braden Granville looked at her with something she could only call contempt. "And what, Jackie, is your version of the truth this week?"

She blinked at him, rather surprised to find that tears had sprung to her eyes. Really. Tears! Jacquelyn hadn't cried for years, not since her father died, and only then because she'd realized she hadn't anyone left to apply to for money on a weekly basis. Feeling that this was almost too good to be true, Jacquelyn let out a slurpy sob, and cried, "Oh! Why must you be so cruel?"

Braden did not look particularly impressed by these theatrics. He said, "Jackie, if you don't want me to do to you what I did to that door, you had better tell me the truth."

This, Jacquelyn felt, was simply too much. Her tears forgotten, she stood up, pulling her dressing gown tightly around her—tightly enough so that no curve of her body was left unseen.

"You brute," she said, with a haughty toss of her head. "I knew you'd strike me one day. You're all the same, you lot from the Dials. You think beating a woman is the only way to exert your power over her."

Braden looked as unimpressed by this speech as he'd been by her tears. "Personally," he said, "I prefer extortion to physical violence, where women are concerned. Jacquelyn, if you don't tell me what you said to Caroline Linford this afternoon, the wedding's off."

Jacquelyn's jaw dropped. This was not an occasion for which she'd practiced an expression beforehand. The one she wore, therefore, was not one of her best.

"What?" she cried, her voice breaking on the word.

"You heard me," Braden said, grimly. "Tell me what you told her."

"You can't—" Jacquelyn forgot to clutch her dressing gown closed. Instead, her hands dropped slowly to her sides. So great was her shock, that she did not even realize it.

"You . . ." she breathed. "You can't call off the wedding."

"Actually," Braden said, "I can. Now tell me."

"I'll sue." Jacquelyn blinked. "In court. I'll file for breach of promise."

He made an impatient gesture. "Be my guest. It doesn't matter anymore. Just tell me what you said to her."

"Doesn't matter?" She hurried across the room, not so unconscious now of her nudity beneath the dressing gown. Quite the contrary. She was pleased that the diaphanous material would make her nakedness beneath all too apparent to him. "How can you say that, Braden? Is that what you want? To see your name in the papers, not because of some new invention of yours, but because you're being sued by your former fiancée?"

He shook his head, in the irritated manner of someone who is being bothered by a mosquito. "I don't care anymore, Jackie," he said. "None of that matters to me. It used to, I'll admit it. The idea of paying you a ha'penny galled me to the core. But now—" Lightwood wouldn't be pleased with this one, but he went on anyway, realizing now that it didn't matter. Nothing mattered, except Caroline. "I'd consider it money well spent, if it rids me of you forever."

She was genuinely shocked. It was a blow to her feminine pride. She said the first words that came to her mind. "But I love you," she murmured.

He held up a hand to silence her. "Not that, Jackie," he said. "You were doing so well before."

She couldn't help herself. "But it's true. I know you don't want to hear it. God knows, the Lothario of London has never uttered those three words before, to any woman. But they're true. I love you."

He looked down at her curiously. "Now, that's going a bit too far, don't you think? Love me? No, Jacquelyn. It's better this way. The wedding's off."

Jacquelyn reached out and seized him by the lapels of his coat. "All right," she cried, desperately. "I'll tell you what I told her, the Lady Caroline, at Worth's today."

He smiled down at her, a soothing smile, a smile that almost made him look handsome.

"Ah," he said. "That's more like it. Well. What, then?"

"It was nothing, really," Jacquelyn said, with a nervous laugh. "I suppose it was a bit cruel, but I've known her since we were at school together, and you know how girls will tease one another—"

"Yes," Braden said. "I imagine Caroline was teasing you terribly, and you had no choice but to retaliate."

His sarcasm was lost on Lady Jacquelyn, who said, "Well, of course. That's precisely how it went. I was rather put out, and so I threw it up in her face, the fact that she's so painfully in love with you—"

But Braden had reached out, and suddenly was gripping her by the arms.

"What," he said, between gritted teeth, "did you say?"

"To Lady Caroline?" Then, seeing his expression, she said, in genuine astonishment, "Oh, don't tell me you didn't know, dearest. You can see it in her eyes anytime your name is mentioned. Caroline always had the most useless eyes. You can read her thoughts in her least little glance—"

His grip tightened.

"And what did she say?" he demanded, giving her a little shake. "What did Caroline say, when you told her this?"

"Well, she denied it, of course, darling." Jacquelyn looked down at his hands. "Braden, you're wrinkling my robe, you know."

"Denied it?"

"Well, she *would* deny it. Embarrassed, of course. I mean, as I very well pointed out to her, what would the great Braden Granville want with little Lady Caroline Linford? After all—the Lothario of London, and sweet innocent Lady Caroline? It's perfectly ludicrous. Of course, she said something about how she thought you might possibly return her feelings—" Here Jacquelyn was embroidering a little upon the truth, but she wanted to see how Braden would react. How he reacted would tell her all. "But I told her you were only playing your little game with her, of course."

He released her so abruptly, she staggered, tripping over a piece of the door. *"A game,"* he murmured. "Oh, God."

So. She straightened, and reached down for the sash to her dressing gown. It was just as she suspected. Really, she thought to herself. Who'd have thought it? The great man himself, conquered by that peculiar, horsey girl.

Well, it wouldn't last. Jacquelyn would see to that.

"Well, obviously I told her that, darling," she said, reaching up to smooth the hair he'd mussed when he'd shaken her so savagely. "What would you expect me to tell her? It's the truth, isn't it? What possible interest could you have in Caroline Linford? She's so dull. And, after all, pet—" Here Jacquelyn's eyelids drooped suggestively, and her voice dropped to a purr. "You belong to me."

There was something almost contemptuous in his expression when he looked at her then. But that, of course, was impossible. And yet . . .

"Not anymore," he said, and then he turned and headed toward the now gaping doorway.

Panic, stronger than any hand, clutched at Jacquelyn's throat. Darting forward, she seized him by the sleeve and cried, "But, Braden, darling, what can you mean by that? You said, quite plainly, that if I told you what Caroline and I talked about, you'd still go through with the wedding!"

He glanced down at her, just once. He said, "You should know better, Jacks, than to believe something one of my lot from the Dials ever said."

And then, with a brief crunching of wood splinters beneath his feet, he was gone.

28

*T*ommy crouched in the dark. He was breathing hard. Too hard. So hard, he feared he might be overheard. He had to be quiet. He had to be quiet, and he had to think.

It was impossible to think, though. His heart was hammering. He thought it might burst. He felt the drum of it too loudly in his ears. That was all he could hear, though. The pistol had gone off so close to him, he was convinced the blast had deafened him.

He *knew* it had deafened him. He'd had to peer hard at the lips of the impossibly large man who'd answered the door of the house near where he now crouched. *No, Mr. Granville was not at home.* At least, that's what he thought the giant had said. There was a negative shake of the head to accompany the giant's reply to Tommy's next question— *no, he did not know when his master was expected.*

And then the thick lips moved rapidly, irritably. The giant pointed to a pocket watch he took from his waistcoat pocket. The hands indicated that it was past one o'clock in the morning. *Shove off, mate. Come back in the morning.*

But Tommy did not shove off. Because he'd be dead by morning.

He'd known how he must have looked to the butler—if that's what the frighteningly large man had been. Covered in mud, from when he'd dove beneath that carriage in front of the gambling hall. His cravat askew, his coat torn. There were flakes of gunpowder embedded in the skin of his cheek. He could smell them. Feel them, too, dozens of raised welts. They burned.

But at least they hadn't managed to put a bullet through him. Not this time.

He couldn't say who'd taken the shot. There'd been the usual crush outside the gambling hall, a mob of people, half of whom were trying to get in, the other half, like Tommy, trying to get out. One minute, he'd been shoving through the throng, then climbing into his waiting chaise, with Slater right behind him.

Or so he'd thought. Because the next minute, he'd tripped, and had gone sprawling on the floor of the carriage.

That was what had saved him. Tripping. Once again, he'd lost his footing, and his clumsiness had saved his life. The shot had been aimed too high, so the bullet grazed his cheek and sailed harmlessly into the seat cushions, instead of into his brains, where it had been intended.

Slater had probably called out. Tommy supposed he must have. But he hadn't been able to hear even the sound of his own breath after that first shot. The world was suddenly, eerily silent. He could no longer hear the incessant chatter of the crowd that streamed around his carriage, the whinnies of the nervous horses, the deep booming voice of his driver, urging the team to remain calm.

He knew what had happened. He knew it at once. And he had moved instinctively, throwing himself out of the chaise's opposite door—only to find, when he dropped to the street, another carriage, filled with drunken boys about his own age, blocking his way.

No matter. He'd ducked, and rolled beneath it.

And then he scrambled to his feet and ran. Ran for all he was worth.

He had not known where to go. Home was out of the question. Go home, when someone wanted him dead? No. He would not risk putting his mother and sister in danger. After the first few streets, he'd realized he was heading in the direction of Slater's rooms. Yes, Slater would help. Slater would look for him there, first thing. Wait there, he thought to himself, as he sprinted past startled flower sellers and ladies of the night. Wait for Slater. Slater would know what to do.

And then something strange happened. He remembered Braden Granville's startled look that morning, when Tommy had mentioned that Hurst had been the one who'd introduced him to The Duke.

And somehow, when Tommy came to the street where his sister's fiancé had lately taken up rooms, instead of pounding on the door for the marquis's surly landlady to let him in, he ducked down an alleyway. He'd stood there, panting in the dark, trying to catch his breath.

Slater had been right behind him, helping him climb into that chaise, one hand on his elbow. He knew the marquis had believed him drunker than he actually was. Tommy had given up gin, however, since the night he was shot. He would drink wine with dinner, and ale with breakfast, but since his injury, he could not abide the taste of hard liquor. Instead, he slipped the waiter a guinea, and whispered for him to bring him water—only water, but in a glass like the gins ordered by others, only with an orange twist in it, so that he could tell it apart.

He had not been half so drunk as Slater had thought him. That was why, he realized, with a growing chill, he was not dead now.

He could not think where to go. He could not go home, and he could not go to Slater's. But he couldn't stay in an alley all night, not deaf as a post, as he was. He had other friends. He was debating which one lived the nearest when he saw the chaise pull up—his chaise, driven by Peters. As Tommy watched, Slater burst from the carriage, and pounded up the steps to his front door, where he stood hammering on the thick portal.

And that's when it really came home to Tommy just how deaf he was. He couldn't hear the hammering. He was standing not a hundred feet away—he could see the worried look on his driver's face—and yet he could not hear the hammering.

The door opened. Slater's landlady stood there in shawl and nightcap, shouting at the marquis, by the contorted twist of her features.

But Tommy could not hear her.

She must have assured the marquis that he had had no visitors, since Slater turned, and dove back into the carriage.

Tommy, in his dank alleyway, almost came forward then. He almost flagged down Peters, and climbed in beside his old friend. Because it couldn't be. It simply couldn't be. Slater was his friend, his best friend. He was marrying his only sister, for God's sake. Why would Slater want to kill him? Slater had saved him back in Oxford, had pulled him back from the brink of death. It was ridiculous to think he might wish Tommy harm.

But at the last minute, Tommy ducked back into the dark alley. His chaise rolled by, moving at a dangerous clip on a street that, even so late at night, still teemed with activity. He let them go by, his heart drumming a frantic beat in his ears. *Idiot*, his heart seemed to say to him. *Idiot idiot idiot idiot* . . . .

Something had held him back from climbing into that carriage with Slater.

He could not say what it was, beyond the expression Braden Granville had worn that morning at the mention of The Duke. The Duke, who had already shot him once, would certainly not hesitate to do the same again. But he had not been in that crowd tonight. Tommy would have recognized him at once. There was no disguising that terrific bulk.

No, it had not been The Duke who'd shot at him. But it had almost certainly been someone working on his behalf. Tommy was as sure of it as he was sure he couldn't hear the orange seller standing across the street, her mouth opening and closing in eerie silence as she hawked her wares. The Duke had appointed someone to assassinate the Earl of Bartlett.

And Slater had been right behind him at the carriage. *Right* behind him. . . .

No. It was impossible. Not Slater. Slater hadn't shot at him. He wouldn't.

Would he?

It didn't matter. It didn't matter who it had been. What mattered was that he'd lived. He needed to go on living. He couldn't go home. No, he wouldn't be safe there, nor was he willing to put his mother and sister's lives in jeopardy by returning home. But he couldn't stay out on the street all night. Before his injury, yes, but not now. He hadn't the strength.

But he also had no money. He had gambled it all away, and then some, at the card tables. He could not take a room anywhere. Where could he go? What could he do?

And then quite suddenly, he knew. There was one man in London Tommy knew for certain wasn't on The Duke's payroll. One man in London he knew he could trust above all others.

And so he headed there, taking back alleys all the way.

Now he huddled by the servants' entrance, in the shadow of the steep steps leading to Braden Granville's front door, hugging himself even though it wasn't cold. It was a warm night, with a heavy layer of rain clouds overhead, pink in the bright lights from the city. It had not yet started to storm, but it would. Rain, Tommy was convinced, would kill him sure as any bullet. He was in shock. He recognized the signs in his uncontrollable shivering, his chattering teeth, his clammy skin. Tommy could only pray that before the heavens burst, Braden Granville would come home.

He must have nodded off, crouched there in the darkness,

because it seemed as if he were in the middle of a prayer about the rain, when suddenly a light shone in his eyes, and he realized the front door, high at the top of the steps, had been flung open.

He said a name—or at least he thought he did. He still couldn't hear himself—and came out from the shadows. A phaeton stood beside the curb, pulled by a magnificent team of grays. Braden Granville's Arabians, stamping nervously, rolling their lovely eyes at him.

And at the top of the steps stood the man himself.

He'd turned questioningly in Tommy's direction. The light from his front entrance fell full across his face, plainly revealing his shock when Tommy finally came stumbling into view.

He said something, Braden Granville did. But Tommy could not hear him. He saw the man's lips move, but he could not hear what he said.

And then—Tommy did not know how it came about—he was sinking, and hands were reaching out to him, trying to keep him upright. Tommy tried to tell them what had happened, only he did not know whether or not he spoke out loud, because he still could not hear his own voice.

But he was certain that he was crying, because he felt wetness on his cheeks, and he had time only to think that it was a sorry thing, when an earl—even a young one—wept before another man, especially a man like Braden Granville.

And then everything went black, and the last thing he remembered was Braden Granville's arms going around him, and his lips moving, his expression one not of shock anymore, but concern.

29

It was at ten o'clock sharp the next morning that Braden Granville raised the elaborate brass knocker on the Earl of Bartlett's door and let it fall back again.

Ten o'clock, Braden realized, was early for a social call. Ladies like Caroline Linford and her mother had hardly risen by that hour, or if they had, they were only just finishing their toilettes or breakfasts, or sitting down, perhaps, to write letters. How vastly different from life back in Seven Dials, where, by ten o'clock in the morning, the day had already been under way five or six hours, since all the women there rose at daybreak, in order to prepare the morning repast for their husbands or fathers and brothers, or stoke the fires for the day's baking, or help to scale the first catch. . . .

And to Braden, who'd been unable to break some of the habits he'd acquired back in the Dials, ten o'clock was rather late in the day. But he was quite conscious that this was not a popularly held opinion with people in his new circle, and so he had restrained his impulse to call on Caroline any earlier—although it had taken everything he had to keep himself from doing so, from doing to Caroline's door what he'd done to Jacquelyn's.

306 · MEG CABOT

But breaking down Caroline Linford's door wouldn't have done at all, no matter how urgently he needed to see her. . . .

And his reason in this case was, he felt, very urgent indeed. Not because he wished to assuage her concern on her brother's account—for he knew she must be frantic with worry for him. No, not that at all. The boy was well enough. He had been sleeping soundly when Braden left his house for Caroline's, with no injuries worse than a powder burn and a ringing in his ears that would last only a day or two.

No, there was another matter far more pressing—to him, anyway—than Tommy's welfare that made him eager to see the Lady Caroline. And it wasn't even a desire to ascertain for himself the truth of Jackie's extraordinary revelation that Caroline Linford was in love with him. No, it was something more important than even that. For as unpleasant as his interview the night before with Jackie had been, there was one thing she'd been right about:

He had never, not in all the years since his first sexual encounter, uttered those three words Jackie had accused him yesterday of not having anywhere in his vocabulary.

He had certainly had them said to him—whispered to him— even screamed at him, once or twice. Plenty of women had told him that they loved him. But he had never returned the favor.

And not because he was incapable of feeling love. He had loved his mother, and his father, and even Weasel, in his own way. But a woman? Never. They had all been pleasant, the women he had known. Unquestionably beautiful. But none until Caroline had kept him sleepless, tossing and turning until the wee hours, going over, in his head, her every word and gesture. None until Caroline had made him feel so completely out of control, as if the world over which he'd once thought he had mastery was slipping inexorably out of his grip. None until Caroline had caused his heart, each time he saw her, to flip inside his chest.

None until Caroline.

And that was why he was standing there at that early hour, knocking at her door. He intended to tell her what he'd told no other woman, what he ought to have told her last night, only he'd thought his kisses might better form the words.

But he would tell her today, and she had better listen, because he only intended to say them just the once. And if she laughed, or worse, turned her back on him again, he . . . well, he didn't know what he'd do. But he could guarantee he'd never say them again, those words. Never.

And then the door to her house was opening, and a tall, hawk-nosed man—a butler, Braden supposed, though the fellow looked a little familiar, causing him to wonder if perhaps they had met before—was looking down at him haughtily.

"Yes?" he drawled.

Braden extended his card with matching haughtiness. "Lady Caroline, please," he said.

The butler did not even glance at the card. "Lady Caroline," he said, "is not at home."

This was not something Braden had anticipated. Oh, not that Caroline would have left the house before ten o'clock. He did not, for a moment, believe she had. But that she would have instructed her butler to say she was not at home to anyone.

Braden, who'd continued to hold out his card, now turned it over, and, removing a pencil from his pocket, hastily scrawled something across the back of it.

"Be so good," he said, when he was finished, "as to give this to the Lady Caroline, and tell her I'll be waiting for her inside my curricle."

The butler glanced at the large black carriage that stood below them, on the street. He said, "I beg your pardon, sir, but you'll be waiting quite some time. Lady Caroline left town this morning. Upon her return, I will, of course, inform her that you called."

Braden stared at the butler in utter disbelief. "Left town?" he repeated. "Left *London*?"

But that was impossible . . . absurd. The girl couldn't have simply *left*.

"When?" Braden heard himself bark. "Where did she go?"

The butler looked disdainful. "Really, sir," he said. "But I am not at liberty—"

Braden hardly heard him. Something had begun to buzz inside his head, as if it had been he, and not the earl, who'd been too close to a pistol blast.

What was he to do now? Caroline, it appeared, was gone. But where? And why?

He knew why. He knew perfectly well why. He had bungled it. In his ham-handed attempt to make her forget about that blasted fiancé, he had only made things worse. She was so unlike the other women in her circle in so many ways—so scrupulously conscientious, unaffected, without a trace of vanity—that he had forgotten that in some ways, she was as absolutely conventional as most girls in the *beau monde*.

And one of those ways was her complete ignorance of all things sexual. Oh, certainly she knew how the thing was done. But she knew nothing of the pleasure that could be had between a man and a woman. And when he'd tried to show her, he'd certainly succeeded in arousing her. . . .

But he'd also, he knew from the way she'd run from him, frightened her witless.

Shaking his head to dispel the buzzing in it, he asked the butler, "Is Lady Bartlett at home?"

The butler's look of disdain now grew openly hostile. "Lady Bartlett is unwell. If you would like to leave a message for her ladyship, I will see that she gets it."

Braden thought about leaving a message concerning the earl. It would, he thought, be politic to let the Lady Bartlett know that her son, whom she'd surely noticed had not come home the night before, was all right.

Politic, but not, Braden thought, wise. The fewer people-who knew the earl's whereabouts, the better—even if it meant causing her ladyship a bit of anxiety.

"No," Braden said. "No message."

He turned to go.

And then, to Braden's utter astonishment, the butler's arm shot out, and his shoulder was squeezed excitedly.

"Dead?" The butler peered down at him, all haughtiness gone from his slightly narrow face. "Is that you?"

Braden, startled, stared at the man. And then quite suddenly, he said, "My God. Wormy?"

The butler's expression had changed from one of extreme boredom to one of the most agitated recognition. "Aye, it's me," he whispered, raggedly, with a quick glance over his shoulder, back into the house.

"My God," Braden said. "I hardly recognized you, all done up in suit and tails. When did they let you out of Newgate, then?"

Paling, Wormy Jones slipped from the house, carefully closing the door behind him, so that they could speak without being over-heard.

"Jesus, Dead," he said, taking a handkerchief from his waist-coat pocket, and mopping his suddenly damp face with it. "I didn't recognize you, either, in that cravat. What's it been, then? Twenty years?"

"At least," Braden said. "But you've done well for yourself. Last time I saw you, Wormy, they were dragging you off to prison for stealing that—"

Wormy flung a finger to his lips. "Shhhh," he hissed. "What are you trying to do? I'm clean now, I swear it. Have been ever since they let me out the last time. I'm not sayin' it's been easy—"

"No," Braden said, thoughtfully. "No, I don't imagine it has

been. But your luck's done a bit of turning, hasn't it? I mean—"
He nodded meaningfully toward the Earl of Bartlett's front door.

Wormy flinched. "Aw, that," he said, dismissively. "Aye, it's not bad. Wouldn't ever've got the post, though, if that bleedin' Lady Bartlett knew a mule from a thoroughbred, which, I can tell you, she don't. But the wages are good, and I get on well with the cook, so . . ." He broke off, with a philosophical shrug.

Braden did not like to take advantage of a friendship as old as this—particularly since he had not seen the fellow since he himself had been knee-high—but he had not lost any of his eager desire to see Caroline. And so he asked, with all the nonchalance he could muster, "I don't suppose you could tell me now where Lady Caroline's gone off to, could you, Wormy?"

Wormy hissed at him, "It's Bennington now. None of that worming me way into tight spots anymore. I'm clean, I tol' you." He glanced furtively up and down the block, as if he expected at any moment the local constable to come tearing toward him. "Look, mate, I can't tell you where she's gone, only because I don't know it. All I know is, I called for the brougham to be brought round at six this morning, on her orders, and had the boys load it up with her bags."

An oddly helpless feeling—a feeling Braden Granville did not like at all—came over him, and when he spoke again, it was in a voice raw with emotion. "You must have some idea where she went, Wormy."

The butler shook his head. "Honest I don't, Dead. In quite a rush she was to leave, though. Didn't look as if she'd slept a wink."

How well Braden knew the feeling.

Then Wormy brightened. "I know," he said. "You want to find Lady Caroline, you've only got to ask the Lady Emily. She's a rum'un. She'll tell you."

Braden blinked. "Lady Emily? Yes. Yes, I suppose she'd know."

Wormy took a step back toward the door, then flung a glance

in Braden's direction. "I swear I wouldn't've known you, Dead. You're that changed. You're one of *them* now." On the word *them*, he nodded back toward the house again.

"No," Braden said, firmly, and without the slightest regret. "That's not true."

Wormy looked distinctly disappointed. "Oh," he said. "Well. Good luck then, Dead."

Braden nodded. "Same to you, Wormy. I mean, Bennington."

And then the thief became a butler once more, and slipped, with chin raised high, back into the house.

And Braden went in search of Lady Emily Stanhope.

Only first, of course, he had something he needed to do.

30

"But Sister Emily," Lucretia Knightsbridge complained. "This beard itches."

Emmy, annoyed, snapped, "Well, what do you expect me to do about it? They were all out of mink beards at the costume shop."

But none of the members of the London Society for Women's Suffrage appreciated Emily's sarcasm, and didn't seem to be inclined to return to rehearsing their tableau, which Emmy had written and was now directing. It was Emmy's hope that by conducting a mimed performance on the steps of the Parliament building of President Lincoln's signing of the Emancipation Proclamation, attention would be drawn to the parallel between the slaves in America and the women of England, and the men inside the Parliament building might be called upon to do as Mr. Lincoln had, and right a wrong that had gone too long uncorrected.

Lucretia Knightsbridge was supposed to be playing Lincoln, but she kept lowering her beard to bleat at Emmy about the discomfort of her costume.

"If Sister Lucretia doesn't have to wear her beard," Chrystabel Hemmings, who was dressed in rags with paper shackles glued around her wrists and ankles, whined, "then I shouldn't have to wear these trousers. The wool chafes me."

Genevieve Kenney sucked in her breath quickly. The prettiest of the members of the London Society for Women's Suffrage, she had been elected to play Lady Liberty, and was dressed in only a muslin toga, with a bough of gilt olive leaves in her golden hair.

"If you think your trousers are bad," she cried, "what about *my* costume? I look like a harlot!"

It was in the middle of the uproar that took place directly following this statement that Emmy happened to notice, over the ladies' heads, a tall and distinctly out-of-place figure at the end of the room. Out of place, of course, because the figure happened to be male, and males did not, as a habit, make their way into the sanctum that was the meeting place of the London Society for Women's Suffrage.

And then, with a gasp of her own, Emmy realized who this particular male was.

And suddenly, she was rushing, as fast as she was able, to escape through the nearest possible exit. . . .

But Braden Granville was too quick for her. He easily barred her way to safety by thrusting a long and powerful arm across the doorway.

"Lady Emily," he said, not bothering to raise his voice above the cacophony of female voices, still arguing vociferously, all around them. He didn't have to. Like a foghorn, his deep voice carried easily above their more high-pitched, seagull-like tones.

"I believe you might be able to enlighten me, Lady Emily," Braden Granville continued, "on a matter in which I have a most personal and burning interest."

Emily swallowed. She had known, of course, that this was going to happen. Caroline had assured her she was wrong, but Emmy had known. A girl simply could not run from a man like Braden Granville and expect to get away with it. It didn't happen.

Still, she'd promised Caro. And so she said, "This is a private meeting, sir. You have no right to be here."

Up went those dark, intimidating eyebrows, including the one with the white slash through it, a scar from some long-ago knife fight, Emmy was quite sure. Pity the knife wielder hadn't held the blade a little lower. She wouldn't then be in this terribly awkward position.

"No right to be here?" Braden Granville asked, sounding amused. "Whyever not? I'm a supporter of votes for women, you know."

Emily blinked up at him with astonishment. "You—you can't be," she stammered. "This is a trick. A ruse, to get me to tell you where Caroline's gone."

He said, "Not at all," and reached into his waistcoat pocket. "It's perfectly ridiculous, one half the population not having the right to a say in its governance. You are, for the most part, rational creatures. More rational, surely, than most men I know. I'd feel a good deal better knowing our government was in your capable hands than, say, Lord Winchilsea's."

Stunned, Emily could only stare at him, her mouth slightly ajar.

"If dues are necessary," Braden Granville remarked, "then I will, of course, pay them. But you, then, Lady Emily, must concede that as a dues-paying member of your organization I have, in fact, every right to be here."

Emily watched in utter disbelief as Braden Granville thumbed through his billfold.

"I trust," he said, pulling out a fifty-pound note, "this will suffice."

Emily reached out to take hold of the bill in the manner of someone in a trance. But Braden Granville pulled it quickly out of reach.

"Wait a moment," he said. "I want to know what I get in return for giving you my hard-earned money."

Emily said, evenly, "A certificate of membership, of course."

"A certificate? For fifty *pounds*?"

"Well, and a sash."

"A sash? What am I to do with a bloody sash?"

"You're supposed to wear it," Emily said. "At our rallies. It says Votes for Women on it."

"Is that all?"

"No. You'll receive our monthly circular—"

"Oh," Braden said. "*That* ought to be entertaining. Will it, perhaps, explain why that woman over there is wearing a false beard?" And then he surrendered his fifty-pound note. "Never mind. I don't want to know. Just tell me where the devil Caroline's gone off to, and don't lie. I can see straight through any attempts at prevarication. Always have."

Emily took the bill, folded it crisply, and tucked it up her sleeve. It was admittedly with some sense of unreality that she did this, since Braden Granville was the first man to join any affiliation of The Movement, that she knew of.

She found herself quite unable to look him in the eye. He had such a penetrating glance, for all his irises were merely brown. Still, there was no mistaking the flecks of russet within them, and that, she thought, was quite unnerving. How Caroline could love this man, she hadn't the slightest idea.

But that she did love this man, Emily knew without a doubt. And since this man, in her opinion, was a good deal better for Caroline than the last one she had had her heart set on, that one being the pinheaded Marquis of Winchilsea, Emily decided to give him a chance to prove to her whether or not he was worthy of her breaking her solemn pledge to Caroline.

"What are you going to do," she asked cautiously, "when you find her?"

Braden Granville set his jaw. "I intend to make her see that marrying that jackanapes Slater would be the worst mistake she could ever make."

Emily folded her arms across her chest. "Oh, and I suppose she'd be much better off as your mistress?"

"Mistress?" He glared at her as if she had said something distasteful. "I intend to make her my wife."

Emily let out a whoop of laughter at this. "Oh, please! You, the Lothario of London? Marry Caroline Linford? I think not."

She ought not to have laughed. She knew it almost the minute the words were out of her mouth. She saw the pain that creased his face, the sudden dark anger that quickly followed it.

Still, he controlled the emotion admirably, saying in a carefully toneless voice, "I know that to you, the idea of a man like me marrying your friend is preposterous. And you're probably quite right. But I think I'd be a better husband for her than that . . . than the marquis. And I intend to prove it to her, if you'll just tell me where she went."

All urge to laugh had fled with the sight of the very real emotion Emily had seen in those dark eyes. He loved Caroline, she realized with something akin to shock. *Really* loved her. She had thought as much outside the Old Bailey, but this confirmed it. Only . . .

"You can't marry Caroline," she pointed out. "You're engaged to Lady Jacquelyn."

"Not anymore," was his terse reply.

"But . . ." Emily shook her head. "Caroline won't be able to testify. If Lady Jacquelyn files for breach of promise, and Caroline is married to you—or even just engaged to you—her testimony won't be counted—"

"I don't care about that," Braden Granville ground out, impatiently. "I'm willing to settle. Whatever it takes."

"If she breaks it off with the marquis," Emily felt compelled to inform him, "her name will be mud. And you can bet a pretty penny he'll sue, too."

"I...don't...care." He was obviously on the verge of losing his temper, that dangerous temper that Tommy had talked so much about. "Just tell me where she is."

Emily blinked. Good Lord. It was true, then. It was perfectly true. The Lothario of London. The Lothario of London was in love with Caroline. Caroline, her Caroline, who could not pass a beggar without giving him half of what was in her purse, or a cart horse without slipping it a sugar cube. She had the most notorious skirt chaser in London so head over heels in love with her, he'd been willing to join the ladies' suffrage movement, because her best friend had told him to.

"Caroline has gone to my country house in Shropshire," Emily said. "Woodson Manor. She said she needed to be alone, to think. I'm not sure if you ought to—"

But Braden Granville had already turned and fled the room like a man with a . . . well, with a pack of angry suffragettes after him.

31

Caroline sat upon the window seat, watching the rain splashing the panes, and wondered if she had lost her mind.

It certainly seemed to her as if she had. For what but madness could have made her behave the way she had with Braden Granville?

It was horrible, what she'd done. Worse than shocking. What had she been thinking?

And the worst thing of all was that she had brought it all down upon her own head. Lessons in how to make love. Indeed!

Well, she was alone at last—quite thoroughly alone, save the caretaker and his wife, and the men who cared for the horses. But they all lived out. Which suited her very well indeed: She needed peace and quiet, solitude in which to think through her dilemma, without any distractions—particularly in the form of Braden Granville.

Especially in the form of Braden Granville.

And now she was alone, and it was raining out, and she had all the time she wanted to sit and think about her horrible mistake, and how she was going to make things right again.

Only she didn't think she could.

She saw that now. She did not love Hurst Slater. She knew now that she had never loved Hurst Slater. What she had felt for him had been nothing more than gratitude, first that he had saved her brother, and then that, from out of all the women in London, he should have sought her out to be his bride. She had been flattered by his attentions, excited by his kisses—passionless, she realized now, though they had been—and gratified at the thought that this dashing young marquis wanted her, and not some prettier girl. Her, out of all the beautiful young women he knew. He wanted her.

And *that* was why, she knew now, that she had not wept when she'd found him in the arms of another. *That* was why she had not confronted him in a storm of jealous rage.

She had not loved him.

But that, of course, was the least of her concerns. Weighing far more heavily on her conscience than the fact that she did not love—and probably never had—her fiancé, was the knowledge that what Jacquelyn Seldon had accused her of yesterday at Worth's was true:

She was in love with Braden Granville.

She didn't want to be. It was horrible, knowing that she was. She loved him, in spite of his horrible reputation where woman were concerned, in spite of the fact that she highly disapproved of nearly everything about him, including his work and style of living. She loved him, in spite of Hurst, and his appealing blue eyes. She loved him in spite of all the things she'd heard, all the things Jackie Seldon had said. She loved him, had loved him since that moment in the hallway at Dame Ashforth's, when her heart had done that odd flip-flop in her chest.

She loved him for being everything no other man in her acquaintance—with the possible exception of her father—had ever been: a self-made man, who'd had the strength and persever-ance to pull himself up out of the gutter, and to the top of his line of work. A caring man, who hadn't forgotten his friends and fam-ily in his meteoric rise to the top, who was not embarrassed to be seen in public with his very eccentric, but sweet, father. A man of honor, who had initially been appalled at her proposal, and had turned her away—she realized now that there were plenty of men out there who would not have been so gallant, who would have made every attempt to take advantage of her innocence. Braden Granville had not. . . .

At least, not at first.

But even then, Caroline was convinced he had not done so cold-bloodedly. She was quite sure he felt something for her. She had seen it in his face the night before, as his father had led her away. A naked longing that had brought home, as almost nothing else had, the gravity of her situation, the fact that she'd been playing, all this time, with fire. . . .

Aren't we? That's what he'd asked her, when she'd said it wasn't as if the two of them were in love.

Aren't we?

And that's when she'd realized what she'd done. Because it had been all very well for her to love Braden Granville—for her to burn for him, and long for him, and sigh over him. It hadn't mattered, because she'd been sure he hadn't returned the emotion.

But for him to love her in return, and to have admitted it— well, sort of—in that voice, that voice that even now, remembering it, made the hairs on her arms stand up. . . .

What else could she do but run? Because it could never be. *They* could never be. She'd pledged herself to Hurst. She could not go back on her word. She could not do that to him, to her family. . . .

And then, as Caroline sat there, contemplating her sanity, or lack thereof, there came a knock upon the door, so loud and unexpected that she actually shrieked, and leaped up from her seat.

Who could it be? she wondered, fighting to get her heart rate back to normal as she stood in the middle of the Stanhopes' front parlor, where the furniture was shrouded in white linen to ward off the dust until the family returned later in the summer.

A message, perhaps? A note from her mother already, though she had not been gone from London above twelve hours yet? Oh, why wouldn't the woman leave her alone? She'd expressly written in the letter she'd left Lady Bartlett that she needed to be alone—though she had not mentioned just *how* alone she'd be, omitting from her note the fact that Emily and the rest of her family were still in the city, something that, if her mother found out, she would not have liked at all.

Pulling her robe about her—she had changed out of her traveling clothes and into her nightgown, though it was only just past teatime, because she had nowhere to go, and there was no one to see her, anyway—she went to the door.

It practically burst open at her touch, the wind from the storm outside had risen so in the last few minutes. Lashed by the rain, a tall figure stood on the doorstep, swathed in a great oilskin coat. The only person from the neighborhood who stood so tall as that was the vicar, who'd been known to drop by from time to time to call on Emily's father. Perhaps he had seen the lights, and thought Lord Woodson was at home—

But then he threw back his hood, and Caroline shrieked. The person underneath the greatcoat was not the vicar at all.

Braden Granville stepped over the threshold, stripping off the dripping garment, and giving the door a shove closed behind him with his foot.

"Good God, Caroline," he said. "What's that you have on?"

Blushing scarlet, Caroline stammered, "It's . . . it's a nightdress. What are you doing here?"

"A nightdress?" Braden looked around, and apparently because there weren't any servants about, hung his coat on the newel post of the staircase that curled from the foyer to the upper stories of the house. "I hardly think that appropriate attire at this early hour—anyone might come to the door—and particularly in weather like this. You must be freezing."

"How," Caroline demanded, in what she hoped was an authoritative voice, "did you find me? What are you doing here?"

"I ought to put the same question to you." Braden looked around at the draped furniture, and the chandeliers wrapped in muslin bags, and declared, "This place is like a tomb. Did you really think you could get any serious thinking done here, Caroline? It's a veritable sarcophagus."

"It isn't a sarcophagus," Caroline said. "It's just closed up for the season. And it's a perfectly reasonable place to come to think. Especially since I came here to be *alone*."

If he got the hint, he didn't let on. Instead, he strode into the parlor, kneeling down beside the cold hearth, and reached up inside the fireplace to open the damper. "I hardly think that was wise, do you? What about those nefarious evildoers Violet's supposed to defend you against? You don't think they have those in the country? You don't think a young woman, all alone, in a big house like this, dressed in a nightdress that leaves very little indeed to the imagination, wouldn't act as a magnet for men like that?"

Caroline reached up and clutched the wrapper even more tightly closed. "How did you find me?" she asked. "I didn't tell anyone I was coming. Anyone except . . ."

"That's precisely how I found you." Braden, having found some wood, appeared to be intent on lighting a fire to ward off the damp chill of the house. "Lady Emily told me."

"*Emmy* told you?" Caroline could hardly believe her ears. Emmy, her best friend, with whom she'd trusted her deepest, darkest secrets, had let spill the most intimate one of all, and to *this* man, of all people?

"No," Caroline said. "No, I don't believe you. Emmy wouldn't do something like that."

"She would," he said, as he carefully lit the pile of tinder he'd built beneath the wood pile. "She's quite reasonable, you know. A good deal more reasonable than you."

Caroline, still very indignant, but grateful, actually, for the fire, which had sprung merrily to life, and was already sending some much needed warmth in Caroline's direction, said, "I have been perfectly reasonable."

"Have you?" He was still kneeling before the fire, on the rather raggedy polar-bear-skin rug that Emily's mother had refused to allow in their London town house, but which her husband, Lord Woodson, had insisted upon keeping, having shot the creature himself—in self-defense, or so he claimed—on a polar expedition in his extreme youth.

When Braden looked up at Caroline, she could see something that very much resembled a sparkle in his dark eyes.

"Then why did you run away?"

Disconcerted by this sparkle, Caroline stammered, "I—I told you. I needed time to think. . . ."

"Not now," Braden said. "I meant last night. Why did you run away from me last night?"

"Oh," Caroline said, faintly. She had not been expecting that particular question. "Because . . ."

"Because why?"

She couldn't tell him. Not there in Lord Woodson's drawing room, with her in her nightclothes, and her feet bare. How she must look to him! She hadn't a shred of dignity left. This was what he'd reduced her to. She was quite sure the tracks of her tears must be showing, all up and down her cheeks. Her eyes could only be red and swollen.

"Because it can't be," she said, her voice raw. "You know it can't be."

The sparkle, she noticed, disappeared abruptly. "Because I'm not gentry?" he asked, quietly.

Caroline, struck to the heart by the hurt in his voice, found herself, without quite being aware she'd moved, sinking down onto the thick fur rug beside him, and reaching for his hand.

"Of course not," she said, keeping her gaze fastened on the hand she held in her lap, since she found it a good deal easier to look at his calluses than into his eyes. "You know it has nothing to do with that. It's true that it would seem as if we come from different worlds, you and I. But they're not so very different. My father wasn't always an earl. He wasn't even always considered a gentleman. But like you, he was one, anyway—from birth. Some men— no matter how low-born—just are."

He had grown very still the moment her fingers had come in contact with his. Now he asked, in a voice that no longer sounded hurt, but was still unimaginably soft, "Then why?"

She didn't have to ask what he meant. He was still waiting to hear why it was they could never be together. As if he didn't know. As if it hadn't been all they'd talked about, since she'd first come to him, that day in his office. Did she have to tell him? Did she have to say the words Hurst Slater, Marquis of Winchilsea?

She looked up then, into his face, meeting his gaze with her own . . . and then hastily looked away again, appalled. For what she'd seen in his dark, normally so inscrutable eyes was a look of such naked longing that it took her breath away.

And that was when it struck her that they were all alone together in the house—that there was no one else around for miles and miles, save her horses—and that outside, the storm had gathered in intensity until the clouds had rendered the evening sky black as night, and the rain was lashing the windowpanes quite savagely. That even if she'd wanted to—and she most definitely did not—she could not have reasonably turned Braden Granville out into such weather.

"Oh," Caroline couldn't help murmuring, "dear."

And then, to her abject horror, she felt him reach up with his free hand, and pull a pin from the complicated pile of ringlets she'd been too tired to brush out.

"Oh," she said again.

He hesitated, his hand, which had been raised to pluck another pin, balanced in front of her eyes.

"Did I hurt you?" he asked, curiously.

"No," she said. "Only . . ."

"Only what?"

"Only I wish you wouldn't."

"Wish I wouldn't what?"

"Touch my head like that," she blurted, in a rush. "It isn't right."

Braden lowered his hand, but his gaze, as he looked down at her, was uncomprehending. "You don't want me to touch your hair?"

She nodded vigorously, and in doing so, realized the pin he'd removed had been a crucial one. She could feel the heavy pile of curls slipping already. "It's wrong," she said. There was an unbearable tightness in her chest, and she was beginning to suspect that she might burst into tears at any moment. "Don't you see it's wrong, Braden? Everything we've been doing . . . it's very wrong. *I* was wrong. No matter what you say."

"Is that," he asked, in quite a kind voice, she thought, "why you ran away?"

"Y-yes." Here they came. She could feel the tears gathering beneath her eyelids. A second later, the room grew watery, as she tried to blink them away. "I couldn't—I couldn't bear it."

The hurt tone returned to his voice. "Couldn't bear being touched by me?"

"No!" She reached up with her free hand, the one he wasn't still holding, the one he wasn't caressing with his thumb, and wiped away her tears with the back of her wrist. "No, that's not it at all. It's just that I'm engaged to be married, and it's very upsetting to be engaged to be married to someone . . . and yet think you might be . . . in love with someone else."

There. She had said it. Admitted out loud, for the first time, what had been weighing so heavily upon her shoulders.

And then Braden Granville was clearing his throat—was it her imagination, or did he sound very uncomfortable indeed?

"That's very interesting," he said. "Because I too find it upsetting to be engaged to be married to someone . . ." He paused, and Caroline, tears still trembling on her eyelashes, glanced up at him questioningly. . . .

And was completely unable to look away. Something in his gaze held hers to it, surer than the strongest magnet or glue.

"And I *know*," he said, deliberately, "that I'm in love with someone else."

This time, when his hand moved toward Caroline's head, she didn't flinch. Nor did she draw breath to protest. Instead, she sat perfectly still as Braden reached for another pin, gave it a gentle tug . . .

And her hair, in all of its dark blond glory, came spilling down her shoulders.

"That," Braden said, in a voice so deep, she hardly recognized it, "is much better."

32

And then his fingers sank deeply into the heavy fall of her hair, and he was bringing her face up toward his . . .

And Caroline didn't protest. How could she? He loved her. Every fiber of her being was pulsing, vibrating, *singing* with this newfound knowledge. Her heart was beating in time to the words. . . .

He loves me. He *loves* me. *He loves me.*

Which was why it was perfectly all right for him to bring his mouth down, with a good deal of proprietary savagery, over hers. And why it didn't bother her in the least when he released her hand and snatched her instead around the waist, bringing her body up hard against his. And the fact that there was only that thin layer of material separating her skin from his? Entirely forgivable.

In fact, Caroline found herself feeling quite relieved that she was wearing so little clothing. Because unhampered by corset or crinoline, she could, for the first time, *feel* things she'd never felt before . . . or at least, hadn't been able to feel in so much fascinating detail. There was the reassuring hardness of Braden's chest, against which he was crushing her own, much softer one. There was the tight wall of muscle that made up his stomach, his skin singeing her, right through the material of his waistcoat and shirt.

And, most interesting of all, there was that rock-hard lump between his legs that last night—had it really only been just twenty-four hours ago?—she'd been so shocked to feel against her, but which now she was rather curious to inspect. It had felt so *strange* . . . and continued to feel strange, since even now she could feel it pressing rather insistently against her, through the thick material of Braden's trousers. . . .

Then Braden, who'd been kissing her more deeply, more intrusively than ever before—until the room was spinning all around her, and the only stable thing in it was him—lifted his head, and whispered down to her, in a voice that wasn't in the least bit steady, "Take this off."

And with his fingers, he plucked at her nightgown.

But Caroline shook her head, so that the golden highlights in her thick hair glimmered in the firelight.

"No," she said, her voice not quite steady, either.

"No?" he echoed, looking a little shocked.

She gave his waistcoat a pluck of her own. "Yours first."

With an alacrity that caused her to lean back in surprise, he stripped off his coat, waistcoat, and shirt, almost in a single motion. Caroline heard a good many buttons pop, and some material being torn, as well.

And then, the firelight bringing into high relief the peaks and valleys of his muscular torso—the golden swell of his biceps, the deep indentations along either side of his stomach, the crisp, dark hair with which his chest was matted—he reached for her again, and this time, when he dragged her toward him, and her fingers touched, for the first time, bare flesh, and not material, Caroline's breath caught in her throat, and her heart began a frantic beat that she could feel being echoed thunderously within the walls of his own ribs.

He was kissing her again, but now it was with more urgency than savagery, and his hands, instead of being around her waist or in her hair, were busy with the ribbons and buttons that held her nightclothes together. For a moment, she thought he was going to rip the garment from her the way he'd ripped his own, but he was more gentle than that, his fingers seeming almost reverent as they brushed her skin. In less time than Caroline would have thought possible, she was naked before him.

Only the fire was so warm, and his hands so capable, that she didn't even realize it until she felt the startling sensation of his naked chest against hers. . . .

This was something so unexpected—and so incredibly wonderful—that Caroline, hardly knowing what she did, pressed even closer to him, as his hands, seeming to delight in her naked-ness, raced up and down her body, as if he were trying to memorize her every line and curve. One second his fingers were molded to her breasts, his touch hot as the fire that burned beside them. The next, they had moved to cup her buttocks, exerting a gentle but insistent pressure that brought her pelvis up hard against his.

And all the time, his lips moved over her, devouring her, as if he would never stop, not until he had tasted all of her, her mouth, her throat, even the rosy tips of her nipples. . . .

Then, quite suddenly, his ink-dark head lifted from where it had been pressed between the valley of her breasts, and, his gaze locked onto hers, Braden started lowering her, slowly, but inexora-bly, to the floor. . . .

Or, rather, the thick white fur upon which they'd been kneeling.

And even then, Caroline did not quail. Oh, her heart was pounding, all right. But so, she knew, because she could feel his pulse leap at her lightest touch, was his. No, Caroline did not lose courage . . . not then.

But when he'd successfully navigated her to the floor, and she lay in the thick white fur, so smooth and warm upon her back, with her hair spread out behind her head like a fan, and Braden, still kneeling—only now it was between her legs—reached for the buttons of his pants, and released that part of him she'd felt pressing so urgently against her. . . .

That was when Caroline's bravery fled, like water from a cracked vase. She simply could not see any physical possibility of what was about to happen . . . well, happening.

Braden, she could tell at a glance, hadn't the slightest doubt. In fact, he seemed perfectly oblivious to her skepticism. His hands were upon her once again, only now they were touching her in that place—oh, that *place*—he'd touched before, sending her to such glorious heights. And it felt glorious again, only he couldn't possibly think . . . he couldn't actually be planning on . . .

But apparently he was, since he was moving over her, the way he had on the swing the night before, only this time, he was naked, and so was she, and the sensation of his flesh against hers was almost more than she could bear, it was so intoxicating, only he couldn't, he really *couldn't*—

And then he was, and Caroline, feeling the tip of that impossibly large, impossibly hard thing pressing against her in that place, froze, and reached up to grasp frantically at his shoulders, those wide, dangerously strong-looking shoulders, to which she'd clung for stability when his kisses had sent the room spinning around her, and which she pushed at now, to get his attention.

He raised his lips from hers—because through it all, he'd been kissing her as if he couldn't stop, as if he'd never get enough of kissing her—and looked down at her, his gaze oddly unfocused.

"What?" he whispered, and Caroline, beneath him, bit one of her beard-burned lips, hardly knowing how to tell him . . . not when she could feel his heart pumping so furiously against hers.

She couldn't tell him. How could she tell this man that she thought there might be something wrong with him, that he was grossly deformed, and that the act of love was never going to be a possibility between the two of them? This was obviously untrue, since he had evidently been making love successfully, despite his infirmity, all over London, for the past decade or so. Maybe it was *her*. Maybe *she* was the one who was deformed. Maybe she had suffered all her life with this hidden malady, and not even known it. Maybe she would never know what it was like to feel a man inside her, because no man, if they were all like Braden, would ever fit—

"Caroline." Braden's voice sounded odd, as if he were biting down on something very hard. A quick glance at him—his face, after all, consumed most of Caroline's line of vision—revealed that he was tightly clenching his jaw. *"What is it?"*

"Nothing," Caroline said, quickly. "Only . . ."

She felt him move closer to her, the tip of that hardened shaft prodding her where his fingers had been before, opening her, moving slickly along that damp and tender spot. . . .

And then, as if by magic, he was inside her. His restraint broken, he'd slid into her, lured by the incredible warmth he'd felt emanating from her, incapable of stopping himself.

He'd meant to go slowly. He'd meant to be patient. But his fine intentions crumbled in the actual face of that heat. Clutching her tightly, he moved, just a fraction of an inch . . . or so he'd thought. All at once, he was burying himself in that slick wet heat, and she stiffened in his arms, and cried out. . . .

And then he was consumed by guilt, because where she'd felt only pain, he'd felt the most magnificent pleasure, was feeling it still, as she closed around him, tighter than any fist. . . .

Beneath him, Caroline opened her eyes, which she'd screwed shut as he'd entered her, and blinked like someone waking from a trance.

"I'm sorry," he said raspily, moving to cup her face in his hands, raining tiny kisses down upon it. "I'm so sorry, Caroline. I love you so much. . . ."

But Caroline, as if she'd come to understand something, responded only by moving beneath him . . . just slightly, but enough to cause him to suck in his breath, amazed all over again by the sweet, enveloping warmth that clung to him so tightly. For Caroline, though she hadn't been able to help crying out at the size of him, at the disturbing length of what he was filling her with, knew now that those times he'd touched her with his fingers, and she'd felt an empty craving within her, that it was *this* she'd craved, *this* she'd been longing for, almost since the moment he'd first touched her.

This realization must have shown on her face, because with a muffled moan, Braden lowered his mouth to hers again, and began to move within her—and not gently, either. He moved like a man who'd come to the end of what precious little control he'd had over his baser emotions, and now, with her surrender, he was abandoning himself to them. He dove into her, as if with each thrust, he could somehow pour more of him into her. One of his hands even curled around her hips, lifting them, so that he could plunge more deeply between her thighs, pillage her more thoroughly.

And then Caroline, both her arms wrapped around his neck, her breath coming in ragged gasps, felt her entire body go taut, as if she were a string on an instrument a musician had chosen at that very moment to tighten. Her heart racing so fast, it seemed it might burst, she pressed herself to Braden as closely as she could, letting him fill her, letting him plunder her.

And then the string broke, and she seemed to go flying in a million different directions at once.

Truly. Suddenly, she was soaring across mountaintops and plains, whitecapped seas and barren deserts, through stuffy British drawing rooms and incense-filled Japanese temples, airy Indian palaces and colorful Bedouin tents. Flying, quite literally flying through them, as if she were a bird, or a passenger on a magic carpet. It was incredible, the most incredible thing she had ever known.

Until, with a jolt that was at once violent and infinitely gentle, she was back within herself, and Braden Granville had just collapsed, with a sort of a shout, on top of her. They were, she saw with a shock, in the Stanhopes' country house, lying across Lord Woodson's polar bear skin rug, where they had apparently been all along.

Braden, not breathing particularly steadily himself, nevertheless asked her, with a curious expression on his face, "Are you all right?"

Caroline, her heart having returned to something like a normal rhythm, was aware that his, pulsing very fast and strong against her bare breast, hadn't yet. She hoped he wasn't going to suffer an apoplexy, and answered worriedly, "Yes, of course. Are *you*?"

He seemed to think her question amusing, since he was smiling as he reached out and smoothed some long strands of her hair from her face. "I," he said, "am very well indeed."

And they lay in companionable silence for a moment, listening to the fire crack and hiss, and the rain, which had slackened somewhat, beat upon the windows.

"This wasn't," Braden said, a bit apologetically, after a while, "exactly how I wanted this to go, you know."

Caroline, very interested to hear that the professor had erred, struggled up onto her elbows, and eyed him brightly. "Wasn't it?"

"No." Braden spoke with a good deal of self-reproach. "Of course not. A young lady's defloration ought to take place in a bed, not on the floor."

"Ought it, indeed?"

"Of course. You'll have to forgive me, Caroline."

She said gravely, "I'll certainly try."

"And now," he said, moving from her, and reaching for her nightgown, which lay twisted beneath them, "put this on—oh, no perhaps you'd better not, it appears to have absorbed some, er. . . . Have you got another?"

"Indeed," Caroline said, observing the evidence of their sin with raised eyebrows. "Upstairs, in the first bedroom to the right."

"Very good. Stay here, and I'll fetch it for you. Then we'll find our way to the larder, and see if there's anything to be had for supper."

Caroline, feeling quite lethargic, made no move to hide her own nakedness as he struggled back into his trousers. She'd already revealed to him the innermost secrets of her heart. Why on earth would she bother hiding her body from him?

"The servants all live out," she informed him, apologetically.

"Thank God," was Braden's prompt reply.

"Yes, but you see," Caroline explained, "we shall have to fend for ourselves in the kitchen. And I must confess, I've never cooked a meal in my life."

Braden grinned down at her. "Fortunately for you," he said, "I have."

It was much later when Braden Granville looked up from the book of sonnets he'd been reading aloud and saw that Caroline's eyes were closed. Her shoulders rose and fell slowly with each deep, even breath she took, her eyelashes curled darkly against her cheekbones, her hair spread out in an amber arc against the pillows.

Smiling, he closed the book, and placed it atop the small table beside the bed they shared. It was the first time the sound of his voice had ever put a woman to sleep. He didn't know whether to be pleased or insulted.

But Caroline, he supposed, wasn't precisely the sonnet-type. She was much too levelheaded to be swayed by poetry. And she'd had a very long, very exhausting day—though she seemed, for the first time since he'd met her, actually happy. At least, she'd *looked* happy enough, sitting there in the Stanhopes' kitchen, watching him as he cooked, and then later, as they were eating.

And of course directly after that, she'd looked very happy indeed, when Braden, possessed by a sudden urge to bend her back across the table and ravish her all over again, promptly did so. Not a word of complaint had escaped her lips then . . . though, he thought now, she might well have cause, since they'd yet to make love in a bed. A carriage, a swing, a bear skin rug, and a rustic table, but no mattress as yet. He'd have to rectify that, at his earliest opportunity.

But Caroline didn't seem to mind. She behaved like a woman who'd had a weight lifted from her. Gone was the veil of worry that she'd seemed to wear almost constantly throughout their relationship. It was as if, by finally saying those three words—those words he'd so long avoided saying to any woman until now, until Caroline—he'd unstopped a bottle, and a different Caroline altogether had come pouring out of it.

A very different Caroline, for this one seemed not to have a care in the world. No nagging mother, no judgmental friends, no wedding looming on the horizon. She did not know, of course, about her brother's recent brush with death—and Braden was certainly not about to tell her. The earl was recovering nicely and was safer in Braden's house on Belgrave Square, with Crutch and Weasel and the rest of Braden's staff to watch over him, than he'd have been anywhere else. Braden had felt no qualms in leaving him there. His only discomfort was in the knowledge that he had kept Tommy's latest adventure from Caroline. . . .

But how could he tell her, when he knew the information would send her running back to London? He would tell her in the morning, he promised himself. For now, let her go on being content to forget about the future, and forget about the past, and live entirely in the moment.

Which was, considering what the future held for them, when they got back to London, the only real option.

His gaze never straying from Caroline's sleeping face, Braden set down the book of sonnets, and reached across the bed to lift a long strand of her silken hair, which he examined in the candlelight. Who would have thought, he mused, that in this innocent-looking girl lay such depths of passion, such a well of sensuality, that he—

Braden Granville, the Lothario of London—had been astounded by it?

It was with this thought that Braden blew out the candle on the bedside table and lay back, wrapping an arm around Caroline and spooning his body against hers, wondering at the softness of her hair, which had spread out across both their pillows.

A second later, Caroline's voice sounded in the darkness.

"Braden?"

"What is it?"

"I suppose there are a good many other ways," she said, sleepily, "of doing . . . what we did, earlier this evening."

He blinked in the darkness, not certain he'd heard her right. "Making love, you mean?"

"Yes. I think we should try them."

Braden was not usually so slow, but it had been a very long day, and they'd already made love twice—if that's what one could call their coupling, which to him seemed more like explosions of too long pent-up passion, particularly when it came to Caroline, who climaxed more quickly than any woman he had ever known. He asked, "Try what?"

His eyes having at long last adjusted to the darkness, he saw Caroline turn her head toward him. He could not, of course, make out her expression, but her voice carried her astonishment at his slow wittedness.

"Why, all of them," she said.

He blinked. Then blinked again. "*Oh,*" he said. "Of course." And he reached, gamely, to pull back the sheets. . . .

But Caroline had rolled over, with a contented sigh, and a "Good," uttered in the dreamiest of voices. A second later, she was asleep again, one arm curled possessively across his middle.

Braden, smiling to himself in the darkness, lay back against the pillows, and closed his eyes.

33

*C*aroline woke with a start.

Two things struck her at once as being terribly wrong. The first was that sunlight was streaming through the part in the curtains, indicating that it was already rather late into the day. Given Caroline's habit of rising before eight to go riding, this was disturbing.

But even more disturbing was the second thing she'd noticed. And that was that there appeared to be a large naked man in her bed.

But after brushing some of the sleep from her eyes, Caroline was able to see, by throwing a glance at the ormolu clock on the mantel, that it was only just after ten.

And the naked man, she realized, as memories of the night before came flooding back, was none other than Braden Granville.

Braden Granville, with whom, she recalled, she had behaved *most* scandalously. Braden Granville, who'd told her not once, but several times throughout the evening, and *very* emphatically, that he loved her.

What's more, he'd also informed her, quite without making it seem as if she had the slightest say in the matter at all—Emily would have been shocked—that they were getting married. That he didn't give a hang what anybody said, or how many people they shocked. That he was procuring a special license tomorrow, and that they would get married on the day after that, and that was the end of it.

And that had all seemed very well last night. Last night had been the most wonderful night of Caroline's entire life. She had been transformed, as if by magic, into someone else entirely, a bold and lascivious creature, quite unlike her normal self.

But in the bright light of day, the spell was broken. She was herself again. And she knew very well that no matter how many times Braden Granville declared that that would be the end of it, there would never be an end to it. How could there be? Because even if he did manage to get a special license today, and they married tomorrow, what was going to happen the day after that?

Caroline knew perfectly well what was going to happen. Her mother was going to have an apoplexy. Tommy was never going to speak to her again. And Hurst would be terribly, irrevocably hurt.

And she would be known throughout London as the girl who had jilted the Marquis of Winchilsea.

And it was no good saying the marquis had jilted her first. It wasn't the same, Caroline knew, when a man did it. It was one of Emmy's favorite topics, one that she frequently chose to bring up, especially at exclusive dinner parties where she could be sure there were plenty of philanderers present: Why was it that a man could have as many illicit affairs as he liked and suffer not the slightest social stigma, but when a woman did it, she was socially ruined?

Which was what Caroline was now. Ruined.

It was just as well, perhaps. Hurst would never take her now, not even on a silver platter. She was used, sullied, another man's plaything. Just thinking about how she'd been used caused Caroline to pull the sheet up over her head to hide her flaming cheeks.

Oh, Lord, what had she done?

It didn't do any good to say to herself that she'd done nothing worse than the marquis had done to her. Somehow, she felt that what she had done *was* worse. Hurst had been a loyal and faithful friend to Tommy, the best anyone could ask for. Even if he had been having an illicit love affair with Lady Jacquelyn Seldon—even if she now knew his kisses had been pale, pathetic imitations of the real thing, his whispered endearments meaningless compared to the gut-wrenching admissions Braden had made, in a voice that had forever seared those words upon her soul—he did not deserve to be treated this way.

They could not, Caroline realized, simply elope. At the very least, she had to write to her mother. She could not risk giving the Lady Bartlett an apoplexy. And Thomas, too, was going to need a letter of explanation and apology. And Hurst. . . . Oh, Hurst! What could she ever say to make it up to him?

Ruined. She was ruined. Caroline Linford, who up until the night before had been perhaps the most virtuous girl in all of England, was now most decidedly not so. And what was more, she'd been proposed to by the most notorious skirt chaser in town, the Lothario of London, Braden Granville.

It was simply too much to be believed. It couldn't possibly be true.

But she had the evidence of it right there in the bed beside her.

She had started to get out of bed to hunt for pen and paper, so that she could begin her letters of apology at once, but was distracted when she noticed that she clutched the whole of the sheet that had covered them, so that Braden Granville lay completely exposed to her gaze . . . exposed and quite gloriously nude.

Caroline, who had never seen a naked man before—well, unless one counted her brief glimpses the night before, when she'd been too preoccupied to get a good look—studied this one with some trepidation. Men were, she had always known, quite different from women. But precisely *how* different, she'd never had occasion to explore. But now Caroline saw these essential differences, and with no little alarm.

Braden Granville was not known as a handsome man. Caroline knew that. But while his face might not have been as attractive as some—being, for the common taste, far too saturnine and brooding, with a nose that had obviously been broken not once, but several times, and that scar, that stark white scar, that sliced his brow—his figure was all that was masculine and, though she knew she oughtn't admit it, pleasing.

How could she not appreciate the impressive size of those biceps, which even in sleep managed to look menacing? And that dark layer of hair swirling across his chest, then fanning down along that flat muscular stomach, to thicken into a nest between his legs, where lay the fascinating object that had afforded Caroline so much pleasure the night before. Her gaze was, of course, immediately drawn to it, and not just because the hair on his torso seemed to taper into an arrow that pointed at it. It really was a most extraordinary organ. Gazing at it in its relaxed state, Caroline wondered how she could ever have viewed it with the anxiety she had. In repose, it looked almost . . . well, harmless.

In fact, Caroline found herself not quite believing that such a relatively small thing could balloon to such enormous proportions. Her letters of apology forgotten for the moment, she reached out a tentative hand—after glancing quickly at Braden's face, to make sure he was still asleep—and touched it.

Her curiosity whetted, she wanted only to . . . well, she wasn't at all certain what she wanted.

But certainly not what occurred, which was that the thing began to grow.

Caroline, throwing a nervous glance at Braden's closed eyelids, quickly moved her hand away. But it was too late. It was much too late.

And then she jumped again, this time with a yelp, when one of

Braden's hands closed over her wrist. Glancing down at him with large and startled eyes, she saw that he was fully awake, and grinning at her in a most unsettling manner.

"Good morning," he said, in a voice that was deeper than usual, and still rough with sleep. "What have you been up to?"

Caroline said, with wide-eyed innocence, "Nothing—"

But the word ended on a note of alarm when Braden seized her free hand, and then lifted her toward him, not releasing her until she rested atop him.

"Now," he said, as if their conversation the night before had not been interrupted by nine hours of slumber. "What was it last night you were saying you wanted to try?"

Caroline blushed scarlet. Not just, of course, because it was broad daylight, and he was referring to things that most people, she knew, did not even discuss under the comforting cloak of night, but also because she could feel that organ that she'd wakened, long and hard beneath her.

"I—" she started to say, but that was all she got out, before he reached up and brought her mouth down upon his.

And then, really, conversation became impossible, because his tongue was making a sweeping inspection of the inside of her mouth, as if he suspected there might still be undiscovered country there. Which was all right with Caroline, since she found that she didn't much feel like talking, anyway. Not when his fingers were lifting the hem of her nightdress, his hands slipping beneath it, up the length of her thighs, across her belly, along her ribs, and then up to her breasts, to tease her nipples into the same ready hardness that she'd—albeit innocently—teased him.

What was it, she wondered, in the small part of her mind that was still capable of thought when Braden Granville's hands were on her, that made her go so weak at this man's slightest touch? He had only to kiss her, and she felt a wave of desire slam through her that was so violent, she was left shivering damply in its wake. Even now, she could feel that familiar tightness, that telltale wetness, between her legs that meant she was ready for him, and all he'd done was kiss her. Well, kiss her, and touch her *there*, and *there*, and, oh, *there* . . . .

And then, her back arching with pleasure, Caroline's half-lidded eyes flew open. For she'd realized that she was so ready for him, he was already halfway inside her, and she hadn't even noticed, she was that wet. And then his hands left her breasts, and settled instead on her hip bones.

Holding her still, his gaze never leaving hers, he entered her completely, and *that* she felt. Lord, did she feel it: she was full of him, more of him, she could have sworn, than there'd been last night.

And then he was moving, with deliberate slowness, still holding her hips, guiding her. Caroline couldn't help gasping at the rigid thickness of him as he eased first in, then out of her tight core. But there was enough slickness there that it didn't hurt . . . in fact, quite the opposite. Caroline felt the same mounting excitement she'd experienced the night before. She moved her hand across his furred chest, so that she could feel his heart beating beneath her palm. As she'd suspected, it was drumming with the same urgency as her own.

Then Braden was tugging her nightdress impatiently over her head.

"What," she demanded, from within its silvery folds, "are you *doing*?"

He succeeded in freeing her from the flimsy tent, and threw it to the floor, before raising both his hands to her breasts again.

"I want," he said, in a voice so guttural with desire, Caroline barely recognized it, "to see . . ."

To see where they were joined together, Caroline quickly realized, by following the direction of his gaze. She would have blushed with embarrassment, but, lowering his hands to her hips again, and pressing her down against him, he quickened his thrusts into her, and she let out a little moan, instead.

And then the bright shaft of sunlight that had found its way through the part in the curtains seemed to wrap around her, engulfing her in an embrace of warm white down. And she didn't mind in the least, because it felt so delicious. She could feel the tiny sunbeams licking her from the scalp of her head to the bottoms of her feet, and every inch of her tensed, delighting in the erotic sensation.

And then she collapsed against Braden's chest, perfectly spent.

Braden, however, was not. Suddenly, he'd rolled her over and, without missing a beat, thrust into her so hard, she thought he might break the bed, since she'd learned by now that he could not break her....

And then he, too, with a convulsive shiver and a hoarse shout, collapsed, quite heavily, upon Caroline.

"Braden?" she said, after a while, when he did not move. She knew this time that he had not suffered an apoplexy, because she could feel his heart beating very hard indeed against her breast.

He leaned up onto his elbows, which was a relief, since Caroline had feared his superior weight might crush her. "Yes?" he asked, in lazy tones.

She looked up into his dark eyes. They were smiling at her, every bit as much as his lips. He looked different than he had when she'd first seen him, that night at Dame Ashforth's, when he'd worn such a frightening frown, and had looked so annoyed. He seemed much younger now, happier, and more relaxed. Was that, Caroline wondered, going to be his married look? If it was, it was going to be quite a bit harder for her to extricate herself than she'd ever thought.

"Nothing," she said.

"That's it?" He cocked an eyebrow at her. "That's all you have to say? 'Nothing?'"

Realizing she must have sounded a fool, she tried, "Is there anything for breakfast, do you think?"

The smile broadened, both in his eyes and on his lips.

"I see you remain stubbornly unimpressed by my lovemaking skills," he said. "I shall have to rectify this matter at once."

34

*A*nd then it all ended.

It was, Braden knew, his own fault. He ought to have insisted upon taking her away from there at once. He ought to have whisked her off to Bath, Brighton, anywhere. Anywhere that she could not be traced.

But it was his first time. Not his first time with a woman, certainly, but his first time with a woman whose mere presence so filled his heart and mind, there wasn't room for anything else . . . rational thought, apparently, included.

If he'd been thinking rationally, of course, he'd have realized the absolute necessity of removing Caroline Linford at once from the reach of her family. But no man, he later consoled himself—small comfort though it was—could have retained possession of his wits when faced with the delightful discovery that the woman he adored, who'd been but a scant few hours earlier utterly virginal, took to lovemaking like a fish to water.

It wasn't the sort of thing a man—at least a man like Braden—could ignore. Even if he'd had some inkling of what lay ahead, he doubted he could have done anything differently. He'd been drugged by love. He'd thrilled at her slightest touch. He'd felt intoxicated simply by the sound of her voice. He'd fallen in love for the first time in his life, and he'd fallen hard.

How could he have guessed that the mewling bastard would not follow his orders? He ought to have known, of course. He ought to have remembered that there was someone of whom the faint-hearted devil was a good deal more frightened, someone whose methods were a great deal more brutal than Braden's.

But Braden had dispatched that particular individual. He hadn't, of course, chosen to share that with the marquis. And that had been another mistake. He had underestimated the man. Vastly, grossly underestimated him.

And because of it—that one, simple mistake—he lost everything.

Even more depressing than that was that when the blow came, he was perfectly unprepared for it. He'd been making breakfast— breakfast!—when it happened.

They'd been in the kitchen. Caroline had been suffering all morning from a guilty conscience; Braden recognized the signs, though he could not think what to do about it, beyond bending down to kiss the slight worry line that he sometimes spied pucker-ing her smooth forehead. When they made love, it was different. Then all her troubles vanished, as if by magic. It was when they were not making love that she seemed to become conscious of the gravity of what she'd done.

He'd tried reasoning with her, telling her that everyone would understand eventually—though he could not, of course, tell her why. He had promised her brother he wouldn't mention the gam-bling, and most especially the two attempts made upon his life be-cause of it. He could only hope that the earl would set things right with his sister in his own time.

And Caroline was trying, he could see, to put a brave face on it. But she was not at all used to going against the wishes of her fam-ily. Small rebellions, certainly: her horses, her support of Emily's cause, her seeking out lessons in how to make love. But this sort of grand scale insurgency was clearly making her uneasy.

And though he didn't like that she should be unhappy, he knew he would not have loved her half as dearly as he did if she'd been callous enough not to care. Lady Bartlett was manipulative, Thomas thoughtless, and her fiancé an idiotic wretch, but Caroline loved them each, in her way, and the thought of causing them pain was upsetting to her.

And so he'd tried to make her forget her troubles by clowning, flipping eggs in the skillet he held—a skill his mother had taught him before her death—tossing them as high as he could, in hopes that one would eventually stick to the ceiling, and speculating on what Lord Woodson's cook would say when she returned, and found fried eggs in the rafters.

And it appeared that he was succeeding, at least in a small way, at cheering Caroline up, since she laughed at his antics, and even went so far as to try her own hand at the skillet. That any woman belonging to so-called Polite Society should have joined in such a silly game, rather than stand and mock him for it, quite boggled his brain. Out of all the supposedly aristocratic women he'd met before Caroline, only Jacquelyn had shown the smallest spark of humor, which had set her apart from all the mind-numbing social-ites in her set. But Jacquelyn's wit had always been at the expense of others, her ideas often lifted from—but never credited to by her—popular writers or politicians.

Caroline Linford, on the other hand, laughed easily and often, and said exactly what she was thinking, borrowing from no one. He had known from the first time she'd described her rather un-orthodox method of supporting the women's suffrage movement that Caroline was an original, quite unlike any other woman he had ever met before. What he had never suspected was the hold she would eventually have over his heartstrings.

Which was why, when the bell to the servants' entrance

sounded midway through his breakfast preparation, he felt his first tug of foreboding. The house was shut up. Who could be calling?

Caroline was holding on to the handle of the skillet, his arms around her as he showed her how to jiggle the pan just enough to send its contents flying. She must have felt him tense at the sound, since she looked up at him, her already deeply brown eyes seeming to go a fraction darker, and said, softly, "I'll go."

He took the pan, moving away from her so she would not realize how deeply his unease ran. His stomach muscles were tightly clenched, his jaw muscles already leaping with suppressed emotion.

"No," he said succinctly, putting down the skillet. "I will. You stay here."

But Caroline surprised him. She pushed a few strands of loose hair from her face and said, determinedly, "No, *I* will. I'm sure it's a message from my mother."

And she went bravely to the back door.

That had been his second mistake. His first, not removing her at once from Woodson Manor, might have been forgivable. But the fact that he hadn't thought to intercept any missives from Lady Bartlett was most definitely not.

Still, he set aside the skillet and followed her to the door, just in case it wasn't a servant with a message from her mother, but one of those nefarious evildoers Caroline had mentioned, from whom she might need protection.

It was, however, only Violet.

"Oh, *hello*, sir," the girl said, brightening perceptibly when she saw him. If it entered the maid's head to wonder what her mistress was doing, entertaining Braden Granville in her friend's empty country house, it did not apparently bother her. She grinned sunnily up at him.

Caroline, however, was far from grinning as she read the contents of the letter Violet had brought to her.

"Caroline," he said, the foreboding he'd felt since hearing the bell ring turning into full blown alarm at her shocked expression. He could not imagine what her mother had written. Something about Thomas, he supposed. Braden had instructed the boy not to stir from his home until it was deemed safe for him to do so by the men Braden had put on both The Duke and the marquis's tails. Had the lad taken matters into his hands? Had some new disaster befallen him?

"What—" he started to ask, but when she turned her gaze toward him, he saw that those brown eyes were filled with tears—and a look of such injured betrayal, he very nearly cried out.

"How could you?" Caroline asked, in a heartbroken voice. "How *could* you?"

Braden couldn't honestly say he hadn't any idea what she was talking about. What he could not imagine was how her mother, of all people, had found out.

"How could I what?" he asked, carefully.

"How could you have shot Hurst?" Caroline wailed, throwing herself down onto a nearby settle, and the letter into a crumpled ball on the floor. "When you promised me you wouldn't?"

Braden, conscious that Violet was still standing in the doorway, blinking confusedly at them, stepped toward the maid, and laid a hand upon her arm.

"Would you mind terribly," he said, giving the maid a gentle push out the door, "waiting outside for a few moments?"

Violet, still staring at her sobbing mistress, murmured, "Oh, but Lady Bartlett said I was to fetch her ladyship home at once—"

"Just a few moments of privacy, if you please," Braden said.

He closed the door as soon as he'd successfully navigated Violet through it, then leaned down to pick up the discarded note. Smoothing out the foolscap, he stared down at Lady Bartlett's strong, looping cursive:

Caroline, her mother wrote, *Your brother did not come home last night or the night before. When I went to look for him at Lord Winchilsea's, I found the marquis suffering from a bullet wound given to him by your "friend" Mr. Granville. Your Hurst is grievously injured. I can't imagine what that horrid man was thinking. And I've still had no word from Tommy, and can only suppose the worst—he's gone to Oxford after all. Everything is in a muddle. Do come home from Emmy's at once. Pettigrew fears my heart palpitations may prove fatal this time.*

Mother

Braden felt something constrict inside him, and realized, with a sinking sensation, that what he was feeling was something he hadn't felt in a very, very long time.

It was fear.

He had dealt, in his lifetime, with every conceivable kind of trouble—generally with a pistol, but occasionally without. And he was no stranger to the feminine variety. He had, he knew, broken far more hearts than he wished to remember.

But those women had been easily assuaged, usually with a diamond bracelet or earrings.

But Caroline's heart, which he held more precious than his own, was not so easily mended.

He tried an apology.

"Caroline," he said, knowing his desperation showed in his voice. "I'm sorry. But for what it's worth, he went for his pistol first. I had to defend my—"

Caroline lifted her face from her arms. He was alarmed at the shiny tracks the tears had made along her cheeks. "You promised me you wouldn't," she said, with a sob. "And then you just went ahead and did it."

Braden, bewilderment tempering his fear, sank down beside her on the settle, and laid his hands upon her quivering shoulders.

"Caroline, sweetheart, what are you talking about? I never promised you anything about—"

She'd torn herself from his grasp, and out of his reach, before the words were completely out of his mouth. She stood in the middle of the entranceway, her chest heaving beneath the bodice of her plain white dress, tears standing out in her long lashes.

"You did," she accused him. "You *did* promise! The whole reason I wouldn't tell you who it was I saw with Lady Jacquelyn was because I knew you would do something like this, and I couldn't bear it—"

In a flash, Braden had left the settle as well, and closed the distance between them in two long strides.

"What are you talking about?" He seized her shoulders again, only this time not to comfort her, but to keep her in one place so he could look down into her eyes.

"You know perfectly well what I'm talking about." Caroline glared up at him, and he realized the tears were only partly from despair. They were tears of anger, too. She was angry with him. "Hurst and Jacquelyn. As if you didn't know. How did you find out? You made her tell you, I suppose. I hoped—I hoped she loved him better than that."

"Hurst?" Dumbfounded, he shook his head. Then comprehension dawned. "It was *Hurst* you saw that night with Jackie?"

"Of course it was," Caroline said, angrily. "Don't pretend as if you didn't know. Why would you have shot him if you didn't know?"

"Are you trying to tell me," he said, stooping down so that he could look her in the eye, "that when you volunteered to act as a witness on my behalf, it was *Hurst* that you had seen with Lady Jacquelyn?"

"Of course." Caroline glared at him through her tears. "Why else do you think I wouldn't tell you his name? I didn't want to see him shot. I knew all about you and your guns. You think pistols are the solution to every problem, don't you? Well, they aren't. They're wicked and wrong. They hurt people. Do you think I wanted Hurst's sister—he has one, you know—to go through what I went through when Tommy . . . when Tommy . . ."

She broke off sobbing. Braden, feeling frightened again, tried to put his arms around her, draw her close—anything, anything at all, to stop those angry tears—when a fresh wave of them came, and she pounded a fist against his chest.

"But you went ahead and shot him anyway! How long have you known? You must have been laughing at me all along. . . ."

He could only stare down at her, perfectly bemused by what she'd said. Hurst? It had been *Hurst* whom she'd seen with Jackie at Dame Ashforth's? Hurst Slater was Jackie's phantom lover, the man because of whom Weasel had been stabbed? The bloke who could melt into shadow and disappear at will was none other than the Marquis of Winchilsea?

If it hadn't been for the tears still marking Caroline's face, and the injured betrayal with which she was regarding him, he might have laughed out loud. Because suddenly, as if a curtain had been lifted, Braden could see. Saw everything, in fact, at last.

Jackie's phantom lover, whom they'd had so much trouble identifying, hadn't been hiding only from Braden Granville. Slater had also been trying to keep from being found by Seymour Hawkins.

It was no small wonder he'd been so desperate to escape detection. The man who'd stabbed Weasel could only have been one of Hawkins's men, sent to track down the marquis, who'd disappeared from Oxford at around the time the Earl of Bartlett had been shot. Hawkins, disliking loose ends, must have realized that the young earl who'd very rightfully accused him of cheating was still alive, and was likely to talk—not to the authorities, of course: the earl wouldn't want to draw attention to his gambling habit. But he'd surely talk to his friends, and that would hurt Hawkins's business.

And so Hawkins had appointed someone to finish the job.

But it wouldn't have satisfied The Duke's twisted sense of justice to have just anyone kill the earl. No, it had to be Slater, to teach him a lesson for sticking his nose in where it didn't belong, and hauling Thomas Bartlett back from death's door.

The earl, of course, hadn't been able to tell Braden for certain that it had been Slater who'd shot at him the night before. But he'd been sufficiently suspicious of his friend to do everything he could to avoid him afterward.

And that had been all the incentive Braden had needed to pay a little social call on the marquis.

He hadn't known then, of course, how things were going to work out between him and Caroline. But he'd known he wasn't going to stand idly by and allow the brother of the woman he loved to be killed—and quite possibly by her own fiancé.

And so he had gone to the rooms kept by the Marquis of Winchilsea and suggested—merely suggested—that if he valued his health, Hurst Slater might want to leave town for an extended period of time.

For, say, a year.

A suggestion at which the marquis had balked. More than balked, in fact. He'd taken umbrage at the idea, and gone for his gun, apparently feeling that ridding himself of Braden Granville was a better alternative.

And Braden had been forced to draw his own weapon—the one he'd brought with him in the unlikely event that gentle persuasion alone proved ineffective with the marquis.

Well, what choice had he had, really? The man had been about to shoot him! And it had, after all, only been a flesh wound. Braden had been careful about that. He could have injured the bloke a good deal more seriously, but hadn't, only because the foolish man had saved Caroline's brother once.

Really, he'd been quite reasonable, he thought. He'd offered the marquis a remarkably fair deal. Exile, rather than incarceration or death. Braden could, he'd pointed out to the marquis, have turned him over to the authorities instead—the same authorities to whom he'd sent word that Seymour Hawkins could be found operating a gambling circle in Oxford, the exact address of which he'd ascertained from Thomas.

Only Braden had left out that tantalizing bit of information.

And that had been yet another mistake. Because apparently there was a force greater than Braden's of which Hurst Slater was frightened. And since he didn't know that that force—Hawkins—was about to be apprehended, the marquis had done exactly the wrong thing:

He'd stayed in London. And he'd talked.

And if the letter Caroline was clutching in her hands was any indication, he'd talked to the Lady Bartlett.

The irony of it all was that the last thing Braden would ever have done was turn the blighter over to the law. Caroline had troubles enough without adding to them a fiancé who'd been hurled into Newgate. That, he knew, she would never be able to live down.

No, better that the bloke simply disappear than be dragged through the courts.

But this is what he'd chosen instead. To stay and fight. A foolish decision under normal circumstances. No one fought Braden Granville and won.

Except that Hurst Slater had a weapon against which Braden hadn't the slightest defense.

Caroline.

"You're hurting me," Caroline said, trying to shrug his fingers off her shoulders.

He let go of her at once.

"Caroline, you have got to believe me." He followed her. For some reason, she'd gone to the door. "I had no idea. You're mistaken if you think it had anything at all to do with Jacquelyn. I did go to have a chat with your fiancé, but—"

"No." She shook her head. There were still tears running down her cheeks, but she stood by the door with her shoulders thrown back, as determined as he had ever seen her. "I was mistaken, all right, but not about that. *This* was the mistake. You're the Lothario of London, after all. I should have known that it was all just a great game to you."

"A *game*?" he echoed, his voice breaking.

"Yes, a game," Caroline said. "All this time, you knew it was Hurst who'd been with Jackie, and you wanted revenge. Well, you've gotten it now, haven't you? You bedded his fiancée, the same way he bedded yours. And then you *shot* him."

"Caroline." He could only stare at her in horror. She was not, he thought, the same person she'd been up until a half hour ago. Suddenly, she was someone he had never met. He supposed she felt the same about him. "Is that what you really think?"

"Well, what else am I to think? Why else would you have done it, Braden? Why *else* would you have shot my fiancé?"

"I told you. He pulled his weapon first—"

"Why?" Caroline's voice was hard. "What were you saying to him, Braden?"

"Caroline—"

"Tell me."

In a small part of his mind—a part detached from the present situation—a voice whispered, *So this is how it feels. This is how it feels to have your heart broken.* He'd heard the sensation described many times, but he had never actually felt it himself. The closest he supposed he'd come was how he'd felt at his mother's death—a panicky, cold feeling, as if he'd been locked in a dank, airless cell, much like the one at Newgate he'd once spent a night in.

Because of course he couldn't tell her. Not without revealing what her brother had made him swear never to tell. If it had all worked out the way it was supposed to, Slater would simply have disappeared. Braden had never imagined that a cowardly, sniveling thing like the marquis wouldn't follow his orders. If he'd had the smallest inkling that Hurst Slater was Jackie's phantom lover, he would never have underestimated the man so badly.

But he hadn't known.

And now it was beginning to look as if he had lost everything.

"I can't tell you, Caroline," he said, knowing even as he said them that the words would never be enough, but praying—yes, actually praying—that she'd understand. He'd given his word. A man lived and died by his word in the Dials. It was so often all he had.

Except in this case, it was his ruin.

"I see," Caroline said.

And then she turned and opened the door before he could say another word.

Violet stood in the sunlight just outside, flanked by two very large, very intimidating footmen.

"I'm sorry, milady," she said, glancing nervously at Caroline. "But I heard the shouting, and I thought I'd better fetch Riley and Samuels. . . ."

"Yes," Caroline said, in a voice Braden had never heard her use before. It was a flat, lifeless voice. "I'm coming."

Violet glanced from Braden to her mistress, and back again. "But . . ." The maid looked horrified. "Your things, milady. And you can't go out without a bonnet, and your gloves—"

"I don't care," Caroline said, in the same dull voice. "I don't care about my things, or my gloves. Come along, Violet."

The maid, after a last, frightened look at Braden, hurried after her mistress.

"Caroline," Braden said, starting forward. He could not quite believe what was happening.

But even as he moved, the two footmen, after allowing Caroline and her maid to pass, moved to fill the doorway, blocking his path.

"God damn it," Braden cursed, as Riley and Samuels stared at him impassively. "Get out of my way or I swear—"

"Let the lady go, sir," the one on the left said. "Don't make us have to hurt you."

"You don't understand," Braden growled. "I don't mean her any harm. I just need to make her see reason."

Glancing pointedly down at Braden's balled fists, the one on the right said, "That's exactly why we ain't moving. Not until she's safe in the carriage."

"By then it will be too late," Braden said, realizing that once she got back to London, and into her mother's clutches, he'd very likely never see Caroline again.

"That, sir," the footman said, unruffled, "is the idea."

35

"For God's sake, Jacks," Hurst said, irritably. "Get away from the window. Someone will see you."

Jacquelyn stayed where she was, gazing down at the pedestrians on the street below. "What does it matter?" she asked, bitterly. "Granville's broken it off. Who cares if anyone sees me here?"

"I care." Hurst glared at her in annoyance from the chaise longue upon which he reclined. "You know *la* Bartlett's been in and out all day. She'll have another one of her fits if she looks up and sees you here. You may have lost your fatted calf, my sweet, but I still have mine. And I intend to keep it that way. I would think you'd support me in that. After all, you're to benefit from the Linford coin as well."

Jacquelyn sighed and moved away from the window, sitting down in the chair she'd pulled up close to the edge of his chaise longue.

"It just doesn't make any sense," Jacquelyn said. "Why would he shoot you like that, if he didn't know about us?"

"I told you, Jacks," Hurst said, for what felt like the hundredth time. He had uttered this lie so often, he could do it by rote now.

"The fellow came stalking in, and quite without preamble, shot me in the leg. There was no discussion."

Hurst twisted uncomfortably on his couch. He couldn't, of course, tell the truth. If he told her that he had been the one who'd gone for his pistol first, Jackie would call him ten kinds of a fool. Because of course Granville was faster with a pistol than any man in England. Going for his gun had been a mistake. A grave mistake.

But a worse mistake would be telling Jackie what had caused him to go for his gun in the first place: Granville's warning that he knew all about what the marquis had been up to with The Duke, and that he had better get out of town, if he knew what was good for him.

No, he could never tell anyone that, not even Jackie. Especially not Jackie. If she knew that her lover was actually a notorious murderer's boot-licking lackey . . . well, her pretty derriere would not warm that seat cushion a second longer. Daughters of dukes—even penniless ones—did not rub shoulders with petty criminals like himself.

"I tell you, Jackie," Hurst said, raising his voice querulously. "I tell you, I've never been more surprised in my life. I ought to go to the law."

"Then why don't you?" Jacquelyn asked, flatly.

"Don't want to distress the in-laws," he said. "Looks bad and all, right before the wedding, me draggin' Granville through the courts. Embarrassing, and all that. Fetch me another glass, will you, darling?"

Jacquelyn complied, though with ill grace, going to his sister's sideboard and pouring him a glass of his brother-in-law's best sherry. "You aren't telling me the whole story," she complained. "There's something missing from all this. It defies logic. Why should Braden Granville stride into your room and shoot you? There's only one explanation for it."

"Jackie," Hurst said, tiredly, taking a sip from the glass she brought him. "He never uttered your name."

"Well, it's the only explanation that makes sense." Jacquelyn settled back into her seat. "He broke it off with me the night before. He came after you next. He must know the truth about us."

"Impossible," Hurst said.

"Someone must have seen us. And I wager I know when. I *told* you it was too risky, meeting like that in the old woman's sitting room. But no, you simply *had* to see me."

Hurst, forgetting his anxiety for a moment, relived their touching reunion in Dame Ashforth's sitting room. "It *was* lovely," he said, with relish.

"But hardly worth your losing your plumber's daughter, and me my gunsmith."

Hurst, brought back to the moment, stirred uncomfortably on his couch. His leg was smarting rather badly, for all he'd kept off of it, as Lady B's surgeon had recommended.

"I haven't lost my plumber's daughter," Hurst said.

"Not yet," Jacquelyn said. "But it shouldn't be long. I swear she's in love with Granville, and it's clear he returns the feeling. In fact, that might even be why he shot you."

Hurst restrained a snort at the idea of anyone being in love with Caroline Linford, who was a pleasant, but thoroughly dull girl—compared to his Jackie, anyway.

"It's too late for me, barring a miracle," Jacquelyn went on, "but if you do anything to jeopardize this match with the Linford girl, I'll shoot you myself, so help me God . . . and you can be sure *I* won't spare any vital organs."

Hurst licked his lips. "You can be very cruel when you want to be, Jacks," he said, admiringly.

She leaned forward to run a finger along his jawline. "You haven't," she purred, "the slightest idea. . . ."

A low tap sounded on the door, and a second later, a mob-capped parlormaid appeared, bobbing an apologetic curtsy.

"Beggin' your pardon, my lord," the child said, "but Lady Caroline Linford's here to see you."

If someone had prodded her with a stick, Jacquelyn would not have moved more quickly toward the door to an adjoining room.

"Good God," she cried. To the maid, she said, "Show her in. Show her in at once." To Hurst, she hissed, "Don't bungle this, Hurst, do you hear? She's our only hope."

And without another word, Jacquelyn slipped out of the room.

Hurst, on his chaise longue, sighed. Jacquelyn had never spoken a truer word. The problem was, she didn't know just how dire the situation had become.

Caroline appeared, looking as she always did, virginal and sweet in blue and white. He had the satisfaction of seeing her pause on the threshold, quite taken aback by his altered looks. Well, and why not? While the bullet had gone right through the fleshy part of his thigh, quite missing bone and a vital artery—almost as if his opponent, Lady B's surgeon had remarked, had purposefully tried to spare him undue damage—it was still a wonder he was alive. Few who'd faced Braden Granville's pistol could make that claim.

"Hurst," Caroline said, as she recovered herself, and hurried to his couch. "Oh, Hurst, I'm so sorry. Are you very badly hurt?"

Hurst fingered the blanket he'd pulled up over his injured leg, its bandage being not quite as impressive as he would have liked. "I'm all right, I suppose," he said, weakly. "It's a flesh wound, really."

Caroline, who'd sunk down onto the chair Jacquelyn had recently vacated, paused in the act of stripping off her gloves. "A flesh wound?" she echoed. "But my mother intimated it was much more serious than that."

Hurst—remembering that this was the image he'd hoped to

convey to the Lady Bartlett when she'd appeared in his rooms literally minutes after Granville had left them, wondering if the marquis had seen her son—allowed his head to loll back against the
chaise longue's velveteen cover.

"Well, I did lose a good deal of blood. . . ." he murmured.

Caroline removed her gloves, and looked at him sorrowfully.

"And it was Braden Granville," Caroline said, "who did this to
you?"

"Indeed," Hurst said. "He must have been having an off-day,
to have missed my heart by such a degree. He's quite a good shot,
I understand."

Caroline's lips, which were quite unlike Jacquelyn's, being
neither full nor rouged, pursed. Hurst recalled having seen her
mother wear the exact same expression, whenever a dish that was
not to her liking was served to her at dinner parties.

"You're lucky," Caroline said, "that he didn't kill you."

Hurst nodded. "I know it. I didn't even have a chance to defend
myself. He simply walked in and—and began slapping me about.
He said a good many ugly things, slandering my person—and . . .
and yours, Caroline."

Caroline blinked at him. "Me? Mr. Granville was slandering
me, you say?"

"Quite. I couldn't stand for that, of course. No man speaks that
way about the future Lady Winchilsea. I almost challenged him
then and there. But instead, next thing I knew, he'd drawn one of
those pistols of his, and shot me."

Caroline looked down at the ring on her finger—his grandmother's ring. "How perfectly horrid for you," she said, tonelessly.

"I didn't get really angry," Hurst said, "until I heard the drivel
he was spewing about you, Caroline. All about how I was lowering
myself, marrying you, a girl whose title was only a generation old."

"I see," Caroline said.

Hurst reached out, and took one of her hands in both of

his, and laid upon it what he fancied was quite a passionate kiss. "There's nothing," he said, emotionally, "I wouldn't do to protect your honor, Caroline."

He had turned her hand over and begun to rain kisses down upon her palm before Caroline was able to withdraw her fingers.

"I see," she said again. "Well, the whole thing sounds as if it were very trying. I'm sorry it happened to you. Did the surgeon say how long it would be before you could walk again?"

"I shall be able to walk down the aisle on our wedding day," Hurst said, letting his blue eyes rest warmly upon her. It was a look that had driven the chambermaids at Oxford quite frenzied with lust, and he supposed it ought to work just as well on the Caroline Linfords of the world. She was, after all, a plumber's daughter, and that was quite near a chambermaid, in Hurst's way of thinking. "Never you fear, my love."

"Well," Caroline said. Rather to his astonishment, she did not seem at all frenzied by his loving look. "That's what I've come here to talk to you about. I had heard, of course, that you were rather more ill than you appear to be. And while I am delighted to find that you are not, as reported, at death's door, I fear the fact that you are not means I must discuss something rather . . . unpleasant with you."

"Unpleasant?" Hurst laughed, as if he could not imagine any such thing. But his laughter had a nervous quality to it. Because inwardly he was thinking, *Oh, no. She knows. Tommy must still be alive. Alive and hiding out somewhere. He must have gotten a message to her. He must have seen the pistol. Stupid. Stupid to have missed!*

"I'm afraid, Hurst," Caroline began, in apologetic tones, "that our wedding is going to have to be called off."

Hurst stared at her. It was his own fault, of course. He shouldn't have missed. How could he have been so stupid as to miss? If only the idiot boy hadn't tripped!

"But." Hurst managed to rouse himself from the paralytic

stupor into which her words had sunk him. "But the invitations . . . five hundred of them . . . already sent out."

"Yes, I know," Caroline said. "And that *is* a shame. I am having a letter drawn up that we'll send to our guests, of course. As for the gifts, I think it would be best if we returned them—"

"No," he said, in a low voice.

She looked up, her brown eyes questioning. "I beg your pardon?"

"You heard me." And Hurst, who had never felt anything much at all for Caroline Linford, felt such an overwhelming dislike—maybe even hatred—for her, he nearly shook with it. "You are marrying me, Caroline, next week, and that's the end of it."

Was he imagining things, or had there been a flicker of anger—actual *anger*—in those normally gentle brown eyes?

"No," Caroline said, with admirable calm. "No, Hurst, I'm afraid not. You see, I know why Braden Granville shot you."

He felt as if an icy bucket of water had been thrown over him. He lay there, utterly stunned.

"You . . . you *know*?" he managed to stammer.

"Yes," Caroline said. "Not that I am in any position to blame you."

This was more than he could reasonably assimilate. He had *shot* at her brother—the boy still hadn't come home, according to Lady B, and might, for all anyone knew, be wandering the streets of London with a head wound—and she didn't consider herself in any position to *blame* him for it?

"Wh—" he stammered. "Wh—wh—"

She was tugging his grandmother's ring from her finger. "Yes," she said. "You see, Hurst, I haven't been faithful to you, either." She placed the ring on the small table beside his glass of sherry. "I am quite ruined," she announced, flatly. "I know you shan't want me now, anymore than I want you."

Hurst stared down at the ring. Ruined? Caroline Linford was *ruined*?

"Who"—the words were hardly more than a ragged whisper through his bloodless lips—"was it?"

"Oh," Caroline said. "It doesn't matter. But it's better like this, don't you think, Hurst? I know people will talk, of course, and Ma will be inconsolable, and Tommy—well, poor Tommy, will be furious when he hears. But I don't think I was ever really meant to marry, you know. And now you'll be free, and can wed your Jacquelyn. I know she hasn't any money, Hurst, but there are more important things—"

"J-Jacquelyn?" He shook his head. *"Jacquelyn?"*

"Yes, of course." Caroline was completely unemotional, simply businesslike. He had never, he realized, seen her like this, so brisk, so sure of herself. It was as if . . . it was almost as if overnight, she'd become . . .

Well, a *woman.*

"I saw you two together, you know," she said, with a shrug. "On a divan at Dame Ashforth's. I probably ought to have made my presence known, but it seemed better to avoid a scene at the time."

It was all slowly beginning to sink in. Sweet, dull, virtuous Lady Caroline— *his* Lady Caroline—was virtuous no longer. She was also, he couldn't help noticing, not very dull anymore.

Ruined. She said she'd been ruined. And that she'd seen him. Him and Jacquelyn, together on a divan at Dame Ashforth's. But she hadn't said anything. All this time, she hadn't said anything.

Until now. Because now, apparently, she was saying good-bye.

She rose to go. "I hope there won't be any unpleasantness about this, Hurst. I really was quite fond of you for a little while. And I like to think you were, too, of me."

He blinked up into her heart-shaped face. She looked . . . older. But that was impossible. He had seen her only a few days earlier. How could she . . . ? *Who* could she . . . ?

"And now I had better leave you," she said. "We still haven't found Tommy. It's quite the oddest thing, and not a bit like him. I don't suppose you've heard from him, have you?"

Hurst, realizing at last what was happening, threw back the blanket that had been covering his legs, and made an effort to stand.

"You can't do this," Hurst declared.

The money. That was all he could think. The money that might have been his. The fortune that, with the earl out of the way, would have been all Caroline's—and his. He hadn't wanted to kill the earl. Lord knew he hadn't wanted to do it. But he'd eventually come to believe he was actually doing the Linfords a favor: the boy would only have gambled away his inheritance when he finally received it anyway. This way—The Duke's way—the money, at least, would be safe.

He hadn't wanted to do it, but he felt he had no choice now. Standing with his weight on his uninjured leg, and holding on to the back of the chair she'd been sitting in, he said, "Caroline, think what you're doing. I . . . I saved Tommy's life. If it hadn't been for me, your brother would be dead."

For a moment, something passed through those eyes. He was certain it was guilt, and felt a rush of relief. He'd won. He'd won.

But then the guilt disappeared, and was replaced by that curious, emotionless mask.

"You did save Tommy's life," Caroline said, calmly. "And for that I'll always be grateful. It's for that very reason, you see, that I can't possibly marry you now. You deserve so much more than . . . well, what I've become."

"I don't care what you've done," Hurst said, desperately. "Or who with, Caroline. I'll take you back. I still want you."

Caroline raised her eyebrows, as if he had said something interesting. "Oh?"

"I mean it, Caroline," he went on. "And . . . and the truth is, well, not to be coarse, Caroline, but you'll never get anyone else.

Not after what you just told me. You'll be publicly humiliated, a laughingstock, when word of this gets out. No man will want you—but I do. I will always want you."

Her eyes—those damned reproachful eyes—were cool. "But I don't want you," she said, matter-of-factly.

And without another word, the Lady Caroline Linford left the room. And his life.

Jacquelyn came bursting from the room next door.

"You fool!" she cried. "You perfect fool!"

"Jackie." Hurst let go of his chair, swinging his injured leg gingerly, and limped toward the window. He felt as if he needed a bit of air. "She saw us. At Dame Ashforth's. She saw us."

"I heard. I'm not deaf. God, you are such an imbecile! If you'd just eloped with her when I asked you to, none of this would be happening. But no. You had to let Granville get his hands on her—"

"What do you mean?" Hurst interrupted, sharply.

"You are such an innocent, beloved." Jacquelyn tossed her head. "Ruined! I'll say she was. And who do you think did it? I'll tell you. None other than the man who put a bullet through your leg."

Hurst's lips moved silently. *Granville?*

"I told you he's in love with her," Jacquelyn said, waspishly. "And it was clear to me—at least when I saw her at Worth's yesterday—that she feels the same way about him. And there you have it. He got her. The Lothario of London got your fiancée. And all because you didn't act quickly enough."

Hurst watched through the window as Caroline Linford appeared upon the street, and entered her waiting carriage. "Braden Granville," he murmured. "She's leaving me for Braden Granville."

"Likely as not," Jacquelyn said. And she went and rang the bell for the maid.

Hurst turned his head to look at her curiously. "What are you doing?"

Jacquelyn regarded him curiously. "Ringing for my things. I'm leaving."

Hurst stared at her. "You're what?"

Jacquelyn looked determined. "I don't like it any better than you, my pet, but we haven't any choice. And we oughtn't waste any time. I noticed that old fool, Lord Whitcomb, looking down my dress the other night. I'm going to go and throw myself at him. He's got five thousand a year, and another two coming when that windbag mother of his finally dies."

Hurst said, through dry lips, "No. No, Jackie—"

His mind was awhirl. He could not quite believe what was happening to him. To have lost so much so quickly was beyond the scope of his understanding. It couldn't be happening. It couldn't.

"I hope you've some other pokers in the fire, love," Lady Jacquelyn said. The maid had appeared with her bonnet and parasol, laid them on a table, and quickly disappeared again. Jacquelyn pulled on a pair of white lace mittens as she spoke. "The Chittenhouse girls are miserably plain, I know, but the eldest has ten thousand a year. If you can bear to look at those teeth every morning, it might well be worth it. Oh, but we can't make the same mistake this time, my pet. I think we should stay away from each other until after the weddings. Don't you agree? We can't risk another Dame Ashforth's." She noticed his expression and said, "It won't be long, love. Surely you can live without your Jackie for a few months, at least?"

And with that, she kissed him briefly on the lips, and floated from the room.

He flinched as the door closed behind her.

Of course he could live without her.

But why should he have to?

He knew why. He knew why only too well. Two names. Two odious, noxious names.

Braden Granville.

Braden Granville, that upstart from the Dials, who didn't know his place any better than The Duke knew his, but who seemed to think he could make up for it with his hefty bank account and a charming way with women.

Braden Granville, whose money was so new, it squeaked, every penny of it earned not by the proper method of accruing income, through careful investment of inherited funds, but by the sweat of his odious, upstart brow.

Braden Granville, who knew far, far too much. Hurst couldn't imagine how—probably because of the highly unsavory circles in which he traveled—but somehow, Granville had managed to learn of the plot to get rid of the Earl of Bartlett.

He had to be gotten rid of. If only Hurst had been quicker the day before with his pistol. . . .

Well, in any case, it was clear now he had to finish what he'd started. Braden Granville had to be destroyed. The alternative was unthinkable. Hurst had to protect himself.

It wasn't going to be easy. He knew that. Granville's performance in his own sitting room the day before had proved how inhumanly quick the man was with a weapon. He was someone who had spent a lifetime sidestepping death, and was well used to having pistols pointed at him.

But Braden Granville had never met an adversary who'd had as much reason to kill him as Hurst. Granville's knowledge of Hurst's activities with The Duke made him supremely dangerous.

And then there was the fact that the man had threatened, manhandled, and humiliated him, then had gone on to bed both the love of his life and, apparently, his virginal fiancée.

Granville had to die. And Hurst was the one who would kill him, wounded leg or not. He could still walk. The surgeon had assured him he could. He'd walk right into Braden Granville's impossibly large house on Belgrave Square, and—

No. No, he'd *slip* into it, the way he'd slipped in and out of

Jackie's house. Slip into Braden Granville's, do his business, and slip out again, avoiding detection. He could do it. He knew he could. He'd been caught unawares the day before, when Granville had shown up at his flat. This time, he'd be the one to show up un-expectedly.

Oh, yes. And he wouldn't be satisfied with a mere bulle through the leg, either. He would have the pleasure, Hurst decided, of watching Granville die.

The Duke, he thought, was going to be proud.

36

*B*raden Granville sat in his library, a glass of whiskey in his hand. He had not drunk from the glass, nor did he recall pouring it. He simply stared into the liquid's amber depths, thinking that its color shifted in the light in quite the same way as a certain pair of eyes he knew. . . .

The Earl of Bartlett's voice drew him back from where he'd gone, miles and miles away.

"So you're saying I can't go home yet." Thomas still spoke a little too loudly. His hearing had not yet completely returned, although the surgeon who'd been summoned to attend him had assured them that it would, in time.

Braden inclined his head. "Yes," he said. "Apparently, there was a slight . . . misunderstanding."

The boy studied him quizzically from the chair in which he slumped. "Misunderstanding? What kind of misunderstanding?"

"Well." Braden Granville wondered how it was that he could go on talking like this, as if he hadn't a care in the world, when inwardly, he was weeping. It sounded dramatic, he knew. But it was the truth. Just not a truth he chose to share with Weasel or Crutch, and most specifically, this boy in front of him.

"The authorities have tracked down and arrested Seymour Hawkins, otherwise known as The Duke." When Tommy's jaw dropped at this piece of information, Braden nodded. "Yes, I thought it wisest to have him incarcerated. You needn't worry, you won't be called to testify against him. The crimes he committed right here in London some time back will keep him behind bars for years. Unless, of course—" This he added almost thoughtfully, "they hang him."

"I had no idea," the earl said, again speaking too loudly. "There was nothing about his arrest in the papers."

"No. There'll be something tomorrow, if my sources are correct. And so you'll have to stay here at least another night. No messages home, either. I'm sorry, but the . . . individual with whom I dealt yesterday proved to be surprisingly intractable, and did not follow my instructions. Your life could still very well be in some danger, at least so long as he thinks The Duke remains at liberty."

The boy eyed him somberly with dark eyes that were disturbingly like his sister's. But Braden tried not to think about that.

"You're talking about Hurst, aren't you?" Tommy asked. "No, don't shake your head. I knew it was him. I knew it was him from the moment the gun went off in my ear. He tried to kill me." His voice did not quaver in the least.

Braden tried for a slight shrug by way of response.

"No," the earl said. "There's no need to baby me. I've been a fool. I see it all now. He felt bad the first time—when The Duke shot me last December, I mean. Because it was his fault, in a way, for taking me to that place. He knew they'd cheat me. He knew it good and well. And so he blamed himself."

Braden said only, "I think so," and that he said softly.

The earl apparently hadn't heard him. "But then it became apparent that I was a liability, wasn't I? Because of what I knew. I might talk. Not just about the cheating, but about how The Duke tried to kill me. And so he determined to get rid of me."

Braden said, "If it's of any comfort to you, I didn't get the impression that Lord Winchilsea relished the assignment of killing you. I believe he was only doing it because his own life was in some jeopardy if he didn't."

"Still," Tommy said, with a good deal of indignation, "he didn't have to go through with it. He could have run away."

"Ah, yes." Braden's smile was brittle. "But then he wouldn't have had the privilege of marrying your sister, you see."

The earl, turning red with anger everywhere but where the gunpowder still lay embedded beneath his skin—it would, according to the surgeon, work its way out eventually—scowled into his lap. "As if I'd let her marry that blackguard now. It was all right, when I didn't know he was in on it. But now—"

"Yes, well." The brittle smile vanished. "That is, of course, for you and your sister to work out."

"I've got to tell her," the boy said. He didn't, however, speak very loudly, and Braden wondered if perhaps he hadn't meant to say the words out loud. "If only there was some way to leave out the gambling, though . . ."

"You'll have plenty of time to think it through." Braden Granville set the untouched glass of whiskey aside. "You're to have no communications at all with your family until we know it's safe."

"But she has a right to know," the earl said, more loudly this time, so it was clear he wasn't speaking to himself. "She has a right to know the kind of man she's marrying. Don't you see? It's all my fault she got involved with him in the first place. He had me fooled—he had all of us fooled. With his title and his connections and his charm. We thought he was gentry."

Braden lifted a brow at the fractious boy. "And he is. Winchilsea is a well-respected title, one of the oldest in the Baronetage." He recalled his father's frequent recitations from that esteemed tome. "The Slaters have managed to maintain their blue-bloodedness from as far back as—"

374 · MEG CABOT

"But underneath all that," the earl interrupted, "he isn't any better than that Hawkins fellow."

"That may be so," Braden said, gravely. "But I don't want you leaving this house, or sending any messages—not to your sister, or your mother, or anyone. Later, if you wish—"

But he broke off, and said nothing more, only busied himself with shuffling the papers on his desk. What was he doing? *What was he doing?* He'd sworn he wouldn't. He'd told himself he wouldn't appeal to this boy to help him with his situation with Caroline. If she refused to believe him when he said his shooting Slater had nothing to do with Jacquelyn, then she was exactly like all the other women he'd ever known: suspicious, contrary, and controlling. He'd washed his hands of her.

And yet he was bleeding inside.

"Later, sir?"

Braden did not even glance at him. "Nothing. Run along. I have a good deal of catching up to do. As you know, I left early yesterday, and came in quite late today. . . ."

The earl said, quite suddenly, "You shot him, didn't you?"

Braden, startled, cleared his throat. "No, no. Well, not really. Just a little." When a broad grin broke out over the earl's face, Braden said, severely, "It isn't amusing. It's quite wrong to shoot people. Guns and violence . . . we are a civilized society, and there isn't any place for them."

The earl's grin vanished. "You sound exactly like my sister."

"Yes," Braden agreed. "Go and visit Weasel now, will you, my lord? I have a great deal to do."

The earl left him then, but there was a determined look in his eye as he slipped from the library.

Not so very far away, the cool, collected young woman who'd so calmly broken off her engagement earlier that afternoon threw herself onto the grass beneath her back garden badminton net and commenced to sobbing.

It was ridiculous, Caroline knew. It was ridiculous that she couldn't stop crying. It was even more ridiculous that she couldn't weep in the privacy of her own home.

But there was enough weeping going on in there, and for entirely different reasons than hers. Thomas had still not been found, nor had they received any word of his whereabouts. Lady Bartlett was beside herself. And her suffering was only going to be compounded when, in a day or two, she got word that Caroline had called off her engagement. Then Lady Bartlett was going to suffer no mere apoplectic fit. Oh, no. She would quite probably succumb to an ague, or even a fever, that would carry her off, ending her travails forever.

But now, knowing only that her son was missing, Lady Bartlett had called for her physician, her apothecary, and a surgeon. These individuals were so busy banging in and out of the house with various remedies for her palpitations and fainting spells, that Caroline had finally realized she'd get no peace indoors, and, knowing Emmy was out on another one of her protest marches, fled to the privacy of her garden.

Where she wasted no time giving full vent to her emotions.

Had her mother's physician seen her, Caroline knew, he would have told her that she was overwrought. The apothecary would doubtlessly have prescribed hartshorn. She had no idea what the surgeon would have said, since there was no way to set a broken heart, but she supposed the man would have felt obligated to try.

But there was nothing any of them could do. Caroline had brought her sorrows down upon her own head. She had had Braden Granville. For twenty-four glorious hours—maybe a little less—she had had Braden Granville, felt what it was like to be loved by him, felt what it was like to be alive, for the first time in her twenty-one years.

And then she'd learned the truth. The bitter truth. That none of it had been real. That it had all just been a game. That she had just been another victim of the Lothario of London.

She sobbed helplessly into the grass, thankful for the veil of twilight which hid her from view, and so kept her mother from sending Bennington out to inform her that earls' daughters ought not to recline weeping in the grass, even in their own gardens.

She was a fool. She knew it. A fool for falling in love with Braden Granville.

But his performance had seemed so convincing! She really had thought he loved her. Only how, she asked herself, for the millionth time, could a man who'd professed his love for her so tenderly still be capable of entertaining feelings for another woman? For he'd have to feel *something*, at least, for Jacquelyn, in order to work up enough rage to shoot her secret lover.

It was exactly as Emmy had always said: Men were rats.

And then, just as she thought her heart might quite literally be breaking, and that maybe she would, in fact, require a surgeon, or at the very least a little hartshorn after all, a familiar voice sounded from the vicinity of the small summerhouse by the garden's back wall.

"Oh, God. What's this then? Did Ma finally sell off all those horses of yours?"

Caroline lifted her head and squinted in the direction of the summerhouse, suspicion momentarily halting the flow of her tears. "Tommy?" she whispered.

She saw a dark shadow disattach itself from the others by the wall, and then her brother ambled across the lawn, and dropped down beside her, putting a finger to his lips.

"Quiet now," he said. "No one's supposed to know I'm here."

Under different circumstances, Caroline might have hugged him. Now, however, she only looked at him, saw that he appeared to be in one piece, and sighed. "Where have you been?" she asked. "Ma's worried sick."

Thomas said, with a wry grimace, "Try to curtail some of your joy at seeing me again, Caro. It's embarrassing."

"Well, you had jolly well better go inside and let her know you're all right," Caroline informed him, "or you'll have seen the last of anything resembling an allowance from her, let me assure you."

Thomas, sitting cross-legged beside her in the grass, said, "I can't let her know I'm all right. And you're not to tell anyone you've seen me. I've got to stay disappeared for a while more. But I had to see you, Caro."

Though the light was dim, Caroline thought she saw a look of genuine concern on her brother's face. Since he was so rarely serious with her, she forgot her own problems for the moment, and peered at him through the twilit air.

"Tommy," she said, softly. "You're in trouble, aren't you?"

"A good deal of it," her brother replied. "And all of my own making. Which is why I had to come see you, even though I promised I wouldn't. You see, Caro—" He leaned forward and did something he'd only done three or four times in his life: he laid his hand over hers. "It's about Hurst."

"Hurst?" Caroline sniffled. Her tears had not yet completely vanished. In fact, at the mention of that particular name, she felt them returning, pricking the corners of her eyes. "Oh, God, Tommy." She had a sickening sensation that her brother had somehow got wind of the Lady Jacquelyn situation. "Please, don't. I already know."

Tommy dropped her hand in astonishment. "You do?"

"Yes, of course. I broke it off with him this afternoon. I ought to have done it long ago, the moment I found out, in fact. Emmy told me to—"

The earl's jaw dropped. "Emmy knows?"

"Yes, of course." Caroline eyed him curiously. "You know I tell her everything. Only Ma wouldn't let me break it off with him."

"*Ma?*" Her brother's face contorted with horror. "You told *Ma?*"

Caroline blinked at him. "Well, of course I told Ma. But she said the invitations had already gone out, and that my reputation would be ruined if I broke it off, and that I could win him back if I just used my womanly wiles, and . . . oh, Tommy, I was such an idiot, I believed her. And I did the worst thing. . . . You wouldn't believe how stupid I was. I went to Braden Granville, and I—"

He interrupted her. "Caroline," he said, carefully. "What are you talking about?"

"What do you mean, what am I talking about?" Caroline asked. "I'm talking about Hurst." She looked at him curiously through the gloaming. "What are you talking about?"

"I'm talking about Hurst, as well."

"Yes," Caroline said. "I thought so. Well, thank you for your concern, but I already know all about it. I walked in on them, you see."

Tommy shook his head. "Walked in on *who?*"

"Hurst, of course," Caroline replied with impatience. "And Lady Jacquelyn Seldon. I saw them making love on a divan in one of Lady Ashforth's sitting rooms."

For a moment, her brother only stared at her. Then he opened his mouth and let out a word that caused Caroline's ears to burn. And she had heard a good many such words from his lips in the past.

"*Tommy,*" she said, scoldingly.

"Bugger *that,*" her brother said. "Are you telling me that Slater and Jackie Seldon were . . . were . . . *trysting* behind your back?" Only the word he used wasn't *trysting.*

"If you must be vulgar about it," Caroline said, primly, "then I suppose the answer to that question is yes." Then she looked at him curiously. "Isn't that what—"

"God, no!" Tommy burst out. "I was trying to tell you why Slater got shot! That's why you were crying, wasn't it?"

Caroline said, "Well, yes, I suppose, in a way. But, Tommy,

that *was* why he got shot." She swallowed, then went resolutely on. "Braden Granville shot Hurst."

"Right. As a warning," Tommy said, "to leave me alone."

Caroline gave a quick, negative shake of her head. "No, Tommy. Why would Braden Granville want Hurst to leave you alone? He shot him because he'd found out, you see, about Hurst and Lady Jacquelyn."

"He didn't," Tommy said, with some indignation. "And I think I should know. I'm the one who started it all. Granville shot Hurst because of me. Hurst was trying to kill me, because the fellow who shot me last winter found out I wasn't dead after all, and could not only identify him, but ruin his business, too. So he told your fiancé he had to finish the job."

Caroline, sitting in the grass under the evening's first smattering of stars, looked at her brother. Looked at him as if she'd never seen him before. Noticed for the first time the circles under his eyes, and the curious dusting of some kind of soot or grime all along one side of his face. He still had on the clothes he'd gone out in the night he'd disappeared, and though someone had obviously tried to clean and press them, there was a rip in the lining of his coat, and the knees of his trousers were still darker than the rest of his pants.

But that wasn't what caused her to reach out and grasp his hand between her own. She did that because her brother was wearing the most serious expression she'd ever seen on his face.

"Tell me," she said, urgently.

He frowned nervously. "You'll be angry with me."

"I won't," Caroline assured him. "Oh, I'm sure I won't."

And so he told her.

37

$\mathcal{B}$ raden Granville sat at his desk, adding up a column of numbers. He finished, then eyed the sum he'd come up with. Wrong. It had to be wrong.

What was happening to him? He'd used to be able to add much longer columns of numbers in his head. Multiply and divide them, too. Why couldn't he seem to do it anymore? Why couldn't he concentrate?

He knew why, of course.

But he refused to think about it. What was there to think about?

It was better this way. He was better off without her. Look at what she'd done to him: he could no longer add the simplest column of numbers. If he'd stayed with her any longer, she might have sapped from him every ounce of intelligence he possessed. That, apparently, was what happened when one fell in love. One's brains were sucked away, or turned gelatinous. At least, that's what the inside of his head felt like at the moment.

Was this love, then? Was this what so many poets had wasted page after page describing? What Shakespeare had extolled? If it was—and he had every reason to believe it, based on his complete inability to think of anything, anything at all, but her—he wanted nothing more to do with it. Not if it meant he had to live the rest of his life with this knot in his stomach, this soreness in the vicinity of his chest.

There was a tap on the door.

How, he wondered, had it come to this? That the Lothario of London should be sitting at his desk, pining for the one woman in England he couldn't have? How many women out there, he wondered, had sat feeling the way he did now, over him? He hadn't known. He hadn't known what it was like. Now he understood the long letters, pleading with him to change his mind. Now he understood the threats, the tears.

Love *hurt*.

What hurt most of all was that he knew that, however many times he told himself he was better off—that if she couldn't trust him now, she never would—it wasn't true. He wasn't better off. He needed her. Needed her goodness, her frankness, her humor, her humanity. Needed *her*, dammit. Needed to feel her close to him, her warmth, her scent, her—

Another tap at the door.

And it was his own fault she didn't trust him. How long had he known of his moniker—Lothario of London—and done nothing to change it? He was notorious for his many love affairs, his charm, his power over women. And he had done nothing to change that, to insist that it wasn't that he'd *wanted* to hurt these women—far from it. Only that none of them—none of them—had turned out to be what he was looking for, what had been right for him.

Until now.

When it was too late.

"Dead." Crutch appeared in the doorway, looking impatient. "I've been knockin' and knockin'. Were you ever going to say come in?"

Braden glanced at his butler. "Why should I bother? I knew you'd come in anyway."

Crutch peered at him. "It's dark in here, Dead. You want I should light the lamps?"

"No," Braden said, realizing, even as he said it, that Crutch was right. The light filtering through the glass panes in the French doors leading to the garden had shifted from the gold of sunset to the lavender of twilight. No wonder he'd added those numbers wrong. He could barely distinguish his own hand in front of his face.

But as usual, his butler didn't listen to him. Slowly, the rosy glow from the sconces along the wall brightened the room. Crutch even turned on the small gaslights that lit the display cases which held various incarnations of the Granville pistol throughout the years.

"That's better," the butler said, with satisfaction. Then he added, "Someone to see you, Dead.'S why I knocked."

Braden sighed. "I told you. I'm out. And if it's Jacquelyn—"

"It ain't," Crutch said. "It's the Lady Caroline—"

Braden felt as if his entire world, which seemed to have been crumbling beneath him, bit by bit, had suddenly shifted back onto solid ground. He stood up hastily—too hastily. He knocked over his inkwell.

"Send her in," he said, as he bent to clean up the mess. "No, never mind this, I'll take care of it. Send her in at once. Don't make her wait any longer—"

Crutch, looking faintly surprised, went away. Braden used his handkerchief to soak up the spill, telling himself the entire time, *She is undoubtedly only here to ask about her brother. It hasn't anything at all to do with you. She hates you. And she has every reason to, for only a criminally blind idiot like yourself would have failed to guess that Slater was the man she was protecting all along. . . .*

And then she was there, standing in front of him, chewing her bottom lip nervously and looking every bit as heartbreakingly lovely as when he'd last seen her.

"Hullo, Braden," she said gravely, in that low-pitched voice he'd come to adore.

He found himself quite at a loss for words, and was astounded by the fact. Very seldom had he ever suffered from being tongue-tied.

Fearful she would think he was being purposefully rude, he hurried out from behind his desk and indicated one of the comfortably stuffed leather chairs in front of it.

"Won't you have a seat?" he asked, and was chagrined when his voice came out sounding oddly uneven.

If Caroline noticed, however, she gave no sign. She sat down, still in her gloves and bonnet. A reticule dangled from one wrist. In the gaslight, he could see her face clearly. Anxiety was swimming in those deep brown eyes.

How often, he asked himself, had he entertained women a thousand times more sophisticated than Caroline, and done it smoothly and with dazzling aplomb? Why was it that this one time, when it really mattered, he found himself gawky as a schoolboy, and floundering to think what to do.

A drink, he thought. Offer her a drink.

It seemed inconceivable to him that a little over twelve hours ago, he'd held this woman in his arms, and poured into her what had felt like a lifetime of need.

"Would you care for a sherry?" he asked her.

"Sherry?" she echoed, in a strangled voice. *"Sherry?* No, I don't want any *sherry.* Oh, Braden, why didn't you *tell* me?"

He stared down at her confusedly. He should, he supposed, have sat in the chair opposite hers, but he was not sure that, at such close proximity, he'd be able to resist reaching out for her. . . .

"Tell you what?" he asked, having only half heard her. His traitorous concentration had fled once more, leaving him only with an ability to gaze at her throat, and remember how smooth it had felt beneath his lips and tongue, soft as silk.

"About Tommy."

That brought him up short. He blinked at her.

"Tommy?"

"Yes, Tommy," Caroline said. "He told me everything. Oh, Braden, if you'd only said that *that* was why you'd shot Hurst. How could you have stood there, and let me think it was because of Jacquelyn?"

He was too surprised to dissemble. "You've spoken with the earl?"

"Yes." Suddenly, Caroline reached up and, as if they were bothering her, untied the ribbons that held her bonnet in place. Then she wrenched the hat off, tossing it carelessly onto the floor. "He told me everything. I couldn't tell him about . . . well, about you and me, of course. So I couldn't ask him the one question that vexes me the most. Braden, why didn't *you* tell me?"

He shrugged his heavy shoulders. "Your brother made me swear I wouldn't."

"He made you—" Caroline looked up at him curiously. "That's *all*? Tommy made you swear not to tell?"

He opened his lips, but again, no sound came out from between them. What was wrong with him?

He knew. He knew what was wrong. The impulse to take her into his arms, to smother that small mouth with kisses, was so strong, his arms were shaking with it.

But he could not allow himself to touch her. All of his resolve to let her go would vanish, he knew, the moment they touched.

And he had to let her go. He knew that now.

They were from different worlds. To prove it to her, he said, pacing toward the French doors, his head down so he wouldn't have to look her in the eye, "I know that in the circles in which you travel, Caroline, it is common to give one's word, and then break it when keeping it no longer becomes convenient." He paced back toward his desk. "But in the Dials, when someone makes an oath, they keep it." He headed back toward the French doors. "Even at the risk of death."

She stood up and met him as he was making his way back toward his desk. "Even," she asked, in the softest voice imaginable, as she lifted her chin in order to look him in the eye, "at the risk of losing me?"

She was close enough now that if he reached out, he'd have been able to touch her, to stroke the light brown curls that had escaped from her hairpins.

"Yes," he said, and though each word tore at his gut, he forced them out, anyway. "Don't you see? That's why perhaps it's better that you and I—"

Hurt instantly flooded her eyes.

"That you and I what?" she asked, her voice unsteady. "What are you trying to say? That because you keep your word, you're better than me? Is that it? Braden, I know I never should have left, but—"

"Caroline," he said, knowing it was for her own good, but feeling that with each syllable, he was hammering a nail into his own coffin. "You know that's not it. It's just that . . . I don't belong here. Here in Mayfair. Don't you see? I'm an imposter. All of this, the house, the business, these clothes I have on . . . they aren't me. I'm not who you think I am. I'm no gentleman. I'm no businessman. I'm from the Dials, Caroline. I don't know the difference between a fish knife and a butter knife. I don't belong in this world, your world, and I never will. What you thought, when you learned that I had shot Hurst . . . it was wrong, but it wasn't far wrong. Not really. Do you understand?"

He saw her eyes widen, and realized that at last, she was beginning to understand. She would never, he knew, understand how much he loved her—so much that he had to let her go, rather than let her be pulled down to his level.

But then he noticed that she wasn't looking at him. She was

peering at something around his shoulder. Something that caused
her to fling a hand to her mouth in horror.

Braden turned around.

Just in time to see the Marquis of Winchilsea open the French
doors and limp into the library, a pistol pointed quite steadily in
the vicinity of their hearts.

38

*B*raden's first thought, of course, was for Caroline. She must be got safely from the room, and at once.

But how? For the marquis did not look at all like a man with whom one might reason. Always impeccably dressed—to the point where he'd occasionally been accused of dandyism—the marquis was not looking his best at the moment. His heavily frilled cravat was loose, its snowy folds flecked with dirt—from scaling, Braden didn't doubt, the back of his garden wall—and his breeches were equally as soiled. His golden hair stood wildly out from his head, and his blue eyes had an unfocused, irrational look about them.

He regarded the two of them with bright interest, however.

"Well, well, well," he said. "Isn't this fascinating. Lady Caroline breaks off her engagement with me, then heads immediately for Braden Granville's private home. Whatever, I wonder, can *that* mean?"

Caroline said, in a voice Braden was sure she meant to be reassuring, but which shook rather badly, "It doesn't mean anything, Hurst. I was only telling Mr. Granville the truth about you and Jacquelyn. I felt he had a right to know."

"But he already knows," Slater said, pleasantly. "He broke it off with Jackie several nights ago."

Caroline, Braden saw, swallowed, and glanced at him. He tried to reassure her with a rueful smile. "See?" he said, lightly. "I told you Jacquelyn and I were through."

"Right," Slater said. "Granville and Jackie are through. And so, it appears, are you and I, Caroline. Which brings me back to the original question. What are you doing here, Caroline?"

Braden cut off further attempts at conversation between the two by stepping neatly in front of Caroline. "That isn't the question at all," he said, coldly. "The real question is what are *you* doing here, Slater?"

The marquis, to Braden's surprise, tossed back his head and let out a whoop of laughter. "Slater!" he cried. "Slater! Now, really, Granville. Is that polite? Is that the way a fellow addresses his betters? Certainly not. But then, I wouldn't expect you to know that, seeing as how you have only just crawled up from the depths of the gutters. Allowances must be made for the underclasses, I suppose."

Braden, wishing heartily he could get to his desk, where he kept a small-sized derringer in his top drawer, leaned back to say casually to Caroline, "His lordship seems to have a private matter to discuss with me. Why don't you go and wait for me in the foyer?"

But even if Caroline had been inclined to leave—which, judging by the stubborn look on her face, she was not—Slater would not have allowed her to. He said, "I think not. Caroline, sit down in that chair there."

But Caroline was not about to go anywhere—not even a chair to which she'd been directed by a madman holding the latest model Granville pistol.

"Hurst," she said. "I know you're upset about my canceling the wedding. But this is hardly the way to—"

She broke off, interrupted by Slater's humorless guffaws.

"Isn't it, though? Isn't *this* the reason you've broken it off, my dear? Because you've fallen for this"—he sneered at Braden—"scoundrel? No, wait, scoundrel's too good a name for him." And now he leveled a look at Braden Granville that might have frozen butter, it was so cold. "What do you call a man who steals another man's bride?"

Braden decided to keep Slater talking. It would, he thought, give Caroline the best chance at a clean break for the door.

"I don't know," he said, politely. "What do you call a man who attempts to murder his fiancée's brother?"

"That is a lie," Hurst said. The indignation in his voice was thick. "A foul lie, meant to besmirch my noble name. But what else are we to expect from a man with so low a character as Braden Granville, except lies, lies, and more lies? You can't trust scum from the Dials, Caroline."

Caroline said, "Hurst, Tommy himself told me—"

"Told you what?" Hurst was holding his pistol, Braden saw, the way a man unused to firearms held a gun—not carefully enough. Every time he swung it in Braden's direction, he had to resist an urge to duck. "Caroline, you know perfectly well I never tried to hurt Tommy. I love Tommy. Wasn't I the one who sat with him all those months he was ill? Read to him when he was unconscious, and we weren't sure if he would wake? Wasn't I the one who pulled him in off the street, where he might have lain bleeding to death, if I hadn't come along?"

Braden saw those brown eyes he'd come to love flash with fire. "Oh, yes," Caroline said, bitterly. "But he wouldn't have been shot in the first place if you hadn't taken him to that dreadful place—"

"I didn't know," Hurst insisted. "I tell you, Caroline, I swear I didn't—"

"You're lying." Caroline's sweet voice was hard. "You're lying to me, the same way you lied to Tommy, and my mother, and everyone else I know. You're nothing but a sneak and a liar, hiding under the guise of a nobleman, and I can't believe how much time I wasted, thinking I loved you!"

It was at this point that Caroline might have made her break for the door. Slater seemed completely stunned by what she'd said. But to Braden's utter chagrin, Caroline stayed where she was.

Still, the distraction she'd provided was all that Braden needed. A split second later, he had hurled himself at the marquis, both hands going for the pistol in his fingers.

The two men fell to the ground with a crash. Braden heard, but only distantly, Caroline scream. His whole being was centered on prying the gun from Slater's fingers.

But for a man who prided himself on his lineage, Slater was not fighting with anything like what his ancestors would have called nobility. He was biting, *clawing* at Braden's hands, trying desperately to knee him in the groin, elbow him in the throat... anything he could possibly do to throw him off.

Braden wouldn't let go, however. It wasn't just his life at stake. Had they been alone, he might have let go of the pistol for a moment, and shoved a fist into one orifice or another of Slater's. But as it was, Caroline was still somewhere in the room. If he allowed Slater to pull that trigger, there was no telling where the bullet might go: harmlessly into the wall . . . or fatally into Caroline's heart.

But that was another thing about the violently deranged: they could have the strength of ten men. Slater was obviously desperate, and desperate men were difficult to subdue. Every muscle in Braden's body was shaking with the effort.

He would not give up, however. He could not. His life depended upon it.

And then, in spite of all his efforts—in spite of the finger he'd thrust behind the trigger, which Slater had kept pulling until it tore a gash in Braden's skin—a shot went off, deafeningly loud.

Smoke filled the room. Miraculously, Braden felt Slater's grip slacken, and for one panicked moment, he thought it was because he'd managed to fire a bullet into Caroline . . . especially since he heard no sound from her.

But then he realized that Slater had not released the gun because he'd managed to shoot anyone. No, he'd released it because someone had drilled a neat hole through his right hand, from which blood was gushing at an admirable rate, directly onto Braden's Oriental rug.

And Slater, after babbling incoherently at the pain of this injury, promptly fainted, quite unnerved by the sight of his own blood.

A second later, Braden felt a soft weight collide with his chest, and suddenly, Caroline's wildly beating heart lay over his.

"Braden," she was crying, clinging to him in an embrace that was rather more of a choke hold than anything else. "Braden, are you all right? You're bleeding!"

He *was* bleeding, he discovered, after taking stock of himself, but not from any serious injury. His finger, where Slater had gouged it by pulling on the trigger so many times, was cut nearly to the bone. And he appeared to have injured his lip, most likely from Slater worrying it with his teeth, something Braden did not in the least wish to discuss.

But other than that, he felt extraordinarily fit. He raised his uninjured hand to Caroline's hair.

"Shhh," he said. "I'm all right. I'm all right."

Her sobbing subsided almost at once, and he was able to ask her, "But wherever did you find the pistol?"

"Over there," Caroline said, pointing in the direction of his desktop, where she'd dropped the smoking derringer. "In a drawer.

I looked everywhere—I knew you had to have a loaded one some-where nearby—"

He smoothed her tumbled hair, unable to think how close he'd come to losing her—not just once, but three times, now.

"That was quite a shot you managed to pull off," was all he said, however. "Especially for someone who claims to hate guns so much."

Caroline lifted her tearstained face from his chest.

"I hate them," she informed him, "but I never said I didn't know how to use them."

And while Braden was still digesting this piece of information, she added, "And I don't care."

He blinked at her, not having the faintest idea what she was talking about, and startled by her sudden vehemence.

"What you were saying before," she said. "About how you're an imposter, and don't know the difference between a fish knife or a butter knife. I don't care. I don't care what knife you use. I love you, and I always will."

And then—he didn't know quite how it happened—she was kissing him the way she had that time in his carriage, when she'd wanted to know if she was doing it correctly.

And this time, just like that time, the answer was yes. Oh, yes. She was.

Braden felt something inside of him break as her lips moved with sweet hunger over his. And it wasn't his heart, he realized, but the knot that had formed in his stomach since the moment he'd thought he lost her. It melted away, and he knew then that, dif-ferent worlds or no, the two of them belonged together. And he would let no one part them ever again.

They were still kissing when the door to the library burst open, and the Earl of Bartlett, Crutch, and a limping Weasel came tum-bling in.

"We thought we heard a—" Tommy came to a halt, stopped in

his tracks by two sights that were, each in their own way, equally astonishing: an unconscious and bleeding Marquis of Winchilsea, and his own sister in the arms of Braden Granville.

"Well," the Earl of Bartlett said, after a moment. "Ma's sure to have an apoplexy now."

Epilogue

They were playing badminton in Braden Granville's back garden.

Not badminton the way it was supposed to be played, either, but a new version, devised by Caroline. Still played with rackets, birdies, and a net, the only difference, really, between regular badminton and Caroline's version was that instead of losing a point when a serve was missed, the offender had to remove an article of clothing.

The only problem, Caroline was discovering, was that certain players enjoyed losing a bit too much.

"Now that was an easy one," she said, of a serve she was convinced Braden had missed on purpose. He had not, in fact, so much as raised his racket in the birdie's direction.

Braden, who'd already lost his shoes and shirt, now began to lower his trousers. "Shame on me," he said.

"Don't think," Caroline informed him severely, "that just because you're naked, I shan't continue to play."

He eyed her through the net, tied between two slender poles not far from the enormous padded swing upon which they'd spent many leisurely hours. She had lost her shoes and gown, and now stood in the dappled sunlight in only her corset and pantaloons, a most delightful sight.

But perhaps most delightful of all was the fact that she was, at long last, his wife.

"I thought," he said, having shed his breeches, "that when one or the other of the players lost all of his or her clothing, the game was over."

"Not," Caroline said, loftily, "if he or she has purposefully missed serves. Now, really, Braden, you've got to *try*. Otherwise, it isn't the least entertaining."

She stepped back to serve, and Braden, quite enchanted by the manner in which her rosy nipples rose up out of the cups of her corset whenever she raised her arms, shot an arm out beneath the net, seized hold of her, and half carried, half dragged her over to his side of the impromptu court, where he unceremoniously deposited her in the grass, then dropped down between her legs, and began to examine the bow which held her pantaloons together.

"On the contrary," he said, pleasantly, as he gave the silk ribbon a tug. "I am prodigiously entertained."

Caroline, not quite as put out by his unsportsmanlike behavior as she pretended, studied the pattern the leaves and branches overhead made against the cloudless blue sky. "If I had known," she informed him, "what a poor loser you were, I would never have insisted on playing."

"What?" Braden asked, as he examined the soft flesh he had uncovered. "And let Emmy's wedding present go to waste?"

"The badminton set *is* the most useful thing we've been given," Caroline observed. "Did you see the silver soup tureen from the Prince of Wales? Whatever are we to do with it? It's big enough to swim in."

Braden's only response was a grunt. This was because he had buried his head between Caroline's thighs, where he was conducting a thorough exploration with his lips and tongue.

"I suppose," Caroline said, a bit breathlessly, after a very short time, "that I oughtn't to complain, however. It's astonishing that anyone gave us anything at all, when you consider how we eloped, and . . . well, everything that came before that."

Braden lifted his head, and regarded her with a wry expression from between her knees. "I realize that after a month of marriage, most wives are well acquainted with, and perhaps even bored by, their husband's lovemaking techniques, so perhaps you'd like me to stop what I'm doing so that you can continue to chatter about wedding gifts?"

Caroline, whose heart had begun to beat a bit unsteadily, sighed. "Oh," she said, closing her eyes. "No. Please carry on."

Braden did so, with a good deal of relish.

Later, luxuriating in their mutually satiated state, it was Caroline who first lifted her head from the grass and asked, "Did you hear something?"

"I did not." Braden, tracing lazy circles with his fingertip along his wife's bare hip, contemplated all the places where she had become tanned during their two weeks honeymooning in Lugeria. It was quite something, he was discovering, having a wife. Even better, a wife who never complained about the sun—or he was discovering, much of anything, for that matter. Except, perhaps, his business. But that was something he'd been working in secret to rectify.

"I'm telling you"—Caroline began to crawl about, gathering up her clothes—"someone's here."

"Impossible," Braden said. He folded his fingers behind his head and stared up into the cloudless summer sky. "I sent everyone to the races with explicit instructions that they were not to return until after dark. It's probably only the neighbors, and they can't see us. The walls are much too high."

And then, bursting through the French doors at the back of the house, waving a newspaper and an envelope festooned with a good deal of ribbon, came his father.

"Braden?" Sylvester Granville called. "Braden, my boy, where are you?"

Caroline, struggling into her gown, hissed, "Oh, Braden, do get up! What if he sees you?"

Braden watched her frantic wriggling, finding it quite charming, despite the circumstances. "What if he does? I'm not doing anything wrong. It's my property, and you're my wife. I assure you that for once in my life, my behavior is well within the parameters of the law."

But to appease her, he rose, stepped casually into his trousers, and pulled them up.

"Ah, there you are," Sylvester said, hurrying up to them a few seconds later. "Enjoying the lovely weather, I see."

"Quite," Braden said mildly. "And what are you doing home so early? I thought you and Lady Bartlett were attending that concert in the park. . . ."

"Oh, we were, we were." Sylvester looked worried. "But unfortunately we ran into Lady Jacquelyn and that new beau of hers, Lord Whitcomb, and would you believe that Lady Jacquelyn *cut* your mother, Caroline? Cut her dead!"

Caroline, who'd come to stand beside her husband, sighed. "Oh, dear. Poor Ma."

"Shocking behavior," Sylvester continued, sadly, "especially coming from a duke's daughter. One might expect better behavior from a lady of her distinguished background. Still, it was good of her not to sue you for breach of promise, Braden. She might have, you know, and been well within her rights." Sylvester grinned at them, and wagged a chastising finger. "Lucky for you she found solace so quickly with Lord Whitcomb. I understand the two of them will be exchanging vows next month. Quite a nice match, I must say, even if his lordship *is* a bit old for her. . . . But the marquis! Oh, my, have you heard about the marquis? Why, he was so devastated, I understand he decamped for America. America, of all places!"

"Lady Bartlett, Pa," Braden said, trying to steer his father from the topic of Hurst. "Is she unwell, then?"

Sylvester looked surprised. "Oh, didn't I say so? No, no, she asked me if I'd mind terribly leaving the concert early. Lady Jacquelyn's behavior quite shocked her, and she went home to rest. Your mother is terribly delicate, you know, Caroline. Why, I don't believe she's yet recovered from the shock of your elopement. . . ."

Caroline, Braden noticed, was beginning to look distressed. While her brother wholeheartedly supported their marriage, Lady Bartlett had not welcomed the news with as much enthusiasm. Even when Hurst's duplicity—and Braden Granville's role in putting a stop to it—had been revealed to her, she could not find it in her heart to forgive Caroline—not for choosing Braden over the marquis, but for eloping: Lady Bartlett was crushed that the Worth wedding dress would now never have occasion to be worn.

Seeing his wife's troubled look, Braden held out his arm. She moved quickly into his embrace, slipping an arm around his bare waist. He smiled down at her, and laid a kiss upon the top of her sun-warmed head.

While Lady Bartlett had been let in on the reason behind the Marquis of Winchilsea's mysterious decampment to America— that faced with The Duke's incarceration, and Braden's threat of certain death if he ever showed his face in London again, he had chosen a clime less hostile—Sylvester Granville had not, primarily because Braden preferred to shield his father from things that would, he knew, only worry him unduly.

"But look," Sylvester cried, "look what I have here, Braden. This might make Lady Bartlett feel a bit better, I would think!" He held up the copy of the *Times* he'd been clutching beneath his arm.

Caroline noticed it first, and gasped as she stepped forward to seize the paper from her father-in-law's hands.

"Braden," she cried. "What is this?" Then she read aloud from the sporting section: "'From Granville Enterprises, a surprise: not a new style of pistol, but a handsome and yet fully functional bridle. A significant improvement over the bearing rein, this harness, with its relaxed bit, allows the animal free movement of his head, without sacrificing driver control.'" Caroline, flabbergasted, turned wide eyes upon him. "Braden!" she cried. "When did you do this?"

He shrugged uncomfortably. "Some time ago, actually," he said. "That night after we all saw *Faust* . . . I couldn't sleep, and I kept remembering your face when you saw the duchess's bearing reins—"

Caroline, shaking her head with wonder, read on. "It says here that the Prince of Wales has ordered a gross of them for his stables!"

"Prince of Wales," Braden muttered, rolling his eyes.

"I'm so proud of you," Caroline said, her eyes shining in the sun as she returned to his side to hug him again. "I knew you could invent something that was actually useful."

"Thank you," Braden said, wryly, "for the crumbs from your table, Mrs. Granville."

"But that isn't all," Sylvester Granville broke in, excitedly. "What do you think was being delivered as I came up the steps to the house, my boy? What do you think?"

Caroline looked at the brightly sealed envelope. "What is it?"

"His letter," Sylvester said, proudly. "Braden's letter of patent from the queen. She's offering him a baronetcy because of his contributions to the science of firearms. My boy—your husband, my dear"—Sylvester Granville puffed out his chest—"is going to be a lord!"

Caroline looked up at Braden with shining eyes.

"But he already is," she said, with a smile. "*My* lord, anyway."

About the Author

MEG CABOT was born in Bloomington, Indiana. Her eighty-plus books for both adults and teens have included multiple best-sellers, selling over twenty-five million copies worldwide. They have been made into numerous films and television series, the most well-known of which is The Princess Diaries. She currently lives in Key West with her husband and various cats.